THE QUESTION OF A KISS

Lady Cynthia had sent Captain Sheffield away. She had not been able to bear the thought that he agreed to wed her solely because of the funds she offered.

But now he was back, and the best she could do was to ask in a cool voice, "Did you forget something?"

"Yes," he murmured, and Cynthia felt the warmth of his breath on her cheek. "I forgot to kiss you."

Before Cynthia could respond, she felt his lips on hers. She went rigid as his free hand drifted down to settle on her hip. "Relax," he told her.

When she felt the warmth of his mouth open over hers, some secret part of her obeyed his command. Her body relaxed against his, adjusting to the shape of him as though she had been there many times before.

Was this kiss proof of the Captain's passion? Or was it merely his first payment of their marriage bargain? Cynthia did not know—and as she melted in his arms, she did not care. . . .

SIGNET REGENCY ROMANCE

Coming in November 1995

Elisabeth Fairchild
The Love Knot

Sandra Heath
Lucy's Christmas Angel

Gail Eastwood
The Captain's Dilemma

An Immodest Proposal

by

Patricia Oliver

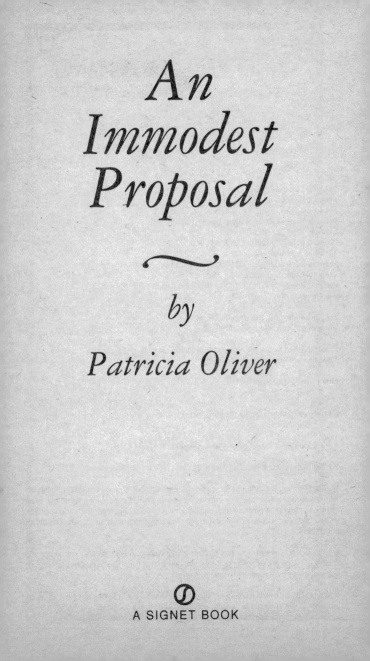

A SIGNET BOOK

SIGNET
Published by the Penguin Group
Penguin Books USA Inc., 375 Hudson Street,
New York, New York 10014, U.S.A.
Penguin Books Ltd, 27 Wrights Lane,
London W8 5TZ, England
Penguin Books Australia Ltd, Ringwood,
Victoria, Australia
Penguin Books Canada Ltd, 10 Alcorn Avenue,
Toronto, Ontario, Canada M4V 3B2
Penguin Books (N.Z.) Ltd, 182–190 Wairau Road,
Auckland 10, New Zealand

Penguin Books Ltd, Registered Offices:
Harmondsworth, Middlesex, England

First published by Signet, an imprint of Dutton Signet,
a division of Penguin Books USA Inc.

First Printing, October, 1995
10 9 8 7 6 5 4 3 2 1

CHAPTER ONE

An Odd Alliance

London, October 1813

"Relax, my dear Robert," Lady Cynthia murmured with gentle sarcasm, her green eyes dancing with amusement. "You are quite safe from me. Much as I love you, Robbie, nothing—absolutely *nothing*—could induce me to accept your so flattering offer, believe me."

The Marquess of Monroyal cast a jaundiced eye on his lovely cousin and raised one dark eyebrow. "I do not recall making any offer, my sweet," he drawled with characteristic nonchalance. As if to set the seal on his disinterest, he drew out a delicate porcelain snuff-box from his lavishly embroidered waistcoat and flicked it open with a polished fingernail. Negligently he took a pinch of the yellowish brown powder specially blended for him by Fribourg and Treyer's, tobacconists, and raised it first to one aristocratic nostril and then the other.

Lady Cynthia observed this flawless performance with amusement touched with awe. Trust Robbie to imbue the ordinary—and if truth be told rather nauseating—habit of snuff-taking with a refined elegance that aroused the helpless admiration of every young sprig down from Oxford and not a few older gentlemen about Town who should have known better.

This pantomime was all a huge bluff, of course. Cynthia knew for a certainty that her cousin did not even like tobacco. He had told her so himself one rainy afternoon a month ago when, bored beyond reason at having to cancel her plans to drive in the Park, the marquess had introduced her to the fine art of taking snuff. Cynthia had mastered her cousin's elegant flick of the wrist immediately, but had shown little interest in learning to identify the various blends currently popular among the *ton*.

He regarded her with hooded gray eyes, a faint smile pulling at the corners of his sensual mouth. Wordlessly he proffered the porcelain box with the air of a master challenging his recalcitrant pupil.

Lady Cynthia shrugged and stretched out her hand. "We both

know you were about to do so, however," she replied tartly. "Why else would you be here at this early hour, Cousin, if you had not succumbed to my father's argument that I am in dire need of masculine guidance?"

She dipped her thumb and forefinger gingerly into the snuff and gently shook off the excess of brown powder before raising it to her nose. "By which he means holy matrimony, as we also know, do we not, Robbie?" she continued, pausing to meet his quizzical gaze. "Although in my limited experience there is nothing holy about parson's mousetrap—a misnomer if ever I heard one—being rather a state of oppression and frustrating dependence expressly designed to gall the female spirit." She threw him a dazzling smile and was comforted by his answering grin.

"So let me repeat, Robbie dear," she said with theatrical flair. "Assuming of course that your so charming offer has been made, I would not dream of cutting short your career as London's premier rake. I do not subscribe to the common romantical myth that rakes can be reformed into diligent and devoted husbands."

Lady Cynthia inhaled delicately from each nostril and sneezed discreetly into a wisp of lace she held at the ready.

The marquess smiled approvingly. "You are becoming rather proficient in your vices, my dear," he drawled provocatively. "Perhaps it is time you had your own mix at Fribourg's. One of the lighter Martiniques, I would suggest."

"I think not, Cousin," Lady Cynthia responded with a laugh. "It is one thing to see the startled expressions on the old Tabbies' faces when you offer me a pinch of your special mix at one soirée or another, but quite beyond the pale to make a spectacle of myself by setting up my own blend to advertise my vices, as you call them. It is mere affectation in any case. I am convinced of it. And a rather vulgar habit into the bargain, Robbie. Deny it if you dare."

The marquess regarded her intently for a moment, a curious little smile on his lips. "Have you never felt the need to advertise your vices, my dear Cynthia?" he mused.

"I have no vices," Cynthia responded quickly, staring at her cousin warily. And that was unfortunately the truth, she thought. After eight uneventful years wedded to a gentleman more than twice her age, Lady Cynthia Lonsdale had an impeccable reputation and a vast fortune, a state of affairs she had of late found rather tedious.

"After nearly a decade with poor old Lonsdale, I am not at all surprised to hear it, love. But don't you sometimes wish you had?" he murmured with a provocative glint in his gray eyes.

Cynthia stared at him in surprise. How could this charming rogue know that she had been assailed by that very thought with increasing frequency over the past four months. Ever since her twenty-ninth birthday to be more precise. It had suddenly dawned on her one morning that here she was, rushing toward middle age with nothing to show for her life except a tidy estate in Surrey and an embarrassingly large fortune. Neither of these possessions seemed to provide the satisfaction she had experienced during the first year and a half of her mourning. For some inexplicable reason the pleasure she had once derived from her status as an attractive, wealthy widow no longer gave her comfort. What good were possessions to her if she were too old to enjoy them? she wondered bleakly, suddenly overcome with visions of herself at sixty puttering around in her beloved rose-garden at Milford Hall with no one to share her enjoyment of the blossoms. With no one to share her life.

"James was neither poor nor old," she retorted sharply, throwing off the fit of the blue-devils that seemed to plague her so frequently of late. "And if you must know, Cousin," she continued daringly, "I have occasionally wished that I might be more like Lady Hartfield, dainty, and blond, and so very beautiful, and . . . and . . ."

"And brazen?" her cousin suggested gently, his gray eyes alight with amusement.

Cynthia shot a reproving glance at him. "No, not brazen exactly. But certainly alluring in a faintly decadent sort of way, if you know what I mean, Robbie. Lady Hartfield must be at least my age, and yet she is always surrounded by a court of dashing young bucks."

"Aha!" the marquess exclaimed delightedly. "So you dream of decadence and dalliance, my sweet? Who would have thought that the proper Lady Cynthia Lonsdale harbored such immodest fantasies in her lovely head? You astound me, love. And if it is Lucy Hartfield's style of decadence you wish to affect, I would be more than willing—"

"No, thank you, Cousin," Cynthia interrupted, feeling her cheeks grown warm at Lord Monroyal's half-formulated suggestion. "I meant no such thing, as you must know. I merely wondered why all the handsome young men flock to Lady Hartfield, while I seem unable to attract anyone but old roués and fortune-hunters desperate to line their pockets at my expense."

Cynthia heard the marquess stroll over to where she stood at the library window gazing down at the small enclosed garden of her father's London residence. A gnarled pear-tree stood stoically in the October breeze, almost denuded of its yellowing leaves. Cynthia felt a tremor of apprehension as she gazed at the old familiar friend of her childhood. How reassuring it must be, she mused, to shed one's tattered autumn splendor with the absolute certainty that with the return of spring one would reemerge in a burst of youthful green leaves, peak in a glorious display of white blossoms, and mature gracefully with the satisfying weight of fruitfulness. Such was the cycle of life, she thought, a cycle in which she had played but a small, singularly unproductive part.

She sighed and glanced up affectionately at the tall man beside her. Robert Stilton had become her childhood mentor and confident after her aunt Sophy had wed his widowed father over twenty years ago. Although not actually related by blood, Cynthia had never thought of Robbie as anything but family, and had come to rely on his caustic humor and sympathetic ear.

"I apologize for being so peevish this morning, Robbie, but the truth is I am overset with old age." She laughed self-consciously at the startled expression on her cousin's handsome face. "Yes, I know it sounds nonsensical, but I cannot forget that I am turned twenty-nine, Robbie. Twenty-nine," she repeated with a hint of desperation in her voice. "And I have this quite lowering feeling that I have nothing whatsoever to show for my life. Nothing!" she echoed, feeling the telltale tightening of her throat.

"I warn you, Robbie," she continued recklessly, overcoming her momentary weakness, "I am ready to do something quite desperate."

Cynthia's tone must have communicated her anguish to Lord Monroyal for he instantly took her hand and lifted it gallantly to his lips.

"My dearest Cynthia," he murmured softly. "I never thought to hear such words from your lips, but I see that there is hope for you yet." His smile widened into a grin as Cynthia glanced at him in surprise. "All this talk of decadence and dashing young men. It is as plain as a pikestaff what ails you, love."

"And what is that, pray?" Cynthia demanded warily, mistrusting the wicked glint in her cousin's gray eyes.

"You are ripe for a lover, my dear," came the answer, even more preposterous than she had anticipated. "I should have seen it months ago."

"Rubbish!" Cynthia exclaimed, annoyed at the flood of heat to her cheeks. "You are quite off the mark, Cousin."

The marquess merely laughed. "Believe me, I know whereof I speak, little one. An ardent lover would put some joy back into your life, and make you forget that unhealthy preoccupation with age, my dear." He pressed his lips to her fingers with a seductive gesture that caused an unfamiliar warmth to uncoil deep in Cynthia's body.

Lord Monroyal smiled possessively, quite as though he could read her mind. "I am entirely at your service, my sweet," he murmured with an intimate smile that made Cynthia's breath catch in her throat. "I would be honored if you would consider . . ."

She gasped and jerked her hand away. "Do not even think it, Robert," she interrupted sharply, startled at the beguiling power of her cousin's seductive charm. "How *could* you? I thought we were friends."

"We are, my sweet innocent. But it is such a short step from friend to lover." He left the words hanging in the air between them, tantalizing her with their implications.

"No!" Cynthia abruptly turned away from the mesmerizing glow of her cousin's eyes, rejecting the dizzy notion that had nudged its insidious way into her mind. Her knees felt weak, and she realized with sudden shock that she had come as close as she ever had to being seduced. And by Robbie, no less! The thought appalled her. For years Cynthia had known of her cousin's success with the ladies; had seen with her own eyes how females of all classes gravitated to his tall, dark figure; had heard preposterous tales of his prowess in the boudoirs of London; but until this moment she had never quite understood the unnerving masculine attraction the marquess exerted on his female admirers. Now she knew, and the knowledge frightened her.

She turned to meet the complacent, predatory stare of her cousin's gray eyes. "Do not do this to me, Robbie," she said tersely, noting from the smug expression on his face, that the marquess knew exactly what was going through her mind. "It is not a lover I need," she admitted, putting into words the truth she had been trying to avoid for so long. "Father was right, you know. I need another husband. I am not cut out for decadence."

She smiled tremulously and the marquess responded with a grin quite devoid of seductive overtones. Cynthia felt the tension ease between them and sighed. "I am sorry to disappoint you, Cousin," she remarked teasingly. "But I cannot help being what I am."

The marquess's grin broadened. "I wouldn't want you any other way, Cynthia," he said seriously. "And perhaps I can still be of service to you, love. If I were to renew the respectable offer I have yet to make, I mean," he added with an entirely different kind of charm.

"Lady Cynthia," he began, taking up her limp fingers again and pressing them tenderly, "would you do me the honor—"

"Robbie!" Cynthia cried in genuine dismay. "I cannot believe you are actually ready to commit the final sacrifice for me. I am flattered, dearest, but I cannot allow you to immolate yourself on the altars of matrimony merely to stave off this fit of peevishness on my part. Perhaps if you were to invite me to drive in the Park instead . . ."

Cynthia never finished her sentence, for the door of the library swung open to admit her father, his ruddy face alight with expectation.

"Well?" he inquired, staring pointedly at the couple standing by the window, hands entwined. "Is it done?" He glanced from one to the other eagerly.

Cynthia withdrew her hand from her cousin's grasp and turned to face her father. "If you mean has Robert made the offer you have bullied him into making, Papa, then the answer is yes, it is done. But do not think to celebrate my nuptials just yet, for I have explained to Lord Monroyal that we would not suit."

Lord Halifax's face fell. He came across the room to stand before his daughter, and Cynthia knew from his pained expression that he was not about to accept her decision without protest.

"Is this correct, Robert?" he snapped, a frown marring his still handsome face. "Have you made my daughter an offer of marriage?"

Cynthia glanced up at her cousin and saw that he was smiling at her, his eyes reminding her of that other offer he had also made. He was a shameless rogue, but she wondered irrationally whether she had made a mistake in refusing such an offer from London's most sought-after womanizer. Her mind shied away from the thought. Robbie was dear to her, but he was incapable of constancy and—she suspected—any real affection for the women he bedded so casually. And Cynthia did not want intimacy with a man for whom love was a game of skill, a game at which he was singularly adept, but one that he could win or lose with equal *sang-froid.*

"Yes, indeed I did, my lord," Cynthia heard her cousin say solemnly, before he looked away and addressed Lord Halifax.

"But the cruel minx has thrown my offer back in my teeth, tossed my innocent heart aside like a discarded nosegay, trampled my sensibilities until I squirmed with anguish, blasted my poor ears with—"

"Enough, Robbie!" Cynthia exclaimed, torn between the desire to laugh and an irresistible urge to box his ears. She saw that her father was regarding Lord Monroyal with a startled expression. "Pay no attention to the rogue, Papa," she said soothingly. "The mere notion of getting riveted has addled his brains, but he has complied with your wishes, and now I hope you will leave the dear man in peace. He is not cut out to be a husband, as you must know if you believe half the gossip in the saloons."

"You are a stubborn puss," said Lord Halifax with a mixture of exasperation and evident affection. "Your mother will be most distressed to hear that you have refused your cousin. She quite had her heart set on it, as did Lady Monroyal. An excellent match it would have been, and I must insist that you reconsider, Cynthia. Robert will take the running of Milford Hall off your shoulders, my dear, and you can be comfortable again. Besides," he added reflectively, "this union will keep everything in the family."

Cynthia knew all too well what her father referred to, and the notion that her life and fortune could be disposed of so cavalierly made her bristle. "I am sure Robert does not need yet another estate to add to his patrimony, Papa," she said crossly. "And he is already as rich as Golden Ball, so my paltry inheritance can make no difference to him."

Lord Halifax glared at her sternly. "You will moderate your language, if you please, Cynthia," he ordered. "Such things are for gentlemen to decide, and if Robert has consented to have you, I strongly advise you to accept his offer. It is the most advantageous arrangement you will get, let me tell you, my dear. So be guided by us if you please."

"There will be no such *arrangement*, as you call it," she responded sharply, her ire now thoroughly aroused. "I am sure Robbie would rather have a tooth pulled than marry me. Or anyone else, for that matter. And besides, we have already agreed that we will not suit. Is that not so, Robbie?" she added, throwing an imploring glance at her cousin.

"*You* have so decided, my dear Cynthia," he murmured facetiously. "And far be it from me to question the wisdom of your choice."

Cynthia could have cheerfully wrung her cousin's elegant neck at that moment, but before she could respond, her father intervened.

"So you are determined to defy me, Cynthia?" Lord Halifax said sternly, and his daughter recognized the signs of incipient anger in his fine blue eyes.

"If you mean do I refuse to marry a man who does not wish to be saddled with a wife, and whom I do not consider an eligible husband, Papa? then yes, I intend to defy you. And neither do I intend to accept one of those venerable gentlemen you insist upon throwing at my head, nor any of the fortune-hunters who are forever hanging at my heels. Better to be single than accept that fate, I say. And at twenty-nine, Papa, I thought I had a choice in the matter."

Lord Halifax stared at his daughter for several moments. "What precisely is your objection to Monroyal, Cynthia?" he asked suddenly, momentarily disconcerting her.

She glanced ruefully at her cousin. "Well, look at him, Papa," she responded with a helpless gesture towards the elegant marquess, lounging negligently against the mantel, a vision in pale gray breeches and a modishly cut morning-coat of blue superfine. "Robbie is all very well in his way, of course," she began, enjoying the pained expression that flashed across her cousin's aquiline features. "But he is not exactly in the first flush of youth. In fact at times he appears utterly weary, no doubt as a result of his obsession with gambling and ladies' boudoirs—"

"Cynthia!" her father thundered wrathfully. "I cannot believe that Lonsdale allowed you to express yourself with so little delicacy. You will keep a civil tongue in your head, my girl. What a husband does outside the home is his business and no one else's. A wife should expect to be provided for according to her station, of course, but—"

"Aye, but there's the rub, Papa," Cynthia could not resist interjecting. "Our dear Robbie has too many other women to provide for—"

"Ah, Cynthia, that was unworthy of you, my pet," the marquess drawled, before his uncle could recover from his shock at Lady Cynthia's audacity. "I'll admit my reputation is not spotless, as yours undoubtedly is," he added with an obvious reference to their previous discussion. "But it is cruel of you to chastise me for minor peccadilloes and to suggest that I am in my dotage. Most unkind, my dear," he murmured with mock dejection.

"I agree with Robert entirely," Lord Halifax exclaimed with

unexpected vigor. "One would suppose, to listen to you, that you are set against a second marriage entirely, Cynthia. Is this true?"

Cynthia gazed into her father's puzzled blue eyes and wondered, not for the first time, why men seemed incapable of understanding a woman's most elemental needs. Could her father not guess that *of course* she wished for a second marriage; she yearned for it ever more desperately as the months drifted by and her dream of a family of her own began to slip into the realm of the impossible. Yet she refused to accept her parents' calm assumption that she must accept a husband of their choice, as she had accepted the wealthy Viscount Lonsdale, bowing to their wishes as though she had none of her own. A stolid, aging husband held no appeal for her, although Cynthia knew that the *haut monde*, no less than her parents, would expect her to make a sensible alliance with just such a man. But in her heart she dreamed of someone quite different. . . . But dare she reach for her dream? she wondered. Dare she even attempt the search for a man more suited to her needs?

Both men seemed to be waiting for her answer. Her father with growing exasperation, Robert with a cynical smile on his lips as though daring her to confess her secret desires.

"No, Papa," she said quietly, turning away to gaze out at the pear-tree in the garden below. "I am not averse to a second marriage. Quite the contrary if you must know the truth."

"Then why the devil must you be so stubborn, Cynthia?" Lord Halifax burst out impatiently. "You have received over a dozen offers in the past six months. What are you waiting for, child? One of the Royal Dukes perchance?" he added caustically.

Cynthia could find no adequate answer for this, and was grateful when her cousin intervened. "If you will forgive me, Uncle," the marquess said diffidently, "I believe we are going about this in the wrong way. You cannot deny that Cynthia very dutifully accepted Lonsdale's offer when you selected him for her ten years ago, my lord."

"She was a good deal more tractable then, it seems," Lord Halifax huffed crossly. "What could a chit of eighteen possibly know about men?"

"Exactly so, Uncle," the marquess calmly continued. "At that time it was certainly appropriate for her to be guided by you. But Cynthia is now a widow of twenty-nine, who presumably does know something about men. And if I am not mistaken, sir, your daughter would much prefer to take a younger man to her bed."

Cynthia felt her face flame and was thankful she could not see her father's reaction to Robbie's quite outrageous suggestion. Outrageous, yes, she thought, marveling at her cousin's perspicacity. But so close to the truth that she wondered if the rogue had indeed read her mind. Obviously, her cousin was one man who could see into a woman's secret heart.

"You are very blunt, boy," her father said gruffly after a long pause, evidently uncomfortable with the direction the discussion had taken. "But I, for one, consider you to be quite young enough to suit her."

"Ah! But your daughter has already written me off as too decrepit, my lord. I wager our Cynthia has someone a good deal younger in mind. Am I not right, Cousin?"

He was giving her the chance she needed, Cynthia realized. If only she were brave enough to take it. It would be a pity to disappoint Robbie when he seemed to understand her so well, and she was reluctant to appear missish. Before she could consider the consequences, Cynthia turned to face the two men.

"Yes, Robbie, but how did you know?" She threw a defiant, glittering smile in his direction before turning to her father. "Robbie is right, Papa. I fancy a younger gentleman for a second husband." She paused and then continued with a rush. "I would have a family, you see," she added, dropping her eyes as the color rose to her cheeks. "And methinks a young man would make a better father." And husband, too, she thought, but dared not say so. Nor did she risk a glance at her cousin, who would undoubtedly read her thoughts again.

There was a pregnant pause, and then her father snorted derisively. "That is arrant nonsense, child, and you know it," he growled.

Cynthia regarded him steadily. "You were but twenty-five when Tony was born, Papa, and I still remember the hours you spent with me and Harry and Samantha at Halifax Park. You gave us a very happy childhood, you know."

The Marquess of Halifax went very still, and his eyes took on a faraway expression. Cynthia gazed fondly on her father, and a tender smile played over her lips. Finally she moved to slip a hand through his arm. "Do you remember, Papa?" she murmured softly. "It seems like only yesterday that Harry's mongrel—what was his name?"

"Demetrius," said Lord Halifax, his eyes on his daughter's radiant face.

"That's right! Demetrius. What a silly name for a dog. Remember the afternoon he got into old Ned's chicken-house and massacred—how many hens was it?"

"Sixteen," her father promptly responded.

"You see what I mean?" she said. "You remember everything we did together. That's important for a child."

Lord Halifax patted his daughter's hand and cleared his throat. "You were a headstrong chit even then, Cynthia. I remember the morning you took out my Spanish barb when I had expressly forbidden you to go near the brute."

Cynthia smiled. "Yes, but did you really expect me to resist the temptation, Papa? He was so very sleek and beautiful, and ran like no horse I had ever ridden before."

"You were a naughty minx," remarked his lordship affectionately.

"And I did not break my neck, as you said I would, Papa," Cynthia added with a laugh. "You never did trust my judgment, even then."

Her father observed her steadily, his blue eyes quizzical, but Cynthia knew he was weakening.

"So now you want a young husband, do you, puss?" he said slowly. "Your mother will not like it, I can tell you, and I confess I find it a little unnatural myself, but if you tell me which one you fancy, my dear, I will do everything in my power to see that you get him. Does that make you happy, sweetling?"

Cynthia smiled radiantly. "Oh, yes, Papa," she murmured happily, standing on tiptoe to kiss his lean cheek. "Very happy."

"Whom do you have in mind, lass?" he wanted to know.

Cynthia glanced over at her cousin and noticed that the marquess was eyeing her with his usual cynical smile. "Why, I have no specific gentleman in mind," she replied. "I was hoping that Robbie would consent to be my mentor in this affair. I have no doubt he knows every eligible gentleman in London. What do you say, Cousin?" she added, unable to repress a saucy smile at the expression of dismay on Lord Monroyal's saturnine face.

"Then I will leave you in his capable hands, my dear," her father said without waiting for the marquess to reply. "I must go and disappoint your mother, Cynthia. She was anxious to welcome Robert into the family."

Cynthia sighed as she watched Lord Halifax hurry from the room and turned to regard her cousin, an anxious frown on her face.

"You *will* help me, will you not, Robbie?" she queried. "I have not been out of my blacks long enough to have met any younger men who are truly eligible and not merely out to line their pockets. I am depending on you to guide me."

Lord Monroyal's lips quirked, and his face took on a resigned expression. "What precise miracle will I be expected to perform, love?" he drawled.

Cynthia could not repress a grin. "Merely to produce a young man inclined towards matrimony and willing to consider an aging female of passing comeliness and a large fortune," she responded with shattering honesty.

The marquess shrugged eloquently. "Consider it done, my dear," he drawled. "No doubt the large fortune will provide incentive enough to offset the advancing years." He ducked adroitly to avoid the cushion his cousin hurled at him, and strolled over to pour himself a glass of his uncle's best brandy.

"I trust it will not be the only incentive, Robbie," Cynthia said, voicing one of her deepest fears.

"If the lucky gentleman has eyes in his head," the marquess remarked confidently, "he may regard the fortune as incidental, my pet. So do not trouble your pretty head with morbid thoughts, Cynthia. Somehow or another we will muddle through, never fear."

Long after her cousin had taken his leave, Lady Cynthia stood at the library window watching the final yellow leaves flutter down from the pear-tree.

Her fortune might well attract a suitable candidate, she mused, suddenly overset by a wave of melancholy.

But could it keep him?

CHAPTER TWO

Desperate Wager

The soft shuffle of cards on the green baize table was the only sound in the room. At least so it seemed to the Honorable Captain Brian Sheffield, as he stared gloomily at the unprepossessing cards in his hand.

He cursed softly under his breath.

At this rate he would never regain the frighteningly large sum he had already lost to the exquisitely dressed gentleman lounging very much at his ease in the opposite chair, Brian thought, his claret-fogged brain refusing to acknowledge the futility of such an endeavor.

"No man in his right senses gambles with Robert Stilton," his friend and fellow officer, Captain Richard Chatham, had warned him as soon as they entered the notorious portals of Watier's on Bolton Street earlier that evening to find a small silent crowd watching the deep play at one of the faro tables.

"'Tis said he has lost and won several fortunes at deep basset," Chatham continued, pausing beside his friend to observe the game that was being played out between a tall, elegantly attired gentleman with classically chiseled features, and a florid individual of considerable girth, whom Brian recognized as Sir Christopher Barkley, a gentleman noted more for intemperance than wisdom.

"I hear that win or lose, the marquess does not crack a smile," Chatham added with a hint of envy in his voice. Brian could well believe it. In spite of the mountain of vowels stacked carelessly beside him, the tall gentleman's expression revealed nothing but boredom and a faintly contemptuous flicker in the depths of his slate-gray eyes, as Sir Christopher lost the game and thrust yet another hastily scribbled note across to his opponent.

"Your luck seems to be elsewhere tonight, Barkley," the imperturbable marquess drawled. "Would you care to try a hand of picquet instead?"

"Picquet? Not on your life, my lord." Sir Christopher laughed shortly. "Piquet is not my game. I thought I was a fair hand at faro, but obviously I was mistaken. Remind me not to take you on again, Monroyal," he added, getting ponderously to his feet. "I shall send my draft around in the morning if that is convenient, my lord?"

"The devil take it!" Brian heard Chatham murmur almost reverently. "I'll wager Barkley dropped over ten thousand pounds in vowels tonight. Monroyal never plays for chicken stakes, that I do know."

Brian grimaced at the thought of having that impossible sum to lose. Or to win, he mused, eyeing the vowels scattered carelessly on the green baize beside the marquess's brandy glass. The captain was considered no mean hand at whist and picquet by his fellow officers on the Peninsula, and had, more than once, lined his empty pockets at their expense during the interminable nights in makeshift bivouacs, waiting for orders to come down from the Field Marshall—an honor so recently bestowed upon the Marquess of Wellington by the Prince Regent after the battle of Vittoria. Perhaps he might be as fortunate here in London as he had been on the Peninsula, Brian thought, his eyes still riveted on Lord Monroyal's winnings. A dangerous assumption, as well he knew, but one that might deliver him from his irksome dependence on his brother.

The crowd of interested observers dissipated, and Brian cast a curious glance at the darkly handsome gentleman who was the focus of so much attention. Although he did not know the Marquess of Monroyal personally, he had heard enough stories of the man's reputation with women and cards to know that Robert Stilton was not a man who did things by half measure. If rumor could be credited, the marquess's immense fortune had recently been increased by an improbable wager with Ball Hughes during a game at battledore and shuttlecock, an entertainment much favored by London's wealthiest dandy.

"He was one of my brother's Oxford cronies," Brian volunteered, as the two young men made their way across the room to the macao tables. "But John never forgave Monroyal for outbidding him on that black barb, Horatio, five years ago. Particularly since the horse proved a consistent winner at Newmarket against John's prize cattle." He gave a short mirthless laugh. "He should have known better than to bid against a man with bottomless pockets," he said bitterly.

"I gather you are still at odds with your brother," Chatham remarked as they settled themselves at a table and called for a bottle of brandy.

"Was there ever a time I was not at odds with that clutch-fisted old skinflint?" Brian growled. He poured himself a brandy and took a large swallow before setting his glass down and glaring across the table at his friend. "I don't wish to hear that bastard's name again tonight," he muttered. "In fact, I would prefer never to see the miserable squeeze-crab ever again. I wouldn't be surprised if he cut me off without a penny after the huge dust-up we had this morning."

The captain grimaced irritably. His leg was bothering him again. It invariably did when he stood about on it for extended periods, as he had this morning in his half-brother's study. The captain wished fervently that he could get a clean bill of health from the army physicians, but only last week they had told him bluntly that he could expect to be on their recuperating list for at least another two or three months. Brian chaffed at this added delay in rejoining his regiment, the 7th Hussars, which, from the latest reports, had been engaged in the siege of San Sebastian at the end of August, and even now must be advancing with Wellington's main army into France.

Military life had not been Brian's first choice as a career, but as a second son his options had been woefully limited, particularly since he had no fortune of his own. The captain could still remember his bitter disappointment when he discovered that his father had failed to make good on their unspoken understanding that Brian would inherit one of the minor unentailed estates in the vast Sheffield holdings. The reading of the will had been a severe shock to the naive twenty-year-old he had been then. And the smug expression on the new earl's face, which John had not even tried to hide, told Brian more clearly than any words who was responsible for their father's change of heart.

It had done not the slightest good to confront his half-brother with his perfidy. Had he not been so devastated by this betrayal, Brian would have realized the futility of appealing to the new earl's better nature. John had no such sense of *noblesse oblige*, and now that he held the trump card, he made no bones about informing his younger half-brother that not only could Brian kiss any thought of sharing the old earl's patrimony good-bye, but that his services were no longer needed in the management of the prestigious Sheffield racing stables.

This stroke of meanness on the part of his half-brother—who had long harbored an overt dislike for the offspring of his father's second marriage—perhaps more than the loss of any hope he might have had of being master to his own land, had driven Brian to join the army. He stayed long enough to see his distraught mother and young sister settled in the Dower House, and to extract the price of his captain's commission from the new earl, who had been unable to find an excuse to deny him their father's last bequest. And then he had left Mulgrave Park for London, determined never to set foot in his brother's house again.

Until now, five years later, when his mother, Lady Agatha, the Dowager Countess, had been unexpectedly joined by her young daughter-in-law, the Countess of Mulgrave, in demanding that her wounded son be tended, as became his station, in Mulgrave House on Belgrave Square. But that, too, had come to an end, if John stood by this morning's threat to throw his half-brother out into the street. Brian believed him quite capable of such barbarity, and had taken measures to avoid the humiliation by hiring a set of rooms on Jermyn Street, close to Chatham's lodgings.

Leaving his batman, the grizzled Nat Hardy, to effect the removal of his scanty possessions from Mulgrave House, Brian had taken refuge in Chatham's company. Together the two had caroused the afternoon away at various dubious establishments, until Brian had overcome some of his simmering resentment at his brother's rejection.

"Where the devil is that fat brother-in-law of yours, Dick?" he demanded irritably, taking a long drink from his glass.

"Toby will be here any moment," his friend replied easily. "But if you get yourself foxed, old man, you will be no match for him. Toby rather prides himself on his luck at macao."

Brian glared at Chatham with a flicker of annoyance. "Are you saying I am foxed, Chatham?" he growled. "Toby had best look to himself unless he wants to lose his fancy waistcoat, let me warn you. I feel lucky myself tonight," he added, wondering if this were indeed true or whether the sight of the winnings on the marquess's table had turned his thoughts in that direction. He took another drink. The thought of being obliged to win at cards to put a little of his friends' money in his empty pockets disheartened him. It was one thing to do so in the army as a distraction from the bloody business of war, but here in London a scion of the powerful Sheffield family should not have to sink so low. Brian cursed his half-brother anew and smiled grimly. If Lady Luck would aid him tonight, he told himself, perhaps the future might not look so bleak.

"There he is!" Chatham explained, pushing back his chair to

welcome the two modish gentlemen who approached their table. "Toby, old man, we were about to start without you."

Brian rose and slapped the corpulent newcomer on the back. "Well, Toby, you fat fiend," he said amicably. "We missed your wit and charm at Vittoria, old boy. And your blunt," he added truthfully.

The Honorable Tobias Tottlefield was one of those rare individuals who could—if one believed the stories bandied about the regiment—make friends with an army mule. He was also very conveniently plump in the pocket and ever ready to accommodate those military cronies less fortunate than himself. Even had Toby not recently married Dick's sister, Brian would have been drawn to the older man's cheerful disposition and calm resourcefulness in the face of danger.

"You may have all three of them tonight, Sheffield," Toby responded jovially. "And I've brought Forsdyke along for good measure. His wife has let him off the leash for a few hours." This witticism was accompanied by a loud guffaw as Tottlefield turned to the tall, sparse gentleman who stood quietly beside him. "You know Sheffield, don't you, Henry?"

Brian recognized Lord Forsdyke as one of the officers attached to Lieutenant-General Sir Rowland Hill's command at Vittoria, and he hastened to shake his hand.

"You were with Hill at Vittoria, I believe, sir?" he said to Forsdyke. "Have you any news from the Peninsula? The last I heard, Wellington was advancing into France."

"You were there also, I gather," Forsdyke replied cordially. "And wounded, too, from what I hear."

"Yes," Brian replied shortly. He did not relish speaking of his disability. "But I am anxious to rejoin the regiment before there are any major encounters in France."

The viscount smiled, his weathered face creasing. "A glutton for punishment, I see," he murmured. "I will be returning myself next month, but the French have already been routed in Dresden, where unfortunately General Moreau was lost, and again at Leipzig with very heavy losses." He paused to regard the captain with a glimmer of macabre amusement. "There will be enough Frenchies for you when you return, Captain, never fear."

"Are we to waste the evening discussing the war, Forsdyke, or shall we play cards?" Toby demanded with bluff heartiness.

Tottlefield's words brought Brian's thoughts abruptly back from his regiment, and he joined the others at the table, determined to banish the blue-devils that had plagued him since morning.

Several hours later, Brian's spirits were considerably revived and his pockets fatter than they had been in several months. With the help of his congenial companions, he had put both his clutch-fisted elder brother and the gambling marquess from his thoughts. He was therefore surprised and a little wary after the game had broken up, and Tottlefield and Forsdyke had gone off to bed, to hear a soft drawl at his shoulder.

"You must be Mulgrave's young brother, if I remember rightly." The voice was light and faintly amused.

The captain glanced up quickly, and was startled to find himself being regarded by a pair of slate-gray eyes that revealed nothing but polite speculation.

Brian blinked in surprise. "Yes, I'm Sheffield," he replied shortly, the mention of his half-brother reviving his surliness. "I trust you do not propose to discuss my brother," he added with deliberate curtness. "Any friend of John's is *persona non grata* at the moment." He stared at the marquess belligerently, wishing him in Jericho.

The marquess ignored the rudeness. "I'm Monroyal," he said dryly. "And no, I have no interest in Mulgrave at all. To be quite honest, I find him a dead bore." He regarded the captain steadily, a cynical smile curling his lips. "I heard you were back from Spain and wondered if you had run across my brother Geoffrey over there. He is a bit of a rattle and no hand at writing. Our step-mother is getting anxious for news, since Geoffrey's last scrawl was dated June 5th. We know he survived Vittoria," the marquess said tentatively.

"Yes, I saw him just before they shipped me home," Brian said. "Nary a scratch, as far as I know. But he had his horse killed under him. A big gray gelding with a white blaze."

"Lionheart," the marquess murmured, as if to himself. "Pity. He was a fine horse." He seemed to recall himself and gestured to the two younger men. "Let me order a fresh bottle." He indicated the empty vessel on the macao table. "I have heard you are good at picquet, Sheffield," he added as an afterthought. "Perhaps I can entice you to play a hand with me."

It had all started as innocently as that, Brian recalled two hours later, staring with an odd sense of fatalism at the cards in his hand. Dick had hinted rather insistently that they should take their winnings from macao and retire for the night. The marquess had merely smiled that cynical little smile of his and said nothing. Finally, when Brian had lost all his winnings and began to sign vowels for the marquess, Chatham had risen in disgust and taken himself off, muttering dire warnings under his breath about the fate of fools and their money.

But Brian had merely refilled his glass and stayed. He knew he was being foolish beyond reason to wager away funds he did not have, but some perversity kept him sitting there, hoping that his luck would miraculously change. Confident that it eventually would do so. It had not done so, of course, and finally Brian had admitted defeat. He had also been forced to face the unpleasant truth that even if he sold his two horses, all his clothes, his jewelry, his commission, and perhaps his soul, he would never cover a quarter of the vowels he had so carelessly signed, and which the marquess negligently stuffed into his pocket without a second glance.

Chatham had been right, Brian thought irrelevantly. The marquess did not crack a smile at the enormous windfall that had come his way. Of course, for such a man, fifteen thousand pounds probably meant nothing at all. A sum to be gambled away the following evening with no thought of the consequences.

"I shall be gone into the country tomorrow for about a week," he heard Lord Monroyal say as though from a great distance. "We can settle when I return, if you prefer."

Numbly Brian agreed, mumbling his adieux as they strolled out into the cold October dawn together.

Brian shuddered at the enormity of what he had done. There was no help for it, he mused as he made his way along the streets awaking to their daily bustle. If he could not come up with fifteen thousand pounds within the next sennight—and there was no conceivable way he could—then he would have to put a bullet through his head.

A sobering thought.

Lady Cynthia sat idly at the piano the following afternoon, unable to concentrate on her favorite sonata. Instead, her fingers drifted of their own accord into the melancholy strains of an old French love song. The words of the famous sonnet that had caught her romantical imagination at seventeen gradually filtered back into her memory, and Cynthia began first to hum, then to sing them softly, lingeringly, feeling the implications of their sadness with a fresh awareness.

> Quand vous serez bien vieille, au soir, à la chandelle,
> Assise auprès du feu, dévidant et filant,
> Direz, chantant mes vers, en vous émerveillant:
> "Ronsard me célébrait du temps que j'étais belle!"

Would that she might grow old in the knowledge that a man had treasured her, celebrated her beauty in his heart as Ronsard had obviously loved the long-dead Hélène, whose name he preserved forever in his poem, Cynthia mused, overcome by a sudden yearning for something she could not name. To her knowledge, no man had ever loved her, much less written love songs to her beauty. The thought, which would never have occurred to her a year ago, now caused her to shudder, and suddenly she felt a stifling melancholy settle upon her soul.

To shake off this unusual fit of the dismals, Cynthia played the song again, but the plaintive refrain—redolent with echoes of unrequited love, lost youth, and loneliness—did nothing to lift her spirits. It spoke too closely of her own fears and unfulfilled dreams. It reminded her too vividly of all she lacked: a man's loving arms around her, a man's warm hands, a man's lips on hers, a man's . . . In short, a man, she thought, her cheeks suddenly pink at the unruly direction of her musings. Even James, with his stern, phlegmatic presence, and ponderous insistence on discussing the diseases of sheep at the dinner table, would have been preferable to the empty restlessness of the past several months.

Cynthia sighed and ran her fingers over the keys, all desire to practice her sonata for Mrs. Summerville's musicale next week evaporating. She was debating whether to try again or give up all pretense of interest in her forthcoming performance, when the door opened and the butler appeared.

"Yes, Hastings?"

"The Marquess of Monroyal, milady," the butler replied, his expression questioning. "I have taken the liberty of bringing him upstairs."

"Thank you, Hastings," she replied, her spirits miraculously revived. If anyone could banish this strange melancholy afflicting her this afternoon, it would be Robbie, she thought. She watched her tall cousin stroll across the music room with studied nonchalance. As always, the marquess was dressed to the nines, his buff coat defining his broad shoulders to perfection, and his pale yellow breeches provocatively snug enough to attract every feminine glance in any room he entered.

Cynthia was not immune to this blatant display of masculine physique, but she refused to feed her cousin's huge vanity. "You are looking very pleased with yourself this morning, Robbie," she said lightly, extending her hand, which he carried to his lips with exaggerated gallantry. "I take it that Mrs. Scanton-Jones has capitulated?"

The marquess regarded her with a pained expression, one finely chiseled eyebrow raised quizzically. "You disappoint me, my dear. I had thought you above the vulgar tittle-tattle of old, disgruntled Tabbies."

Cynthia laughed. "You cannot fob me off so easily, Cousin," she said. "I heard it from my mother, no less. I doubt she would be overjoyed to hear you call her an old Tabby."

A lazy smile hovered on her cousin's lips, and Cynthia was struck, as she had been so many times in the past, with the sheer animal magnetism of the man. Poor Mrs. Scanton-Jones had not stood a chance against this charming rogue, she thought. Cynthia could tell from the satisfied smirk on his handsome face that she had guessed correctly, and was startled at the stab of envy that caught her off guard.

"Do you never tire of these everlasting conquests, Robbie?" she said peevishly, motioning him to a chair beside the piano. "I would suppose that such unmitigated success might pall after twenty years of being on the Town."

The marquess laughed. "I am not yet that old, my pet. And I am not always successful, I must confess. You yourself gave me a superior set-down only the other day. I am still reeling from the shock of it."

"Pooh!" Cynthia exclaimed inelegantly. "You are roasting me, Cousin. But I am glad you are come, Robbie," she remarked, changing the subject abruptly. "I have been blue-deviled all morning and stand in urgent need of your charming wit."

"It is yours to command, my pet," the marquess responded smoothly. "And incidentally, the object of my call is to bring you good tidings regarding your hunt for a husband."

Lady Cynthia flinched. "You make me sound like some old fright who is reduced to using subterfuge to attract the attentions of an eligible gentleman. Not exactly an uplifting notion, my dear Robbie."

The marquess grinned sardonically. "You can hardly deny that dangling a fortune in front of a man's nose is a subterfuge of sorts, my dear. However, I would draw the line at suggesting you are a fright, much less an old one." He paused and Cynthia caught a devilish flicker in his gray eyes. "At least not yet," he murmured under his breath, but loud enough for her to hear.

"A backhanded compliment if ever I heard one," Cynthia responded crisply, refusing to be drawn into her cousin's word-play. "Tell me your news," she added, suddenly apprehensive at the speed with which her cousin had undertaken his inquiries. "Who is he?" she demanded, more eagerly than she had intended.

Lord Monroyal smiled his cynical little smile, and Cynthia felt

herself blushing. "I had never before considered the vicarious delights to be gleaned from playing pander, my dear Cousin," he
drawled softly. "You have opened new dimensions of pleasure to
me, Cynthia. I shall be forever in your debt." He paused as the
butler entered with a tray of refreshments.

"Thank you, Hastings," he said, accepting the proffered glass
of sherry and sipping it while the butler served his mistress.

"You are being utterly provoking, Robbie," Lady Cynthia burst
out as soon as Hastings had closed the door behind him. "And it
is unfair of you to tease me. Marriage is not a joke to me, as it undoubtedly is for you, heartless wretch that you are. I should have
known you would make a mockery of the whole idea." She
stopped, suddenly and inexplicably on the brink of tears.

"I am sorry I upset you, Cynthia," he said, his face instantly
sober. "You are right that marriage means nothing to me. To be
honest with you, I intend to avoid parson's mousetrap entirely, although I beg you will say nothing of this to my mother." He
grinned briefly. "But I am also a man of my word, and if I
promised to find you a suitable husband, I shall do so, my dear.
Trust me in this."

Cynthia drew a deep breath and glanced down at the keys, the
echoes of Ronsard's sad refrain ringing in her ears. Had she done
the right thing to entrust her promiscuous, hedonistic cousin with
her most secret desires? she wondered. Could she really trust him
not to turn the whole adventure into a farce for his own amusement?

"I do trust you, Robbie," she said hesitantly. "But I have serious doubts about the wisdom of this venture," she confessed. "I
would not wish to appear forward or immodest or—"

"Nonsense, love," her cousin interrupted smoothly. "Ultimately
this will be a marriage of convenience, no better or worse than
hundreds of others that are contracted every year. Money cannot
buy love, of course," he added with a condescending quirk of his
eyebrows. "But you already know that, I presume. Applied judiciously, however, it can generate a healthy amount of respect, and
in many instances, a considerable degree of loyalty and congeniality which is, as I see it, all one can hope for in a marriage in
any case."

This piece of worldly wisdom, intended—Cynthia was convinced of it—to bolster her flagging spirits, had quite the opposite
effect on her already melancholy state of mind.

She sighed. "You make it all sound so . . . so mercenary," she
protested weakly. "And I had enough respect and congeniality

from James to last me a lifetime. He was nothing if not congenial," she continued, warming to her subject. "But his idea of congeniality was to discuss nothing but topics of his own choosing at
the dinner table, regardless of what our guests might have preferred. I remember one particularly grim evening during which he
waxed loud and long on the finer aspects of curing a certain strain
of murrain which had infected the flocks that year. I nearly died
from the mortification of it."

"Poor darling," the marquess murmured sympathetically. "But
cheer up, Cynthia. Neither of the two young men I have selected
for you would put you to the blush with their table conversation.
Count on it, pet."

Cynthia was immediately distracted from her less than happy
memories of the late viscount. "Who are they, Robbie?" she demanded. "You have actually found two eligible gentlemen for
me?"

A teasing light danced in her cousin's eyes, and he smiled com-
placently. "There must be dozens out there waiting for you to notice them, my dear," he said nonchalantly. "I have merely selected
two of the most promising for your consideration."

"That is wonderful, Robbie," Cynthia responded impatiently.
"But will you please get to the point and tell me who they are?"

Unable to delay any longer, the marquess sighed and took another sip of sherry. "The first likely victim is young Thornton," he
said, smiling at Lady Cynthia's suddenly pursed lips. "The Honorable Theodore Thornton, known to his cronies as Teddy. Toothsome Teddy, to be more precise." He paused to grin at her with a
touch of malicious amusement. "Teddy is the possessor of a bewitching pair of blue eyes, I am informed by a lady of my acquaintance who should know all about bewitching eyes, having
bewitched me with her own only recently."

"I have no interest in the color of your ladybird's eyes," Cynthia interrupted crossly.

"And indeed you should not, my dear coz. Not at all the thing,
old girl," he protested in just the condescending tone of voice that
Cynthia most detested.

"Our Teddy has not a feather to fly with, of course, but that
should present no obstacle," her cousin continued blandly. "I
imagine his sire will be only too glad to sanction the match if you
can prevail upon your father to put it forward."

"If you are talking about the Earl of Strathford's youngest son,
Robbie, you can cease this instant," Cynthia said disgustedly. "I
understand that he is a confirmed gambler who, when his pockets

are to let, employs those bewitching eyes you mention to inveigle
the ready from susceptible matrons who should know better."

The marquess shrugged his elegant shoulders. "That is quite
true, love, I cannot deny it. But with a wife to supply the blunt,
our Teddy would not need to resort to such tactics, now would
he?"

"Perhaps not," Cynthia said shortly. "But I do not fancy a husband who will bleed me dry within a year with his extravagances,
Robbie. Let us leave Teddy to the matrons, I beg of you. Tell me
about the other gentleman."

The marquess smiled, and Cynthia felt a sudden tremor of excitement. "Perhaps Teddy is rather too expensive to make a reliable husband, Cousin," he admitted. "Even though I am sure old
Strathford would be delighted to let you have him. But now that I
think on it, Teddy is not the man for you, my dear. Now my second candidate is very much more the thing."

He paused and eyed her teasingly as he sipped his sherry.

"Is fifteen thousand pounds too steep for you, Cynthia?" he
asked abruptly.

"Fifteen thousand pounds?" Cynthia raised her eyebrows
quizzically. "You sound very much as though you wish to sell me
a horse, Robbie," she said with a laugh. "And I confess that fifteen thousand is rather steep for a horse. Or even twenty horses,"
she added, her eyes alight with humor."

"I am talking about a man," the marquess said soberly.

Cynthia felt her smile fade and a spiral of panic begin in her
stomach and rise insidiously into her throat. She could not find
the words to respond to her cousin's outrageously blunt statement. Was this, then, the price of a man? she wondered, strangely
uncomfortable with the thought. Was it going to be as easy as
this? Suddenly Cynthia realized that this course she had embarked
upon held hidden shoals and dangerous currents she had not taken
into consideration. If she would succeed, she must take the risks.
Either that or remain forever on the fringes of life, watching the
years pass by until one day, perhaps in the not so distant future,
she would bend to her father's will and accept another husband of
his choosing.

Her cousin must have misread her hesitation for he grinned
wickedly. "An upstanding, reliable husband is very much like a
good horse, coz. He does not come cheaply. But perhaps you
might tempt him with less."

"Oh, it is not the amount that bothers me, Robbie," Cynthia
said. "James left me very well provided for, as you know. But if

you want to know the truth, I am beginning to have second thoughts about the wisdom of this venture."

The marquess took another sip of sherry and regarded her for a long moment over the rim of his glass, his gray eyes sober. "No, my dear," he said finally. "The truth is that you have lost your nerve, Cynthia. You are suddenly more concerned with what people will think than you are with reaching out and taking what you want from life. You have the means, my dear, and the opportunity. What you lack is the courage." He smiled gently, and Cynthia knew that she had disappointed him.

"It is all very well for you to say I lack courage, Robbie," she said in a small voice. "You are a man, and society is unlikely to chastise you for bending the rules to suit yourself. But that kind of courage is not usually appreciated in females; the *haut monde* will see it as immodesty, and I run the risk of being labeled a managing female, or worse, a harridan."

"So? What does it matter what the old Tabbies say if you get what you want, Cynthia? And what if I were to tell you that the man I have in mind is a soldier, a man who can appreciate courage and has taken more risks in his life than you will ever know of. A young, vigorous man who can be yours for an insignificant sum, which, by the way, is a debt he owes and cannot pay."

Cynthia felt herself blush at the vision her cousin's words conjured up in her mind. Only the unknown soldier's debt rang a discordant note in the picture. "Never say he is another Toothsome Teddy, Robbie," she said ruefully.

The marquess shook his head and finished off his sherry. "No more than an occasional gambler, I would say. But he could still go to Debtor's Prison, you know."

"Fifteen thousand pounds sounds rather steep for a soldier to fritter away in a game of chance," she mused, her interest aroused in spite of herself.

"Yes. I thought so, too. But it appears he was more than halfway foxed and very reckless. Perhaps he was reaching out for something he wanted desperately from life, my dear. Just as you wish to do. The difference being, of course, that our soldier miscalculated the risk and lost. Whereas you, my dear Cynthia," he drawled softly, "cannot fail to win if only you will take the risk."

Cynthia rose slowly and wandered over to the window. The music room was at the back of the house, and as she looked down into the walled garden, her eyes were drawn irresistibly towards the pear-tree. Startled, she noticed that the old tree was almost completely denuded of its autumn leaves. Even as she watched, a gust of wind loosened the two lonely yellow flags that clung tenaciously to their bare branch and sent them fluttering—the last reminders of a productive cycle of life—down to settle comfortably among the colorful carpet of leaves that blanketed the earth.

With sudden insight Cynthia saw the mute scene in the garden not as an ending of the tree's cycle, but as the promise of a new beginning. Abruptly she turned and trod back towards her cousin, her step light and a smile on her face.

"Tell me all about this soldier of ours, Robbie," she said eagerly. "I am ready to take that risk you spoke of."

CHAPTER THREE

Immodest Proposal

Captain Sheffield groaned inwardly as the bespectacled Mr. Matthew Hamilton, junior partner of the London firm of solicitors MacIntyre and Hamilton, regarded him accusingly over his steepled fingers. He should never have come, Brian thought dejectedly. He had known how it would be and was not the least surprised when the solicitor shook his head in dismay at the request Brian had so reluctantly made.

"Fifteen thousand pounds?" Hamilton repeated, his tone fluctuating between outright disapproval at the audacity of a younger son to make such demands upon the Sheffield estate, and condemnation of the irresponsibility that had brought a Sheffield, even a younger one, to this sad pass.

"Completely out of the question, Captain Sheffield, sir, if you want my candid opinion. Mr. MacIntyre would never sanction advancing such a sum."

"It is money that will come to me anyway," Brian protested, loathing himself for the note of desperation he heard in his own voice. "It is not as though I would be depriving my brother of his income, or anything like that," he added, rather more belligerently than he had intended.

Mr. Hamilton closed his eyes in a pantomime of long-suffering resignation that made Brian yearn to smash a fist into his smug, pinched face. "At one thousand pounds per annum," the solicitor intoned ponderously, "the sum you request, sir, accounts for the next fifteen years of the income established in your name by your esteemed father, the late earl. To advance this income in a lump sum would circumvent the conditions of your father's will, which clearly stipulates that—"

"The devil fly away with what the will stipulates," Brian burst out, unable to control his frustration at all this legal twaddle the solicitor was using to cloak the ugly fact that his family's agents were quite prepared to see him in Debtor's Prison before they would release a single groat to save him from this final disgrace.

Angrily, he rose to his feet, scraping the chair against the highly polished floor. "I shall speak to MacIntyre about this," he growled.

He turned towards the door, but Mr. Hamilton's prosy voice made him pause. "Much as I commiserate with your unfortunate predicament, Captain," the solicitor said unctuously, "I can assure you that Mr. MacIntyre, were he here to receive you this afternoon, would merely corroborate my evaluation of your request, sir. There is no possible way in which the estate can meet your demands. I am sorry, Captain, but I am certain your brother, the earl, would agree."

"Oh, I am sure he would, the stingy bastard," Brian muttered under his breath as he flung out of the solicitor's office and rejoined his friend Chatham, who awaited him below in his curricle.

"No luck, eh?" Chatham stated the obvious as he guided his team out into the flow of traffic clogging the streets in that part of London known as the City.

"No, it's Debtor's Prison for me after all," Brian said shortly. And in truth there seemed no other solution to his dilemma short of the melodramatic shot in the brains, which Brian had already ruled out as cowardly to the extreme. "I trust you will keep me supplied with brandy, Dick," he added sourly. "I imagine a man might happily drink himself to death in such a place."

"There has to be another way out of this bramble," Chatham remarked, turning his horses in the direction of Hyde Park. "Monroyal is rumored to be as rich as Croesus, old chap. Perhaps if you threw yourself on his mercy, he would . . ."

"Do not even think of it, Dick," the captain snapped harshly. "This is a debt of honor we are talking about, not some measly tradesman's bill. I cannot do less than honor my vowels."

"I wish I could help you, Brian," Chatham said with evident embarrassment, "but I am overdrawn myself, and you won my last guineas from me yourself at macao last night. Of course," he continued after a pause, "I might be able to get a thousand from my mother, and there is always Tottlefield. He has mighty deep pockets, you know."

"No," Brian said sharply. "Thanks, Dick," he said, softening his tone. "I have only myself to blame for this bumblebroth. You did try to warn me, you know. I was so convinced I would come about . . ." His voice trailed away into a sigh.

"At least you are cured of reckless gambling for a long time to come," his friend remarked with forced cheerfulness. "So perhaps something good will come out of this after all."

Brian laughed and it was not a pleasant sound. "Unfortunately I ceased to believe in miracles when my father died and left me at the mercy of that stingy bastard," he muttered.

"Perhaps you underestimate your half-brother's sense of family responsibility," Chatham suggested as they tooled down Piccadilly towards the Park. "Are you quite set against applying to him for relief?"

Brian grimaced at the very thought of asking John for help. "He would enjoy raking me over the coals, and then he would deny me on some trumped-up excuse or other. If I have to listen to his parsimonious drivel once more, Dick, I swear I shall plant him a facer."

No, he thought morosely as they entered Hyde Park from Piccadilly Street. The chance of a miracle happening before Lord Monroyal returned from the country and Brian would be expected to redeem his vowels was so slight as to be nonexistent.

For perhaps the sixth time that afternoon, Lady Cynthia stood before the cheval mirror regarding herself with a critical eye. She felt uncommonly nervous. In truth she had suffered severe qualms of missishness ever since Lord Halifax had announced at the breakfast table that he had—at her Cousin Robert's instigation and much against his better judgment—approached Captain Sheffield at Watier's last night.

At this startling and unexpected news, Cynthia's stomach had tied itself in knots, and she had lost interest in the substantial helping of kippers and coddled eggs Hastings had just served her. She had toyed with a piece of toast and sipped her tea, but her appetite was irrevocably gone.

Typically, her father had not elaborated, and Cynthia had been obliged to extract the details of his encounter with the captain in bits and pieces.

"What did you say to him, Papa?" she wanted to know.

"What do you think I said to him?" Lord Halifax replied gruffly. "I told him that he might find relief from his debts if he called here this afternoon at four o'clock."

"Is that all?" Cynthia asked, appalled at her father's bluntness.

Lord Halifax paused in the process of shoveling a forkful of York ham into his mouth to glower at her. "What did you expect me to say, girl?" he snapped. "That I have an addle-pated daughter who fancies a strapping young man like him for a husband?"

"An aging daughter, Papa," Cynthia added dryly. "You forgot the part about aging."

"None of your impertinence, miss," Lord Halifax said sternly. "I told you that I cannot like this nonsensical start of yours, Cynthia. It is highly unseemly for a gently bred female to propose such an arrangement to any man, much less a total stranger. It will serve you right if the captain takes you for a wanton and laughs in your face."

Cynthia cringed. Her father had voiced one of her own greatest fears, and she would have given anything to postpone this encounter until she had screwed up her courage to sticking point. It had never occurred to her, when Robbie had proposed the captain's name to her yesterday afternoon, that things would proceed with such implacable speed. She had barely had time to accustom herself to the sound of his name before she must confront the man himself and say things to him that she had never said to any man, not even her husband.

Most definitely not her husband, she thought. Her papa had taken care of all the arrangements for her first marriage. She had barely exchanged a dozen words with Viscount Lonsdale before the ceremony. All she need do, she remembered her father telling her, was to look beautiful and be obedient. Her mother had augmented this oversimplified masculine advice on what a perfect wife should be with more practical information, most of which had terrified Cynthia out of her wits. But it had all been for the best, she thought, just as her mother had said. Knowing what James was going to do to her had somehow lessened the shock of him actually doing it. And after the initial fright had worn off, Cynthia had enjoyed the tenuous influence this nightly possession of her body seemed to exert over her husband. At least he had never brought up the subject of murrain while he was in her bed, she recalled.

"And what did the captain say, Papa?" she inquired, determined to wring the last bit of information from her reluctant parent.

Lord Halifax threw her a disgruntled glance. "He looked at me as though I were daft, of course. As any right-thinking man would do under similar circumstances. And believe me, girl, I felt daft accosting a total stranger with an invitation to call on my daughter. Dashed uncomfortable it was. This whole notion of yours is as queer as Dick's hat-band."

"You never told him to call on *me*, surely?" Cynthia exclaimed fretfully. "You promised not to mention that part of it until later."

"Well, of course I did nothing of the sort," Lord Halifax said huffily. "I am not a complete flat. I had no wish to appear as though I had escaped from Bedlam."

"But what did he *say*, Papa?" she repeated stubbornly wishing that her father would be more forthcoming.

Lord Halifax chewed for several moments before responding. "He wanted to know if this was some kind of a hoax, of course. And I can't say that I blame him. He seemed surprised that a stranger should know about his private business, I'll say that much. Deuced awkward it was, let me tell you."

"Robert said it was fairly common knowledge at the clubs, so actually it is not surprising at all. But tell me, Papa, what else did he say?"

"He asked me what kind of relief I was talking about. Only natural to want to know, after all." He motioned to the butler to serve him another thick slab of ham, causing Cynthia to take a deep breath to curb her impatience.

"And what did you say, Papa?" she murmured with deliberate sweetness.

The marquess glanced at his daughter sternly. "I told him that it was not for me to say," he answered sharply. "Which is what you wanted, is it not, Cynthia?" He paused again, and his expression softened perceptibly as he gazed on his daughter's anxious face. "I wish you would allow me to handle this matter, my dear," he added in gentler tones. "Let me talk to the captain and put the matter to him man to man, as it should be done, child. It is not seemly for you to appear so immodest. These arrangements are better handled between gentlemen, Cynthia. I am better equipped to look out for your interests in any case. Only think how well I arranged everything with Lonsdale. We do not know anything about this captain fellow, except that he comes from an unexceptional background and has spent the last five years in the army. We do not want him to take advantage of you, now, do we?"

Cynthia smiled affectionately at her father, understanding his concern. "I feel as though I am taking advantage of *him*, Papa," she said ruefully.

"Bah!" Lord Halifax exclaimed impatiently. "Your wits have gone begging, girl. If giving a fellow fifteen thousand pounds is taking advantage of him, then I am a Chinaman."

"Then am I to assume that the captain is coming to call this afternoon?" she inquired, her heart beating uncomfortably in her throat.

"Of course, he is coming," the marquess responded impatiently. "Haven't I been telling you so? Only a blithering idiot would whistle that kind of money down the wind. And from what I could ascertain, the captain is nobody's fool."

"What does he look like Papa?"

"You will find out soon enough this afternoon, my dear," her father said testily. "But let me warn you, Cynthia," he added on a serious note, "this man is not Lonsdale. He is an officer in the King's Army and more used to giving orders than receiving them. Especially from a female."

"I have no intention of giving Captain Sheffield any orders at all, Papa," Cynthia responded mildly.

But her father's warning rang in her ears for the rest of the day, and as four o'clock drew closer, Cynthia wondered if such a man as the captain, accustomed to the excitement and rigors of military life, would adapt tamely to the tranquil country existence she was about to offer him.

"This may well turn out to be one of those miracles you have ceased to believe in, Brian," Captain Chatham needled his friend as the two men turned into Berkeley Square. "Perhaps you have a fairy godmother lurking in the background somewhere, although I admit it is well nigh impossible to imagine Lord Halifax in that role."

Captain Sheffield grinned wryly. "Sorry to disappoint you, old chap, but I do not believe in fairy godmothers either," he retorted, gazing about him at the stately town mansions that lined the exclusive square. Brian had grown increasingly uneasy the closer his friend's curricle came to Halifax House. "There must be something the old cadger wants from me, but the devil take it, Dick, I cannot imagine what it might be."

"It is well known that Halifax is highly connected with the present government," Chatham remarked, guiding his curricle around an elegant barouche disgorging a smartly gowned matron and three young beauties fluttering and giggling about her. Both gentlemen tipped their hats at the group, eliciting a fresh outburst of giggles from the young ladies.

"So?" Brian prompted as the girlish voices receded behind them.

"I was wondering if perhaps Halifax has singled you out for a special mission of one sort or another."

"As a spy, you mean?" Brian said, startled at the novelty of his friend's notion, and not at all displeased at the prospect, which would mean his imminent return to the Continent. "Well, that would certainly get me out of London, but it would do nothing to cover my debt to Monroyal," he pointed out, still reluctant to assign any such significance to his lordship's odd invitation.

"Didn't Halifax say you would get relief from your debts if you showed your face here?" Dick Chatham reminded him. "What other debts do you have besides Monroyal's?"

"None at all," Brian replied. "But I cannot believe that spy notion of yours, Dick," he said after a pause, during which they bowled along beside the well-tended, neatly fenced gardens in the center of the square. "What else do we know about Halifax, anyway?" They had gone over much of this same exchange last night after the marquess had delivered his unexpected and somewhat mysterious ultimatum, but had been unable to find a plausible motive for such a summons.

"My mother told me this morning that Lady Elizabeth, the Marchioness of Halifax was a celebrated Beauty in her time," Chatham contributed. "Said it was touch and go between the Duke of Attlebridge—you remember, Jack Hampton's father-in-law—and Halifax. But Halifax won her and 'tis said they have a happy marriage."

The mention of marriage raised an uncomfortable specter in the captain's mind, and he glanced uneasily at Chatham. "And what about offspring? Does Halifax have any marriageable daughters, by any chance?" he demanded. "Perhaps one with a harelip or a squint that he cannot place among the first-born scions of his tonnish friends?"

Dick Chatham gave a crack of laughter. "Relax, old chap," he said with a wide grin. "As far as I know, there is only one unmarried girl still in the schoolroom and an elder daughter, Viscount Lonsdale's widow, who does not go about much. His lordship's heir, Viscount Holt, was attached to Wellington's retinue in Spain. Cut rather a dash with the señoritas as I recall."

Brian felt himself relax. He had been rather popular with the Spanish señoritas himself, he recalled, and his knowledge of the language had given him a decided advantage over his less-gifted fellows.

"Besides," Chatham drawled with a wicked grin. "When you get right down to it, old chap, a wife with a squint might be a small price to pay to get out from under that kind of a debt. Fifteen thousand pounds is a sum not to be sneezed at, if you ask me. I might even be tempted myself," he added unexpectedly. "Particularly if the chit is as well endowed as Lady Elizabeth is reported to have been when she caught Halifax's eye."

Brian laughed, amused at his friend's ability to make light of even the worst situations. He himself was less sanguine. Waking up yesterday morning to discover that his game of picquet with Lord Monroyal had not been a bad dream after all, had come as a severe shock to him. He could not recall ever having gambled beyond his means before, and the nebulous threat of Debtor's Prison had suddenly become an ugly reality. Lord Halifax's mysterious invitation at Watier's last night had offered a straw of hope at which Brian was tempted to grasp unquestioningly. But Dick's careless banter about squinty-eyed chits had raised a specter he found difficult to ignore.

Captain Sheffield much preferred his friend's first explanation, that there was some mysterious, important assignment waiting for him at Halifax House. The second explanation was much less palatable, and as Brian jumped down from the curricle and knocked on the marquess's front door, he did not dare ask himself if he could stomach a squinty-eyed wife—or any wife at all for that matter—in exchange for his financial freedom.

He was not at all sure that he could. But the alternative could not bear thinking of either.

Although Lady Cynthia Lonsdale had assiduously prepared herself, both in mind and spirit, for Captain Sheffield's call, when he was announced shortly before four that afternoon, she felt woefully unprepared for the task she had set for herself. In a moment of cowardice, she entertained the notion of calling upon Lord Halifax to receive the captain in her stead. It would be so comfortable, she thought more than once during the afternoon, to allow her father to take charge of everything, as he had repeatedly offered to do.

Disgusted at her own missishness, Cynthia paused briefly before the mirror on the landing to touch a hand to her impeccably dressed hair before descending with deliberate steps to the first floor, where the unknown gentleman awaited her in the Yellow Saloon. It had been pure vanity that had prompted her to instruct Hastings to put the caller in this particular saloon. The gold furnishings would provide a pleasing background for her new and very expensive walking-gown, she thought. Cut in the latest fashion only two days ago by London's most sought-after modiste, the gown of soft lustring matched the blue-green of her eyes almost exactly, and Cynthia had the satisfaction of knowing she looked her best.

Stifling a momentary feeling of panic when Hastings threw

open the ornate doors to the saloon, Cynthia took a deep breath and swept into the room, a polite smile fixed on her face.

The tall gentleman standing at the window turned sharply at her entrance, and Cynthia's first fleeting impression was that the captain looked older than his twenty-five years, perhaps because he appeared so much larger than she had imagined. He immediately came across the carpet to meet her, and Cynthia took this as a good omen. Her smile widened, and she held out her hand.

"Captain Sheffield," she greeted him warmly. "I am glad you decided to come."

He bowed rather stiffly over her fingers, barely touching them with his own. "Did you imagine I would not, ma'am?" he said dryly, his blue eyes fixed on her face.

Cynthia stared at him, startled and vaguely troubled by the echo of bitter amusement in his voice. Without consciously thinking about it, she had been afraid that at the last minute, Captain Sheffield would shy away from accepting her father's blunt invitation. That she would have to send for Robbie again to find another suitable candidate.

But he *had* come, she thought, repressing a sudden glow of excitement.

"Perhaps not," she acknowledged, a smile hovering on her lips again. "My father's invitation must have sounded rather mysterious to you."

He did not return her smile.

Cynthia saw him glance towards the door of the saloon and knew that the moment had come to take matters into her own hands.

"I admit it did sound rather odd," he remarked dryly. "So you are Lord Halifax's daughter?" he added, one eyebrow quizzically raised.

"Yes," Cynthia responded quickly, suddenly embarrassed at her failure to introduce herself. "I am Lady Cynthia Lonsdale. My father did not mention me?"

He was regarding her again, and Cynthia felt herself blush. "No, my lady," he said coolly. "Is there any reason why he should?"

This interview was not going well at all, Cynthia decided, and was relieved when Hastings appeared at the door to ask if she would require refreshments to be served.

After the butler had served their sherry and withdrawn, Cynthia settled herself on the yellow brocade settee and regarded the man who stood to one side of the hearth, his booted feet planted firmly on her father's Axminster carpet. His face was rugged rather than handsome in the smooth, classical style so prized by London matchmakers, she noted. His blue coat—well cut without being flashily modish—needed no padding to enhance the breadth of shoulders she guessed owed nothing to the regular sparring at Jackson's Saloon affected by so many London gentlemen of athletic inclinations. And his buff-colored breeches defined—as Cynthia caught herself noting in a single knowledgeable glance— a pair of thighs that must be the delight of his tailor and the envy of less well-endowed gentlemen.

Tearing her mind from this dangerous train of thought, Cynthia raised her glass. "Here's to the future, Captain," she murmured pleasantly, "and whatever it might hold."

Captain Sheffield hesitated a fraction of a second before raising his own glass in a similar salute. But his eyes were wary, and his well-shaped lips did not return her smile. "To the future, my lady," he said dryly.

He is as nervous as I am, Cynthia thought with sudden clarity, and the notion comforted her. "And to answer your question, Captain," she continued, taking her courage in both hands, "I asked my father not to mention the purpose of his invitation because, since it concerns me so closely, I felt I should be the one to broach the matter to you."

She saw the captain glance uneasily towards the door again as though he sought to escape from this uncomfortable interview. Cynthia did not blame him. She could tell from his shuttered gaze that he was on his guard. Papa was right, she mused; this man was nothing like James and would not submit tamely to having his future rearranged for him by a strange female. Nor was he anything like her cousin Robert, who could—when it suited him—be cajoled into any manner of outrageous schemes, particularly by females.

She took a sip of sherry to steady her nerves and pulled her lips into a faint smile. "Do not look for my father, Captain Sheffield," she said with more calm than she felt. "Much as he wished to take charge of this transaction"—she flinched inwardly at the word— "claiming that such matters are best discussed between gentlemen, I trust that you are a man of enough common sense not to dismiss my proposal out of hand merely because I am a female."

She smiled encouragingly, but once again the captain gave no sign of relaxing his cool demeanor.

"I trust you will find that I keep an open mind, my lady," he said cautiously. "And if this proposal you speak of can provide the financial relief Lord Halifax mentioned, I would be foolish indeed not to listen to it."

The captain's mouth quirked up at one corner, and Cynthia felt her anxiety ebb. It was an attractive mouth, she noted irrelevantly, and the laugh lines etched in his bronzed cheeks suggested that Captain Sheffield was not always as grimly serious as he appeared today.

"That is exactly what my father said," she remarked, remembering Lord Halifax's blunt evaluation of the captain as nobody's fool. She only hoped that he meant what he said about having an open mind.

She took another sip of sherry and regarded the captain speculatively. The very worst he could do was turn her down flatly, she thought, and if he did so, there were doubtless other young men who might not be so punctilious in accepting money from a female.

"Let us get to the point, Captain," Cynthia said abruptly, suddenly tired of this roundaboutation. "I gather that you are under the hatches to the tune of fifteen thousand pounds, sir. Is that correct?"

All trace of humor vanished from the captain's face, and Cynthia saw his jaw clench. She met his eyes unflinchingly, however, and in their startling blue depths she fancied she saw a glimmer of resentment.

After an uncomfortable pause, he spoke in clipped tones. "That is correct."

"These misfortunes become common knowledge more quickly that one would wish, as I am sure you know, Captain," she said gently. "This is London, after all, where gossip is one of the chief diversions of the *ton*." Cynthia smiled faintly, but the captain's face remained rigid with distaste, and her heart took a downward spiral.

"And you are one of those who delight in hearing about the misfortune of others, I must assume," he said harshly.

Cynthia quailed inwardly at the bitterness in his tone. "Not in the general way of things, no," she replied, striving for calmness. "But in your particular case, Captain, your predicament interested me for quite another reason." She paused, but this confession elicited no response at all from the captain, whose blue eyes had turned a hard, flat gray.

When he did not respond, Cynthia drew a deep breath and continued recklessly. "You see, I know a good deal about you, Captain Sheffield. I know that you are five and twenty, a younger son

who is at odds with his family. You have been in the army fo
five years and decorated several times. And recently wounded a
Vittoria, of course, hence your presence in London. You have
small income from your father's estate which will not cover one
tenth of the debt you have incurred." She paused and a smil
flickered on her lips. "And, of course, I know that you stand in ur
gent need of fifteen thousand pounds."

If anything the captain's stance became more rigid, and hi
blue-gray stare even more glacial.

"I have also heard from reliable sources that you are an honor
able man, Captain," she ploughed on, determined to get throug
this dreadful interview. "They tell me you are a man whose wor
can be trusted, a man whom a woman might trust . . ." Her voic
trailed off, and Cynthia wondered bleakly whether she was per
haps wasting her time on this taciturn captain her cousin had rec
ommended so highly.

"But perhaps I have been misinformed, sir," she murmure
with a touch of sarcasm, her temper beginning to simmer at hi
continued silence.

"And perhaps not," the captain responded unexpectedly. "Yo
are certainly right on the mark about one thing, my lady. I am s
deeply under the hatches that by next week I would not be sur
prised to learn that there is a fastener out for me." He let out a
crack of laughter then, but Cynthia cringed at the bitterness in it.

"And if the debt were to be paid?" she asked tentatively.

He stared, his eyes revealing, for the first time, a flash of inter
est. "By Lord Halifax, you mean?" he said brusquely.

"By me," Cynthia corrected him calmly, watching the captain'
eyes widen as the implications of her admission sank in.

"You wish to pay my gambling debts, my lady?" His tone wa
mocking, bordering on the incredulous, and Cynthia read disbe
lief, perhaps even derision in his blue eyes. Before she coul
reply, he laughed cynically and drained his glass. "And wha
would I be required to render up to you in exchange, my lady?"
he drawled. "My soul?"

No, only your body, Cynthia found herself thinking with more
pleasure than she had bargained for. The notion of having access
to the captain's lean hardness caused an unfamiliar flutter of de
sire to distract her. Cynthia had always considered the pleasures
of the marriage bed vastly overrated, and James had done nothing
to shake this conviction in the eight years they had shared that
state. But suddenly, as she gazed on this man's broad shoulders,
tapering hips, and long legs, the immodest thought nudged at her

consciousness that perhaps there might be something more to lying with a man than the dutiful couplings she had shared with the late viscount.

Cynthia felt the warmth rise to her cheeks at these wayward thoughts, but she could not help smiling at the captain's reaction. "Nothing quite so Mephistophelean, sir," she said lightly, anxious to deflect his anger. "All I am asking, if you choose to give it, is your name."

In the absolute silence that followed this blunt pronouncement, Cynthia saw various emotions flicker across the captain's rugged face. Evidently she had taken him by surprise, but gradually the implications of her words seemed to sink in and the captain's eyes—no longer tinged with gray—drifted down her person and back up to meet her gaze squarely.

He cleared his throat. "Am I to understand you are speaking of marriage, my lady?"

Cynthia let out the breath she did not realize she had been holding in a long sigh. There was no going back now, she thought with an odd sense of relief. She had made her extraordinary—and if her father was correct, highly improper—proposal, and the sky had not fallen in on her. True, the captain appeared nonplussed, but he had not run screaming from the room, nor had he laughed at her. At least not yet.

"That is correct," she murmured, meeting his gaze boldly, and wondering just what was going on behind those startlingly blue eyes. Was he disgusted and trying to hide it? Amused perhaps? Or worst yet, did the captain pity her? Cynthia cringed inwardly. Did this young, virile man feel nothing but pity towards her, in spite of the best efforts of her expensive modiste and French hairdresser? In spite of her fortune? The notion appalled her, and she wondered why she had not counted on having to face the embarrassment of a man's pity.

"I see," the captain replied slowly. "You wish to purchase a husband for fifteen thousand pounds?" His voice was expressionless, and Cynthia could not detect his feelings from these blunt words. She was grateful that he had not mocked her.

She rose to her feet, clutching the empty glass with cold fingers. "That is indeed how it must appear to you, sir," she murmured, summoning a shadow of a smile. "And naturally, you are partially correct. But things are not always that simple, Captain." She walked over to the window and pulled aside the rich gold curtains. Like the library directly beneath it, the Yellow Saloon overlooked the walled garden, and Cynthia gazed down at the now completely denuded pear-tree below. The sight of it, bare arms lifted to the cold October skies as if in silent prayer for a fruitful rebirth, gave her a surge of hope. A similar rebirth was within her grasp at this very moment. She would not even have to wait for the warmth of spring to make her fruitful. Captain Sheffield could do so within weeks, perhaps even days, if he could be persuaded to accept her terms. And Papa had been right, she thought wryly, the proposal she had in mind was immodest, but not nearly as immodest as the thoughts that flitted through her mind as she turned from the window to gaze speculatively at the tall man standing by the hearth.

Cynthia smiled, suddenly determined to put scruples aside and reach out for what she wanted. "Let me tell you a little about myself, Captain," she said briskly. "Perhaps then you will understand what has driven me to take this unusual step." She returned to the settee and settled herself comfortably. "I am nine and twenty," she began, "and a widow, as perhaps you already know. I was married at eighteen to a man almost thirty years my senior. He was not my choice, of course, but I cannot complain. Lonsdale gave me everything I could ask for except the one thing I really wanted: a family." She paused and lowered her eyes, feeling the warmth rising to her cheeks at this brash confession. "I . . . well, I wish to fulfill this dream before it is too late," she continued, forcing herself to meet his gaze. "Call me unnatural or immodest if you will, but the thought of playing aunt to my brother's offspring for the rest of my life does not appeal to me at all. I would prefer to be a mother," she said defiantly, raising her chin a notch as if daring him to censure her.

For the first time since his arrival, Captain Sheffield smiled, and Cynthia was quite swept away by the unexpected sweetness of it. "I can well believe that, my lady. My sister Caroline talks of nothing else." His face lost its stern expression. "In her last letter from Scotland, where she is spending a few months with our uncle, she was planning on three boys and three girls, although she has yet to be wed." His mouth twitched into something very like a grin. "She is just turned seventeen, of course, and given to romantical dreams."

"I hope they all come true for her," Cynthia said with a sincerity that came straight from her heart. "I had such dreams, too, when I was eighteen, but at nine and twenty, I feel my life slipping by. It has made me rather reckless, I am afraid. At least so my father believes." She stopped abruptly, hoping she had not frightened him off with such desperate prattle.

"A second marriage should not be difficult to achieve for someone of your rank and fortune, my lady," the captain remarked, a quizzical note in his voice.

Cynthia laughed softly. "Without resorting to this Cheltenham farce, I suppose you mean, Captain," she completed the thought he had probably been too polite to utter. "That is true enough. Except that my father, in his obsession to see me safely and comfortably settled is determined to choose another old man for me," she said bluntly. "And the younger men who have approached me are all wastrels of the worst sort. Like George Wooster, the Earl of Yarmouth, for example, a man who has run through two fortunes already and would like to run through mine as well." She shuddered involuntarily and moved to refill their glasses.

When she handed the captain his glass, Cynthia's fingers touched his briefly. The contact seemed to startle him, for he drew back and his expression became grim once more.

"So," he said, and Cynthia flinched at the brutal frankness of his words. "I agree to wed you, Lady Cynthia, and you will discharge my debt?"

She was standing so close to him that when she looked into the changing blue-gray of his eyes, Cynthia fancied she saw a riot of emotions warring within him. But perhaps she merely imagined that the captain cared a fig for her or anything she might propose, she thought, uneasy at the sudden fear that he might reject her. His harsh summary of her proposal grated on her nerves, particularly since he had—in typical masculine fashion—twisted it to sound like a mere convenience for both of them.

"No," she said firmly, determined to clarify her position at the risk of appearing naive and foolish. "You have it backwards, Captain." She laughed at his expression of disbelief. "First, I will discharge your debt, and then you will promise to give serious consideration to the second part of my proposal."

"Are you telling me that all you ask is that I *consider* your proposal, my lady?" he asked in amazement. "What if you never set eyes on me again?"

Cynthia smiled. "I trust you to tell me your decision in person," she said simply.

He was silent for a moment, regarding her intently. "You are indeed reckless, my lady," he said at length, one corner of his mouth hinting at a smile. "This is an expensive gamble you take. You stand to lose fifteen thousand pounds."

"Yes, I know," she agreed, unaccountably cheered by the hint of a smile. "But no more than the gamble you took playing for

high stakes at Watier's, Captain. I assume you had your heart se
on something you valued highly; something you lost instead. It i
no different for me. I am more than willing to gamble for what
want, Captain. If I win . . ." Cynthia smiled her most glitterin
smile, as if anticipating that happy event, "the risk will have bee
worth it."

"And if you lose?"

"If I lose?" Cynthia repeated, eloquently raising one elegan
shoulder. "If I lose, Captain, then I shall have to try again, will
not?"

CHAPTER FOUR

Uneasy Decision

Dick had been right about the miracle, Captain Sheffield realized as he descended the broad steps of Halifax House later that afternoon, his face set in a bemused expression. He strode briskly along, leaving Berkeley Square behind him as he made his way towards Bolton Street and Piccadilly where Dick Chatham had agreed to meet him at Watier's for an early dinner. His thoughts caught up in the events of the past hour, the captain saw little of his surroundings, and by the time he stepped into the portals of the club, his mind was as befuddled by Lady Cynthia's preposterous proposal as when he left Halifax House.

The woman had an incredible nerve, he thought wryly, glancing about the reading room for his friend's distinctive ginger head. Rather more forward than he would have wished, of course, but honest and direct. To his surprise, Lady Cynthia Lonsdale had employed none of the flirtatious glances or simpering smiles he found so insincere and calculating in females of her class. Indeed he had found himself admiring her fortitude and determination to reach out for that dream that seemed to have escaped her in her first marriage.

But marriage? Brian shivered involuntarily. He conceded that the fulfillment of Lady Cynthia's dream must necessarily involve marriage. If it was a family she yearned for, then a husband was a necessary appendage unless the lady was prepared to be ostracized by the *haut monde*. Somehow he could not imagine the viscountess contemplating such a flagrant breach of convention. Her demeanor and air of consequence spoke of a deeply rooted sense of family pride, besides which he knew that Lady Cynthia was possessed of an impeccable lineage and a fortune in her own right. And on top of all these advantages, she was undeniably beautiful, Brian admitted grudgingly.

But marriage? The notion intruded once more upon his consciousness, a vaguely annoying presence, like an ill-fitting boot, which disturbed the already precarious balance of his well-being.

The captain gave a mental shrug. He had ceased to believe that marriage had any place in his future the day he had listened, disillusioned and full of futile resentment, to the reading of his father's will. Without land of his own, without a reasonable income, without prospects of any kind except the career he might forge for himself in the army, Brian Sheffield could not hope for a respectable alliance with any female of his acquaintance. Even the enchantingly naive Miss Corianna Hornby, whose pale, fairylike beauty had enthralled his boyish heart at twenty, would be considered above his touch by her doting parents. Without the promised gift of Seven Oaks, whose borders marched with those of Hornby Hall, Sir William Hornby's prosperous manor, Brian had been deprived of any hope that even Corianna's wealthy parvenu father would countenance a match between them.

"Sheffield!" a hearty voice called out; the captain shook himself free of the past and turned to see his friend Chatham sitting with a group of fellow officers in the far corner of the room. They signaled him to join them, and as Brian strolled across the room, he hoped that Dick had not discussed his mysterious invitation to Halifax House. He had no desire to broadcast the odd proposal he had received from Lady Cynthia.

"What about a hand or two of *vingt-et-un*?" Toby Tottlefield suggested in his usual jovial tone, as soon as Brian had taken a seat.

Brian flinched and shook his head ruefully. "Sorry, Tottlefield, but my pockets are to let at the moment," he replied, glancing at Chatham, who gave him a conspiratorial wink.

"Your luck is bound to change, old sport," Chatham remarked innocently, although it was clear to Brian that his friend referred to his recent call at Halifax House.

"That may well be true," he replied, knowing that Dick was anxious to learn the outcome of that mysterious invitation but unwilling to speak of it before the others. "If one believes in miracles, that is," he added with a grin.

"And *do* you?" Chatham demanded, his blue eyes twinkling with repressed curiosity.

Sheffield's grin broadened, and he returned his friend's wink. "That might very well be," he said enigmatically.

Further exchange was impeded by the sudden arrival of Major Sir David Laughton, who was immediately beset by questions regarding the latest activities of Wellington's forces on the Peninsula. So it was not until much later that evening that Brian was able to unburden himself over a glass of brandy in Chatham's lodgings.

As the captain gave a clipped, much abbreviated version of his interview with Lady Cynthia, he was not surprised to see his friend's expression change from eager curiosity to amazement and then to alarm.

"Marriage?" Chatham repeated in a dazed voice. "How preposterous, old chap. She must be all of thirty if she is a day."

"Nine and twenty," Brian corrected him curtly. "Although she hardly looks a day over two and twenty."

Chatham looked increasingly alarmed. "You cannot seriously be considering parson's mousetrap?" he demanded in horrified tones. "Hang on a bit, old chap. Surely there must be another way out of this bumblebroth short of casting yourself upon matrimonial waters."

"If there is, I cannot see it," Brian replied despondently.

Chatham served the captain another stiff brandy and clasped him compassionately on the shoulder. "Steady on there, Brian," he said bracingly. "Ten to one you misunderstood her intentions. What in tarnation would the daughter of a marquess want with you?" After a moment's pause, he seemed to realize what he had said. "Not that you ain't the best of fellows, of course," he added hastily, as Brian let out a crack of cynical laughter. "But wealthy widows rarely wed men like you and me; second sons with nothing but good looks and a few battle scars to recommend us. Come to think of it, I cannot recall anyone who did."

"You are wrong there, Dick," Brian commented sourly. "My mother tells me that the Duchess of Ware snared poor old Major Hampton only last summer."

"I would hardly call Jack Hampton old," Dick remarked. "And from what I hear, he is besotted with the girl. A regular Beauty by all accounts."

Brian waved Major Hampton's good fortune aside impatiently. "Hampton was not in the market for a rich wife," he argued. "He put his neck in the noose with his eyes open, the poor sod." The bitterness in his voice put a pall on the conversation, which petered out into uncomfortable silence.

Chatham regarded him steadily for several moments, then shook his head. "It sounds to me as though you should send her packing, Brian," he said hopefully. "She is too old for you in any case, and more than likely a managing female into the bargain."

"I cannot see that I have any choice in the matter," the captain burst out viciously. "Unless you can tell me where else I am to obtain fifteen thousand pounds by next Wednesday."

This desperate outburst was followed by a heavy silence during which both young gentlemen took refuge in their brandy. All that could be heard in the comfortable masculine untidiness of the small room was the halfhearted crackling of the fire in the hearth.

Brian could not remember being quite so hard-pressed to know which path to take. During his five years in the army, the captain had learned that split-second decisions often meant the difference between life and death. So far he had been lucky, and his ability to make the right decision with a minimum of fuss had earned him the respect and loyalty of his men. Why then could he not make up his mind now, he wondered, when the outcome concerned him so nearly? If this were a military decision, what would he do? Brian mused, idly swirling the amber liquid in his glass. Risk an alliance with the enemy or face the shame of defeat and possible death? Hardly an apt comparison, of course, because a military alliance often turned out to be a temporary agreement, whereas any alliance he made with Lady Cynthia Lonsdale would be permanent. Frighteningly permanent.

The captain took another large swallow of brandy and shuddered as the fiery liquid burned his throat. In military terms, the choice would be so simple, he thought, because he understood the rules, as did his opponent. But when the opponent was a female, by what rules was he expected to play? Brian had no idea, and this fact undermined his self-confidence, made him unsure of his ground. He had the uncomfortable feeling that he had been routed before the skirmish had even begun. With sudden insight the captain saw himself ambushed, outmaneuvered on his weakest flank, with surrender his only option.

In which case, he though grimly, gulping the last of his brandy, there was no decision to make at all. It had been made for him, and the realization of his vulnerability aroused a bitter resentment in him such as he had not felt since the reading of his father's will.

"At least the she isn't an ape-leader," he heard Chatham observe in a thick voice. "If what you tell me is true. She might well have been, you know, Brian, and then you would have been forced to pack her off to the country and get her with child as painlessly as possible."

Chatham's crude comment snapped the captain out of the drunken stupor that was beginning to make his predicament recede into a drowsy haze. For no apparent reason he took offense at the picture of married life Dick had painted.

"Have a care, Chatham," he said curtly. "You are speaking of a lady who may well become my wife, so I will thank you to watch your tongue."

"Pardon, old chap," Chatham spluttered, his pale blue eyes blinking owlishly. Then his handsome, freckled face split into a grin. "So you are going to marry the wench . . . eh, lady, that is?" he drawled, enunciating each word carefully. "May I be the first to offer my condolen . . . that is to say, congratulations—"

"Oh, do shut up, Dick," Brian cut in impatiently. "You are giving me the most god-awful headache." He pushed himself out of the chair with some difficulty. "Gotta go home." He slammed his tall beaver onto his head, accepted his gloves and cane from Dodson, his friend's batman, and turned towards the door.

"And do not bruit this about, Dick," he muttered peevishly. "It ain't settled yet by any means," he added with a defiance that had a hollow ring to it.

But of course it was, Brian thought resentfully as he walked down Jermyn Street to his own digs, where Hardy, his batman for the past five years, received him in disapproving silence. And in spite of the unusual quantity of brandy he had consumed, sleep would not come. Chatham's last words rang persistently in his ears, and Brian lay there considering—with distressing clarity—the other side of this alliance he was obliged to enter with Lady Cynthia.

He would have to bed her. The startling thought chased all possibility of sleep from his tired body. Why had he not thought of it before? He would be expected to divest that shapely form of its indubitably expensive clothing, lay the lady on her bed, and commit that ultimate and most intimate act of male possession, which would make her irrevocably his wife for the rest of his life.

Brian shuddered, whether from the terror of surrendering himself with such finality, or the anticipation of that pleasurable possession, he refused to consider.

In either case, when sleep eventually came, it was neither restful nor refreshing, but when the captain arose the next morning, he had come to terms with the uneasy decision he must make.

"It is kind of you to spare the time to drive with me, Willy," Lady Cynthia remarked cheerfully as she led the way into the hall of Halifax House and allowed Hastings to wrap her in a warm, fur-lined cloak. "I am anxious to have your opinion of this new team, and . . ."

"My dear Cynthia," the Honorable Willoughby Hampton interrupted jovially, accepting his tall beaver and gloves from the butler. "Happy to be of service, I assure you. My pleasure entirely, coz. I cannot for the life of me imagine a greater pleasure than driving out with a beautiful woman and a spanking team of high-steppers on a brisk afternoon. What more could a man want, indeed?"

Cynthia glanced over her shoulder at her cousin's smiling face and laughed from pure pleasure. "You are a complete quiz, Willy," she protested. "And here I was trembling in my half-boots wondering whether you would give me the cut direct when you heard that I had sought Monroyal's advice on the merits of this team. I understood you would not be back in Town before mid-November, and by then the grays would have been snapped up by another."

"Beckwith's breakdowns, I presume?" Hampton remarked as the butler ushered them out of the front door. "Cannot go too far wrong there, my dear. Old Reggie has an excellent eye for a good bit of blood. Pity to see such prime cattle sold off at Tattersall's, but I hear Reggie had a run of bad luck at the tables and was in sore need of the ready."

"So you agree with Monroyal that the grays are worth the money, Cousin?" Cynthia inquired. "I confess I am delighted with them."

"Robert knows his cattle," Hampton replied with a hint of reluctance. "Leans towards the flashy himself, of course. Only have to look at those bays of his. Sixteen-mile-an-hour tits, all right, but bokickers if ever I saw any. Would not have them in my stables, I can tell you that, coz."

"Which is just as well, Cousin," Cynthia replied gaily. "For Robert would not part with them for all the spice in India. Very taken with them he is. But tell me what you think, Willy," she added, gesturing towards the four splendidly matched grays that stood with well-bred aloofness awaiting her pleasure.

Her cousin had barely finished his examination of the first wheeler, running his hands knowledgeably over the animal's withers when Cynthia was distracted by the sound of an approaching horseman. The rider dismounted lithely and came towards her, the reins of his big roan gelding looped nonchalantly over his arm.

Cynthia felt her cheeks grow pink with pleasure as she extended her gloved hand, a genuine smile of welcome on her lips.

"Well met, Captain Sheffield," she said with admirable composure. Inwardly, Cynthia chaffed at the blush that had taken her by surprise. He seemed so much larger than he had yesterday in her father's drawing room that she felt a little breathless. She was not in the habit of being overwhelmed in a gentleman's presence, but something about the captain's lean features and inscrutable blue eyes flustered her.

To cover her discomposure, Cynthia turned to her cousin and found his merry brown gaze fixed on her quizzically. "Willy, let me make you known to Captain Sheffield. Captain, my cousin Willoughby Hampton." She watched the two men shake hands and marveled at how different they were. As always, Willy was dressed to the nines, verging on dandyism with his gold-tasseled Hessians, green-striped waistcoat, fastidiously tied cravat, and many caped greatcoat. The younger man was plain by comparison. His blue riding jacket was well cut but eschewed the nipped-in waist sported by the most daring Town Tulips, and his cravat was tied in a simple fall over a dark blue waistcoat. His buckskin breeches were creaseless and revealed an alarming expanse of well-muscled thigh, as Cynthia noticed without seeming to dwell overlong on that portion of a gentleman's anatomy ladies most often found fault with.

"Wounded at San Sebastian, I take it?" Hampton inquired with that offhand tone of voice gentlemen used when referring to male activities of importance.

"Vittoria," the captain replied shortly. "Last June to be precise. I have been back since early July. Recuperating, the army sawbones call it." He gave a brief laugh. "I call it a great waste of time when there is so much still to be done before Boney is routed for good."

"Eager to be back there, are you?"

Cynthia was conscious of a distinct pause, during which she felt her heart stand still. The whimsical smile on her cousin's lips suggested that he had asked the question deliberately, and she wondered what rumors regarding the captain had reached his ears.

The captain smiled grimly. "The army is my profession, sir," he said in neutral tones, without so much as a glance in her direction. When it became apparent that he would say no more, Hampton broke the silence.

"I understand the Sheffields are connoisseurs of horseflesh,

Captain," he said with natural good humor. "What do you think of these grays?"

The captain let his eyes wander over the four horses, who were beginning to show signs of restlessness. "I would say that is one of the finest rigs in London," he said with genuine enthusiasm. "I envy you, sir."

"Oh, do not envy me, Captain," Willy retorted before Cynthia could prevent him. "This is my cousin's rig. She is an enviable whip, as you probably know, almost as good as I am," he added with deliberate condescension. "Drives to an inch. Although perhaps a tad unpredictable for true greatness."

"What an odious creature you are, Willy," Cynthia exploded, mortified that her cousin had both praised and denigrated her before the captain. "Pay him no heed, Captain," she added, turning towards Sheffield. "He is envious that I got my hands on this team while he was out of Town. Shame on you, coz."

Seeing that she was truly put out, Hampton caught her gloved hand and raised it elegantly to his lips. "A thousand pardons, my love. I was but jesting. You are the best all around horsewoman I know, Cynthia, and that is a fact. Your stables at Milford Hall are proof of your enviable expertise in raising prime cattle, as I am sure you know."

Her good humor restored, Cynthia laughed and glanced at the captain, who was regarding this little scene with a bemused expression.

"Now I suggest that you take Captain Sheffield up beside you for a turn in the Park," her cousin said unexpectedly. "As a breeder himself, his opinion of the grays is probably more to the point than mine. I am, after all, merely a dilettante," he lied facetiously.

Lady Cynthia looked at her cousin in astonishment. "Perhaps Captain Sheffield does not wish to drive in the Park with an unpredictable female," she said acidly, mortified that Willy would have the audacity to play match-maker with her.

"Of course, he does, you silly widgeon," Hampton said affectionately. "And besides, who knows, perhaps in a week or two the captain will go back to his regiment. You must not deprive him of the pleasure of driving behind such a team, my dear Cynthia. Too cruel by half, coz."

Cynthia glared at him and then turned to the captain, detecting a glint of amusement in his blue eyes. Would he, as Willy had suggested, rejoin his regiment as soon as she had paid his debt? she wondered. What she had told him yesterday was true, of course. She was willing to gamble. Willing to risk fifteen thousand pounds against a young soldier's sense of duty and loyalty to the army. If the pull of adventure, excitement, and advancement in his chosen career proved stronger than the fortune and position she had to offer, then she would lose. If what she had to offer was not enough to tempt a man like Captain Sheffield—and quite suddenly Cynthia faced the very real possibility that the captain might decline her assistance altogether—then she would be obliged to look elsewhere for a husband.

The prospect was more than daunting, it was downright painful, for quite unconsciously, Cynthia had set her heart on Captain Sheffield. Rashly and quite without encouragement of any kind, she had set her heart on a man she hardly knew.

All the more reason to fight for him, Cynthia told herself stubbornly. "Pray do not allow my obnoxious cousin to tell you what to do, Captain," she murmured, flashing the gentleman in question a sweet smile.

"I do not allow anyone to tell me what to do," the captain replied pleasantly but in a tone of voice that left little doubt in Cynthia's mind that he included more than Willy. Cynthia's smile became fixed, and she wished she had held her tongue. And then the captain smiled one of his rare smiles, and Cynthia's incipient anger melted.

"Mr. Hampton is right in one thing though," he continued easily. "It would indeed be too cruel of you to deprive me of the pleasure of driving out with you." He reached out and ran a hand over the nearest leader's glossy neck, and Cynthia was stunned at the odd sensation this simple gesture aroused in her. "And unpredictable or not," he added, his eyes looking straight into hers, "I am willing to take the risk, my lady."

For the space of a heartbeat, Cynthia stared at him, not daring to breathe, not daring to attribute more to the captain's words than he had meant. But exactly what had he meant? she mused. Was he ready to risk more than the drive in the Park? Or was he merely teasing? The wisest course, she decided, was not to rush her fences with a horse as skittish as the captain showed signs of being.

"You are most welcome, Captain," she said with cool politeness. "That is if you really do not mind, Willy?" She looked inquiringly at her cousin and was chagrined at the roguish twinkle in his brown eyes.

Willy made her a rakish bow. "I am delighted to relinquish my place to our gallant captain," he murmured, a wide grin on his round face. "Allow me to assist you, my dear cousin," he added, moving lazily towards the smart, burgundy-lacquered curricle behind the grays.

But it was the captain's hand that was extended to steady Lady Cynthia when she stepped agilely into the sporting vehicle. If she knew anything about her devious cousin, Cynthia thought, no doubt Willy had deliberately maneuvered the younger man into this show of gallantry, and when she experienced the strength of the captain's large hand on hers, Cynthia could not bring herself to regret it.

When the captain climbed into the curricle and settled his weight beside her on the green leather seat, Cynthia threw her cousin a grateful smile, and, on impulse, dismissed the stocky groom who usually rode up behind her.

"Take care of the captain's horse, Jem," she ordered, ignoring his censorial scowl and giving her horses the office to start.

Cynthia was glad the grays were in a mettlesome mood, for they required her full attention, and she had little to spare for the disturbing presence beside her. Only when they reached the Park did she relax sufficiently to glance at her companion. If she was disappointed to find his gaze fixed admiringly on her horses rather than on herself, Cynthia refused to acknowledge the fact. For the moment it was enough that he had come back to see her. Undoubtedly he had reached some conclusion about the matter that lay unresolved between them.

If her father was correct—and Cynthia had little reason to believe otherwise—the captain would indeed agree to consider her proposal. But considering marriage to a strange woman several years his senior was a far cry from actually entering into such an alliance. Since yesterday Cynthia had become painfully aware of that difference. Perhaps she had been foolish not to have insisted upon marriage in return for the fifteen thousand pounds she had promised to pay, she thought wryly. But the dice were cast; she had played her hand. And after the captain played his own, she would know whether she had gambled and lost, or won the first round of this uneven game they were playing.

And if she lost, Cynthia told herself philosophically, it would probably be all for the best.

Above all else, Lady Cynthia did not want a husband who came to her unwillingly.

Despite his determination to accept the hand that Fate had dealt him with good grace, Captain Sheffield had approached Berkeley

Square with a certain amount of reluctance that afternoon. Any way he looked at his present dilemma, there appeared to be only one way out, so Brian had screwed up his courage over a large helping of coddled eggs and York ham, numerous rashers of bacon, thick slices of toast, and a large mug of ale served by a glum Hardy on the cluttered table in his rooms at an unusually late hour that morning.

The food had appeased his physical appetite, but Brian's spirit was still troubled. In the end he called for his roan gelding, Hannibal, and rode over to Halifax House, determined to invite the Lady Cynthia to ride with him in the Park. Undoubtedly it would be easier to say what he had to say to the lady from the safe distance of Hannibal's back, he thought—half ashamed of his own cowardice—than standing, ill at ease, in the Halifax drawing room.

The sight of the team of splendid grays poled up to an expensive racing curricle standing before Halifax House gladdened his heart. But when the front door opened to reveal Lady Cynthia herself, dressed in an equally expensive fur driving cloak and accompanied by a stoutish gentleman who appeared to be on excellent terms with her ladyship, Brian felt his spirits rise. Perhaps the lady had fixed her interest on another candidate, he thought, surprised that this notion was not altogether a pleasant one. As he came closer, the captain recognized the gentleman as the Honorable Willoughby Hampton, grandson to the influential Earl of Belton and one of London's wealthiest bachelors. Very much a confirmed bachelor, from what Brian had heard, which must surely eliminate Mr. Hampton from the competition, he thought, oddly comforted.

Her smile had been genuine when she turned to greet him, and the pink blush that tinted her perfect cheeks delighted him. Whatever her faults, Lady Cynthia had a quiet beauty and unconscious elegance that set her apart from other society females the captain had met during his brief stay in London.

Brian had not been surprised to learn that the foppishly dressed Hampton was the lady's cousin. Dick Chatham had told him that the Savilles were connected to many of England's prominent families. What did surprise him—and make his decision to accept the lady's terms more palatable—was the discovery that not only was Lady Cynthia a notable whip but that the Lonsdale stables were recognized for the quality of their thoroughbreds.

With his years of breeding Sheffield hunters, perhaps he could be of some use to her ladyship after all, Brian mused wryly—beyond that of stud service as Dick had so crudely put it. It was this prospect that persuaded the captain to take the dandy's place beside her ladyship in the curricle. Brian was well aware of the quizzical gleam in Hampton's eyes as he bandied words with Lady Cynthia and wondered how much, if anything, the elegant fribble knew or had guessed about the captain's presence at Halifax House.

Lady Cynthia must have guessed the drift of his thoughts, for they had barely entered the gates of the Park before she mentioned the purpose of his call.

"My cousin knows nothing of the matter between us, Captain," she said briefly, casting him a faint smile. And to Brian's surprise, that was the only time Lady Cynthia gave any indication that there was any other reason for this outing than to take advantage of the fine October afternoon. And enjoy each other's company, he reflected, gradually becoming aware that he did indeed enjoy the companionship and comfortable conversation of the lady who had come so unexpectedly—and providentially—into his life. Lady Cynthia was more than superficially knowledgeable about horseflesh, he soon discovered. Her expert handling of the mettlesome grays gained his instant admiration and respect. She had the nervous team well in hand from the very start of their drive and never once did she waver from the cool control she displayed in tooling the highly-bred cattle through the noisy London traffic.

"Hampton was niggardly in his praise," he remarked once they entered the Park, and Lady Cynthia began to relax. "You are a superb whip, my lady, not merely an enviable one."

She flashed him another of her open smiles. "Thank you, Captain," she responded, without a hint of false modesty. "Willy is a sad tease, I am afraid. We were very close as children. His Uncle George, Viscount Dillon, was married to my father's sister, Aunt Sibyl. Unfortunately she ran afoul of a green hunter in their fifth year of marriage, many years ago, and took a fatal fall. A neck-or-nothing rider, like all the Savilles, but rather more reckless than most of us, I am afraid. I still remember how much I envied her. She had a bright red habit I particularly fancied, and a matching red shako with a curling black feather. All very dashing and romantical to the child I was at the time, of course. Poor Dillon never stood a chance, and as far as I know, still mourns her."

She was quiet for some time after that rather intimate confession, perhaps regretting that she had revealed so much of herself in the telling. Brian felt the sudden need to ameliorate the regret he had detected in her voice.

"The red habit is easy enough to replicate surely," he remarked.

Lady Cynthia laughed wryly. "Ah, yes, Captain," she said in a lighter voice. "But I lack Aunt Sibyl's flair, you see, so I have never had one made."

"That I doubt very much, if your present performance is any indication of your competence," he said smoothly.

"Thank you again, Captain. But competence is one thing; flair is quite another. I used to dream—when I was very young and foolish—of wearing a scarlet habit and riding a white horse along Rotton Row, dazzling all the quizzes with my horsemanship. Luckily I have outgrown that rather childish ambition," she added apologetically, a faint blush of embarrassment blossoming on her cheeks.

If Brian had hoped that Lady Cynthia would broach the matter that lay between them and demand to know his response to her proposal, he was disappointed. A full hour after they had left Mr. Hampton standing, in his pale yellow breeches and gold-tasseled Hessians, in front of Halifax House, they arrived back to find her ladyship's groom waiting for them.

"Might I impose upon you to join us for tea, Captain?" Lady Cynthia inquired politely, when they found themselves standing before the great front door, held open by the stiff-necked butler.

"I think not, my lady," he replied, suddenly anxious to regroup his tangled emotions. "But I would like your permission to call upon you tomorrow, if I may?"

She looked him directly in the eyes and smiled gently, her blue-green gaze inscrutable.

"Of course." Her smile deepened. "Until tomorrow, Captain. Hastings," she called, turning to mount the shallow steps. "See to the captain's horse, will you?" And without a backward glance, Lady Cynthia disappeared into the house.

Was she so sure of his acquiescence? he wondered, watching another groom lead Hannibal round from the stables. Or was she as unsure as he was himself about the possibility of a shared future?

The captain wished he could be sure of his own mind.

CHAPTER FIVE

Invitation to Tea

"Well, well!" Lord Halifax exclaimed gruffly as Lady Cynthia entered the drawing room before dinner that evening arm in arm with her mother, Lady Elizabeth. "Here are the ladies, Robert. A sight for sore eyes, would you not agree? Not a day over twenty either of them," he added, moving forward—a doting smile on his handsome face—to escort his wife to her chair.

"What Spanish coin you do give me, James," Lady Halifax protested, laughing up into her husband's eyes. "I do declare you are as big a rogue as Robert here." She held out her hand to her nephew, who bowed over it with consummate grace, murmuring the faintly risqué compliments that never failed to delight the marchioness.

Lady Cynthia was not as pleased as she might have been to see her handsome, flamboyant cousin, and while she watched the courtly little scene he played out with her mother, she wondered what had brought him. When he turned to greet her in an equally flattering manner, Cynthia noted that his gray eyes glittered with secret amusement.

"You are looking quite, quite ravishing, coz," he murmured, running his gaze over her golden silk-gowned figure with brazen admiration. "You take a man's breath away, my love, and no mistake."

As always when the Marquess of Monroyal flirted with her this openly, Cynthia felt positively unclothed by his caressing stare, and her cheeks flushed with embarrassment.

She nodded stiffly and removed her hand from his grasp. "I trust you are not foxed tonight, Robert," she said waspishly, accepting a glass of sherry from Hastings. "You run on like a positive Jackstraw."

"Cynthia!" her mother exclaimed in shocked tones. "Why must you always think the worst of our darling Robbie? What has he done this time to throw you into high dudgeon?"

"Darling Robbie, indeed," Cynthia muttered scathingly. "The

rogue delights in putting me out of countenance, Mama. And tonight he appears to be in a particularly odious mood."

"You flatter me, I fear, coz," the marquess countered, his gray eyes drifting once more over her person, lingering overlong—or so it seemed to Cynthia—on the fashionably low neckline that revealed more than the usual expanse of ivory bosom.

"I trust I pass muster, Cousin," she said with a touch of sarcasm.

Lord Monroyal raised his eyes and smiled one of his rare, sweet smiles, which Cynthia trusted as much as she would trust a snake. "Complete to a shade, coz," he murmured. "As always."

"Enough of this teasing, Robbie," the marchioness chided gently. "Your father and I are eager to know how your siege of Captain's Sheffield's heart progresses, Cynthia. Has he capitulated yet?"

"For fifteen thousand pounds, he would be a deuced fool not to," her father said bluntly. "If the man refuses to take that kind of bait, I would wash my hands of him, child. In fact, I will insist that you do so."

Lady Cynthia closed her eye briefly and drew a deep breath. It was all too obvious that neither of her parents approved of her determination to select a younger man as her second husband. A freakish start, her mother had called it when she learned what her eldest daughter proposed. Lady Halifax had been sorely disappointed that her favorite nephew Robert—for whom she had a decided partiality—had not been Cynthia's choice, and, as Cynthia knew full well, her mother had not yet lost all hope of bringing her daughter to her senses.

"I am not a child, Papa," Lady Cynthia began patiently. "And it is not a siege I am conducting, Mama. As far as I know, the captain has not made up his mind one way or the other."

"I fear my cousin is too modest," Lord Monroyal interrupted. "I ran into our mutual cousin, Sweet Willy, in White's this afternoon, and he told me a quite different story, my dear."

"Willy is prone to exaggeration, as well you know, Robbie," Cynthia said flatly, unaccountably annoyed to learn that her affairs were being bandied about in the clubs. "I am surprised you pay any heed to him, Cousin."

"Our Willy has it that the captain is definitely épris, coz," the marquess drawled suggestively. "He tells me you cast him off quite heartlessly and took up the captain in his place this afternoon, my dear. Quite cut up about it was our poor Willy. I trust the captain was aware of the singular honor you bestowed upon him, Cynthia, and showed his gratitude appropriately."

"Do not tell me the man has accepted already, Cynthia?" her mother exclaimed anxiously. "This whole affair is being conducted with unseemly haste, child. I do not like it above half."

"You will have to ask the captain himself, Mama," Cynthia said through clenched teeth. "I have asked him to take tea with us tomorrow."

This defiant announcement was received in silence by her parents, but Lord Monroyal let out a delighted crack of laughter. "Splendid, coz," he remarked with a cynical smirk. "The unhappy fish is practically in the net already. Congratulations!"

Cynthia turned on him furiously, and would have made an acid retort to this unflattering comment, had not Hastings chosen that moment to swing open the doors to announce that dinner was served.

Although the marquess had threatened to grace his aunt's tea-table with his presence the following afternoon, Cynthia only half expected the rogue to keep his word. Robert was not—as she knew from long experience—particularly fond of China brew, and only rarely put in an appearance at her mother's afternoon gatherings.

It was, nevertheless, with some trepidation that Lady Cynthia made her way down the curving staircase to her mother's Chinese drawing room the next day. She had dressed with considerable care, choosing a new afternoon gown of sea-green silk, trimmed sparingly with ruffles at the hem and a lavish Brussels lace collar. She had allowed her French abigail to gather her auburn ringlets into an elegant cluster on top of her head, with enough loose curls escaping from the knot to lend her small features a fragile, feminine appearance. Cynthia had been pleased with the result. Annette had achieved a simple elegance that suited her mood, she thought wryly, and gave her the confidence she would need to weather the captain's first official encounter with her parents.

Lady Halifax was already ensconced on her favorite dragon-footed settee when Cynthia strolled into the room, and the assessing look her ladyship gave her daughter conveyed both approval and speculation. There were three other ladies sitting with the marchioness, and when Cynthia recognized them, she moved forward to greet them, an eager smile on her face.

"Aunt Sophy!" she exclaimed gaily, leaning over to place an affectionate kiss on the Marchioness of Monroyal's smooth cheek. "I am glad to see you back in Town so early. Robert did not say a word to us yesterday when he dined here."

"How like my ramshackle son to forget he has a mother," Lady Monroyal observed with a chuckle. "But to his credit, I must admit that he did not expect us until next week. I was just telling my dear Elizabeth," she added, turning to smile at Lady Halifax, "that the girls insisted they simply had to enjoy this unusually sunny October weather driving in Hyde Park to ogle the gentlemen."

Lady Cynthia turned to her two cousins, who had risen at her entrance, with a welcoming smile. "Unless I am very much mistaken, I expect it will be the gentlemen doing the ogling, my dears," she teased, embracing the two young ladies enthusiastically.

"You see, Mama," the seventeen-year-old Lady Letitia cried out excitedly, "I told you that Cousin Cynthia would agree that driving in the Park in bang-up style is all the crack in London."

"Pray do not use stable language in the drawing room, Letitia," her mother scolded, somewhat plaintively, Cynthia thought, watching her irrepressible cousin dance about like the schoolroom miss she had been until so recently.

"And you, Constance?" Lady Cynthia interrupted, turning away from Letty's childish prattle to gaze fondly on her other cousin. "Am I to understand that you, too, wish to ogle bucks in the Park?" No sooner had the words left her mouth than Cynthia wished she could withdraw them. Lady Constance's pale face had turned red, and her eyes dropped in confusion.

"Oh, I persuaded Constance to leave her musty old piano and try her luck again in the Little Season," Letitia blurted out in her thoughtless way. "We are counting on you, Cousin Cynthia, to introduce us to all the most dashing gentlemen you know."

Lady Cynthia smiled at this nonsensical chatter. "And what makes you think I know any dashing gentlemen?" she responded dryly.

"Because you are obviously all the crack, that is why," Letitia said, gesturing towards Cynthia's elegant gown.

"Letitia!" her mother exclaimed.

"Oh, Mama!" Letty pouted charmingly and glanced at Cynthia from beneath her lashes. "Do you really mean it, Cousin?" she demanded. "Do you not know dozens of young, eligible gentlemen who are simply dying to meet me? And Constance, too, of course," she added belatedly, throwing a stricken glance at her sister, who seemed absorbed in the writhing dragons in the green and red carpet.

"The gentlemen I know are either married or in their dotage, Letty," she confessed blithely. "They are all your brother Robert's age or even older. So do not count on me to produce dashing bucks at the drop of a hat."

"Oh, dear." Letitia's tone was so downcast that all the ladies laughed. Except for Constance, Cynthia noted, whose gaze was still abstracted. "Are you not acquainted with any young men at *all*, Cousin?"

Involuntarily, Cynthia's eyes sought her mother's, and the quizzical expression she saw there surprised her. Her thoughts went instantly to Captain Sheffield and for the first time, Cynthia realized the task she had set herself. Men like the captain would naturally be drawn to Lady Letitia, who was quite lovely and highly eligible. Also young and virginal, she thought wryly. Besides that, both her cousins had dowries more than sufficient to take care of the captain's present or future debts. Quite suddenly Cynthia found herself praying that the captain would delay his appearance until her cousins had gone. The thought disturbed her, and she put it aside hastily.

"No, I cannot say I do," she lied tentatively. "At least none who would look twice at a sad romp like you, Letty."

If anyone had told her that she would welcome the departure of her favorite aunt, Lady Cynthia would have roundly denied it, but that afternoon she sighed with relief when Lady Monroyal took her leave earlier than expected, promising to join the Halifax theater party two days hence.

In the end she need not have worried. When Captain Sheffield was finally announced, the hour was so advanced that Cynthia had quite given up on him. At the sound of his name, she turned and met his startling blue eyes across the room. Her expression must have betrayed her, for when she approached him, he took her hand in both his and smiled down at her with unexpected warmth.

"My apologies, Lady Cynthia," he murmured as he raised her fingers to his lips. "I fear I am late."

Though he offered no excuses for his belated appearance, Cynthia bit back the caustic rejoinder that trembled on her tongue. She was too glad that he had come at all to quibble over minutia. Furthermore, when he smiled at her as he was doing now, Cynthia felt the floor shift beneath her slippered feet. She tore her gaze away, feeling intensely naive, as she had at her first encounter with Lonsdale; but somehow her husband had never made the floor move, nor had he left her tongue-tied as a schoolroom chit.

"My mother will be glad to see you," she murmured, striving to regain her poise. "She does not approve of you entirely, I should warn you, Captain, but she is not immune to flattery."

"And are you, Lady Cynthia?"

She looked at him in alarm. "Immune to flattery, sir?"

"No, glad to see me?" he murmured, his mouth curving into another provoking smile.

Cynthia gazed at him for a long moment, uneasy at his teasing tone. "I am *surprised* to see you, Captain," she said coolly. "I thought you had quite deserted me." Why she had spoken right from her heart, Cynthia could not imagine, but she had indeed feared the captain's defection. With a light laugh, she tried to dissemble her indiscretion. "That would not have surprised me at all, if you want to know the truth, sir."

"How unflattering of you, my lady," he murmured, without taking his eyes from her face. "What have I done to deserve such distrust?"

Cynthia could think of no glib response to this remark, but as she returned his gaze, she became suddenly aware of the expectant silence in the room behind her.

"Come, Captain," she said hastily, "My mother is anxious to make your acquaintance."

"Now that is a bouncer if ever I heard one," Cynthia heard him mutter behind her as she led him towards the dragon-footed settee, where Lady Halifax awaited them in regal splendor.

Cynthia put her chin up and met her mother's eyes defiantly, struggling not to appear as smug as she felt.

It had been the wrong thing to do, Captain Sheffield realized no sooner had the stiff-necked butler announced his name, and every eye in the room turned to stare—or so it seemed. He should not have listened to Chatham, he mused, his eyes seeking out the only person in the room he had any wish to see. Brian had almost convinced himself that he need not, after all, put in an appearance at Lady Halifax's afternoon tea. Such gatherings were—at least among the officers' wives of his acquaintance, who held them regularly—an excuse to exchange gossip and flirt with single men like himself and Dick Chatham.

The captain had no use for gossip, and flirting was the last thing on his mind, that is until Lady Cynthia turned to regard him with her sea-green eyes. Then the urge to tell the lady that he found those eyes bewitching hit him like a physical blow. Before he could recover his breath, her gaze widened with surprise, and Brian could not refrain from smiling. He had not meant to smile. Quite the opposite, if truth be told. During their two previous interviews, Brian had kept himself deliberately aloof, although his resolve to maintain his distance had faltered during their conversation in the Park. Her own coolness had dissolved, too, when she spoke of her childhood, he remembered, and he had glimpsed the woman of flesh and blood behind the elegant mask she wore.

No, he had definitely not meant to smile as warmly as he did. Nor had he intended to apologize and press her small fingers to his lips as intimately as he found himself doing. His action startled her, he saw, watching with amusement and delight as the varying emotions chased one another across her face. And he had certainly not intended to flirt with her. He had no idea how the words had formed in his mind, much less how he had dared to utter them; but it suddenly seemed important to know if Lady Cynthia was glad to see him. So he asked her.

That had surprised her, too, he saw, but she recovered her poise and brushed the question aside. Nevertheless, Brian was left with the distinct impression—whether she would admit it or not—that Lady Cynthia was definitely glad to see him. This thought gave him the confidence to face the other people in the room, whose presence both of them had momentarily forgotten.

The introductions passed in a flurry of faces, but the captain paid particular attention to Lady Halifax, the mother who did not approve of him. He was taken aback by her extraordinary beauty and found himself smiling down into her eyes—a truer blue than her daughter's and far more assessing—and allowing his admiration for the marchioness to show in his own eyes as he bowed over her hand. Lord Halifax shook his hand heartily and advised the captain to take a glass of sherry in lieu of maudling his insides with tea. Brian politely declined, expressing a preference for tea—a polite untruth that earned him a blinding smile from the marchioness.

"Glad you could come, Sheffield," drawled the Honorable Willoughby Hampton appearing at his side and clapping him on the shoulder, quite as though he were already one of the family. The familiarity of the gesture unsettled him, but he answered politely, ignoring the frankly speculative glance in the jovial gentleman's brown eyes.

"I trust Cynthia did nothing untoward yesterday," Hampton

remarked with a wicked grin. "She has been known to indulge her penchant for racing when she has a fast team in hand."

Brian saw a frown gathering on Lady Cynthia's brow, and quickly intervened. "I certainly would have noticed had her lady-ship done anything outrageous," he drawled laconically, won-dering again how much the wily Hampton knew or guessed regarding his presence at Halifax House.

"You have just been given a set-down, Willy dear," Lady Cyn-thia said with deceptive sweetness, before whisking the captain away to meet the remaining guests. "Pay no attention to my cousin," she remarked as she led him back to his hostess, where Lady Halifax handed him his tea. "He likes to think he is *au courant* in everything that goes on in London, and obviously he is put out to find that, in our case at least, he is not."

Brian liked the way she referred to the tenuous connection be-tween them as *our* case. It was the first time she had acknowl-edged the link, and it reminded the captain forcibly that he had come to Halifax House with the express purpose of accepting Lady Cynthia's proposal. The thought of making such a commit-ment caused his stomach to knot, and he put his half-finished cup down on the intricately carved wood mantel beside which they stood, his palms suddenly damp.

"I would speak with you, Lady Cynthia," he said curtly, before he lost his nerve. "But not here . . ." He gestured around the room, where a few stragglers, among them Mr. Hampton, still clustered about their hostess.

Lady Cynthia looked at him for a moment, her gaze in-scrutable; then she nodded. "When you take your leave, instruct Hastings to show you to the Yellow Saloon," she said evenly. "I shall join you presently."

Less than ten minutes later, the deed was done, and Captain Sheffield found himself standing in the intimate saloon with its gold brocade furnishings and gilded ceiling. The impassive butler poured a glass of sherry before leaving, closing the door silently behind him.

The captain had not long to wait. Lady Cynthia's face was deli-cately flushed when she came into the room and closed the door, leaning against it briefly before coming slowly across the carpet towards him. It was then that Brian realized the lady was nervous, too, a discovery that spurred him to state his case bluntly, before anything else deterred him from the step he knew he must take.

"I have decided to take advantage of your generous offer, my lady," he said with a brusqueness he had not intended. He saw her flinch and wished there had been some other, less crude, manner of telling a female he was willing to sell his freedom for fifteen thousand pounds. No, he thought, that was unfair. All she had asked was that he consider her unusual proposal, not that he necessarily agree to wed her. She had no way of knowing that to a man of honor—as Brian considered himself to be—there could be no half measures. If Lady Cynthia settled his debts, he would wed her. As far as he was concerned, the lady had won her gamble. Brian Sheffield was not the kind of man to take her money and run.

Lady Cynthia ran her tongue over her lower lip, and Brian wondered if he would be expected to kiss her. The notion was not unpleasant, particularly when his eyes followed the unconsciously sensuous movement of the lady's tongue across her moist lips. The sight of her slightly parted lips made Brian wish he had enough address to act on his impulse to touch them with his own, but his feet seemed to be rooted fast to the golden roses in the carpet. His mind would not be still, though, and he could almost feel the softness of her mouth under his, hear the sigh that would escape her as he took her small waist in his hands and drew her against him. Gently at first, and then with greater urgency as his body reacted to the feel of her— The devil take it, he thought with sudden panic, wrenching his unruly mind away from these indiscreet longings, if he did not cease acting like a moonstruck looby, he would embarrass himself before her.

He cleared his throat self-consciously.

"If you mean that you will give my proposal serious consideration, Captain, then I thank you." She smiled, almost shyly, he thought, and was suddenly aware that he had brought her happiness. Even though Lacy Cynthia did not know that he had just agreed to wed her, she was obviously content with the little she thought he had promised. Her naiveté touched him deeply.

"It is I who should thank you, my lady," he said sincerely.

"Not at all, Captain," she protested. "I thank you for placing me one step closer to winning my gamble." The idea must have amused her for she laughed lightly, and indicated his untouched glass. "You have not drunk your sherry, sir," she said suddenly. "Would you object to a toast, Captain? Another toast to the future, perhaps?"

She turned towards the sideboard, but Brian—his feet abruptly uprooted from the carpet—reached for the sherry and poured her a full glass. "I do not mind if I do," he replied, handing her the delicate-stemmed glass. His fingers brushed hers lightly, and quite irrationally, Brian wanted to tell her that, as far as he was concerned, they were betrothed. Then he might certainly presume to kiss her, he thought, watching the green of her eyes become more intense as he raised his glass and gazed into them.

"To the future, my lady," he murmured softly.

And may all your dreams come true, my lovely Cynthia, he added to himself, wondering which of his own dreams might have to be discarded in the process.

Long after Captain Sheffield had taken his leave, Cynthia sat alone in the Yellow Saloon, sipping the dregs of her sherry and daydreaming. She had always daydreamed as a child, and as she approached marriageable age, her dreams had, with increasing frequency, included romantical images of dashing young gentlemen on white chargers. It had come as a distinct disappointment to her, at the age of sixteen, to discover that she did not even like white horses. She had never owned one, nor had she wanted to. And she could not see Captain Sheffield mounted on a white charger.

The notion made her smile. The captain had appeared to best advantage on his own roan, an animal Cynthia had instantly recognized as a prime goer. It had pleased her immeasurably that he shared her love of horses, and her present daydreams centered on the rosy picture of the two of them planning together to enhance the breeding program at Lonsdale Stables. Except that it would no longer be Lonsdale, would it? she thought, for the first time giving substance to the direction of her daydreams. It would be Sheffield, and she would be Lady Cynthia Sheffield, and the prospect delighted her beyond anything she had felt when James had made her a viscountess ten years ago.

The delicious novelty of finding her most cherished hopes suddenly almost within her grasp colored Lady Cynthia's dreams that night, and she awoke early the next morning, her heart dizzy with anticipation. Cool reason soon exerted itself, however, and after ringing for her chocolate, Cynthia slipped into a warm robe and sat down at her escritoire. She would have to face reality sooner or later, she told herself, selecting a new nib from the dish and a sheet of pressed paper from the drawer. The captain's decision to give her proposal his consideration was undoubtedly motivated by the need to settle his debt. Cynthia had no idea when the debt came due, but she was fairly certain that debts of honor, such as the captain's, had to be settled promptly.

So, daydreaming aside, she told herself prosaically, Captain

Sheffield had come for the money yesterday, not for her. She had been a silly goose to allow her imagination to run on as it had. In a widow of nine and twenty such girlish fantasies were inappropriate if not downright indecent. Theirs would be a marriage of strictest convenience—if indeed it ever came to marriage—and to pretend otherwise would be to invite heartbreak.

It would serve no useful purpose to remember the captain's marvelous blue eyes, and the way he looked at her in the Yellow Saloon yesterday. Quite as though he wanted to do something outrageously male, like kiss her, for instance. Cynthia had held her breath in exquisite anticipation, but he had thought better of it. Or, more to the point, he had not intended to kiss her at all. Her face warmed at the thought of how it might have felt to be kissed again by a man, particularly a man like Captain Sheffield.

The door opened behind her, and Betsy set the cup of chocolate down on the escritoire. "A right good morning to ye, milady," she said in her cheerful country brogue. "Up early ye be this morning, to be sure." She regarded her mistress sharply, her brown eyes suddenly serious. "Coming down with somethin' be ye?" The little maid peered closer. "Too flushed by half, ye be and no mistake. Best get back to bed, milady, and let me call . . ."

"No, thank you, Betsy," Cynthia interrupted quickly. "It is a little warm in here, that is all."

Although she looked askance at her mistress, Betsy withdrew and Lady Cynthia took up her pen again, setting down her terse instructions to the Lonsdale agent in London. As she wrote out the sum to be expended immediately in redeeming the captain's vowels, Cynthia visualized the disapproving expression that would cloud Mr. Broadstone's parsimonious countenance. He would do as she instructed, nevertheless. During the past two years of her widowhood, she had impressed upon the solicitor that she would not be swayed an inch from her set course by what he facetiously referred to as his superior masculine experience.

She left it to Mr. Broadstone to contact the Sheffield solicitors and make arrangements to pay off the holder of the captain's vowels. Cynthia preferred not to know such details, considering this information an unnecessary encroachment upon the captain's privacy.

Lady Halifax had no such scruples. Cynthia was sharing a light nuncheon in her mother's private sitting room when the slim packet was delivered to her that afternoon, and Lady Halifax, divining the nature of the contents, demanded to be told the name of the lucky beneficiary of Cynthia's largesse.

Cynthia placed the packet on the low gate-legged table without opening it. "I do not wish to know, Mama," she said firmly. "I have kept my side of the agreement. The debt is paid, and Captain Sheffield is no longer encumbered with it. That is all that matters."

"You are an idealist, my love," Lady Halifax said with an affectionate smile. "Very well, I will not plague you about it, but promise me you will not be too disappointed if the good captain does not keep his side of it."

"And you are a cynic, Mama," Cynthia replied, shaking her head. "I am convinced that Captain Sheffield will do exactly as he promised."

"I can see why, my dear," her mother remarked. "He is a handsome rogue, like so many of them, but I wonder if he will stand firm when the cards are down. What is to stop him from reneging on his promise?"

"He is a man of his word," Cynthia said simply.

Her mother sighed gustily. "I do believe you have developed a *tendre* for the handsome devil," she murmured, regarding her daughter reproachfully. "Indeed, I find him quite charming myself, dear. A little rough around the edges, perhaps, but charming nevertheless."

There were times when Cynthia wished her mother were not so perceptive. "I am no inexperienced chit in her first Season to be dazzled by a pair of handsome eyes, Mama," she said quietly. "I do not ask for miracles, you know."

"If you do not ask for them, you will not get them, that is for sure," Lady Halifax said forcefully, startling her daughter with this abrupt change of direction. "And if truth be told, I rather fancy the captain for you, Cynthia. Not that I do not believe you would be better off with Robert, of course, but there is something about the captain that is, what shall I call it? Appealing perhaps? No, stalwart fits him better. And definitely reliable, a quality which even I must confess our darling Robbie is sadly lacking." She broke off, and Cynthia observed her mother's beautiful face cautiously, surprised and pleased with her sudden reversal in favor of the captain.

"What would you say if I sent round a note asking him to join us at the theater tomorrow evening?" Lady Halifax suggested, a conspiratorial glitter in her lovely blue eyes. "In my experience, miracles often need a nudge in the right direction."

Lady Cynthia laughed softly, vastly relieved at this sudden turn of events.

"Splendid!" she exclaimed. "With you to do the nudging, Mama, a miracle might not be so impossible after all."

"Yes, indeed," murmured the marchioness, her mind already on other things. "But what will you wear, Cynthia? I suggest the new green velvet. And you will wear my diamonds, naturally."

Naturally, Cynthia told herself later, after they had discussed every minute detail of their attire exhaustively, and she had retired to her room to rest for the ball they were to attend that evening.

But would Captain Sheffield appreciate the glittering spectacle she would present? she wondered. Or would her finery merely remind him of the disparity between their fortunes?

The romantic in her wanted to believe the former, but the realist feared the latter.

CHAPTER SIX

Contretemps

Captain Sheffield did not receive Lady Halifax's missive until late the following evening, having spent the day with Dick Chatham and several of their military friends out near the village of Twickenham, attending a mill. Word had got around the clubs that one of Captain Barclay's aspiring champions was engaged to test his mettle against a challenger from the colonies, and in short order, the clubs had emptied of their younger members, and the Richmond turnpike was soon clogged with sporting vehicles of every description.

After an exhilarating afternoon, during which—for the first time since his disastrous card game with Lord Monroyal—the captain was able to forget his financial troubles, he agreed with Chatham's suggestion that they bespeak a meal at the Golden Hind in Richmond.

"Ain't no sense in trying to fight our way back to Town through a mêlée of cow-handed, half-foxed, aspiring young bloods," Dick had pointed out as he struggled to turn his curricle around in the churned-up mud of the field where the fight had taken place. "Doubtless half of them will come croppers before they reach London, in any case."

"A hot rum punch does sound rather good," Brian agreed, chaffing his cold hands, which had suffered from the chill October breeze in spite of his York gloves.

"Not engaged to attend Lady Cynthia this evening, are you, old man?" Chatham asked, as if suddenly remembering his friend's interest in that quarter. "We could push on to Town if you wish?"

"No," Brian replied shortly. "I have already done my duty there, as you well know, Dick. Let me enjoy what freedom I have left."

Chatham's hearty laugh grated on the captain's nerves, and he wished he had held his tongue.

"Buck up, old chap." Dick leered knowingly. "Pleasanter duties await you after you are well and truly riveted to her. I could envy you myself were it not for the leg shackles. The lady is a prize of the first stare, as you must have realized by now."

The captain glanced at his friend uneasily. "You are not bruiting this affair about, are you, Dick?" he demanded.

Chatham looked affronted. "Of course, I ain't bruiting it about," he replied gruffly. "What sort of loose screw do you take me for? It will have to come out sooner or later, of course," he added as they drove into the bustling courtyard of the Golden Hind. "Unless . . ." Chatham turned to fix Brian with a steady gaze. "You ain't thinking of playing nip-shot with the lady, are you, lad? There's many a man who would not think twice about it, let me tell you, but you ain't one of them, I trust."

Brian swung down from the vehicle and turned to watch Dick throw the reins to his groom. He had a sudden, violent urge to plant his friend a facer, not for what Chatham had implied, which was clearly insulting, but because Dick had given voice to an unworthy thought that had flickered intermittently at the back of his own mind during the afternoon. Hearing the ugly thought spoken aloud caused a rush of self-disgust to engulf him.

"If anyone else had suggested that," he growled, "I would have darkened his daylights for him." Turning abruptly away from the startled Chatham, Brian stalked into the inn and demanded a private parlor in such harsh tones, that the innkeeper glanced at him uneasily before ushering them into a low-ceilinged room where a bright fire crackled warmly in the grate.

An abundant, well-cooked meal went a long way towards restoring his spirits, and by the time the captain had put away large helpings of pigeon pie, roast goose, and a rack of lamb, followed by rhubarb and currant tarts, the whole washed down by generous tankards of local ale, Brian was feeling more the thing.

When Chatham's curricle drew up in front of his lodgings shortly before seven o'clock that evening, the captain readily accepted his friend's suggestion that they drop in at his mother's box at the theatre to ogle the ladies if not to enjoy Kean's much praised performance of Macbeth.

The heavy white card, closed with a blue wafer and bearing the Halifax crest, lay on top of the stack of invitations on the hall table. Brian picked it up and held the missive in his hands for a moment before breaking the seal and looking at the signature. For several seconds, he had experienced a pleasant tingle of anticipation, imagining the note had come from Lady Cynthia. But the invitation was from Lady Halifax, evidently written in the marchioness's own hand, begging Captain Sheffield to honor them with his presence at the theatre the following evening.

Brian smiled cynically. *Honor them with his presence*, indeed, he mused, savoring the irony of fate. A scant week ago, the Halifaxes had been unaware of the obscure existence of Captain the Honorable Brian Sheffield, younger son with no prospects to speak of, and now—thanks to a young woman's daring to make him an immodest proposal, he was elevated to the status of honored guest. And it was for *her* sake that he had been included in the party, Brian reminded himself wryly. Would it always be thus? he wondered.

There was no question that he would accept Lady Halifax's invitation, Brian decided, speculating on what part, if any, Lady Cynthia had played in it being extended. What would his friends say, he wondered, when they saw him in such exalted company? As some of them surely would, Drury Lane being a favorite gathering place for young officers on the loose in London. He would have to tell Dick of his change of plans, of course, but the others were bound to draw their own conclusions.

Or John? The captain had not considered his half-brother's reaction to his impending connection with Lady Cynthia, but had to admit that the prospect of provoking Lord Mulgrave's astonishment, and perhaps envy, was rather gratifying. John and his family were certainly in London for the Little Season and might well choose tomorrow evening to attend the theatre.

As the captain followed an usher's directions to the Halifax box the following evening just before the curtain rose, he kept reminding himself that he was—if only in his own mind—betrothed to Lady Cynthia, and should accustom himself to the inevitability of that promise.

And he should also accustom himself to acting the part, he mused, stepping into the box to find it uncomfortably full of people. That might not prove difficult at all, he realized, taking advantage of the first moment to gaze at Lady Cynthia's lovely profile as she chatted amiably with a very young miss in soft primrose muslin. Brian's eyes slid down her graceful neck and he drew a deep breath at the flawless expanse of bosom her dark green velvet gown offered to his view. The diamond necklace she wore must have cost a king's ransom, he estimated, reluctantly acknowledging that—even at his most flush, he could never afford a bauble to rival it.

As if conscious of his intrusive gaze, Lady Cynthia looked up and caught his eye. She smiled and touched her mother's arm.

Instantly Lady Halifax turned to greet him, with more effusive-
ness than he had expected.

"My dear Captain Sheffield," she said, her brilliant smile blinding him with its intensity. "How good of you to come. My dear
Sophy," she said, turning to the pleasant-faced woman at her side,
"this is Captain Sheffield, who is back in England on a recuperating leave. Captain, my dearest sister, Lady Monroyal. And this is
Lady Constance Stilton, the musical genius of the family. Mr.
Hampton you already know. And that saucy miss is Lady Letitia,
a sad romp if ever I saw one."

"Aunt Elizabeth!" the young lady protested loudly, her perfect
cheeks dimpling charmingly, and her eyelashes fluttering
provocatively. "Do not believe a word of it, Captain, for it is not
true at all," she continued naively. "I am the very model of pro-
priety, would you not agree, Cynthia." She appealed prettily to
her cousin who seemed to be unaffected by this display of pert-
ness.

"You are a romp just as your Aunt Elizabeth says, Letty, so do
not try to bamboozle the captain into believing anything different."

Lady Letitia was about to protest again, but his hostess drew
the captain down beside her. "I have saved this chair for you,
Captain," she explained with a smile. "Here between me and
Cynthia, you will be safe from Letty's prattle." Since almost immediately Lady Halifax turned to continue her conversation with
her sister, Brian was free to turn his attention to his betrothed.

Tonight she was indeed the grand lady, poised and elegant as
only a woman sure of her fortune and rank could be, he thought,
listening to her spirited account of the Beresford ball she had at-
tended the previous evening during which the Prince Regent had
disgraced himself again by ogling a young widow not yet out of
her blacks.

"I wonder the old lecher did not select you for his attentions,
my lady," he said pleasantly.

"He would not *dare*, Captain," Lady Letitia cut in from her
place beside Mr. Hampton, who—to give him credit—had en-
deavored to keep her from flirting quite shamelessly with the captain.

"Cynthia would have given Prinny a sharp set-down, believe
me," Letty explained eagerly, delighted to have captured the gentleman's attention. "Prince or no Prince, Cynthia would have rung
a peal over his head or boxed his ears. I'm not quite sure which,
but in any event, he would have realized his mistake soon

enough." Lowering her voice provocatively, Lady Letitia added, "To tell the truth, Captain, Cynthia can be quite the harridan when she is crossed. Just as I can be the tiniest bit of a hoyden upon occasion, you know." This spiteful piece of childishness was accompanied by a quite dazzling smile demurely directly at the Captain.

One glance at Lady Cynthia told Brian that she was not amused, although her face remained expressionless. Her eyes betrayed her, though, and he saw a flicker of mortification, and perhaps pain, in their green depths.

"Spoken like a true hoyden," he drawled, casting Letitia a dismissive glance. "But I will never believe that Lady Cynthia is a harridan. The notion is quite laughable." He smiled with deliberate warmth into that lady eyes until she acknowledged his compliment with lowered gaze and a faint smile.

As her betrothed husband, Brian thought, he might have touched her, squeezed her clenched hands, and reassured her that she had no cause to allow the conspicuous pettiness of the younger girl to overset her. As it was, he did his best, during the short time before the curtain rose on the stage, to show her that he found Lady Letitia's chatter and childishness tedious in the extreme.

When the play began and the house lights were doused, Cynthia—as he had begun to think of her—turned her attention to the stage, and Brian could gaze his fill. Dick was right, of course, Lady Cynthia was a prize of the first stare, and he should be thanking his lucky stars that the lady had selected him in her search for a second husband. Ah, he thought stubbornly, and that was precisely the rub. She had chosen him. Lady Cynthia would not have been his choice for a wife—if he had ever reached the point of thinking about marriage at all. Indeed, she was too far above his touch. He would never have dared present himself before Lord Halifax to demand her hand. The Marquess of Halifax, no less, well known in political circles, confidant to Lord Castlereagh, and one of the Regent's intimate friends. This was an illustrious circle he had stepped into, and Brian doubted that his own half-brother, a belted earl, would have been admitted here.

. All this should have been vastly gratifying to a lowly captain, but Brian found no comfort in the reflected glory. As he gazed in bemusement at the woman who was to make it all happen, his mind drifted once more to that ugly suggestion Dick had made yesterday during their return from the mill. Would it be morally possible for him to renege on his promise? he wondered. Could he live with himself if he did?

Perhaps it was because his mind was occupied with these unworthy thoughts that he reacted as he did when the curtain closed on the first act of *Macbeth*.

He had heard two latecomers enter the box midway through the act and had recognized Lord Halifax's voice greeting his wife. The other man did not speak, and when the lights were raised, he found himself staring into the faintly mocking eyes of the Marquess of Monroyal.

Monroyal! Of course, he thought, why had he not made the connection when he was presented to Lady Monroyal? The man who had invited him to gamble and then calmly taken fifteen thousand pounds from him was the lady's son. And if he was Lady Monroyal's son . . . Brian's ire began to rise at the connection his mind still refused to make. But there could be no doubting it. This hardened gambler was Lady Cynthia's cousin. The man who had created the debt that had driven him neatly into Lady Cynthia's net.

The implications of this discovery were so explosive, that the captain rose without a word to his hostess. Casting one scathing glance at the lady he had thought to wed, Brian moved past the Marquess of Monroyal, muttering under his breath as he did so.

"A word with you, my lord, if you please."

Stopping a short distance from the Halifax box, Brian spun to confront the man he believed had set in motion the sequence of events which would lead him to the altar before his time, with a female who was not his choice.

"Sheffield," the marquess drawled in a bored voice. "What ails you, man? Has my cousin said something to send you up into the boughs?"

"Then you admit she is your cousin?" Brian felt he could not trust himself to speak the lady's name.

The marquess raised one dark eyebrow and his gray eyes darkened superciliously. "If you are referring to Lady Lonsdale, then no, actually she is not a true cousin. Her aunt is my father's second wife," he drawled in that mocking tone Brian detested.

"Ah, but can you deny that between the two of you, you have plotted to ruin me, my lord?" Brian challenged.

The blasted man raised his eyebrow a notch higher and looked down his nose with a haughty sneer. "I think you forget yourself, Sheffield," the marquess said with dangerous softness, his gray eyes cold as slate. "It is my cousin you speak of, and I fail to see how marriage to her would ruin you."

Brian smiled grimly. "So you admit you know of the lady's plans for a second nuptials?"

The marquess shrugged his broad shoulders with studied nonchalance. "How could I not?" he drawled. "My cousin confided in me. I warned her against it, naturally, but she would have her way. She knows nothing of our little game, by the way," he added carelessly.

Brian snorted in disbelief. So the entire incident, which had cost him his freedom, had been nothing but a *little game* to this arrogant wastrel. "You can hardly expect me to credit that," he said bitterly.

"Credit what you please," the marquess replied in his bored voice. "I should call you out for your impudence, but I shall spare you for the lady's sake."

"Can you deny that—" Brian began, fury making his voice tremble.

"You are becoming tiresome, Captain," the marquess drawled, his lip curling into a sneer. "I deny nothing; neither do I admit anything. If you had any sense, you would keep your mouth shut and enjoy the windfall."

Brian was so enraged by this insolence that he could hardly trust himself to speak. Abruptly he knew he had to get away from this vitiated atmosphere where elegance and beauty seemed to mask nothing but deceit and boredom. "Give my regrets to her ladyship," he said with icy stiffness, his mind churning with rage and a sudden sense of regret that knotted his stomach. "Under the circumstances, I cannot stay to enjoy the performance."

The marquess said nothing, merely giving Brian the briefest of nods before he turned to saunter back to the box.

Brian stared at the man's receding back, wishing he had had the foresight to darken the arrogant fop's daylights for him.

Then he turned and walked out into the cold night, his back ramrod straight.

In the days that followed Captain Sheffield's abrupt disappearance from the Halifax box at Drury Lane, Lady Cynthia became increasingly convinced that she had lost him for good. When her cousin Robert had taken the captain's place beside her at the beginning of the second act, Cynthia knew that something had gone dreadfully wrong. Robert had been noncommittal, as always, and the harsh set of his mouth warned her that he was very angry indeed.

"Where is the captain?" she demanded, when he offered no explanation for his presence.

The marquess regarded her expressionlessly in the half-light, and had Cynthia been less preoccupied with the captain's absence, she would have recognized, from the hard glitter of his eyes, that her cousin was in a dangerous mood.

"What have you done to him, Robert?" she hissed as the noise from the pit subsided marginally, a sign that the curtain had risen on the second act.

"I have done nothing to him, Cynthia," the marquess replied curtly. "Although I wish I had."

"Then where is he?"

Her cousin shrugged nonchalantly. "I have no idea, my dear Cynthia," he drawled, "neither do I care." He settled back in his seat and gazed down at the stage, giving every indication that the subject was closed.

Lady Cynthia laid a gloved hand on his sleeve. "Tell me what happened, Robert, or I swear I shall box your ears for you."

This sally elicited a thin smile. "That might be rather amusing, my dear," he murmured, fixing her with a cold stare. And then, after she had lost hope of receiving an answer, he added in an expressionless voice, "You do not want to know, Cynthia. Believe me."

More he would not say, and since he studiously avoided her for the next several days, Cynthia had no way of knowing what had caused Captain Sheffield's abrupt departure and his subsequent silence.

Every evening, in the relative peace of her own chamber, Cynthia would take the flat package of the captain's vowels out of her escritoire drawer and sit with it in her hands, sometimes for as long as an hour at a time, wondering if its contents held the answer to the captain's odd behavior. But although she was often tempted, Cynthia did not open it. She had promised herself that she would respect his privacy, and she was determined to do so.

Cynthia had intended to deliver the vowels to the captain in person; she had looked forward to it, but when he had not called by the fourth day after his unexplained absence, she took the package out of the drawer for the last time, wrapped it in a sheet of brown paper, and sent one of the footmen to deliver it to the captain's lodgings.

Now she could wash her hands of the whole business, she

thought bleakly, knowing in her heart that it would be a long time before she would be able to banish the captain from her thoughts. And from her heart, she admitted with sudden honesty. If only she had followed her original plan to maintain a cool distance from the man—whomever he might be—who would accept the conditions of her proposal, she would not now be in the embarrassing position of having to admit she cared more than she ought for a man who did not want her.

Her heart had betrayed her, Cynthia realized, now that it was too late to draw back. And now that she had returned the captain's vowels, she had relinquished the only hold she had ever had over him. Her money had held him, she acknowledged with a cynicism unusual in her. And now that he had his vowels back, there was no further need for her money, was there? No further need for Lady Cynthia Lonsdale, an aging widow who had the temerity, the monumental audacity and conceit to believe that she could purchase a man's . . . A man's what? she thought, knowing where her mind was leading her and unable to stop. His loyalty? Perhaps even his friendship and eventually his affection? And certainly his body. Cynthia took a deep breath and closed her eyes. Yes, she had wanted the captain's body, she thought, allowing the truth to crystallize in her mind, conscious of the warmth that spiraled slowly up through her own. She wanted his strong arms about her, his mouth—a tremor shook her when she recalled the provocative fullness of his mouth—over hers, demanding in its intrusive possession everything she wanted to give. Everything she needed to give.

Cynthia opened her eyes abruptly and sat up. This would never do, she thought. This was maudlin in the extreme. The captain had chosen—or so she had to believe in light of his continued absence—to remove himself from her life, but Lady Cynthia could not, indeed she *would* not, allow this contretemps to turn her into a mopish, ill-tempered recluse. Glancing purposefully through the heap of invitations on her dressing table, she selected one at random and opened it. Yes, indeed, she told herself firmly, she would be delighted to accept the Earl of Yarmouth's so gracious invitation to drive in the Park this afternoon. Resolutely putting her troubles aside, Cynthia picked up her pen and dashed off her acceptance before she had time to regret her decision.

But regret it Cynthia eventually did, for it was while she was tooling along Rotton Row at the fashionable hour that afternoon with the flashy and flatteringly attentive Earl of Yarmouth, that she saw Captain Sheffield for the first time in over a week.

The sight of her erstwhile suitor did nothing to ease Cynthia's aching heart, however, nor did it provide an acceptable answer to the question of why he had chosen to eschew her company. In point of fact, the sight of Captain Sheffield in animated conversation with the Incomparable Miss Georgina Crenshaw, a young chit barely out of the schoolroom and one of the current darlings of the *ton*, made Cynthia positively ill.

She had no doubt whatsoever that the errant captain had seen her; the flash of his laughing blue eyes told her so. But, cut to the quick by the sight of his curly chestnut head bent solicitously over Miss Crenshaw's delectable pale ringlets, Cynthia deliberately turned towards her companion with a smile of such artificial brilliance that she thought her face would crack.

Much later, having refused to accompany her parents to a musicale she had actually been looking forward to, Cynthia retired to bed with the megrims, wondering if it had not been her heart rather than her face that had cracked at the captain's perfidy.

"Are you telling me you are going to play nip-shot after all?" Richard Chatham's voice was heavy with censure, and Brian flinched.

"There's no need to bite my nose off, Dick," the captain said gruffly, slamming the tankard of ale down on the coffeehouse table with such force that the dark liquid sloshed over onto his hand. "What choice do I have, can you tell me? I've been played for a fool, and no mistake. What would you have me do? Put my head tamely into the lady's net?" His lip curled disdainfully.

Chatham helped himself to another serving of mutton with pickled mushrooms, replenished his own tankard from the large brown jug, and regarded his friend curiously.

"How can you be so sure that Lady Lonsdale knew anything about your dealings with Monroyal?"

The captain raised his eyes ceilingwards, his expression one of exasperation and impatience. "Have I not told you six times already, Dick?" he growled. "The bloody villain as much as admitted they were in the plot together."

"In so many words?" his friend insisted.

"He would not deny it. I asked him point-blank if between them they had planned to snare me, and he would not deny it." The memory of the marquess's sneer was still so fresh in Brian's mind that his fists clenched of their own accord. "I should have drawn his cork for him," he muttered belligerently.

Dick grinned good-naturedly. "That would have been a mill

worth seeing, old chap," he remarked enthusiastically. "I know for a fact that Monroyal spends considerable time at Jackson's Saloon, so he is bound to be handy with his fives." Then his pleasant face sobered. "But do not go making a Jack-pudding of yourself over this, Brian. Refusing to deny something, as you say Monroyal did, is not the same as admitting to it, you know. So don't go off half-cocked, old man. A lady's reputation is at stake here, and you would not wish her any harm, now, would you?"

Dick was right again, of course, the captain had to admit to himself several hours later as he changed for an evening at Mrs. Crenshaw's musicale, the kind of insipid affair he usually avoided, but which Dick had talked him into attending. Mrs. Crenshaw, Brian knew, was one of those abrasive, encroaching matrons who were always trying to edge their way into the *ton*'s notice. Mrs. Crenshaw had been more successful than most, Dick had informed him that afternoon, because she had traded on a distant Yorkshire connection with the Duke of Ware, now deceased. But the lady's chief attraction was indubitably the possession of a daughter of quite startling loveliness, whom even Sally Jersey, not particular known for praising young chits just out of the schoolroom, had pronounced a "diamond of the first water."

"But I am not the least interested in young chits," Brian had protested mildly, after listening to his friend rave on for all of twenty minutes about the enchanting attributes of Miss Crenshaw.

"You will be when you see this one, my lad," Dick replied with an exaggerated leer. "A prime article indeed, is little Georgina Crenshaw. A blond perfection, a veritable paragon of loveliness," he rhapsodized. "And rich as Croesus into the bargain," he added slyly. "Although old Crenshaw's fortune comes from Trade, of course. Shipping, actually. Made an indecent amount of the ready, I am told, with the East India Company. But Georgina will be the prize of the Season when she is presented next April."

Brian grimaced. "And without two thoughts to rub together in her pretty head, I would not wonder," he said crushingly. "And besides," he added, "I do not like blondes."

"Prefer redheads, do you?" Dick remarked with a knowing wink.

And Dick had been right about that, too, Brian thought morosely as he allowed Hardy to assist him into his evening coat. The auburn-haired Lady Cynthia had never been far from his thoughts since he had walked out on her four days ago. And since he had returned that evening to find a small package, with his name neatly inscribed upon it in a lady's hand, waiting for him on the hall table, he had been thrown into a turmoil of indecision.

Had the cool, lovely Lady Cynthia been a willing partner—as Brian was still inclined to believe—in Lord Monroyal's nefarious plot to coerce a respectable, though destitute, gentleman into a marriage of convenience with his cousin? Or had she, too, been a victim of the marquess's devious game?

The latter supposition had given him food for thought, and he halfway convinced himself that the lady might be innocent after all. He had actually begun to believe he had done her a terrible injustice before he returned that evening to find the package awaiting him. He had torn off the wrapper, only to find a second wrapped package, addressed to her ladyship, inside. The seal was unbroken, and the captain's anger flared afresh. Why had her ladyship not bothered to open the package addressed to her? The only answer he could think of to that revealing question was that Lady Cynthia had known both the remitter and the incriminating contents of the package. And if she had known that . . . His thoughts trailed off incoherently as he tried to deny the truth that was staring him in the face.

The lady he had committed himself to wed had coldly manipulated him into parson's mousetrap. The humiliation of knowing himself the dupe enraged him.

In a burst of vicious fury, the captain tore open the second wrapper and a cascade of notes, written in his own hand to the Marquess of Monroyal, fluttered to the faded carpet.

Fifteen thousand pounds worth of vowels, he thought. And she had paid all of them. Or had she? The ugly suspicion of her possible complicity with her ruthless cousin nagged at him again. Had the marquess merely handed Lady Cynthia the package of vowels without demanding any redemption? he wondered. Brian knew for a certainty that the arrogant marquess had no need of the money. And if it had all been a game to him—a *little game* he had called it—then he might well have played that game for the sole purpose of amusing himself. Brian clenched his fists.

"The devil take the arrogant bastard," he exclaimed aloud, startling his batman into dropping his master's tall evening Beaver and turning to regard the captain suspiciously.

"Beg pardon, sir?" Hardy inquired.

The captain grinned wryly. "Nothing of any moment, Hardy," he said shortly. "Blue-deviled, that is all."

"I take it we are out of the briars, Captain?" the batman asked, with the familiarity born of their years of service together.

Brian hesitated. Hardy's question had raised another specter. Could he in all fairness accept the redeemed vowels Lady Cynthia had sent him if he intended to play nip-shot with her—as Dick had so bluntly phrased it? But if he did not return them, he would have to pay her the fifteen thousand pounds. His honor would demand it.

Or he could wed the lady, he told himself bleakly and live with the knowledge that he had been caught and reeled in like a dashed fish.

"Perhaps," he muttered to Hardy as the batman handed him his hat and gloves. "Perhaps we are, at that."

His emotions were still in turmoil as he ascended the staircase at Mrs. Crenshaw's ostentatious mansion on St. James's Square later that evening in the company of Dick Chatham. Both young gentlemen, despite their lack of titles and favorable prospects, were received volubly and effusively by their hostess, and with a charming fluttering of eyelashes by the lovely Miss Crenshaw.

Dick was visibly smitten, Brian discovered as they spent a tedious hour listening to a dubious Italian contralto rendering the most popular arias of the day. The captain himself was unimpressed by the demure Miss Crenshaw, even when the precocious chit showed unmistakable signs of singling him out for an innocent flirtation.

Although mildly amused by Chatham's chagrin when Miss Crenshaw broadly hinted—while her redoubtable mama was fawning over the old Dowager Countess of Hartford—that she was in the habit of driving in the Park every afternoon, weather permitting, Captain Sheffield found himself unwilling to be drawn into dalliance with the chit. The memory of the auburn-haired Lady Cynthia had inexplicably dampened his appetite for prattling blond misses.

It was only because Chatham had stepped in to assure the blushing damsel that, by an odd quirk of fate, it was also their custom to frequent the Park at the fashionable hour, that the captain found himself strolling there the following afternoon. He was not surprised when they were hailed from a passing barouche by Miss Georgina herself, fortuitously in the company of a stiff-necked companion rather than her sharp-eyed mama.

"Captain Sheffield!" Miss Crenshaw trilled in her little-girl voice, her heart-shaped face delightfully pink, and her pansy-blue eyes sparkling vivaciously. "And Captain Chatham, too," she added when Dick cleared his throat pointedly. "What a delightful surprise!"

"The delight is all ours, Miss Crenshaw," Chatham put in quickly with an ingratiating smile, and Brian was amused at his friend's attempt to capture the Incomparable's attention.

"Will you be attending Lady Mannering's Venetian breakfast tomorrow, Captain Sheffield?" she asked naively. "Or Lady Hereford's ball next week, or perhaps Mrs. Canning's rout on Friday evening?" Her purpose was so transparent that the captain felt a momentary pang of regret that he could find nothing to admire in Miss Crenshaw except her undeniably dazzling beauty.

But suddenly he realized that the young lady's superficial brilliance was not nearly enough to intrigue him. There was no mystery in the chit, no depth of emotion such as he had felt pulsed beneath the surface of Lady Cynthia's enigmatic countenance. Miss Crenshaw reminded him forcibly of his sister Caroline, utterly lovable—much like a playful kitten—but all inconsequential chatter and not a serious thought in her head. And females who reminded him of his sister held no appeal for him at all.

Brian wondered when he had acquired such fastidious tastes. He could well remember the time—not so long ago either—when he would have welcomed a flirtation with a pretty little chit like Miss Crenshaw. Had not his childhood flirt, Miss Corianna Hornby, possessed those same pansy-blue eyes and entrancing gold curls? Why then did this untouched innocence now pall on his senses? he wondered. His ideal had undergone a subtle change without his noticing, and he now demanded sophistication and a lively mind in his women. And a pair of sea-green eyes, he thought wryly.

His attention returned to Miss Crenshaw's hopeful face, and he realized she was waiting for his response.

"I rather think not . . ." he began with feigned regret.

"On the contrary, Brian," Chatham burst out impulsively. "I distinctly recall that we both received invitations to Lady Hereford's ball next week. I hope you will save a dance for me, Miss Crenshaw, because I shall be devastated if you do not."

Miss Crenshaw nodded politely at Chatham, but her pansy-blue eyes returned to focus anxiously on Brian's face. "And you, Captain Sheffield?" she murmured shyly. "Shall I save a dance for you, too?"

Disarmed by this ingenuous and entirely inappropriate remark, Brian smiled ruefully. "I would be honored, Miss Crenshaw," he murmured, favoring the young lady with an elegant bow.

It was as he raised his head, the smile still on his lips, that Brian saw the lady who had taken up so much of his thoughts during the past week. Lady Cynthia appeared to be in prime gig. Her auburn curls enhanced by an outrageously modish green bonnet, and her wonderful greenish eyes fixed, with what seemed perilously like adoration, on the floridly handsome countenance of one of London's most expensive and profligate bachelors.

Brian saw the Earl of Yarmouth throw his head back and laugh uproariously at something his fair companion had said, just as the earl's fancy curricle passed the Crenshaw barouche. Lady Cynthia seemed to have consoled herself remarkably well, he thought. Perhaps she had decided on a man of her own rank, after all, he mused with considerable bitterness.

The thought of Cynthia in that rogue Yarmouth's arms caused a strange, unidentified pain to shoot through his chest, and the captain's smile, when he forced himself to return his gaze to Miss Crenshaw's fair face, felt strained and insincere.

CHAPTER SEVEN

The Ball

"What do you *mean* I cannot waltz, Cousin?" Lady Letitia exclaimed in such affronted tones that Lady Cynthia had to smile.

"You are not yet officially out, dear," she said calmly. Calm and infinite patience were the two most effective defenses against her volatile young cousin's often unseemly exuberance, Cynthia had discovered long ago. During the past two hours, however, she had begun to wonder whether a sound thrashing might not have been more effective in curbing Lady Letitia's penchant for shocking her elders into spasms with her hoydenish starts.

Now if only Letty could be more like her well-behaved sister. Lady Cynthia met the elder girl's wide brown stare and saw a glimmer of understanding there.

"But I have been so looking forward to dancing my first waltz in the arms of one of those dashing gentlemen in uniform," Lady Letitia said, her voice bordering on a whine.

"Well, you will not do so here," Lady Cynthia said firmly. "Only consider how upset your mama would be if she could hear you."

"But she is *not* here," Letty said, now definitely whining. "And who is to tell her?"

Lady Cynthia regarded her youngest cousin with disapproval. "I am ashamed of you, Letitia Stilton," she said coldly. "And I refuse to be seen in the company of an impertinent chit who insists upon making a cake of herself." She rose abruptly from the settee she had occupied with her two charges at one end of Lady Hereford's brilliantly lit ballroom, and shook out her green silk skirts.

She turned to Lady Constance, who had also risen. "I think we had better leave before this rag-mannered sister of yours brings the censure of the *ton* down on our heads, my dear," she remarked.

Letty's reaction was immediate and charmingly contrite. "Oh, *please* do let us stay, Cynthia," she pleaded, her blue eyes filling with tears. "I promise to be good. Truly I do," she added, her voice trembling convincingly. "I promise, promise, *promise*—"

"Do not believe a word of Letty's promises, my dear Cynthia," a lazy voice drawled at her elbow. "They are all a hum, believe me. I have been hoaxed too many times to be taken in by them."

Lady Cynthia turned to meet Lord Monroyal's cynical gaze and smiled briefly. "I am about to take the naughty minx home," she explained. "She is giving me the megrims with her peevish starts."

"Cynthia will not let me waltz, Robbie," Letitia murmured, slanting her eyes at her half-brother flirtatiously.

"Then you will not do so, brat," Lord Monroyal drawled with a noticeable lack of sympathy. "If you are spoiling everyone's enjoyment, I shall take you home myself, my girl. And believe me, you will regret it."

Lady Letitia's expression became sullen. "I merely wished to dance with one of our gallant officers," she muttered. "Indeed, surely it is my civic duty to do so, Robbie. Is it not?" Her face brightened suddenly as a fresh group of young men in their brilliant red uniforms came into the ballroom, laughing and scanning the assembled guests eagerly.

"You see, Robert, they all need partners, poor things," Letty exclaimed, her spirits entirely restored.

"Enough!" her brother said curtly. "I will endeavor to find partners for both of you; that is if Cousin Cynthia can be persuaded to stay?" He glanced quizzically at her, and Cynthia nodded mutely.

The truth was that she cared little whether she stayed or left. She had been rather reluctant to attend Lady Hereford's ball and would not have done so had her Aunt Sophy not begged her to accompany the two girls in her stead. Since that disastrous afternoon when Cynthia had seen Captain Sheffield smiling at Miss Georgina Crenshaw as he had never smiled at her, Cynthia had thrown herself into a whirlwind of social activity, accepting far too many of the invitations that came to rest on the hall table at Halifax House. This frenzied pursuit of amusement had merely fatigued her without bringing the relief she had hoped to find.

Try as she might, Cynthia had not been able to persuade her stubborn heart that any number of other men would suit her purposes as well, if not better, than Captain Brian Sheffield. The fact that she had not set eyes upon that elusive gentleman since the day in the Park did nothing to ease her distraught emotions. On the contrary, she had spent an inordinate amount of time wondering where he had taken himself off to, and whose eyes he was smiling into now. The painful thought that perhaps he had gone back to his regiment without a word to her also plagued her. But no, she kept reminding herself, had he not himself said the army surgeons had refused to release him for at least another month?

A delighted cry from Lady Letitia roused Cynthia from these morbid thoughts. "Oh, look, Cynthia," the young girl exclaimed excitedly. "Is that not that handsome Captain Sheffield we met at the theater two weeks ago? Over there with that dreadful lady in the purple turban."

"Do not stare, Letitia," Cynthia warned, her heart suddenly beating in double time. Much as she wanted to stare, too, she kept her eyes averted from the other end of the hall.

"Oh, I think he has seen us," Letty said happily, bouncing up and down in her seat. "Shall I signal to him do you think, Cynthia?"

"No!" Cynthia hissed, her voice unsteady. "You will do nothing so rag-mannered if you please. Do you wish me to die of mortification?"

"Well, he is coming over here anyway," Letty said happily. "And he has another officer with him. One with a ginger moustache of all things. How droll!"

And then, before Cynthia had time to compose herself, he was standing before her, his blue eyes inscrutable, and Cynthia heard herself mumbling meaningless pleasantries.

"Lady Cynthia," he began in that too well-remembered deep voice. "My fellow officer, Captain Richard Chatham, is most desirous of standing up with your cousin."

After that first brief glance at Captain Sheffield, Lady Cynthia focused her gaze on the ginger-haired gentleman, who was smiling at her with open admiration. "Delighted to make your acquaintance, my lady," he murmured, raising her fingers as he made his bow. "I believe you have met my mother, the Viscountess Chapman?"

"Yes, indeed," Cynthia replied through stiff lips. "But I take it you have not yet made the acquaintance of my two cousins, Lady Constance and Lady Letitia?"

"Sheffield has done nothing but extol their charms," Chatham said smoothly, his eyes on Letty's rosy cheeks.

"Did he truly do so?" Letty broke in with a dazzling smile at Captain Sheffield.

"Indeed he did, my lady," Chatham answered with a grin. "But I swear his praise does not do you justice."

The orchestra started tuning up for a cotillion at that moment, and Letty jumped to her feet. "May I, Cynthia?" she exclaimed.

"Please." The chit smiled enticingly up at Captain Sheffield, but it was Chatham who took her hand to lead her out onto the floor. Cynthia hoped the ginger-haired gentleman had not noticed Letty's rudeness.

Cynthia had barely nodded her consent, before Captain Sheffield turned to Constance. Through a haze of emotions, she heard him say, "I had hoped to persuade you to stand up with me, Lady Constance." And before she could gather her thoughts, she was sitting alone, watching the two officers join a nearby set with their partners. Letty was a good match for Chatham, she thought. The child had already forgotten her disappointment and seemed to be on easy terms with him, for the captain was grinning down at her in amusement. Constance was more reserved, of course, and in this she more closely resembled Captain Sheffield, whose expression was serious as he took his place opposite her in the set.

And then the captain smiled at Constance, and Cynthia could have cheerfully strangled her unsuspecting cousin.

"Playing wallflower, love?" a caressing voice murmured close to her ear, and Cynthia jumped. "I see that you have found uniforms for both your charges."

"You startled me, Robert." She glanced up at him and saw that he was laughing at her.

Her cousin handed her a glass of lemonade, which she took gratefully. "So," he drawled, "Captain Sheffield has come crawling back on his belly, I take it."

Cynthia grimaced in distaste. "What a vulgar expression, Robert," she remonstrated. "And hardly to the point. The captain came to dance with Constance, as you can see for yourself."

"You deceive yourself, fair Cynthia," he said softly.

Cynthia shook her head and regarded her flamboyant cousin steadily. "Will you not tell me what passed between you and the captain at the theatre, Robbie? You frightened him off, I suppose you realize that."

"If a man scares that easily, my dear girl, he is not worth having. You deserve the best, and I will see that you get it, Cynthia. So do not, I beg you, trouble your lovely head about anything except fending off that hoydenish sister of mine, who is trying to steal a march over you with the captain."

He grinned wickedly down at her and Cynthia did not realize until later that her cousin had not answered her question. Her attention was drawn—as no doubt the rogue intended it should be—to the dance floor, where the music had come to an end. The couples were milling around and moving slowly in various directions. With a pang of envy, Cynthia saw the tall captain say something to Constance that brought a shy smile to the girl's too serious face. She looked around for Letitia and was not surprised to see her at the center of a group of young officers. She was laughing delightedly and hanging on Chatham's arm with unseemly familiarity.

Cynthia grimaced and turned to her cousin. "You had better rescue your sister from the army," she remarked acerbically. "She appears to be under siege."

Lord Monroyal swore under his breath and moved away towards the wayward Lady Letitia and her cortege of admirers. Cynthia relaxed and cast her gaze around for Constance. The girl was actually talking quite animatedly with Captain Sheffield as the couple strolled towards her. Cynthia's eyes moved irresistibly to the gentleman, and her breath caught in her throat. For the first time that evening, Cynthia was able to look her fill of the captain, and what she saw confirmed what she had already suspected since that fateful day in the Park. Her eyes ran over his tall frame hungrily, lingering on every delightfully masculine inch of him, from his unruly chestnut hair, which curled around his small ears and over his collar, stopping briefly to admire the breadth of his shoulders before slipping down his gold-braided chest to his lean hips, and then sliding breathlessly over the white expanse of muscled thighs to the highly polished Hessians with their jaunty gold tassels.

Cynthia let out her breath slowly and closed her eyes. This was simply too much, she thought, valiantly trying to steady her racing pulse. How could it happen that the mere sight of a gentleman could make her feel so utterly defenseless, so vulnerable, indeed, that she doubted she could have raised a finger to resist had the captain taken it into his head to . . . Ashamed at the immodest nature of her riotous thoughts, Cynthia mentally shook herself and opened her eyes to find Captain Sheffield bending over her solicitously.

"Are you feeling unwell, my lady?" The deep voice was full of concern, and the startling blue eyes were far too close for comfort. Cynthia sat up abruptly, wishing she could drown in their warm depths. In the back of her mind she was aware of the orchestra tuning up for a waltz.

"Can I get you anything, Cynthia?" Constance's voice was sharp with alarm.

"No, thank you, dear," Cynthia said in a rush of embarrassment. "I am feeling very well indeed."

"I am relieved to hear you say so, Lady Cynthia," the captain said and Cynthia wished he would move away from her. She could feel his eyes warm on her face, and she was sure that, from his position, he could see more than her low décolletage was intended to reveal.

"I had hoped you might be persuaded to grant me the next dance."

The strains of the forthcoming waltz were clearer now, and Cynthia felt a sudden pang of regret that she would have to deny herself the delight of feeling the captain's arms around her.

"I am afraid that is impossible, Captain," she said, with a faint smile. "I have two young ladies to watch over tonight, so I am not dancing at all."

"Nonsense, Cynthia," the marquess drawled from behind them.

Cynthia turned and saw that her cousin's gray eyes were full of amusement again. He had Letty firmly in tow but this young lady looked unrepentant, since several officers had followed her, including Captain Chatham.

"I insist you amuse yourself, my dear," the marquess added, casting an enigmatic look at Sheffield. "I shall take it upon myself to watch over this little minx."

Before she could protest, Cynthia found herself on her feet, the captain's large hand warm on her elbow as he guided her onto the floor.

The muted sounds of music and dozens of Lady Hereford's guests all talking at once increased substantially in volume when Captain Sheffield, accompanied by Dick Chatham and several other officers in the colorful regimentals, paused at the entrance to the brilliantly lit ballroom. He glanced around him skeptically. The crowded dance floor was already liberally sprinkled with red uniforms since Lord Hereford, a retired colonel of the 9th Regiment of Hussars, made it a point to issue blanket invitations to all footloose young officers who frequented The Guards' Club on St. James's Street. Lady Hereford had, over the years, tired of protesting her lord's eccentricity and her balls and routs had become known among the young officers as excellent opportunities to ogle young ladies they might otherwise never meet.

"I hope I am not too late to claim my dance with Miss Crenshaw," Dick muttered, scanning the room anxiously.

"It appears the Incomparable has not yet arrived," Brian suggested, wondering if he could avoid dancing with the chit himself without giving offense.

They stood silently for several minutes watching the crush of couples on the dance floor going through the paces of a lively cotillion. Suddenly Brian heard his friend exhale audibly.

"I say, old man," Dick murmured in an awed voice. "Take a gander at that little Beauty over there on the yellow sofa. The angel in white. Do you see her? I think I'll try my luck in that direction if I can wangle an introduction. What do you think?"

The captain's gaze followed his friend's admiring stare towards the end of the room. There were several ladies seated on the yellow sofa, but only one drew his eyes, and it was not the young lady in white.

Brian held his breath for several seconds before letting it out regretfully. "Yes, I see her," he said softly, his gaze riveted on the lady in green silk, whose auburn curls framed a face that had haunted his thoughts ever since he had last seen her, tooling in the Park with that Jackstraw Yarmouth. "Yes, indeed." He tore his eyes away abruptly and took his friend by the elbow. "I need a drink," he muttered. "Let us pay a visit to the refreshment room before we get carried away with the ladies."

Dick agreed readily, and it was not long before they were joined by others with similar notions. The captain drank his first cup of champagne in two gulps and was halfway through his second when he felt a light touch on his sleeve.

"Well met, Captain Sheffield," Mr. Hampton said heartily, his brown eyes twinkling speculatively. "I have not seen you for so long, I had begun to think the army surgeons had sent you back to the Peninsula."

Brian grimaced. "No such luck," he said shortly. Hampton's comment had sounded like any other piece of idle conversation, but the captain had an odd feeling that it was nothing of the sort. He could not forget that Hampton was another of Lady Cynthia's close relatives, who might be expected to take an interest in her affairs. "I am stranded in Town for another month it appears."

Hampton smiled ingenuously. "I trust you are tolerably well entertained, Captain."

The faintly caustic tone of Hampton's voice confirmed what Brian had already suspected. This was no chance encounter.

"Tolerably," he replied shortly, meeting the other's gaze squarely. "But I doubt you are interested in my entertainment, Hampton. What precisely do you wish to know?"

Hampton smiled beguilingly, but Brian was not fooled. That cherubic face, the simpering smile, and the innocent brown eyes were a convenient mask for a keen, intelligent mind. Brian had suspected it, but when the smile dropped away, and the twinkle disappeared from Hampton's eyes, he was not surprised.

"I do not know what there is between you and Lady Cynthia, Captain," the shorter man began, "because she has not confided in me. But I do know, since I am so well acquainted with my cousin, that she is unhappy." He paused to regard the captain with unmistakable hostility. "Vastly unhappy, I might add. And I can only suppose, from what I have observed, that her unhappiness has something to do with you."

After a slight pause, Brian demanded, "And just what have you observed, sir?"

Hampton smiled, and his expression was once again fatuously innocent. "Enough to suspect that you are perhaps laboring under false delusions and behaving rather childishly," he said mildly. "No, no! Do not take offense, Captain," he added hastily as Brian balled his fists menacingly. "I do not mean to pry, but let me suggest to you, my boy, that an apology—even if one is convinced one is not at fault—goes a long way towards achieving one's goals."

"And let *me* suggest," Brian said harshly, suddenly furious at the older man's condescension, "that you cease to concern yourself with my affairs, Hampton."

Hampton merely shrugged and strolled away, leaving the captain with a sense of having indeed behaved rather childishly. This did not improve his temper to any noticeable degree, so when he was accosted, on his way back to the ballroom, by the Marquess of Monroyal, he tried unsuccessfully to brush past him.

When he found his path effectively blocked, he glared at the marquess belligerently. "I am in no mood to have another peal rung over my head," he said harshly. "I have been out of shortcoats for too many years to take that tamely."

The marquess held up his hand at this intemperate outburst. "If my cousin Hampton said what I believe he did, in the prosy manner he has of saying such things, then I can sympathize with you entirely, Sheffield," he drawled. "What I have to say to you can be done much more succinctly. You are a bloody fool to believe, even for a moment, that Lady Cynthia would lower herself to the deceit you seem to have laid at her door. She does not have—as I have told you before—any knowledge that your vowels were made out to me."

"Are you trying to tell me that she paid them without looking at them?" Brian's tone was edged with sarcasm.

"Obviously she did, for if she had discovered the truth, she would have been about my ears like a swarm of hornets. That I can guarantee."

Brian wanted to believe the marquess's words, but his natural dislike of the man made him hesitate. "You received her ladyship's draft?"

"No," came the surprising reply. "I received a draft from your family solicitors, MacIntyre and Hamilton, I believe. In a letter requesting the return of your vowels. The whole affair is over, Sheffield, and I am heartily bored with the entire incident, I can tell you." The marquess raised a bejeweled hand to stifle a yawn.

"No, it is not over," Brian responded harshly. "Lady Cynthia sent the vowels to me."

The marquess raised an elegant eyebrow. "Of course, she did, Captain," he drawled. "I rather thought that was the whole idea. At least from your standpoint, was it not? To discharge the debt and retrieve the evidence?"

"Yes, in a manner of speaking," the captain admitted. "But you do not understand the whole."

The marquess made a dismissive gesture with one shapely hand. "Oh, I think I understand your dilemma all too well, my dear Captain." He smiled thinly, and Brian thought the grimace oddly sinister. "I suggest the next move is up to you, Captain," Lord Monroyal drawled softly. "She is here tonight, you know," he added enigmatically, before he turned and sauntered away towards the ballroom.

Brian followed more slowly, pondering the odd coincidence that both of Lady Cynthia's relatives had taken up cudgels in her defense. If what they said were true, and the lady innocent of any deceit, could it not be possible that her unhappiness might be laid at his door? The notion was entirely too presumptuous, he thought, for it assumed that his absence had in some way upset her. It was ludicrous to imagine that Lady Cynthia had missed him, of course, but the idea would not let go of Brian's imagination, and when he reached the entrance to the ballroom, his eyes sought out her trim figure on the yellow settee.

"She is still there," Dick Chatham said at his elbow. "Looking our way, too, dash it. Unfortunately I have been unable to obtain an introduction."

"I can introduce you, old man," Brian said aloud, before he knew what he was going to say. Without stopping to explain, he started across the floor where a country dance had just come to a close.

And then he was standing before her, gazing down at the flawless expanse of neck and shoulders, faintly pink cheeks, and auburn hair so silky he yearned to touch it. He could not see her eyes, for Lady Cynthia kept them fixed on Chatham and that saucy minx, Letitia. Without recalling how it happened, Brian found himself leading Lady Constance onto the floor to join the set with Chatham and Letitia.

The set seemed to last forever, but as he returned his shy partner to her chaperone, Brian felt Lady Cynthia's green eyes upon him. Let her look, he thought, instinctively straightening his shoulders and tightening the muscles of his stomach. It was all he could do not to swagger, like the young boy he had once been trying to impress the local lasses. When at last he did look at her, he was startled to see her eyes closed and an expression on her face such as he had never seen before. Soft, it was, and somehow vulnerable. He had the sudden urge to take her in his arms. And then she opened her eyes, and Brian felt himself drowning in their sea-green depths.

The strains of a waltz brought him to his senses and he asked her to dance, knowing as he did so that she would refuse him.

"Nonsense, Cynthia," a familiar voice drawled from behind him, brushing aside the lady's refusal. And then she was in his arms. Miraculously, enchantingly. Brian might have thought he was dreaming but for the warmth of her waist under the palm of his hand.

"You are very quiet, my lady," he ventured, after they had circled the room twice in silence. Her gloved hand resting on his sleeve was feather-light, and her eyes appeared glued to the gold braid on his uniform. She seemed not to have heard him.

"If you cannot bring yourself to look at me occasionally, my lady," he said with a smile, "people will believe you are still angry with me."

She looked up then, her eyes round with surprise. "What makes you think I am angry with you, Captain?"

What a fool he had been to imagine, even for a moment, that this woman could be anything but innocent, he thought, mesmerized by the blue-green gaze. Much as Brian hated to admit it, Monroyal had been right. He was a bloody fool to doubt her. And his doubt had brought her pain, if Hampton could be believed.

"If you are not, my dear, you should be," he said, noticing how the unconscious endearment brought color to her cheeks.

"It sounds to me as though you have been talking to my cousin Willy Hampton," she said hesitantly. "You must not pay him any mind. Dear Willy is overly protective with me, particularly since Lonsdale passed on."

"You do not lack for protectors, my lady," he said, wanting to tell her that soon she would have yet another champion.

For Brian had suddenly understood what he must do. Monroyal had been right in that, too. The next move was his, and he knew exactly what it would be.

Lady Cynthia awoke the next morning to the sounds of Betsy pulling aside the heavy curtains and to the tepid warmth of the late October sun on her face. She opened her eyes and yawned.

"What time is it, Betsy?"

"Almost one of the clock, milady," the little maid replied with her ready smile. "Her ladyship went down to nuncheon nearly an hour ago."

"Why was I not awoken at my usual time?" Cynthia demanded in a startled voice. She was not in the habit of lying abed so late, and felt cheated out of the best part of the day.

"Her ladyship forbade it, milady," Betsy explained, her cherry-colored cheeks growing ever pinker with embarrassment. "Said ye needed the rest, she did. Claimed ye was running yerself ragged with all this gallivantin' around. And happens I agree with her ladyship, I do." The little maid came across to the bed, holding out Cynthia's silk brocade robe. "Lookin' a wee bit peaked ye be, milady. 'Tain't a good thing to wear yerself to a frazzle, my sainted mother used to say."

Cynthia slipped out of the big four-poster and into the warm robe. She shivered as her feet groped for her woolen slippers.

"I am starving, Betsy," she complained. "Would you ask Cook to send up a tray for me?"

"Mr. Hampton is with her ladyship," Betsy said with studied casualness, her hand on the door.

"I saw quite enough of Mr. Hampton last night, Betsy," she replied shortly.

"Such a nice gentleman 'e is, milady," the young maid said coaxingly, her cheeks glowing rosily.

Cynthia glanced at her suspiciously. Apparently her father's staff was as anxious to see her wed as she was herself. She laughed. "Very well, Betsy," she capitulated. "Send Annette up to me, if you please, and I will join her ladyship and Mr. Hampton."

"My dear Cynthia, what a sight for weary eyes." Willy Hampton rose from the table with a broad smile on his cherubic face when Cynthia entered the small dining room twenty minutes later.

He took her hand and carried it to his lips with a dramatic flourish.

"Weary?" Cynthia echoed, after greeting her mother affectionately. "If you are so weary, Willy, why is it that you are here at this early hour?" Without waiting for her cousin's reply, Cynthia turned to her mother. "I hear I have you to thank, Mama, for missing my ride this morning. And my breakfast," she added, helping herself liberally from the chafing dishes on the sideboard.

"Willie assures me that your young charges quite burnt you to the socket last night, my pet," Lady Halifax said gently.

"Nonsense, Mama," Cynthia answered spiritedly. "I am not yet in my dotage."

"No, indeed you are not, coz," Hampton remarked, his twinkling brown eyes regarding Cynthia with some amusement. "You were quite ravishing last night, my dear. And I warrant I am not alone in that opinion, Aunt Liza."

Cynthia caught the speaking glance her cousin exchanged with Lady Halifax and sighed. Cousin Willy was a dear, but he had the annoying habit of gossiping with her mother, with whom he was on excellent terms.

"Oh?" Lady Halifax exclaimed expectantly. "And what might you mean by that, Willy?"

Hampton glanced at her slyly. "It appeared to me last night that our friend Captain Sheffield was enchanted with your lovely daughter, madam. Would you not say so, my dear Cynthia? The poor chap seemed to be quite struck dumb with admiration."

"Not every gentleman is a chatterbox like you, Willy," Cynthia said scathingly, motioning to Hastings to fill her cup with fresh tea.

"So the captain is still in London, is he?" Lady Halifax murmured. "I do hope you told him how cross I am with him for not attending my dinner party last week, Cynthia. Perhaps we can invite him to dine *en famille* with us this week, dear. Would Wednesday be too soon?"

"We are both promised to Aunt Sophy's rout on Wednesday," Cynthia said dryly.

"Thursday, then?"

"Mrs. Summerville has asked me to play at a small musical gathering on Thursday."

"I thought you played for Amelia Summerville last week, dear."

"That was almost three weeks ago, Mama. This will be a much

smaller gathering to honor her cousin, Madame Lavoisier, who has just arrived from Paris."

"Well, we shall plan to invite the captain on Friday, then. And do not tell me you are engaged, Cynthia, for I shall not hear of it."

Lady Cynthia smiled ruefully at her mother. "Lady Mansfield is holding her autumn ball on Friday, Mama. Surely you would not have me miss that?"

Lady Halifax rose from the table with an angry flounce. "If I did not know that the idea is ridiculous, I would think you are deliberately avoiding the man, Cynthia. You cannot hope to fix a gentleman's interest if you never allow him to set eyes upon you."

"Ah! You sly puss, Cynthia," Mr. Hampton drawled, his merry eyes lighting up at his aunt's indiscretion. "So there *is* an intrigue in the making here. I thought as much, my dear, when I saw old Robert giving the poor captain the rough edge of his tongue last night. A rare set-to they had, and the captain did not look too happy about it, I can tell you." He paused to regard her accusingly. "Monroyal is in the thick of it, I suppose. Trust *him*. Although why you elected to confide in that rakehell instead of coming to me, Cynthia, I shall never know."

"You were not in Town, Willy," Cynthia replied truthfully. "And furthermore, I absolutely forbid you to breathe a word to anyone about this secret that Mama seems to have let out of the bag."

Mr. Hampton looked offended. "My lips are sealed, coz. But only if you promise to tell me the whole. And since the reason for my presence at Halifax House is to invite you to try out a new team I am thinking of purchasing, we shall have both time and opportunity for a full confession, my dear." He smiled at her engagingly.

"Yes, my love," her mother put in. "Do run upstairs and change. I think it is high time you told dearest Willy all about this mad scheme you have embarked upon to snare our poor, unwary captain. You would have done far better to accept dear Robbie's offer—"

Mr. Hampton stared at Lady Halifax, mouth half a-cock. "Robert made you an offer, Cynthia?" he repeated in a dazed voice. "Now you are bamboozling me, Aunt. I know for a fact that Robert has no intention of getting riveted, so this must be a Banbury tale."

"Why do you not let Cynthia tell you all about it," Lady Halifax murmured, rising hastily from the table. She cast an apologetic glance at her daughter and vanished from the room.

"Well, well," Mr. Hampton remarked with lively amusement. "I see we shall not want for entertaining conversation during our drive, Cynthia."

But far from being entertained, Cynthia was more than a little mortified at having to answer her cousin's perceptive questions that afternoon. So much so, in fact, that her enjoyment of Mr. Hampton's superb team of Welsh-bred chestnuts was quite dampened. In the retelling, her plan to attract a second husband—which had seemed so unexceptional when she had conceived it weeks ago—began to appear rather questionable if not downright tawdry.

Her mood was not the least bit mollified when she returned home to find a magnificent bouquet of white lilies awaiting her. The note that accompanied the flowers was in an unfamiliar hand. Cynthia tore it open, thinking that perhaps it was from the Earl of Yarmouth, whose repeated invitations to drive in the Park she had turned down. But it was from Captain Brian Sheffield, who informed her that he would call at Halifax House the following afternoon, on a matter—as he phrased it—of immediate importance to both of them.

Cynthia's heart did an awkward somersault and plummeted to the soles of her feet. So, the captain had made his decision, she thought, an unexpected wave of sadness welling up inside her. And from the somber tone of his note, she could guess what that decision must be.

Captain Sheffield was in no mood for matrimony.

Cynthia suddenly knew that she did not wish to hear him say those dismissive words to her. Too many of her most intimate dreams had crystallized in the dashing figure of the elusive captain, and Cynthia was not prepared to give up those dreams. The feel of his hand on her waist last night, as they had danced the waltz together, was too real, too warm, too intimate to be ignored. But he had disappeared after that one dance, and she had not seen him again. She recalled every single word he had spoken during that magical time, but suddenly his remark about her being angry with him took on a different meaning. Could he have meant that he was angry with her instead? Or perhaps he had tried to prepare her for the crushing blow he was about to deliver? *If you are not, you should be*, he had said, possibly implying that she soon *would* be angry with him, when he cast her proposal back in her teeth.

Up in her chamber, Cynthia cast off her warm cloak and removed the fashionable green bonnet with its curling feather. Then she sat down at her dresser and examined the pale, set face that stared back at her.

No, she thought wryly, glancing down at the crumpled note she still held in her hand. She certainly did not wish to hear the captain say he did not want her.

No, she would not admit defeat so easily. There must be some other card she could play in this game they were engaged in.

On sudden impulse, Cynthia pulled out a sheet of pressed paper and scribbled a note to her cousin.

Robbie would know what to do, she decided. He would be able to advise her.

After Cynthia had rung the bell and entrusted the note to Hastings, she felt a weight lift from her heart.

No, she mused, smiling at herself in the beveled glass. She would not give up her dream that easily.

CHAPTER EIGHT

Illusive Lady

Captain Sheffield was feeling rather pleased with himself as he mounted the steps to Halifax House the following afternoon and rapped smartly on the door. He had followed up on the decision made the night of Lady Hereford's ball, and the interview he had sought with Lord Halifax had gone remarkably well, he thought. Lady Cynthia's father received him in his study and had been forthright almost to the point of bluntness.

"To tell you the truth," the marquess had confessed as soon as the butler had served their brandy and left them alone, "I had expected to see you before this, young man."

Somewhat taken aback by the implications of these words, and the uncomfortable realization that Lord Halifax must be fully aware of the proposal his daughter had made to a complete stranger, Brian responded more brusquely than he had intended. "I can understand your assumption that I would jump at the obvious advantages an alliance with your daughter would entail, my lord," he said rather stiffly. "But I am not a man to make such decisions lightly; indeed, the notion of taking a wife at all was so far removed from my future plans that the viscountess's proposal came as rather a shock."

Lord Halifax smiled faintly at this admission. "That is exactly what I tried to explain to my daughter, Captain," he said, regarding Brian intently. "A female cannot expect a man to change the direction of his life at a moment's notice and dance to her tune. I warned her that a young man like you, who has already distinguished himself for bravery, may well have a bright future ahead of him as a career officer. Such ambitions of fame and glory are difficult to set aside for the tamer existence of husband and father. I had military ambitions myself as a young man, as does my son, Viscount Holt, who even now defies me to serve with Wellington."

The captain grimaced at this plain speaking, and took a swallow of the marquess's excellent brandy. "I met Lord Holt briefly during the march on Burgos in early June," he said, wondering how he could bring his host's attention back to the matter at hand. He soon discovered that he need not have worried, for Lord Halifax resumed the subject with his customary bluntness.

"So?" he said abruptly, stepping forward to replenish his guest's glass. "Am I to understand, Captain, that you have come to a decision on whether to remain a military man or become a married one?"

"Yes, sir," Brian responded quickly, glad to have the matter phrased in such prosaic terms. "The military was never my first choice as a career, but after my father died, there was little else open to me." He paused, the taste of his father's betrayal still bitter on his tongue.

Lord Halifax must have caught the echo of disappointment in Sheffield's voice, for his smile warmed noticeably. "And now there is, I take it?" he said quietly.

"Yes, sir," Brian repeated. And what else was there to say? he wondered, knowing that there must be something he should add to lend this odd interview a sense of reality. "I had hoped to obtain your approval, my lord," he said tentatively.

"You have no need of my approval, my boy," the marquess remarked dryly. "My daughter is of age and controls her own fortune. She conceived this rather unusual arrangement, and I will admit that although I counseled her against what seemed to me a rather immodest venture, I can find no fault with her choice." He smiled briefly. "It also appears that you have won over Lady Halifax, who was—I must confess—quite adamant in her desire to see a match between Cynthia and her cousin, Lord Monroyal. However, I am glad you sought this interview," he continued, "for it gives me the opportunity to become better acquainted with my future son-in-law."

And his lordship obviously meant what he said, for he proceeded to question the captain in considerable detail, not only about his military exploits, but also about his experience in running the Sheffield stables for his father.

"I always wondered why that brother of yours did not keep you in charge of the stables after the old earl died," Halifax said, when the conversation turned to horses. "I can remember when Sheffield horses were famous for stamina and conformation all over England. I have one of them myself, you know. A big chestnut with four white feet that will take any hedge you care to put him up to. My daughter claims he is rather too long in the back for a truly great hunter, but he has carried me well."

"Do you mean Trumpeter, sir?" Brian asked, showing real enthusiasm for the first time. "That horse was a three-year-old when I left for the Peninsula, and I always wondered if he lived up to his promise. I raised him, you see, but as a colt he had a tendency to rush his fences." He paused, remembering again the pain of being practically disinherited by his father, and rejected by his half-brother. "I would have stayed on at Mulgrave Park after father died, but John and I never hit it off."

Lord Halifax was silent for a moment, then he remarked casually, "I suspect you will find Milford Hall a congenial place, then. My daughter is horse-mad and has built up the stables there until they rival your brother's, I imagine. Mulgrave is rather too fond of spending his blunt on any fancy stud that takes his eye and leaving the actual breeding plans to his steward with indifferent results, I am afraid."

Two hours later, the captain emerged from Halifax House considerably more reconciled with his decision to accept Lady Cynthia's proposal than he had been upon entering it. The prospect of approaching the lady with an offer still presented a major hurdle to be taken, Brian suspected, at full gallop and without further hesitation. It was with this purpose in mind that he repaired immediately to a flower shop and ordered a bunch of white lilies to be delivered to Berkeley Square.

Armed with Lord Halifax's tacit approval, and his courage bolstered by Dick Chatham's assurance that flowers always put ladies in a receptive frame of mind, the captain presented himself at Halifax House the next afternoon, fully intending to get the matter settled without any further delay. His neatly contrived plans were set awry by the information, imparted by the venerable Hastings, that her ladyship was not at home.

Disconcerted by this unexpected news and unwilling to make further inquiries as to the lady's whereabouts, Captain Sheffield strolled back to his favorite club where Chatham had promised to meet him.

"What the deuce?" exclaimed that officer in surprise as soon as he spotted Brian entering Watiers's. "Not done already, surely?" He put down the *Weekly Dispatch* in which he had been perusing the favored contenders in an upcoming mill, and waved at a passing waiter. "That must be a record for popping the question, old man. Am I to wish you happy?"

The captain threw himself into a leather chair and grinned ruefully. "Not yet, Dick. The lady was not at home."

"But . . ." Chatham regarded him owlishly, and Brian noticed

that his friend had made substantial inroads into the bottle of
brandy on the table before him. "I thought you had written the
wench a note, Brian. You are bamming me, are you not?"

The captain shrugged. "I wish it were so, Dick, but according
to Hastings, the lady chose to ignore my note." He watched the
waiter pour a glass of brandy and took it gratefully. He had yet to
sort out his reaction to Lady Cynthia's apparent disregard for his
express intention of calling upon her. Surely she must have
guessed—although he had not explicitly stated it in his note, he
recalled—what the purpose of this particular interview would be?
Brian vacillated between relief that the betrothal was not yet official, and disappointment at the lady's nonchalant attitude towards
him. Did she believe him so securely within her clutches that she
chose some other, quite possibly frivolous, engagement over his
declaration?

The thought was unpleasant, and Brian could not rid himself of
it, even after he had ordered another bouquet of lilies delivered to
Berkeley Square. Neither could he seem to forget the role played
by the ubiquitous Marquess of Monroyal in his projected marriage. The man's influence was everywhere, and now Lord Halifax had let slip the unsettling information that a match between
the obnoxious marquess and Lady Cynthia had been contemplated—nay, actively sought—by Lady Halifax.

The connection was unsettling and the captain attempted to
keep it at bay by embarking on an evening of rowdy diversions
with several fellow officers of the 7th Hussars. But the truth of
the matter, he admitted to himself, returning to his digs in the
early hours more than halfway bosky, was that the gaily dressed
opera dancers who had made up their party at a private supper
had not amused him at all. The brassy-haired lovely who had attached herself to him expressed her disappointment loudly and
eloquently when he refused to go home with her, and the captain
had felt an odd relief to find himself alone in his own bedchamber
except for a sour-faced Hardy, who insisted upon attending his
master even at that advanced hour.

The following morning, he arose at his usual hour and enjoyed
a gallop in the Park on Hannibal, who was growing fat and frisky
at so many weeks of Town living. Brian longed for an extended
ride in the country to shed the cobwebs accumulated during these
past weeks of forced idleness, and this notion inevitably chan-
neled his thoughts back to Lady Cynthia and the kind of life a
union with her offered.

But once again he was disappointed. Hastings eyed him with

more benevolence than butlers at great houses were wont to do, the captain thought, but the result was the same.

"Her ladyship drove out less than an hour ago, sir," Hastings surprised the captain by volunteering. "With her cousin, Lord Monroyal, sir," he added, and then, as if acknowledging his indiscretion, the butler resumed his air of stolid indifference.

The captain had no option but to retire from the field, increasingly puzzled and showing the first signs of impatience at the lady's cavalier treatment.

By the following morning, Brian had decided that firmer measures were in order, so the next time he called at Halifax House, at an hour when her ladyship must certainly be expected to be home, he asked for the master of the house rather than his daughter.

Lord Halifax received him cordially, but when the captain explained his predicament, the marquess's expression clouded.

"Changed her mind, did you say, Captain?" he repeated in astonishment. "Not to my knowledge. Although to tell the truth I have not laid eyes on my daughter for two or three days."

"It is the only explanation I can think of, my lord," the captain said stiffly. "And if this is indeed the case," he added bluntly, "I would appreciate being informed of the fact. I have no wish to be kept kicking my heel for the rest of the Little Season."

Lord Halifax strode purposefully to the bell-rope and tugged it vigorously. "We shall determine the state of my daughter's intentions this very instant," he said shortly. "And I shall insist that she inform you herself if she has, as you say, changed her mind."

"Hastings," Lord Halifax ordered, as soon as the butler appeared, "inform Lady Cynthia, if you please, that I wish to see her in my study on a matter of some urgency."

When the door had closed behind the butler, Lord Halifax turned to his guest. "This is most unlike my daughter, Captain," he said. "Cynthia was never one to put on airs or play the coquette. Are you certain she knew you intended to call?"

"There is no doubt about it whatsoever, my lord," Brian replied briefly. "I had hoped to have the matter settled by now."

"And so you shall, my boy," the marquess said gruffly. "So you shall." He moved to the cherry-wood sideboard and unstoppered the decanter of brandy. "In the meantime, Captain, let me offer you a drink."

The captain had no time to respond to his host's invitation, for at that moment the door opened to admit an expressionless Hastings.

"Well?" Lord Halifax inquired impatiently.

"Milord," the butler intoned stiffly, "her ladyship left barely ten minutes ago. Her ladyship's abigail informs me that Lady Cynthia was engaged to ride in the Park with his lordship, her cousin."

The captain felt his face stiffen, whether in disappointment or outrage he did not stop to consider.

"At this time of day?" he heard Lord Halifax demand in none too kindly terms. What the butler replied, Brian neither heard nor cared. The ugly notion that Lady Cynthia—*his* Cynthia—was far too often in the dubious company of that conspicuously immoral rakehell and gambler made Brian clench his teeth in fury. Was she caught—as he had heard so many of London's young matrons had been—in the seductive coils of the marquess's notorious charm?

The thought that his future bride might have been sullied by the touch of a man who had—if such rumors could be believed—boasted that he could gain entrance into any boudoir in London, slipped unbidden into Brian's already troubled mind.

Brushing the unworthy notion aside, the captain turned, stony-faced, to his host.

"I shall try once more at four of the clock," he said with deceptive calm. "If her ladyship declines to receive me, I shall not return."

"If you had accepted my offer three weeks ago, my dear Cynthia," the marquess chided in a languorous voice, "you would even now be planning your bridal clothes and all those other far-radiddles that females set such store by. Instead of which, you are resorting to behavior that can only be regarded as maudlin in the extreme."

Cynthia brought her mare down to a walk and turned angrily to her cousin. "Offer! What offer?" she repeated. "You never did make me an offer, Robert, so do cease this sanctimonious twaddle."

The marquess drew his big bay gelding to a halt and sat regarding her with a decided twinkle in his gray eyes. "A mere oversight, my dear, I assure you. If you wish it, I shall make you my offer here and now, in the middle of Hyde Park."

With a gesture of annoyance, Cynthia checked her mare and wheeled to face the marquess. "Now you are being ridiculous, Robbie," she snapped.

Her cousin assumed a downcast expression. "I had never thought to hear those cruel words from your fair lips, coz," he murmured. "Here I am ready and willing to offer you my poor heart—such as it is—and you throw it back in my teeth. You wound me, Cynthia."

"Oh, fiddlesticks!" Cynthia replied acidly. "You have no heart to give, Robert, as we both know. And as for making me an offer, I thought I had made it plain to you that you are quite safe from me. I shall die an ape-leader before I contemplate such an addle-pated notion. And well you know it, rogue that you are. If you imagined for a moment that I could be persuaded to take such a disastrous step, you would disappear faster than poor Teddy Thornton when the bailiffs are after him."

Lady Cynthia wheeled her mare and trotted off in high dudgeon. She had sought her cousin out on the spur of the moment this morning when her abigail had conveyed the unexpected information that her father demanded her immediate presence in his study. At her mistress's surprised reaction, Annette had added, with a speaking look, that Captain Sheffield was with Lord Halifax. Instead of the delighted response the abigail had evidently expected from her, Cynthia ordered the removal of the pale yellow lustring gown she had spent all of thirty minutes selecting that morning, and instructed the startled servant to bring out the new military-styled riding habit in dark plum. The exchange was made in record time, and Hastings sent down to his lordship with the message that Lady Cynthia had but that instant departed for a previous engagement to ride with her cousin, Lord Monroyal.

Leaving her groom to hold Queen Mab, her dappled-gray mare, Cynthia had burst in upon the marquess at the breakfast table, much to that gentleman's consternation.

"I have come to ride with you, Robbie," she announced loudly, quite as though she were in the habit of invading the breakfast rooms of single gentlemen at that hour in the morning—or any hour at all for that matter—alone and in a state of high agitation. "I trust you received my note."

Lord Monroyal rose slowly from his chair and regarded his cousin with a quizzical stare that succeeded in disconcerting her more than she liked. "All of ten minutes ago, my dear Cynthia," the marquess replied laconically. "And naturally, I am delighted to accompany you, coz, but I must say that it would have been vastly preferable had you given me the opportunity to call at Halifax House at a more reasonable hour."

"Oh, pooh!" Cynthia exclaimed, knowing that her cousin was perfectly correct, but unwilling to admit the impropriety of her actions. "Do not be so stuffy, Robbie. It is nearly ten of the clock, and I had to see you on a matter of great import. It cannot wait," she added hastily somewhat upset at the unaccustomed censure in his lordship's eyes.

"I must take issue with your choice of simile, my dear," Lord Monroyal drawled, when he pulled his bay up beside her. "In fact, I find that your comportment has deteriorated to the point where I fear for your sanity, dear child," he added with a condescension designed—as Cynthia had every reason to suspect—to set her back up.

"Do not, I beg of you, Robert, give me one of your odious lectures," she said sharply. "I am in need of your assistance, not your censure. And I am not a child."

"So glad to hear it, love," the marquess drawled at his most exasperating. "And I must say that color becomes you, Cynthia, although perhaps a trifle dark for perfection. But the bonnet is a masterpiece. Makes you look no more than twenty, not a day more, I swear."

Cynthia glanced warily at her cousin. The Marquess of Monroyal was not wont to bestow his praise lightly, and her feminine vanity was touched in spite of herself. "Thank you, Robert," she said more cordially, "but I did not come here to talk about fashion." She hesitated, not quite sure how to broach the subject of Captain Sheffield's intentions.

"I did not suppose you had," the marquess responded. "Perhaps you will enlighten me as to the real purpose of this precipitate encounter, my dear."

"It is Captain Sheffield," Cynthia blurted out.

"Hmm. I thought as much," he said matter-of-factly. "Has the poor fellow not yet come up to scratch?"

Cynthia shot her cousin a withering glance. "No, he has not come up to scratch, as you so elegantly put it," she retorted. "And I fear that he has no intention of doing so."

The marquess gave a crack of laughter. "Well, you know what they say, coz. The path of true love runs not smoothly."

To her own surprise, Cynthia felt her eyes fill with tears. "It is all very well for you to make a jest of it, Robbie," she snapped. "But it is no jest to me. I had quite set my hopes on . . ." Much to her mortification, her voice broke and she turned her face away to avoid her cousin's gaze.

Quite unexpectedly she felt her cousin's arm around her shoulders as the horses came to an abrupt halt beneath the bare branches of an old maple tree. Gratefully, Cynthia rested her head briefly on the inviting shoulder. "I am being exceedingly missish about this," she murmured, raising her face to gaze into the gray eyes, which held an arrested look she had never seen there before. "I had no intention of turning into a watering-pot, Robbie, truly I did not."

She closed her eyes, thoroughly ashamed of the tear edging down her cheek. Suddenly the brush of soft lawn against her face caused her to open her eyes in time to see her cousin using his own handkerchief to wipe away the errant tear.

"Hush, love," he said in a voice devoid of his usual banter. "The man must be an arrant fool if he has not yet spoken. And no man is worth a single one of your sweet tears, Cynthia. No, not even *me*," he added, his lips curling into a deprecating grin.

Cynthia assayed a weak smile at this unusual modesty, and the marquess's grin disappeared. His arm tightened about her, and before she could guess what he was about, he bent his head and kissed her firmly on the mouth.

"Robbie!" she exclaimed in shocked tones, pulling away from her cousin and glancing uneasily around the sparsely populated park. "Whatever are you about? You must be quite mad to make such a spectacle of yourself in the middle of Hyde Park." She urged her mare forward so sharply that the startled animal danced about nervously.

The marquess did not appear at all repentant. "Sorry, sweetheart. It was an irresistible reflex, I assure you. I always kiss damsels in distress, Cynthia," he added with deplorable nonchalance. "So think nothing of it, my pet." He grinned so charmingly that Cynthia relented.

"What if someone had seen us? It was quite inexcusable of you, you know."

"Why, then perhaps we shall be obliged to make a match of it after all," he answered flippantly. "Now, tell me why you are so convinced that Sheffield intends to hedge off. Has he not called on you at all?"

"Oh, yes," Cynthia had to admit. "But I denied myself." Now that the thing was stated in so many words, she began to recognize her own foolishness.

"You denied yourself?" The marquess stared at her in surprise. "You are a silly twit, Cynthia. How is the man to declare himself unless you receive him?"

"I just know that he merely wishes to withdraw from the agreement," she confessed, knowing that she must sound entirely irrational. "And I could not bear it, Robbie. I simply could not bear to hear it."

Lord Monroyal stared at her for a long moment before shaking his head incredulously. "I have met any number of hen-witted females in my time, coz, but this piece of foolishness beats the Dutch, let me tell you. Besides," he added philosophically, "there are any number of good enough fellows around who would jump at the chance—"

"I do not want any of them," Cynthia interrupted pettishly. "So do not mention your good fellows to me, Robbie. They simply will not do."

"I see," her cousin said resignedly. "In that case, coz, consider this. If your captain had been inclined to hedge off, surely he could have done so days ago by simply disappearing? The fact that he has called on you at all suggests that his intentions are honorable. If you had the brains of a sparrow, you must have seen this, my pet. And another thing, I suggest you do not keep your precious captain kicking his heels too long, Cynthia. As I told you before, he does not strike me as the kind of man to take kindly to such coquettish tactics."

"I am not playing the coquette," Cynthia retorted angrily.

"Then I suggest you receive the man and let him say his piece. It is pointless to put off the evil hour any longer."

Upon her return to Halifax House, Cynthia heard the very same advice from her father, who appeared extraordinarily aggrieved at his daughter's prevarication.

"If you no longer wish for this match, it behooves you to let the man know, Cynthia," Lord Halifax told her in sterner tones than she was accustomed to hear from him. "I forbid you to shilly-shally around like some hen-witted peagoose. Do you hear me?"

Naturally Cynthia could not deny that she did indeed hear her father's advice, which sounded suspiciously like a command. So it was that when the captain was announced shortly before four that afternoon, she was ready and waiting for this fateful interview.

She had spent more time than usual on her appearance, changing her mind three times, and severely trying the patience of her abigail, before she settled on a slim gown of light green merino, with long sleeves tightly fitted from wrist to elbow with tiny pearl buttons, and embellished with a delicate ruff at the neck and a velvet bow beneath the bosom. Fortified by this impeccable elegance, Cynthia descended the stairs with her heart in her mouth and swept into the Yellow Saloon with far more confidence than she could lay claim to.

"Captain Sheffield," she said brightly, advancing into the room with a polite smile pinned to her lips, "how good of you to call. But Hastings should have taken you to the Chinese drawing room. Lady Halifax always holds her Wednesday teas there, you know. It is quite my mother's favorite room."

The captain moved across the room to meet her and bowed stiffly over her proffered hand. Then he straightened to his full height and, without releasing her hand, gazed down at her searchingly.

Cynthia's heart faltered under the intensity of that blue stare, and she wondered what form this man's rejection would take. She had every reason to believe that the captain was a considerate man and would not crush her sensibilities unnecessarily. But he was also blunt, as she had had the opportunity to discover for herself, and it was unlikely that he would waste time with polite roundaboutation. Her hand still lay imprisoned in both his, and she made no move to reclaim it, content to enjoy the fleeting comfort of warmth and the illusion of closeness between them she had so hoped to make into a reality. Defying all notions of modesty, Cynthia gazed back at him, seeking some small sign of softness in the startling blue depths but finding none.

"I did not come to see Lady Halifax," he said, after what seemed like an age. "My business is with you, Lady Cynthia."

Business. The word made her heart cringe, and she withdrew her hand abruptly, turning away towards the butler, who stood awaiting her instructions.

"In that case, allow me to offer you some refreshment, Captain," she said, conscious of the artificial brightness of her voice. "A glass of sherry, perhaps? Or Madeira?" She kept her eyes fixed on Hastings as he moved silently towards the sideboard where the decanters were ranged. Did she imagine it or was that a flicker of approval she glimpsed in the butler's eye before he veiled them and busied himself with serving the captain? Could it be that the entire household was cognizant of the nature of the *business* the captain had with her? Accustomed to the ways of domestics, Cynthia knew that it was useless to attempt to keep matters of any import from the staff, but she was nevertheless surprised that Hastings had so far forgot himself as to reveal his knowledge.

The captain maintained a rigid silence until the butler softly closed the door of the saloon. Then he moved to a position before the hearth and, raising his glass, took a large draught before setting the glass down on the mantel. Although the captain's demeanor was calm, Cynthia felt the tension in him and suddenly realized that his position must be a good deal more awkward than her own. This unexpected insight enabled her to repress her own distress and take refuge in the role of hostess.

"Can I not prevail upon you to sit down, Captain?" she said with a genuine smile.

"What I have to say is better said standing up, my lady." His tone was so solemn that Cynthia had difficulty keeping her smile in place.

"I see," she said softly, wracking her brains for some way of postponing the inevitable. "Before you say anything, Captain, you must allow me to thank you for the beautiful flowers." She gestured towards a low table by the window, where a large bowl of tall white lilies displayed their regal beauty. "Lilies are quite one of my favorite blooms. They make me nostalgic for the gardens of Milford Hall." Which is where she ought to be at this very instant, she thought wryly. Instead of sitting here making a cake of herself. How she ever came to delude herself that a young, virile man of the captain's stamp could be brought to wed a female already verging on middle age, Cynthia could not imagine. She had been foolish beyond reason and would have to face the consequences of giving rein to her immodest fantasies.

"The pleasure is all mine," the captain responded with a brief smile. He took another drink of sherry, and an uneasy silence descended upon the saloon.

Unable to bear the suspense a moment longer, Cynthia threw herself into the breach. "I presume you have reached a decision regarding . . ." she began, then paused, unhappy with the word trembling on the tip of her tongue, but at a loss to find a more suitable one.

The captain seemed to find his voice. "Reached a decision? Yes, my lady, that is exactly the matter I wish to discuss with you. I have indeed reached a decision." He stopped abruptly, as if regretting this admission.

"Then let me assure you that you may speak your mind freely, Captain," Cynthia said in what she hoped were encouraging tones. "I am not given to enacting Cheltenham tragedies"—she smiled faintly at the futility of such a notion—"and I believe I can accept your decision without reproach and wish you well with all sincerity."

Captain Sheffield stared at her for a full minute before he grinned ruefully. "I see you have anticipated my course of action, my lady," he said gently.

Cynthia felt her fantasies crumble into dust about her feet, but schooled her expression to keep her disappointment from showing. "I have given the matter some serious thought, Captain, and have been brought to the realization that it was ill-advised, not to say downright foolish of me to suppose I could arrange my life to my own liking." She drew a deep breath and paused, conscious of an odd expression in the piercing blue eyes regarding her steadily.

"It is evident that you anticipated a negative decision, my lady," he murmured. "Can it be that you *wished* for it?"

"Oh, no!" Cynthia responded before she could control her tongue. "That is to say, I had hoped for a resolution agreeable to both of us, but I can quite see that your idea of agreeable, Captain, might not be mine."

His gaze softened, and he smiled. "You are quite prepared to lose your gamble, I gather?"

Disappointment shot through her again, but Cynthia returned his smile gamely. "I believe I made that clear at the outset, Captain. You need not fear that I will turn into a watering-pot."

"And are you equally prepared to win, my lady?" he said softly.

Cynthia's heart gave a wild leap, and she felt herself go pale. She was glad to be seated, for the implications of the captain's words had produced a sudden weakening in her knees. She licked her dry lips.

"You are mocking me, Captain," she managed to stammer. "That is not well done of you, sir."

The captain shook his head. "You are mistaken, my dear. I hope I am not such a brute as you seem to think. I meant exactly what I said, and would like an answer to my question. Are you prepared to win your gamble, my lady? In plainer language, are you still disposed towards marriage?"

CHAPTER NINE

The Kiss

Captain Sheffield closed the door of the Yellow Saloon behind him and stood for a moment trying to get his bearings. Nothing had occurred as he had expected, and he felt somehow bereft, as though he had lost one of the most important skirmishes of his life. As indeed he had, he thought ruefully. Instead of leaving the room a betrothed man, one who had, after considerable vacillation and soul-searching, decided that marriage to Lady Cynthia Lonsdale would offer him everything a second son with no other prospects of advancement could possibly hope for, he had been given his congé.

The lady had refused his offer.

Brian was at a loss to understand how such a thing had happened. He rubbed one hand across his eyes, trying to banish the odd feeling of disorientation that overcame him. What had he done to deserve this? he wondered, listening distractedly to the faint sounds of callers in the front hall. He felt vaguely misused. The prize had slipped through his fingers. Prize? In a flash of cynicism, the captain wondered which of the advantages of the alliance he had anticipated making—now inexplicably snatched away—he would regret the loss of most. The lady herself? Lady Cynthia had looked particularly fetching this afternoon, and Brian had allowed himself the luxury of imagining how her shapely mouth would taste when he kissed her. He fully intended to kiss her. Was that not one of the privileges accorded to a betrothed man?

He had not kissed her, of course. A gentleman does not force such attentions upon a lady who has just informed him—in a tone that brooked no argument—that she released him from any obligation—real or imagined—he might have felt himself constrained to honor. So, however much he had wanted to—and Brian freely admitted that he had wanted to very badly—he had not done so. He felt deprived of a pleasure he had already considered his by right.

Yes, he thought, he would regret losing the lady. But he would also regret the horses. The captain had looked forward to working with horses again, and marriage to Lady Cynthia would give him possession of the famous Lonsdale stables. The idea of becoming a serious rival to his half-brother had played no small part in the captain's decision to accept Lady Cynthia's proposal. It had been his ambition at twenty to breed the best horses in England, and Brian had been surprised to discover that this dream had not died, as he had always imagined, when his father died, and the management of the Mulgrave stables had been taken from him.

Yes, he admitted, the loss of the opportunity to put his considerable knowledge of horse breeding to work again ranked up there with the loss of the lady. The notion made him smile rather grimly. And then there was always the fortune, the captain thought. For some reason Brian had been reluctant to think of Lady Cynthia's wealth as part of the bargain; but of course it was. He had no very clear idea of how much the lady's fortune entailed. Wealth had never been much of an issue with him, Brian suddenly realized. At Mulgrave Park he had been content with little for himself, although he had always spent lavishly on his horses. Things were pretty much the same with him today, except that he would have no horses on which to spend Lady Cynthia's fortune. A fortune he no longer could lay any claim to, he reminded himself.

Quite suddenly it dawned on the captain that he had—without conscious thought—been looking forward to the changes in his life marriage to Lady Cynthia would bring. A return to the country would have been the most welcome, and the lady's reference to the gardens at Milford Hall had triggered a nostalgic longing in him for the open countryside of his youth. For the turning of the leaves in the autumn. The first snowfall in the winter. The bringing in of the Yule log at Christmas time. The daffodils and crocuses in the spring.

The captain glanced over his shoulder at the closed door. Had she realized that, in sending him away, in rejecting him, she had deprived him of the life he most wanted to live? he wondered. No, how could she? He had not mentioned a word of how he really felt, of what he really wanted. Perhaps if he had . . .

Brian shrugged his shoulders and turned to stride down the corridor towards the front hall. No, he would not beg any woman to take him, he told himself firmly. He would not sink that low.

The sound of a familiar drawling voice addressing the butler made him hesitate. He cared little enough for the Marquess of

Monroyal at the best of times; this afternoon the captain would have avoided the encounter had it been in his power. A meeting was inevitable, however, and as he approached the front door, Brian saw the marquess sauntering towards him, his jeweled quizzing-glass dangling from his long fingers.

"My dear Sheffield," the marquess remarked, coming to a stop directly in the captain's path. "Why so downcast, old man? I was under the impression—"

Brian cut him off abruptly. "Then you are under the wrong impression, my lord," he said brusquely, trying to push past the other man.

"Am I not to wish you happy, then?"

"No, indeed not, sir," Brian snapped. "Now, if you will allow me—"

"Have you spoken to Cynthia?"

The captain glared at him. "I fail to see what business that is of yours, my lord," he said stiffly.

"Cut line, man," the marquess said curtly. "Have you spoken to my cousin or not?"

"Yes." The captain watched the other man's eyebrows rise in surprise and a flicker of annoyance flash briefly in his gray eyes. "And her ladyship will have none of me, as perhaps she informed you this morning." The idea of any kind of intimacy between this man and his Cynthia—now no longer *his* Cynthia—made Brian's voice sound harsh to his own ears.

The marquess regarded him searchingly. "You made my cousin an offer of marriage?"

"What other kind of offer do you suppose I would make to a lady?" the captain said harshly.

The marquess smiled grimly and brushed the question aside. "You must have made a mull of it, old chap," he drawled in that patronizing tone that set Brian's teeth on edge. "Are you telling me that she actually declined your offer?"

"She declined my offer," the captain repeated curtly.

The marquess stared at him for a moment, his quizzing-glass swinging idly to and fro. "How extraordinary," he murmured softly. "This morning, my cousin was definitely of a mind to accept you."

"Then she changed her mind," the captain said bluntly. "Females have been known to do so, or so I hear."

Lord Monroyal smiled knowingly. "If given enough provocation, some females will," he agreed. "But not this one." He paused, regarding the captain from beneath hooded lids. "Tell me, Captain. Did you kiss my cousin?"

Sheffield drew himself up and glared at the older man. "Mind your own bloody business," he growled.

The marquess sighed audibly. "Just as I feared. You did not even kiss her," he remarked disgustedly. "No wonder she sent you to the rightabout. Cannot say that I blame her."

"How could I be expected to kiss a lady who has just informed me that she will have none of me?"

"Very easily," Lord Monroyal drawled, evidently much entertained. "One places an arm snugly around the lady's waist, another behind her head, and then, to preclude any protest—"

"I am well aware of the mechanics of kissing," the captain interrupted brusquely. "But I am not in the habit of mauling unwilling females."

The marquess grinned. "I am not suggesting anything so uncouth," he protested. "But I find it hard to believe that my cousin—whom I have every reason to believe is a passionate woman—was unwilling."

The captain stared at him in astonishment. "I can assure you that Lady Cynthia gave no indication—"

A crack of laughter interrupted this protestation, and the marquess shook his head in mock despair. "You are more of a fool than I had supposed, Captain," he said gently. "We are not dealing with some innocent schoolroom chit here, you know. Did it not occur to you that after eight years of marriage to as dry a stick as you could wish for, and two years of widowhood, my cousin might be ripe for a kiss from a young buck such as yourself?"

Brian could not believe his ears. "I am sure her ladyship entertained no such improper thoughts, my lord," he said stiffly. "She is every inch a lady."

Lord Monroyal raised his eyes to the ceiling in mock resignation. "Forgive me for saying so, Captain, but you know very little about females if you believe that ladies do not harbor improper thoughts." He smiled as Brian's face took on a mulish expression. "But enough of this *badinage*," he drawled. "Tell me something, Captain. Do you still wish to wed my cousin?"

"What business is that of—"

"Yes or no," the marquess cut in impatiently. "I am about to lose interest in this whole affair, Captain," he warned. "But since my cousin's welfare is at stake, I am willing to give you the benefit of my experience in winning her. If that is what you wish, of course."

The captain glared at him, unwilling to accept assistance from a man he detested, but his imagination captured by the veiled promise of success with Lady Cynthia. "I am sure I do not envy you your experience, my lord," he began, but the marquess waved this censorial remark aside.

"Do you wish to wed my cousin, Captain?" he repeated.

The memory of Cynthia's sweet mouth flashed unbidden across Brian's mind, and he quickly repressed it, uncomfortable with his own desires. Could he trust this libertine to give him the key to winning her consent? he wondered. The seconds ticked by, and the captain saw the familiar expression of boredom settle on the older man's countenance.

"Yes," he said quickly, before he lost his nerve.

Lord Monroyal's face broke into a smile, and he gently took the captain's elbow and turned him back towards the Yellow Saloon. "Then come with me," he drawled, "and do as I say."

They reached the door and Brian paused, turning to look inquiringly at the marquess. "What do you expect me to do?" he demanded uneasily.

The marquess laid a manicured hand nonchalantly on the door handle and turned to smile at the captain. "Simple," he said. "All you have to do is go in there and behave like a man who will not take no for an answer."

The captain stared at him in disbelief. "You cannot mean me to force myself upon the lady?" he asked, appalled at the notion, but vaguely titillated by it at the same time.

The marquess cast him a pitying look. "My dear boy," he drawled in a weary voice, "must I remind you of the old saw about faint hearts and fair ladies? If you truly wish to win this lady, you will have to be considerably more forceful in your approach. If you cannot bring yourself to do so, then I wash my hands of you. And so, I doubt it not, will Cynthia."

So saying, the marquess took the captain's limp hand and placed it on the door handle. Then he made a mock salute and sauntered off down the hall towards Lady Halifax's Chinese drawing room.

After the briefest of hesitations, the captain turned the handle and entered the Yellow Saloon.

No sooner had Captain Sheffield left the room—his rugged face set in granite lines—than Cynthia knew she had made the biggest mistake in her life. What did it matter if he had offered for her under a misguided sense of obligation? What if he had been driven by some obscure masculine notion of honor? Or even worse, by that ever pressing motivator of men, greed? Had she not dangled her fortune in front of him as a bait? Had she not tempted him, deliberately and knowingly? Had she not wanted him, desired him quite shamelessly, at any price?

Then why, oh why, she asked herself repeatedly after he was gone, had she refused him?

Nothing had occurred as she had expected. Lady Cynthia remembered steeling herself for the inevitable interview with Captain Sheffield, emptying her mind of emotion in preparation for the rejection she had anticipated. It would never do to betray the slightest disappointment, she had told herself firmly. And indeed, she had been quite pleased with her fortitude and the game little smile she had kept fixed on her face when he had talked of her losing her gamble. Her heart had gone cold, of course, but she had kept on smiling, explaining that she was prepared for the captain's negative decision. But she had been wrong, of course. Being prepared for rejection was not the same as being able to bear it. She could not remember anything quite so painful ever happening to her before. But thank goodness, she was still able to smile.

And then he had asked her if she was prepared to win the gamble, she remembered with a shudder. That had been much much worse, for the captain had obviously been toying with her. His marvelous blue eyes had smiled at her, but Cynthia had been quite unable to believe him. So she had rallied her flagging spirit, and summoned up her shattered pride to the rescue. She had informed him—quite as though she really did not care a fig for this bronzed young man who had captured her heart—that there was not the least need for him to sacrifice himself in a marriage of convenience when it was obvious that he had a brilliant career in the Army ahead of him. Refusing to listen to his protestations, she had absolved him from any obligation he might feel towards her, and freed him from the onerous decision she had asked him to make.

In effect, she had rejected him.

Cynthia moaned aloud as she recalled the captain's expression of chagrin when he began to realize the tenor of her words, preceded—she was sure of it—by a flash of relief in those captivating blue eyes of his. His pride had been hurt, she supposed, but he would soon get over it. Within a few days, at the most a week or two, Captain Sheffield would be back in his regiment engaged in those deeds of bravery he was reputed to perform so admirably,

and the memory of rejection by an eccentric, aging widow would
fade until it became a source of merriment to him and his friends.
Cynthia shuddered at the thought.

Whereas her own pride had been salvaged, had it not? She had
not had to suffer the indignity of being rejected—perhaps out of
contempt for her foolishness—or worse yet, accepted out of pity
or greed or even a sense of obligation, by a man who must regard
her, at best, as a very immodest female indeed.

Yes, Cynthia thought, her spirits lower than ever. Her pride
was intact, but what good would it do her, this pride she had
placed—in a rash moment of cowardice—above any hope for
happiness with the man of her choice, in those long years stretching ahead of her at Milford Hall?

Of course, she could always bow to her father's will, she
thought bitterly, and settle for another husband twenty years her
senior. But that would never happen now, she saw with awful
clarity, suddenly aware of all that she had thrown away when she
dismissed the captain. Having admired his muscular figure, felt
the warmth of his touch, and the caress of his gaze, Cynthia knew
that no other man would do for her.

Like the simpleton she was, she had thrown away any chance
of happiness.

At this disturbing but indisputable revelation, the tears she had
been holding back for the past hour started to flow. Cynthia
walked over to the window and gazed down at the pear-tree in the
walled garden below. She made no move to check the warm wet-
ness that betrayed her inner agitation. Had not her presence been
expected in Lady Halifax's Chinese drawing room to pour tea for
the Wednesday callers, Cynthia would have escaped up to her
chamber to cry her eyes out. The temptation to do so anyway was
great, for she had so much to regret. Unlike the pear-tree, there
would be no rebirth and fruitfulness for her, she thought, so lost
in melancholy that she hardly heard the door open and close behind her.

"Hastings," she murmured, hearing footsteps on the carpet behind her, "has my cousin, the marquess, arrived yet?"

There was rather a long pause, and then a deep masculine
voice, which was definitely not the butler's, spoke from immediately beside her.

"Yes, indeed. His lordship arrived some minutes ago."

Cynthia whirled to face the intruder, her hands flying to her
wet cheeks, her swimming eyes wide with astonishment.

"Captain!" she exclaimed tremulously. "Oh dear." She dropped her eyes immediately and turned back to the window, in a vain attempt to hide her ravaged face.

She must be living through some terrible nightmare, Cynthia thought, desperate to deny the presence of the man she had despaired of ever setting eyes on again. But the firm grasp of his hands on her shoulders dispelled that fantasy. Cynthia felt herself turned to face him although she kept her eyes firmly fixed on his pale blue waistcoat, inches from her nose. She must look a complete fright, she thought, willing the floor to open and swallow her.

"My dear Cynthia," he said in a husky voice she had never heard him use before. "Tell me what has distressed you so. What caused these tears, my dear? Is it something I did? Have I offended you in some way?" His fingers tightened on her shoulders, as if impelling her to answer.

"Oh, n-no," she stammered, swallowing the lump that seemed to impede her speech. "I must be a little overset, that is all. I n-never cry," she added, giving the lie to that statement with a sob that escaped her before she could stop it. "I c-cannot imagine what is the matter with me." She dashed her hand across her cheek in a vain attempt to divert another tear from trickling down. "It is n-nothing, I assure you."

For the life of her Cynthia could not step back from the captain's grasp. Her feet seemed to be rooted to the floor, and her limbs would not obey her. Quite the opposite, in fact. Some invisible force seemed to hold her in thrall, and the urge to cast herself upon his broad chest was becoming more compelling by the minute. She offered no resistance whatever when one of his arms slipped about her shoulders, pulling her close, and he took out his handkerchief to wipe her tear-stained cheeks.

"There, my dear," the captain said huskily, pocketing his handkerchief and running his knuckles down the curve of her cheek.

"I feel utterly foolish, behaving in this maudlin manner," she murmured, reveling in the unexpected caress and wishing that he would keep his arm about her forever.

She felt his hand cup her chin, urging her to raise her head. Cynthia resisted, fearful of seeing derision or pity—for what else could he be thinking of her shocking missishness?—or perhaps something worse in his eyes.

The pressure on her chin became more insistent.

"Look at me, Cynthia."

"I cannot," she whispered, but her resistance faltered, and her chin tilted up, exposing her face to his gaze. No amount of cajol-

ing would tempt her to open her eyes, Cynthia vowed, suspecting
that they must be red from crying. She must really pull herself together, she thought, suddenly recalling the awkward scene so recently played out with the captain. Why had he returned? she
wondered. She was glad that he had, and that he had seen fit to
put his arm about her in this comforting manner, and dry her
tears. But it would be foolishness indeed to imagine that . . . Cynthia refused to speculate further along those lines, and resolutely
opened her eyes.

The captain's blue gaze was fixed upon her intently, and Cynthia saw neither derision nor pity in his eyes. In fact, if she did not
know better, she might have said . . . but no, she must cease de-
luding herself.

"Please release me, Captain," she said with tolerable calm.
"This is most improper of you, and I cannot imagine why you
came back," she continued, when he paid no attention to her request. "Did you forget something?"

He grinned at her then, and Cynthia's heart lurched uncomfortably. He had never grinned at her in quite that way before. It was
an entirely masculine kind of grin, hinting at suppressed excitement, at possessiveness, at incipient desire. Cynthia closed her
eyes again quickly.

"Yes," he murmured huskily, and Cynthia felt the warmth of
his breath on her cheek. "Yes, my dear," he added softly, "I forgot to kiss you."

Before Cynthia could react to this utterly outrageous confession, she felt his arms tighten around her and the firm pressure of
his lips on hers. She went rigid with shock as his free hand drifted
down to settle on her hip.

"Relax, love," he murmured against her mouth. The pressure of
his lips increased as he explored the contours of her mouth. Cynthia seemed quite unable to resist, and when she felt the warmth
of his open mouth over hers, some secret part of her, long denied
the full expression of her passionate nature, obeyed his command,
and of its own accord, her body relaxed against his, adjusting to
the shape of him as though she had lain there many times before.

After an indeterminate length of time, Cynthia was able to confirm what she had suspected all along. Intimacies with a young,
virile gentleman would be far superior to the perfunctory attentions of an elderly man more interested in his sheep than in his
wife. If only she could have another chance, she thought, she
would snatch what happiness she could find in this man's arms at
any price.

When the captain finally raised his head and gazed down at her with eyes heavy with unmistakable passion, Cynthia waited expectantly, unwilling to break the spell of intimacy the kiss had woven around them.

Finally he grinned at her, the same possessive, male grin, but this time there was satisfaction in it, and triumph, too.

"I think you had best reconsider my offer, my lady," he murmured against her ear. "In fact, I insist that you do so. I doubt I can take many more such kisses without running amok."

"Who said you will get any more of them?" Cynthia demanded, hope flickering brightly in her heart. "I am not in the habit of—"

"Yes, I know," the captain interrupted. "But you will soon become accustomed to it. And it will cause less strain on both of us if we are married, my dear."

Cynthia opened her mouth to protest this high-handed attitude in her beloved, but the captain effectively put a stop to any resistance with another deep kiss.

"What about your Army career?" Cynthia managed to ask during a pause, while the captain ran his lips slowly down her neck.

"The devil fly away with the Army," he murmured in the hollow of her throat.

"And your family?"

"The devil may fly away with them, too."

"Are you sure you really want to do this, Captain?" Cynthia ventured to ask, not quite ready to believe what the captain's words seemed to imply. "You do not have to, you know," she forced herself to say.

"You have already made that point quite clear, love," he replied, bending his head to taste her lips again. "But I think we have settled that question to your entire satisfaction, have we not?"

"Yes," Cynthia responded, rather more meekly than was her wont.

"Good," he said. "Then it is all settled?"

"Yes," she repeated, wondering if she would wake up later and find that this whole blissful episode had been a dream.

Much as he disliked having to admit it, Captain Sheffield thought three days later, as the well-sprung Lonsdale traveling chaise bore him out of London, the Marquess of Monroyal had been right. The lady had been won by the forceful approach suggested by the notorious rake, and Brian could not help wondering how many female scruples the marquess had overcome with similar tactics.

Impatiently, the captain banished all thoughts of the ubiquitous marquess from his mind and turned his gaze towards the woman sitting across from him. His *wife*, he thought, tracing her soft profile with his eyes. The sound of the word was still so new to him that he had to keep reminding himself that the elegant creature in the red velvet cloak, its sable collar snuggled warmly against her cheeks, and fur bonnet framing her small face was actually his wife. Her hands were hidden in a voluminous sable muff, but the captain could still feel the softness of her fingers in his as they had stood together in Lord Halifax's drawing room only hours ago. The Reverend Miller's words still rang in his ears as he had placed the plain wedding band—purchased in haste the day before at Duval & Carrier's on Piccadilly—on her small finger.

They had been warm, his wife's fingers, the captain recalled. Warm and slightly clinging as she had made her response in a low, steady voice. The memory of that moment stirred him. Those simple words had made her his, he mused, astonished that such a brief ceremony could so utterly change his life, and yes, his whole attitude towards her. Brian felt a rush of protectiveness he had never experienced before. Cynthia was truly his now, and he had vowed to honor her for the rest of his life. Rather than inspire him with the resignation he and his friends had always associated with parson's mousetrap, marriage to Cynthia had given his life a new direction, a sense of purpose it had never had before. Brian saw clearly for the first time that the decision he had made three days ago—at the instigation of the despicable marquess, of course, but the decision had been his alone—would benefit him in more ways than he had imagined possible.

His eyes traveled down from his wife's profile across her breasts, barely discernible beneath the heavy cloak, to rest again on her muffled hands. The captain knew that Cynthia wore a warm gown of deep blue merino under the cloak, a high-buttoned gown that boasted a modest frill of lace at the throat and a velvet sash beneath her full breasts. It was her wedding gown and quite unexpectedly, Brian's fingers itched to unfasten, one by one, the row of buttons from throat to hem until it fell, a pool of blue at her feet. His pulses throbbed at the thought of what lay beneath the blue gown, his imagination running rife with anticipation of that act of possession which would make her his in more than name only.

The captain took a deep breath to steady himself and calm the racing of his blood. He raised his eyes to find Lady Cynthia staring at him, a flicker of apprehension on her face. Brian pulled himself together and smiled at her. This woman was not one of his Spanish camp followers ready and willing to be tumbled whenever the fancy took him, he reminded himself, suddenly ashamed at the lascivious yearnings that had assailed him. This was his wife, a lady born and bred, a female to be treated gently and with respect. His smile broadened.

"Are you cold, my dear?" he inquired solicitously.

Lady Cynthia pulled the fur collar of her cloak closer around her and shook her head. "No. Although I am glad Papa insisted on ordering hot bricks for my feet. And it is not as though we were traveling to Yorkshire or some other remote spot. Milford is little more than six or seven miles from Guildford, and if the weather holds, we should be home by four of the clock."

Home, Brian thought. That had a nice ring to it. He had had no real home since his father died. The old earl had not been cold in his grave before John had made it quite plain that his half-brother was no longer welcome at Mulgrave Park. His mother had wanted him to move into the Dower House with her and Caroline, but Brian had found the notion intolerable. He was a Sheffield of Mulgrave Park, and if he could not live there, he would not make a home anywhere else. His mother, the dowager, had pleaded his case with John, and so, not surprisingly, had Lady Mulgrave, but his half-brother had been adamant.

Poor Margaret, the captain thought, her small kindnesses to him had invariably angered her husband. Marriage to his half-brother could not be much fun, even if it had made her a countess. And Margaret had been so young, barely eighteen he remembered, when John had brought her to Mulgrave Park as his bride. Over the next seven years, she had presented the earl with five children, all of them girls, and John had grown progressively more frustrated and belligerent with a wife who seemed incapable of giving him the heir he so desperately wanted.

The thought of his brother's dilemma caused the captain to smile again at Lady Cynthia. With any luck at all, he mused, he would be a father himself by the middle of next summer, and the notion of having a son of his own to carry on the Sheffield line suddenly added an unsuspected dimension to his life. For perhaps the first time, Brian understood John's frustration with his five daughters. Without an heir, Mulgrave Park would come to Brian's son, if and when he had one. He grinned at the thought.

"What do you find so amusing, Captain?" Lady Cynthia demanded, breaking into Brian's pleasant ruminations.

The captain's grin broadened. "I was imagining my brother's chagrin if our first child is a boy," he said, amused at the instant pink flush that suffused his wife's cheeks.

"My mother has five granddaughters already, you see," he added gently. "I think the least we could do is present her with a grandson, do you not agree, my dear?"

"Lady Mulgrave told me that the countess fully expects the next to be a boy," Cynthia replied, smoothly avoiding his question.

"Really?" Brian said, not much surprised at this information. "John will not admit defeat, apparently. Poor Margaret. I pity her if she produces yet another girl."

"I would be quite happy with a daughter," Cynthia said softly, her eyes taking on a faraway expression. "And your brother would do well to remember that without daughters there would be no sons."

"I shall endeavor to remember that, my dear. But I do think we should hope for a son to offset all those daughters John has loosed upon the world," Brian replied with a smile.

The captain wanted to add that they would begin that very night to work on the son he had suddenly set his heart on, but he feared to offend Cynthia's sensibilities with such crudeness. He did not forget it, however, as Lady Cynthia's team of prime cattle ate up the miles, nor did it get lost in the bustle of arrival at the neat Tudor manor-house on the outskirts of Milford, which was to be his new home.

And when the captain climbed the stairs later that evening after a hearty dinner and a sustaining glass of brandy in Lady Cynthia's elegantly appointed drawing room, warmed by a blazing fire in the marble hearth, it was uppermost in his mind.

Only after he opened the door to Lady Cynthia's bedchamber and saw his wife waiting for him in the middle of the wide four-poster, tucked up with the covers tight about her chin like the little girl she had once been, did Brian forget all about his desire for a son and concentrate all his energy and rising passion on the female he had so fortuitously taken to wife.

CHAPTER TEN

The Rift

Lady Cynthia awoke the morning after her arrival home feeling lethargic. She must have been more exhausted by the journey than usual, she thought, turning over drowsily to snuggle more deeply into the feather mattress. It was then that she felt a twinge of soreness, which made her come fully awake, her eyes instinctively seeking the pillow beside her. What she saw made her smile. How could she have forgotten? Tentatively she stretched out a hand to touch the clearly indented pillow. All trace of warmth had long gone, but as her fingers traced the indentation, Cynthia saw in her mind's eye the face of the man who had made it.

Her wedding night had been everything she had hoped it would be. And more, she thought, letting her mind drift back to that anxiously awaited moment when Captain Sheffield had opened her chamber door and stepped inside. He had already removed his coat and cravat, and Cynthia had stared quite shamelessly, fascinated by the sight of so much male presence clearly outlined beneath the thin lawn shirt.

She had been quite unable to tear her gaze away from his lithe body as he stalked—with an unconscious grace that had stirred her own blood—across the room to stand beside the bed. He had looked down at her with amusement and desire in his blue eyes, and Cynthia had let out in a long, trembling sigh the breath she had unconsciously been holding. And then in one swift motion, the captain had peeled back the covers, his eyes turning a deeper shade of blue as he looked his fill. Cynthia had momentarily regretted the decadent impulse that had made her don the sheerest of her night-rails, but that rapt expression on her husband's face had told her, more clearly than any words, that he was utterly captivated.

He had smiled then, and looked straight into her eyes. Cynthia had held her breath again, awed and a little frightened at the intensity of passion she saw reflected in his gaze. When he spoke, however, his voice was husky and caressing.

"I have an astonishingly beautiful wife," he said slowly, his gaze holding hers steadily. "Are you ready for me, love?"

Never having experienced so direct and erotic a request for her favors, Cynthia was momentarily unable to utter a word. The late viscount had invariably snuffed all the candles before climbing unceremoniously into bed and reaching for her. She had soon learned that Lonsdale was not given to unnecessary discourse and rarely noticed anything about her unless it was her absence when he required her presence. Never in the eight years they had lived together had he looked at her as the captain was looking at her now—his gaze hot and unequivocal—and told her that she was beautiful.

Cynthia had held out her hand to him and smiled shyly.

"Yes!" she whispered, acutely aware of her own breathlessness and the ache spiraling up inside her. "Oh, yes!"

The captain had needed no further encouragement. Throwing off his clothes, he slid into the bed, and Cynthia had been immediately enveloped in the touch, and smell, and taste of him. She had been prepared for instant possession, had anticipated the weight of him, and felt herself grow weak with desire. Instead, she had felt his hands and mouth all over her, teasing her, enticing her, inflaming her until she moaned and arched in ecstasy. Only then had he entered her, taking her to heights she had never known possible.

And then—to her intense surprise—he had done it all over again.

And much later, once more.

Cynthia shivered as the recollection of all that her new husband had demanded of her during their first night together came back to her. Where did he get the energy to rise so early? she wondered, as he evidently had. Very early indeed if the cool pillow did not lie. His warmth was gone, but the warmth he had left in her heart still glowed strongly, and Cynthia had to tell herself firmly that she must not allow these pleasant memories to make a slug-a-bed out of her.

She reached out to ring the bell vigorously.

By the time Cynthia came down to the breakfast parlor, it was past nine o'clock and she was not surprised to find that Captain Sheffield had breakfasted an hour ago and gone down to the stables. The November sun shone more brightly than usual, at least so Cynthia imagined as she made her way through the herb garden and into the stable-yard by the back way. Perhaps the sunshine was a good omen, she thought, leaning on the wooden fence that surrounded the open-air jumping arena.

The captain was taking her most promising gelding through his paces, observed closely by Jake Waters, her taciturn head trainer. Old Jake was a veteran of the Lonsdale stables, and had been the late viscount's head groom before Lady Cynthia had taken over the haphazard breeding program initiated by the viscount's father years ago. Cynthia was quick to recognize the old man's knowledge of horses and had made him head trainer against her husband's advice. Old Jake had not disappointed her, and after eight years of hard work and a considerable amount of the viscount's money, they had moved the Lonsdale stable from three brood mares and one ancient stud up to its present count of twenty mares and two stallions prized for their elegant conformation and stamina on the hunting field.

The captain rode with a fluid grace that drew Cynthia's eyes and gladdened her soul. During their drive down into Surrey, Cynthia had discovered the extent of her new husband's passion of horses, and it had warmed her heart to know that they had this love in common. She had been surprised to learn from her father that some of the best hunters to come out of the Mulgrave stables had been bred, not by the present earl but by his younger brother Brian. The captain had been modest about his own achievements but was visibly gratified when Lord Halifax complimented him on the performance of a favorite hunter, Trumpeter, one of the captain's most promising geldings. Cynthia knew the horse well and had ridden him often during her Christmas visits to Halifax Park in Hampshire. If Trumpeter was any indication of the captain's expertise in breeding, Cynthia looked forward to placing the management of her own stables in his capable hands.

"What do you think of Tom-Boy, Captain?" she asked when her husband brought the chestnut gelding to a halt beside her. She looked up into his deep blue eyes and, in spite of her firm resolution not to be missish, Cynthia felt the telltale color rise to her cheeks.

"Jake and I believe that with a more rigorous exercise schedule, he will be ready for the spring sale," she added, all too conscious of the presence of the old trainer, who had ambled up to join them. Cynthia refused to lower her gaze and found herself marveling at the subtle changes she was learning to detect in the blue shades in her husband's eyes. At the moment they were dark and half hooded, and Cynthia could have sworn, when his mouth curled up at one corner, that he was thinking of their first night together. As she was herself, Cynthia had to admit guiltily, turning to acknowledge the trainer. "Is that not so, Jake?"

"Indeed it is, milady," Waters replied in his abrupt way. "And with the captain 'ere to 'elp us, we should make a fine showing come spring."

"Would you have my saddle put on Merrylegs for me, Jake? I am anxious to see how he has progressed while I have been in London. Well?" she insisted, after the old man had gone off towards the stable. "Am I mistaken in thinking that Tom-Boy should bring a record price, Captain? He is quite my favorite, you know," she added, fondling the soft muzzle nuzzling at her sleeve.

The captain swung lithely out of the saddle and came to lean on the fence beside her. "He is in splendid form. As are you, my lady," he added, lowering his voice to a husky whisper. "I hope I did not tire you out last night."

Unaccustomed to hearing bedroom matters discussed so openly, Cynthia flushed scarlet. Never in her eight years with the viscount had his lordship so much as referred obliquely to the more intimate aspects of their relationship. For all intents and purposes, Cynthia had often thought, their nights together might not have existed at all. Her new husband obviously practiced no such reticence. After one startled glance into those warm blue eyes, Cynthia focused her gaze on Tom-Boy's velvet lips, that the horse was using dexterously to mangle the sleeve of her riding habit.

"Naughty boy," she scolded, pushing the horse away. What was she expected to reply to such an indecorous question? she wondered. Anything she might say could well lead the captain into even more embarrassing disclosures. Flustered at the notion, Cynthia dug into her pocket and brought out the carrot she had begged from Cook on her way through the kitchen.

"Here you are, you greedy wretch," she murmured, thrusting it at the horse, who daintily snapped it in half and munched contentedly. "I did not forget your carrot, old boy." Determined to ignore her husband's immodest remark, Cynthia fed the remains of the carrot to Tom-Boy, who nodded his head up and down as he crunched on it.

"No carrot for me, my lady?" the captain murmured in the same husky voice that sent thrills up and down Cynthia's spine.

"How unkind of you, love. I suppose I shall have to settle for a kiss instead." And before Cynthia could gather her wits, the captain had taken her chin in his hand and planted a kiss on her upturned lips.

Cynthia jerked free and glanced guiltily around. "You forget yourself, sir," she said frostily, "I am not accustomed to being mauled about in front of the servants."

To her chagrin, the captain laughed. "I must remember to maul you about only when we are alone, Cynthia. That is what you get for marrying a common soldier, my dear. We are not overburdened with lordly airs and graces."

Cynthia was saved from having to reply to this piece of outrageousness by Waters, who came up leading a frisky roan. "Ain't been out for two days, so have a care with 'im, lass," the old man warned before tossing her up into the saddle.

"I shall be quite all right, Jake," Cynthia murmured, wondering how many of her stable hands had witnessed the unexpected kiss her husband had just given her. Without a glance in the captain's direction, she wheeled her horse and trotted out of the stable-yard. Once she was free of the cobblestones, she put Merrylegs to a canter and took the bridle-path that would lead her through a number of jumps built explicitly to put the hunters through their paces in the open field.

After taking the first two jumps at a canter, she urged the roan to lengthen his stride until he settled into a steady rhythm which she would later increase until the horse hit the stride demanded by a strenuous hunt across open country.

It was not long before she heard the thunder of hooves behind her and by the time her roan took the fifth jump over a stone wall bordering a small stream, she glimpsed Tom-Boy's nose edging up beside her. They continued thus for several more hedges until they came to a low hill where Cynthia was wont to pause beneath an old oak tree to allow her horse to take a breather.

The captain pulled up beside her. "You are a bruising rider, my lady," he said admiringly. "And that roan should bring a good price at the sale." When Cynthia made no response, he drew Tom-Boy closer until his knee brushed hers. "I owe you an apology for my conduct back there," he said lightly. "We soldiers are an uncouth lot, my dear. I confess that I am unused to keeping a rein on my tongue around females. If my crudeness shocked you, Cynthia, as I can see it did, I beg you will forgive me. I promise to be more circumspect in future."

He edged his horse closer and Cynthia knew—from the quickening of her pulse and the odd thumping of her heart—that her husband was about to kiss her again. She should move away instantly, she knew, but her hands lay idle on the reins. This kind of behavior—kissing in the stable-yard, or even in the open field where any passing traveler might see them—was the kind of folly one might expect from young lovers. And one thing she and the captain were not, she told herself firmly, was young lovers. Love did not enter into their relationship at all, of course, and she would do well to remember that prosaic fact.

Nevertheless, when the captain placed an arm about her shoulders and drew her firmly against his chest, Cynthia raised her face for his kiss without the slightest hesitation.

She could make-believe a little, could she not? she thought, abandoning herself to the delight of her husband's embrace.

Towards the end of November, the captain rode the twelve miles into Guildford one chilly morning to look over some young rams offered by a local sheep breeder. Sir William Greenley was noted in the district for the quality of his animals, Lady Cynthia had informed him the day before at the breakfast table.

"We are lucky to get the chance to obtain some of Sir William's stock," she explained enthusiastically, "and I plan to drive into Guildford with the steward tomorrow to make sure I get first choice." She had smiled at him in that open, radiant way she had, and Brian had marveled, as he did every day since his marriage to Lady Cynthia, at the stroke of fortune that had placed her in his path. She had filled out a little, he noticed, and her skin had a healthy glow to it that reminded him of a freshly picked apple, crisp, sweet-smelling, and infinitely tempting.

And he was definitely in a position to know just how tempting his Cynthia could be, he mused, smiling back at her until she blushed and lowered those mesmerizing sea-green eyes of hers. Not a single night had passed since his arrival at Milford Hall that he had not visited his wife's bed and been so well received that he had often lingered until the cocks began to crow in the stable-yard.

"Hugh Hurley is a distant cousin to Sir William's first wife," Cynthia continued, spreading her toast with a thick layer of strawberry jam. "He took the position of steward to Lonsdale's father nearly twenty years ago, but he has kept up the connection, and that is how I heard that Sir William is going to auction off a surplus of young rams next week."

"I do not care to have you driving over to Guildford in an open carriage in this weather, Cynthia," the captain remarked, still captivated by the rosy glow of his wife's cheeks. "If you think you can trust me, my dear, I would prefer to go myself. If Hurley goes with me, I am not likely to buy a ewe for a ram."

He smiled, not entirely sure how his wife would accept this suggestion, which he had been careful not to phrase as an order. In the past month, Brian had made the rather alarming discovery that Lady Cynthia was possessed of far more business sense than he usually gave a woman credit for. Not only did she manage the Lonsdale stables, which had grown over the years into a considerable enterprise, but she also supervised the estate, which, while not large compared to the sprawling Sheffield holdings, was more profitable than small estates usually were, thanks—Brian was beginning to realize—to Lady Cynthia's astute management of her land. On top of this, which the captain considered more than sufficient to keep any landowner busy the year round, Lady Cynthia was in frequent communication with her London man of business regarding her shipping and import interests, and her dealings on the London Exchange. Brian had been both impressed and vaguely intimidated.

Lady Cynthia had been amused rather than offended by the captain's offer to go sheep-trading in her stead. "I must say that Hurley knows a good deal more about sheep than I do," she confessed, "and you can depend upon his judgment entirely."

The captain had been particularly pleased when his wife accepted his offer to spare her the cold drive into Guildford, which, added to his gratification at her request that he take an active part in the running of the stables, went a long way towards making Brian feel that his decision to wed the rich widow had been fortunate indeed.

So, in spite of the chill November wind, the captain had ridden to the market town in excellent spirits, accompanied by the garrulous steward, who was only too pleased to entertain his new master with local gossip. The captain concluded his business with Sir William in good order, amused at the bluff old gentleman's uninhibited tongue.

"Glad to see her ladyship is taking an interest in upgrading her flocks," Sir William remarked as soon as Hurley had made the introductions. "She has done wonders with the horses over the years, but the old viscount would not let her have any say-so with the flocks. Poor judgment, if you ask me. Bought his breeding stock over in Wiltshire instead of coming to me, as Hugh here advised him to. Isn't that right, Hugh?" The baronet obviously did not expect a response, for he continued with barely a pause.

"Why go all the way over to Salisbury when everyone knows my lambs take first place at all the county fairs for fifty miles around? Have for years. But that was his lordship for you. No flair for breeding." He paused and glanced at the captain from under his bushy brows, a speculative twinkle in his eyes. "Glad to see her ladyship has done better for herself this time, Captain," he said bluntly. "Let us hope the breeding at Milford Hall is not limited to sheep and horses, young man. It is high time that gel dropped a young'un of her own, if you get my meaning, sir."

"How could I not do so, sir," Brian replied, not a whit discomforted by the baronet's pointed reminder of what was expected of him. Lady Cynthia had made no secret of her desire for a family, he recalled. It had been the primary reason for her wish to marry again, had it not? And in his nightly enjoyment of his wife, Brian had forgotten that he himself wished for a son to carry his name, he thought, recalling his own ambition to outperform his half-brother.

"I shall keep it in mind, Sir William," he assured the baronet, a remark that seemed to tickle the old man's fancy, for he let out a huge crack of laughter and thumped the captain on the back most heartily.

After leaving Greenley Manor, the captain rode back into Guildford satisfied that he had made at least one friend in the neighborhood. He was feeling so pleased with himself that as they approached the Blue Swan Inn, Brian impulsively suggested to Hurley that they should stop for a tankard of the inn's famous ale before leaving Guildford.

As they entered the inn yard, the captain noticed a spanking team of flashy chestnuts harnessed to a yellow curricle standing in the shelter of a giant oak. Something about the equipage seemed familiar, but he did not recall where he had seen it before until he entered the public taproom and came face-to-face with the Marquess of Monroyal.

The marquess raised an eyebrow with calculated insolence. "Well met, Sheffield," he drawled, rising with feline grace and extending a manicured hand. "And you, too, Hurley," he added, casting a languid glance at the burly steward, who touched his forelock respectfully and moved off to chat with two farmers of his acquaintance.

The captain glowered at the impeccably dressed marquess, feeling very countrified in his worn buckskins and serviceable coat.

"My lord," he said, nodding stiffly. "What brings you down to the wilds of Surrey in this weather?"

"You do not sound overjoyed to see me, Captain," the marquess remarked, his voice betraying his amusement. He waved imperiously at the host. "Bring us another tankard, Henderson, will you." As the innkeeper hurried away to do his bidding, the marquess turned back to regard the captain through hooded eyes.

"To answer your question, my dear boy, I am on my way to visit my cousin." He smiled slightly, but Brian noticed that the amusement did not reach his eyes, which remained darkly gray and enigmatic. "And you, too, naturally, Sheffield. I have been invited for some pigeon shooting in Hampshire, and I never pass so close to Milford Hall without stopping for a day or two." His smile widened but did not warm appreciably. "Cynthia always insists upon it. We are quite the best of friends, you know."

Brian pulled himself together. He must not allow this conceited, arrogant popinjay to provoke him into losing his temper, he thought. The news that the disreputable marquess was on his way to Milford Hall angered him, but there was little he could do about it if Cynthia welcomed her cousin, as he was sure she would. But nowhere was it written that he had to like the connection, nor that he had to be polite to a man he distrusted and disliked.

"Really?" he said softly. "How odd. I would imagine a female might prefer someone nearer her own age. How many years are there between you, my lord? Must be ten if I am not mistaken."

The marquess's smile thinned noticeably, and his eyes took on the coldness of slate. "Then you imagine wrong, my friend," he drawled. "I give her no more than six. My cousin will be thirty next April—but perhaps you already know that, Captain?"

No, Brian had not known it, and evidently the marquess had known that the captain was ignorant of his wife's birthday, for his smile returned, this time perilously close to a smirk. "Ah, perhaps not? Then I should warn you, Captain. Cynthia, like many of her sex, is highly sentimental and sets great store by these anniversaries. I myself have never been able to understand the attraction of celebrating the passage of time so tenaciously, but females being what they are, we must humor them. Would you not agree, Captain?"

Brian would rather have cut his tongue out than give the marquess the satisfaction of agreeing with him on anything, so he merely shrugged and picked up his mug of ale. The realization, brought home to him by his lordship's taunting words, that this Town Beau knew far more about his Cynthia than he did himself caused the captain to grit his teeth in frustration. Even after a month of intimacies shared nightly with his wife, Brian did not know, had not made it his business to find out, had shown no interest in this side of Cynthia's life. He made a silent vow to mend his ways that very evening as soon as they were alone together.

He finished off his ale and set the tankard down with a satisfying smack. "I am sure Cynthia will be glad to see you, my lord," he said, gamely attempting to appear polite, although he could hear the latent hostility in his own voice.

"Oh, I am quite sure she will, Captain," the marquess purred in his cultivated voice, which grated on Brian's nerves like a discordant note. "And by the way, Sheffield," he continued, tossing a silver coin to the host and standing up. "Have you no other interesting news to impart, I wonder? It has been nearly a month since the wedding has it not? I trust you have not been wasting your time in the stables, old man."

If they had been in a less public place, Brian would have liked nothing better than to land a facer on that arrogant nose. But under the interested scrutiny of the innkeeper, he could do nothing but smile thinly and shrug his shoulders again.

"This is hardly the place for that kind of discussion," he said curtly. "You had best ask the lady." With that he turned on his heel and strode out of the inn, calling impatiently for his horse.

Although the captain cut across the fields and through Milford Wood to reach home before his unwelcome guest, he had barely handed over Tom-Boy to one of the under-grooms, when he heard the clatter of racing wheels and the marquess's yellow curricle flashed around the corner of the house and came to a prancing halt in the stable-yard.

As the under-groom led his horse into the stalls, the captain heard a snort of disgust at his elbow, and turned to find Jake Waters staring belligerently at the newcomer.

"So," the old man muttered under his breath, "'is 'igh and mighty lordship is with us again, is 'e? I can tell you one thing, Captain," he said, turning his somber gaze on his new master. "'Tis mighty glad we be around these parts that ye saved 'er ladyship from the likes of 'im." The trainer motioned towards the marquess with his chin. "Afeared we was that she would be taken in by 'is fancy airs and graces. The poor wee lass dinna see what that born devil 'ad in 'is black 'eart. I'd be willing to swear to it, I would, Captain. And it weren't no weddin' bells, if ye ken what I mean, sir, or me name ain't Jake Waters."

With another disgusted snort, the old man ambled off into the stalls, leaving Brian to ponder a puzzling dilemma. What was Lord Monroyal's true relationship with Lady Cynthia? Was he merely the rejected suitor—Lady Halifax's unsuccessful choice for her daughter's second husband? Or was he—and Brian's stomach knotted at the thought—a bastard of the first water, one whose friendly visits to Milford Hall masked the intent to seduce his innocent cousin into the kind of dalliance at which the marquess excelled?

Given his lordship's widespread reputation, the captain was more than willing to believe the latter. The question that bothered him, however, was far more disturbing.

Had the lecherous marquess succeeded in his venture?

Lady Cynthia observed the arrival of the two men from the window of her study, where she had been composing a letter to Mr. Jeremiah Broadstone, her solicitor and man-of-business in London regarding the advisability of increasing her investment in shipping. It had been through Broadstone that Cynthia had made the acquaintance, over six years ago, of Mr. George Walters, a wealthy ship owner with numerous interests in China and India, with whom the late viscount had sporadically conducted business. After James's death, Cynthia had been inclined to drop the association, but a chance meeting with Mr. Walters himself in Mr. Broadstone's London offices had piqued her interest in foreign trading, and she had embarked on several highly profitable ventures under the guidance of the wealthy Cit.

Seeing the two men walking towards the house together reminded Cynthia of the unbridgeable differences between them, particularly in their reactions to her dealings with Mr. Walters. She had hoped, ever since the day she had accepted Captain Sheffield's offer of marriage, that her new husband and the cousin she loved and trusted as a brother might become friends. That had been a vain wish, she thought wryly, for two less compatible characters it would be hard to imagine. Robbie had been unaccountably stuffy about her decision to pursue the affiliation with a Cit, and had expended more effort than he usually did to persuade her to place her money in more respectable investments, such as the Consols. Brian, on the other hand, had been more knowledgeable than she had expected about foreign trading and had encouraged her to follow her instincts.

Cynthia sighed and rose from her desk by the window. She was delighted, as she always was, to see her cousin, but as she ran down the stairs to greet him, she hoped he would avoid those patronizing airs that seemed to be so much a part of his nature.

"Robbie!" she exclaimed as the marquess emerged from the back of the house. "How marvelous to see you again. I hope you intend to stay a few days with us and not go jauntering off on some hunting spree or other." She flung her arms impulsively round her cousin's neck, and as he leaned down to kiss her cheek, Cynthia was suddenly aware that her husband had come up behind the marquess and was staring at her strangely.

Telling herself that it was merely a quirk of her imagination, Cynthia led the way up to the dining room where she had ordered a light nuncheon to be served upon the captain's return.

"You are just in time to eat with us, Robert," she said gaily, taking her place at one end of the table. She looked expectantly at the captain, and was unable to conceal her disappointment when he made his excuses and left them so abruptly that Cynthia turned accusingly to her cousin.

"Whatever have you said to send the captain up into the boughs, Robert?"

"Nothing at all, love," the marquess drawled, helping himself to a thick slice of cold capon and motioning to a footman to cut him some ham from the sideboard.

"I find that hard to believe," Cynthia said, suddenly finding that her appetite had disappeared. If it had been at all possible, she would have left her guest to his own devices and sought out her husband to discover the reason for his churlish behavior. But politeness precluded such a move, and she served herself a small slice of pigeon pie, which she proceeded to toy with absentmindedly.

"I am mortified to think that your husband does not care for me, my dear," the marquess drawled as soon as the footman left to bring up a pot of tea. "But no other explanation presents itself, so what else am I to think?"

"That is the greatest piece of nonsense I have yet to hear," Cynthia replied crossly. "What reason has the captain to dislike you, Robbie? unless you have done something to provoke him, of course."

Lord Monroyal regarded her with faint amusement. "You are a sweet but innocent goose, my pet," he said affectionately. "Cannot you see that the poor man is jealous of my new coat? Which is not surprising when you consider that it was made by Stultz himself only last week. This cut is all the crack, you know, and the captain is not alone in his envy, my dear. Fully half the bucks in London would doubtless share his feelings if they could cast their eyes on this masterpiece." He ran his elegant fingers lovingly down the cunningly fitted lapels of the blue superfine creation.

While Cynthia struggled to find a suitably cutting set-down for this piece of outrageous arrogance, the marquess changed the subject abruptly.

"Are you happy with your soldier, Cynthia?"

His voice was totally devoid of its habitual teasing tone, and Cynthia stared at him for a moment before responding impetuously. "Oh, yes!" she breathed, not caring if her cousin found her unseemly enthusiasm amusing. "Oh, yes, indeed," she repeated dreamily. "I cannot begin to tell you how wonderful he is, Robbie. I m-mean to say . . ." she stammered, her cheeks flaring pinkly at the knowing look in the marquess's gray eyes.

"I can guess very well what you mean, love," he drawled softly. "So I gather the match is to your liking, my sweet?"

"Yes," Cynthia confirmed, concentrating her attention on the half-eaten pigeon pie. "And I have you to thank for it, Robbie. I cannot help but—"

"Nonsense!" the marquess cut in, waving one hand negligently. "No need to thank me, Cousin. It appears that you have turned this young man's fancy into the right channels without any help from me. And although I applaud the effort the captain is evidently putting into the matter, I cannot but wonder why there is still nothing to show for it."

With what Cynthia considered a deliberately provoking gesture, her cousin raised his quizzing-glass and raked her person, pausing significantly on her flat stomach.

Cynthia rose to her feet in a fury. "If you are going to be odious about everything, my lord," she said stiffly, "I shall bid you a quick farewell and a pleasant journey."

Afterwards—her momentary flare of temper pacified by adroit flattery on his part—Cynthia allowed herself to be cajoled into conducting her cousin on a tour of the stables. But her heart was not in it. She found herself unaccountably disturbed by the marquess's oblique reference to her possible barrenness. The subject was one that had not given her any concern, at least none that she would admit to herself. Cynthia had always assumed that becoming *enceinte* was a natural process that—given the proper conditions—would occur as a matter of course. Why then had Robert made it sound unnatural that she did not already find herself in an interesting condition? she wondered uneasily. Never having been in that happy state before, Cynthia was not perfectly sure what to expect. Could the fact that her courses were overdue by two weeks mean anything? She had been overdue before a time or two but nothing had come of it.

She glanced up at her tall, handsome cousin, lounging very much at his ease against Tom-Boy's stall, and wished that she could confide in him. The notion was unthinkable, of course, although he probably knew everything there was to know about such matters. Perhaps she should tell the captain, she mused, but Cynthia shrank from raising false hopes, particularly in her own heart. Perhaps if her courses had not resumed by Christmas time, she would speak to her mother about it. She would also be able to tell her husband, she thought, rejoicing at the possibility of sharing such joy.

The marquess's amused voice cut into her meditations. "You have not heard a single word I have said, Cynthia," he said accusingly.

Cynthia blushed. "Oh, yes I did, Robert," she protested, moving on to another stall. "We were discussing the prices my geldings might bring in the spring sale."

"What a bouncer, love. I disremember hearing you mention any spring sale." He sauntered up to stand beside her at Merrylegs's stall. The roan nibbled playfully at the sleeve of Stultz's fashionable coat, but the marquess did not seem to notice. "Is something troubling you, Cynthia?" he demanded, his voice for once entirely serious.

"No, of course not, silly," she responded without hesitation. "Everything is wonderful." She smiled affectionately. Trust Robbie to sense that all was not well, at least not well enough to be called wonderful as she had just tried to do.

That evening, Cynthia discovered that things were even less wonderful than she had imagined, when she waited and waited in the wide bed for her husband's nightly appearance.

That evening the captain did not come.

Neither did he come to her on the following night. Or the next.

It was not until three whole days after Lord Monroyal had taken his leave of them and driven his yellow curricle off down the drive behind his flashy chestnuts, that Cynthia's husband opened the door to her chamber and stepped inside.

It nearly broke her heart when he came over to the bed and peeled down the covers, just as he had on their first night together. The hunger in his eyes was there, too, and his voice was as husky as ever when he repeated the same words.

"I have a remarkably beautiful wife."

But he did not smile, and Cynthia could not stand it. With a little sob of despair she rolled away from him, her eyes filling with all the tears she had not shed for him during the past six lonely nights.

Instantly she felt the bed sink under his weight and his arms come around her, holding her so fiercely against his lean body that she wondered that her bones did not crack.

"Please, Cynthia," he murmured against her ear. "Please, sweetling, do not cry."

She shuddered as he buried his face in the curve of her neck, and slowly Cynthia felt herself relax into the warmth of his embrace, until the chill of the past six nights dissipated, and her pulses began to hum in response to his urgent caresses.

He took her quickly this time, quickly and forcefully. But Cynthia was more than ready for him and reveled in this indisputable evidence of her husband's need for her. In the absence of love, she thought later as she lay cradled in his arms, listening to the pounding of his heart, she must make do with passion. If she could keep her husband's passion alive, keep alive his physical need for her, surely in time the miracle would happen? And then she would have a child to love. Perhaps several children, she thought, smiling into the darkness. Someone to love openly, without reservation, with all her heart. Without hiding the need for love deep inside her, as she must endeavor to do with this man, who imagined himself wed to a wife who wanted only a child from him. A child in exchange for a fortune, of course.

She could not, would not ask for more, Cynthia vowed, slowly drifting off into sleep in the arms of a man who had already touched her heart as no other ever had.

And no other ever would, she thought drowsily.

CHAPTER ELEVEN

Christmas Fiasco

Two weeks after Lord Monroyal had left Milford Hall, Lady Cynthia allowed herself to believe that the miracle had happened. Never before had she missed two courses in a row, and as the days passed, she could no longer doubt that she had finally been blessed.

Annette was the first to guess her mistress's secret, but although the abigail's confirmation of her suspicions gave Cynthia confidence, she yearned to share her joy with her husband. Yet a vague feeling of unease held her back.

Every morning when she awoke after a night of passion, Cynthia told herself that today she would do it. Had not her relationship with the captain returned to the level of comfort she had enjoyed before her cousin's visit? she asked herself. Had he not resumed his nightly visits to her bed? Had not his passion grown in intensity rather than diminished? But still Cynthia hesitated. Occasionally she felt her husband's gaze linger on her speculatively, and once or twice she had surprised a strange look in his eyes that had alarmed her. So she knew—although she refused to admit it even to herself—that all was not as wonderful as she had claimed between them.

One morning, no longer able to stand the anguish of keeping her joy bottled up, she sat down in her study and dashed off a note to her cousin. It was true that he would find out soon enough when the family gathered at Halifax Park for their annual Christmas celebrations, but her need to share her joy with Robbie was so intense that Cynthia could not resist dropping a hint about the surprise she had in store for him.

It was only after the letter had been sealed with a wafer and given to Turpin to send off to the village, that Cynthia wondered if perhaps her impulsive gesture had not been misguided. Perhaps she should have written to her mother as well, she thought, although Cynthia knew that Lady Halifax was not likely to return from her annual visit to her aging parents in Scotland until just before Christmas. She picked up the pen again and drew a fresh sheet towards her. After dipping the pen in the ink for the second time without setting a single word down, Cynthia laid it aside impatiently.

The captain's voice from the doorway made her jump. "Still writing letters, my dear?" he asked, strolling up to stand beside her.

Cynthia waved at the blank paper and smiled up at him. He looked marvelous today, she thought, as he did every day after a morning spent with Waters at the stables. Her husband was really an attractive man, she realized with a start. His chestnut hair tousled and his blue eyes dancing with enthusiasm gave him the air of a much younger man. What more could a woman want? Her smile broadened.

"I had wanted to write to my mother, but I seem to have left it so late that we will probably arrive at Halifax Park before my letter." She rose and, linking her arm in her husband's, walked with him down the hall to the dining room where a light nuncheon was laid for them.

"Looking forward to seeing your parents again, are you?" he said laconically, taking his place at the head of the table.

"Oh, yes," she replied. "And all my aunts and uncles and cousins, too, of course." The moment she mentioned cousin, Cynthia could have bitten her tongue, for the captain's eyes lost their warmth.

"I can well imagine it," he said briefly and gave his attention to the cold mutton Turpin had placed before him.

After a lengthy silence, Cynthia tried to regain that easy camaraderie with the captain that so often of late seemed to slip through her fingers. "I am sorry that your mother, the dowager countess, will be unable to join us in Hampshire for Christmas, Captain," she remarked rather stiffly. "Your sister Caroline seemed eager to do so when I met her in London, but it is unlikely that your mother will allow her to come alone all the way down from Shropshire."

"Highly unlikely," came the curt response. After a pause, he added almost brusquely, "And since my mother dotes on her granddaughters—all five of them—you may give up any notion of tempting her to visit us, my lady. Unless, of course, there is something you have not yet told me." The captain stopped abruptly. "But I was forgetting, my dear," he continued with cutting directness, "your so amiable cousin made it his business to remark on the absence of anything of that nature. So we have nothing with which to tempt my mother down from the north."

Cynthia went quite still with shock. It was several moments before the enormity of what the captain had said sunk into her dazed mind. She could not believe it. She did not *want* to believe it. Those cruel words could not have come from the man who was in a fair way to stealing her heart away.

"I cannot believe that Robert would be so indiscreet," she managed to say through stiff lips.

"Then you do not know your depraved cousin quite as well as you thought you did," came the cynical response.

Through the latter part of this exchange, the captain had not so much as glanced at her, but suddenly he looked up straight into her eyes, and Cynthia experienced the curious sensation of gazing at a stranger. Her husband's eyes had turned so dark, they reminded her of the heavy, gray clouds that heralded a snowstorm, and she shivered at the cool remoteness she saw in them.

Now was the time to tell him, she told herself distractedly, her mind spinning with conflicting emotions. Tell him now, immediately, to make that coolness disappear and the blue warmth return to bathe her wounded heart in its comforting heat. But her lips would not move to speak the words she longed to utter. Had the captain's eyes shown the slightest hint of softening, had his lips relaxed into the merest shadow of a smile, Cynthia might have found the courage to speak.

But nothing of the sort happened. After a moment, the captain's attention returned to his plate, and he served himself another thick slice of ham.

Defeated, Cynthia rose unsteadily to her feet, leaving her food untouched on her plate. She moved out of the room in a trance, holding herself together rigidly least her control crumble and she make a foolish spectacle of herself. It was only when she reached the safety of her bedchamber that the tears came. Tears for herself, for the child she carried, and for the man whose strange moods threatened to destroy her dreams of happiness.

At least one decision had been removed from her shoulders, Cynthia thought as she slipped out of her gown and crawled between the covers. Now she knew that there was no question of sharing her good news with her husband. She would wait until they were at Halifax Park, where, with her mother to support her, she could tell the captain that he was to be a father without fear of provoking one of these strange moods she could not understand.

No sooner had Cynthia closed the door behind her than the captain regretted his hostile outburst. What had provoked him to speak with such bitterness to his wife he could not tell, but the ugly words rang in his ears for the rest of the afternoon. If only he could bring himself to seek her out and beg her forgiveness, he thought, striding down to the stables to seek solace in working with a promising gray mare that had, according to the report of the assistant trainer who had taken her out yesterday, refused the water jump three times that morning.

Brian drove himself tirelessly, and had the satisfaction of seeing the mare overcome her fear of that particular jump and of starting her on the even more dangerous stone fences in a neighboring field. He took his mug of tea in the large, warm tack room with the stable-hands and by the time he returned to the house to change for dinner, Brian was fully prepared to make his apologies to Lady Cynthia and beg her to excuse his churlishness.

When he entered the drawing room an hour later, his step light at the prospect of seeing Cynthia's sweet smile reappear, an apology ready on his lips, the captain learned from Turpin that he would be deprived of the opportunity to excuse his deplorable behavior.

"Her ladyship will not be down for dinner this evening, sir," the butler informed him while serving the captain's sherry. "Her abigail informs me that her ladyship is feeling a mite feverish and has retired early."

The captain was not deceived by Turpin's toneless voice, and not for a moment did he believe that the real reason for Cynthia's indisposition was unknown to her butler. The uneasy realization that his wife's servants might judge him and find him wanting caused the succulent roast partridge, which he had shot himself yesterday afternoon on a hunting forage into Milford Wood with the gamekeeper, turn to ashes in his mouth. And that was part of the problem, he thought, eating his way doggedly through Cook's tender broiled duck with pickled mushrooms, and vegetable marrow stuffed with minced veal. He still regarded the staff as Lady Cynthia's servants and often felt that they had yet to accept him as the master of Milford Hall.

The captain refused the trifle and waved away the port, returning to the drawing room for a glass of Madeira. The room felt oddly empty without Cynthia's presence, the rosewood pianoforte she was wont to play for him in the evenings accusingly silent. It occurred to Brian with something of a shock that he had grown accustomed to his wife's company, particularly in the evenings, when the prospect of escorting her up to bed hung like a secret promise of joy between them. And yes, he had to admit, Cynthia had brought him more joy than he had anticipated from this marriage based strictly on convenience. He had already benefited greatly from the union. Not only had marriage to Lady Cynthia brought him land and fortune, but it had allowed him to get away from the army and back to his first love, horses. Yes, he had achieved his dearest ambition, but had Cynthia achieved hers? he wondered. All she had asked of him was a family to bring fulfillment to her life. And had he given her a child? he asked himself, uncomfortable with the negative response that rose to mind. But he would, Brian vowed. He would do everything possible to keep his side of the unusual marriage contract he had made with her.

On impulse, the captain decided to take his tea with his wife. He was suddenly impatient to be with her again, to hear her voice and see her smile up at him in that sweet way she had. After instructing Turpin to have the tea-tray sent upstairs, Brian almost ran up to scratch on Cynthia's door.

The door was opened a crack by a truculent Annette.

"Her ladyship is resting, Captain," the abigail informed him curtly, and Brian felt that had she dared, Annette would have slammed the door in his face.

"Who is it, Annette?" he heard Cynthia's voice inquire and, without waiting further, the captain pushed past the servant and entered the room.

"I thought perhaps you might invite me to drink my tea with you, love," he said mildly, dismissing the abigail with a curt gesture. "It is lonely downstairs without you," he added softly, as soon as they were alone.

Brian saw conflicting emotions flit across his wife's face and cursed himself for causing her distress. The initial flash of alarm had been quickly repressed, followed by surprise and something else he could not identify. Whatever the expression on Cynthia's face might have been, it was not the welcoming smile he had unconsciously been hoping for. And why should she be happy to see him? he asked himself dourly. He had been nothing if not uncouth to her earlier, and even now felt as though his presence in her chamber was intrusive and unwarranted. The notion that he was unwanted made him uncomfortable, and Brian vowed to restore himself to Cynthia's good graces. It surprised him considerably to discover that his wife's approval mattered to him.

"I have asked Turpin to bring up the tea-tray, but I can have it put in the sitting room if you prefer, my dear."

The captain was further surprised to hear the hint of pleading in his voice, a note he had definitely not intended to allow there. He glanced at the practically untouched food on his wife's supper tray.

"You have eaten very little, Cynthia," he said, glad of the chance to regain the initiative. "Perhaps we should ask Cook to send up some trifle. I know that is one of your favorites, and you must keep up your strength, you know."

Was it his imagination, or had his wife's green eyes suddenly filled with apprehension? Brian wondered. She seemed pale, and abruptly he was overwhelmed by a strong desire to protect her from the world at large and from his own unverified suspicions in particular. Impulsively he sat on the edge of the bed and clasped her hand. It was cold and lay limply unresponsive in his.

"I am a perfect brute to disturb you when you are feeling poorly, Cynthia," he said huskily, raising her fingers to his lips and then holding them against his cheek to warm them. Yes, he thought disgustedly, he was a brute to suspect this beautiful creature of consorting lewdly with her rakish cousin. Was it his wife's fault that her close relative was indisputably a libertine of the worst sort? Did Monroyal's depravity make Lady Cynthia guilty, too? So what if she evidently cared for the rogue far more than he deserved? She had, after all, chosen to marry him, Brian reminded himself, a younger son with very little else but his youth to recommend him. Had Cynthia wanted rank, a title, and a secure position among the *ton*, she would have accepted her cousin, would she not? But she had not done so, and the thought cheered him.

If truth be told, he mused, watching his wife's sea-green eyes fill with shadows, the Fates had smiled upon him the day they had placed Lady Cynthia within his grasp. He smiled wryly at the woman who had become his wife under such unusual circumstances and knew in his heart that had he been granted a choice, he could not have made a more suitable selection.

Cynthia blushed charmingly, her pale face coming to life before his eyes. Brian had the irresistible urge to kiss her, but before he could do so, there was a scratching at the door. The captain rose quickly and took the tray from Turpin, dismissing the butler and setting the tray down on the buhl table beside his wife's bed.

He could not recall ever having served tea for a female before, but Brian found it oddly satisfying to go through the normally feminine ritual of pouring for his wife. His movements felt awkward, and he spilled some of the brew on the embroidered tray cloth, but Cynthia's smile when she accepted the cup from his hands gladdened his heart. For the first time since he had made his vows, the captain felt at peace with his decision to accept Lady Cynthia's unusual proposal.

She was his, he thought, surprised at the possessiveness that surged through him. And if she could smile at him thus, surely his Cynthia must care for him a little?

The journey to Halifax Park was accomplished a week later without mishap, although after changing horses at the Rose and Crown in Winchester, they encountered an icy rain that dogged the Lonsdale traveling chaise all the way south to Eastleigh where they branched off the few miles to the family seat of the marquesses of Halifax.

Cynthia had mixed feelings about returning to her childhood home with her second husband. For so many years she had come to these family celebrations as the Viscountess Lonsdale in the company of the dour-faced James, who no sooner arrived than he would closet himself with Lord Halifax and any other elderly guests interested in affairs of state and argue for hours on the futility of current government policies.

This year she came as Lady Cynthia Sheffield, and Cynthia felt a deep contentment that she had never, even in the early years of their marriage, been able to feel with Lonsdale. And she knew that she owed this inner happiness to the captain, who had helped her to realize her dream of motherhood. The only cloud on her happiness was the nagging reminder that the captain did not yet know about the impending event.

Cynthia glanced up at her husband as he handed her out of the carriage and noted that his mouth was set in a grim line. Was he dreading this family reunion? she wondered, suddenly wishing that she had confided her secret joy to him. Perhaps she would not wait until Christmas Eve after all, she decided. The captain had a right to know before anyone else, even before her own mother perhaps, that he was to be a father. Yes, she thought, suddenly aware that she had been selfish not to share her early suspicions with him. She would tell him this very night as soon as they retired. This impromptu decision lifted a weight from her heart, and Cynthia smiled shyly up at him, rejoicing in the faint answering smile that crinkled the corners of his eyes and banished their coolness.

"Glad to be home again, Cynthia?" His voice was casual, but Cynthia sensed a reticence there.

"This is not my home," she responded firmly. "My home is in Surrey with you." Cynthia had no idea she was going to say anything quite so revealing, but as soon as the words were out, she was glad they had been said. They needed to be said, she thought, conscious of the color rising in her cheeks.

"I am glad to hear you say so, my dear," he said after regarding her for several moments in silence.

She wanted him to say more, something that would confirm the tenuous emotional bond she needed to feel between them. But he did not, and soon they were interrupted by her mother's butler, who threw open the great front door and came bustling down the steps to greet them.

"Welcome home, milady," he said in that deep, sonorous voice Cynthia remembered so well from her childhood. "We are glad to have you back at Halifax Park again, milady."

As they followed the butler's portly figure up the shallow steps, it occurred to Cynthia that Morgan had spoken as though she still lived here, thus giving the lie to her own assurances to the captain. She glanced at him and saw that his smile had faded.

"Her ladyship is in the Blue Saloon, milady," the butler said, leading the way up the wide marble staircase and throwing open an elaborately carved door to announce them.

Cynthia did not realize just how apprehensive she had been until she found herself glancing around the room without encountering the familiar tall figure of her cousin Robert. Then she let out a sigh and came forward to embrace her mother and her Aunt Sophy, who sat together, as they usually did, on a settee before the roaring fire.

"My dear Cynthia," Lady Halifax scolded, regarding her daughter with a frown on her beautiful face. "I hope you are not coming down with something, child. You look positively peaked, love. Do you not think so, Sophy?"

"Nonsense!" Aunt Sophy said bracingly, enfolding her in an affectionate hug. "Our dear Cynthia is looking quite ravishing as usual. You fuss too much, Elizabeth. The sweet child is doubtless weary from the journey. Morgan," she turned peremptorily to the butler, hovering in the doorway, "be so good as to send up a pot of fresh tea. That will set everything to rights again." She turned with a gracious smile to draw the captain into the circle around the fire.

Cynthia felt the telltale flush stain her cheeks and wished her mother had been rather less observant. The momentary embarrassment quickly passed when her two cousins came forward to smother her with hugs and pelt her with questions about Milford Hall. Cynthia was grateful when Lady Constance drew her down beside her on a small settee and demanded, in her quiet way, to know whether her cousin was happy.

"You must be happy, Cynthia," the younger girl observed shyly. "I cannot recall ever seeing you in such looks."

Cynthia glanced across at her husband and once again marveled at her good fortune. Yes, she was certainly happy, she thought, watching the captain's mouth curl into a smile as he listened to something her mother was saying. Not as happy as she would be that evening, naturally, after she had shared her secret joy with the father of the petit paquet she carried within her. Cynthia smiled gently to herself in anticipation and turned her gaze back to her cousin.

"Yes, I am certainly happy, Constance," she admitted candidly. "The captain is everything I could possibly wish for, and I only hope that one day soon a gentleman will come along who will make you happy, too, love."

Lady Constance smiled and shook her head ruefully, but before she could reply, the door burst open and Lord Halifax strode in followed by four young lads who immediately converged upon Lady Cynthia and vied with one another boisterously for her attention.

"George!" Lady Constance scolded mildly, "you are getting too old to behave like your madcap brother William. It is high time you learned to comport yourself like a gentleman, dear. Whatever will Cousin Cynthia think of you?"

"Pooh!" the tall, gangly youth replied scornfully. "Will is the only madcap in this family. Besides Letty, that is." This incendiary remark caused a heated argument among the siblings that drew Lady Letitia away from her mother's side, where she had been hanging on the captain's every word.

"That is exactly the kind of nonsense one might expect from you, George," she declared scathingly, an observation that drew a chorus of jeers from her younger brothers and an ominous scowl from George.

"Do not imagine for a moment that you are the chief attraction, my dear," Lord Halifax murmured in his daughter's ear as he embraced her heartily. "Your young cousins are all agog to meet the captain. They have been impossible to handle since they learned that we were to have another real live soldier in our midst."

"Is Tony to come home after all then?" Cynthia demanded, her spirits lifting at the thought of seeing her only brother again. Viscount Holt had been unable to get leave to attend her wedding, but had promised to wheedle a few days off to join the family at the end of December.

"Aye," the marquess replied with a sigh, and Cynthia knew that her father was thinking not of his eldest son, but of Harry, his youngest, who had been lost in July 1812 in the battle of Salamanca, serving in the cavalry under Lieutenant-General Sir Stapleton Cotton. She gave her father an extra hug, suddenly determined to name her child after her lost brother if she were blessed with a boy.

"Where is Robbie?" she asked, under cover of the clamor her four young cousins were raising in their eagerness to wheedle war stories out of Captain Sheffield.

"Your cousin Robert is a guest at a house-party down in Devon, but he promised to be here in good time and not arrive on Christmas Eve as he did last year.

As if on cue, the doors of the Blue Saloon swung open and Morgan's deeply sonorous voice announced the Marquess of Monroyal. All eyes swiveled in his direction and Cynthia could not repress a smile at the quelling effect—quite intentional she was sure—her cousin's entrance caused on the company gathered in her mother's saloon. The marquess paused on the threshold and raised his jeweled quizzing-glass to survey the room through a grotesquely enlarged eye. Cynthia had to admit that only a gentleman of her cousin's address could have reduced the whole room to silence with this outrageous performance, including his four boisterous half-brothers who had ceased their chatter to stare at him in admiration mixed with a fair amount of awe.

"By Jove, Robbie," the more daring of them breathed reverently, "that is a bang-up coat you have there. Do you suppose Weston would make one just like it for me?"

"No, I do not, brat," the marquess drawled, returning the quizzing-glass to his waistcoat pocket and sauntering across the room towards his hostess. "Weston does not waste his talents on halflings, George, so put the notion out of your head."

Cynthia could not but agree that the perfectly fitted coat in blue Bath wool, which defined her cousin's muscular shoulders without a wrinkle, and the pale gray kerseymere pantaloons clinging to his thighs with revealing intimacy would certainly be wasted on George's gangling, half-grown frame. At fifteen, the eldest of Robert's half-brothers was still a boy, an obstacle that did not prevent the lad from attempting to imitate the cut of his idol's clothes and the elegance of the marquess's cravats.

With a half smile on her lips, Cynthia turned back to Constance. "George will not be content until he can turn himself out like his brother," she remarked, watching as the marquess made his bow to Lady Halifax and placed an affectionate kiss on Lady Sophia's pink cheek.

Constance sighed. "Yes, and more's the pity," she replied. "And I do believe that Gerald is showing distressing signs of following George's lead in aping Robert's every sartorial extravagance. Only yesterday he confided to me his ardent wish to own a quizzing-glass. Next thing you know, they will want to start using snuff as well."

"Thirteen is rather young to start that odious habit," Cynthia said with a laugh. "And so I shall tell them if you like."

"I wish you would. But I doubt it will make an impression. If you ask me, the boys would do far better taking the captain as their model. Robert is all the crack, of course, but I sometimes wish he were less of the peacock."

Cynthia pulled her gaze away from the exquisite figure of her cousin and sought out her husband. She found him standing listening to something Lord Halifax was saying, but his blue eyes were fixed on her face. The expression was not reassuring, and Cynthia's spirits faltered when he failed to acknowledge her smile.

After their first brief greeting, which Cynthia later realized was rather warmer than she felt was prudent, she made a point of staying as far away from her cousin as she could. The marquess made no attempt to seek her out, but Cynthia caught his amused gaze resting on her several times as she sat assisting her mother in dispensing tea and cakes to the many neighbors who came to pay their respects to the new Lady Sheffield. Cynthia wondered impatiently how long it would be before she could slip away to rest before dinner. Her newly married state had caused more comment than she liked and a particularly blunt remark from old Lady Biddleton, who demanded to know—in the loud whisper she affected every time she attempted to be discreet—when they could expect a happy announcement from their dearest Lady Cynthia.

Cynthia felt her cheeks burn and forced herself to smile as she murmured something appropriate, but she was acutely conscious of the marquess's sardonically raised eyebrow, although she dared not meet his gaze directly. Her husband's eyes were upon her, too, she knew instinctively, as were those of half her mother's guests. She sighed gratefully when her aunt Sophy deftly turned Lady Biddleton's chatter into a less personal channel, but her relief was short-lived.

"By Jove," ten-year-old William exclaimed suddenly in awed tones, one of Cook's gooseberry tarts suspended midway between his plate and his mouth, "is Cousin Cynthia starting her nursery *already*?"

In the dead silence that followed this highly improper pronouncement, not even Aunt Sophy seemed to find words to cover her youngest son's abysmal faux pas.

It fell to Peter, dredging up the wisdom of his twelve years, to jab his brother viciously in the ribs. "What a cabbage-head you are, Will," he hissed contemptuously. "What else would she be doing, anyway?"

Lady Biddleton let out a shriek and groped in her reticule for her vinaigrette. Lady Halifax rose precipitously to assist her elderly guest to the nearest chair, while Aunt Sophy swooped down on her two youngest and propelled them forcefully from the room.

Ignoring the hubbub around her, Cynthia gazed determinedly into her empty tea-cup and wondered what Lady Biddleton's reaction would be if she blurted out the truth, here in front of everyone. Would the old Tabby really swoon away as she was threatening to do even now? But such a course was unthinkable, naturally. She had yet to inform the captain. He would hardly take kindly to learning of his impending fatherhood in front of so many strangers. And her family and neighbors still were strangers to him, Cynthia reminded herself.

Abruptly she found herself wishing that they had stayed at Milford Hall. Idly she rearranged the tea-leaves in the bottom of her cup by swirling the dregs about. What did the future hold for her? she wondered. Would the captain welcome their child as much as she did?

She felt a light touch on her shoulder and looked up into her husband's anxious eyes.

"You look pale, my dear," he said, bending over her until she felt his breath on her face. "I suggest you rest for a while before it is time to dress for dinner. I would go with you, but I am recruited to examine a litter of spaniels down in the stables with the boys."

A wave of happiness washed over her and Cynthia suddenly felt much better. Then the full import of the captain's words sank in, and she blushed. But no, she told herself firmly, the captain was merely being kind. He could not mean what she had, for a fleeting moment, imagined he had implied. Not at this time in the afternoon, surely? She felt herself blush at the immodesty of her thoughts.

She lowered her eyes. "I do feel rather tired," she said hesitantly. "I believe I shall take your advice."

And so she had escaped from the noise of the Blue Saloon and gone up to her chamber, where Annette had removed her gown, brushed out her hair, and tucked her into the big four-poster.

She must have slept for over an hour, Cynthia realized when she opened her eyes, for she noticed that Annette had placed a branch of candles on the small mantel above the crackling fire and pulled the heavy curtains across the dark windows. She felt cozy and secure. The December darkness had been shut out, and one of the servants had built up the fire while she slept until it cast a rosy glow over the counterpane.

Cynthia sat up and glanced at the ormolu clock on the oval rosewood table by her bed. She gasped when she saw the time and swung her legs from under the covers. Annette should have been up ten minutes ago to help her dress for dinner. Slipping into her blue brocade robe, Cynthia picked up the brush and tugged it through her tangled curls, wincing as the bristles caught in the knots.

The door opened abruptly behind her and Cynthia turned, a reproach for her abigail ready on her lips. But the scolding died in her throat, for it was the captain who stood there, his face set in granite lines, his cold blue eyes raking her angrily.

Cynthia quailed as he slammed the door and strode across the room to stand behind her, fists balled at his sides.

"Why in Hades did you not tell me?" The words seemed to escape with difficulty from between the captain's clenched teeth, as if they were spoken under intense stress. "Or did you plan it this way, Cynthia?" he continued harshly. "Did you imagine I would find it amusing to be quizzed by that bloody popinjay, in that supercilious manner he affects, about an event I could neither confirm nor deny? Answer me, damn you," he growled when Cynthia rose unsteadily to her feet and gazed at him in horror. "I would rather not believe it of you, Cynthia, but I can only do so if you tell me there is no truth to this rumor your cousin is bandying about."

Cynthia gripped the hairbrush with fingers that shook visibly. "What are you talking about?" she murmured, hoping against hope that Robbie had not betrayed her and done the unspeakable.

"Do not pretend innocence, my dear," the captain said with an unpleasant smile. "You know very well what I am talking about."

"What is this rumor of Robbie's that has made you fly into the boughs?"

"Do not play me for a fool, Cynthia," the captain said in a dangerously quiet voice. "Is the rumor correct?"

"Unless you tell me what rumor it is, I can hardly answer you," Cynthia replied with a hint of exasperation. "What did my cousin tell you?"

The captain glared at her for several moments, and Cynthia felt her spirits sink. She could no longer deceive herself. Her darling Robbie had committed another careless, thoughtless act and betrayed her secret to the one man he should never have told. Not that she had actually told her cousin in so many words, she remembered, but Robbie was quite capable of reading between the lines and the notion of teasing the captain would be quite irresistible to a man of her cousin's jaded sense of humor.

"You would not wish to hear his exact, tasteless words, my dear," the captain said shortly, "but in essence he congratulated me on your condition. And then he had the effrontery to laugh when he saw he was before me with this interesting piece of news."

Cynthia could well imagine how her cousin must have laughed. When she got her hands on him, she thought viciously, she would tell him exactly what his careless amusement had cost her. But in the meantime, she must try to brush through this uncomfortable interview as lightly as possible.

"I did not tell him—" she began, but was cut short by an explosive exclamation from the captain.

"Then it is true?" he demanded, looking, if possible, more ferocious than ever. "And Monroyal knew it?"

"No," Cynthia said quickly. "He may have guessed, of course, but all I wrote was that I had a special secret to share with him on Christmas Eve." She paused and continued quickly when the captain's mouth drew into a thin, foreboding line. "And with the rest of the family, too, naturally," she said, hoping that she had not made things worse.

"So you are increasing, I take it?" His voice was icy with rage.

Cynthia nodded. "But I was not sure until quite recently—"

The captain cut in again. "And exactly when did you intend to share this *special* secret with your husband, my lady?"

Cynthia felt the tears well up in her throat. "I had hoped to tell you tonight, Brian," she whispered, painfully aware that she was making no headway against his anger. "I would have done so before, but—"

"But his lordship had to be the first to know? Is that it?"

She reached out a hand to him, but let it drop when the captain stepped back. "No. That is not the way it was meant to be. It is just that Robbie knows me so well, he must have guessed the truth."

"And I do not know you at all, it seems. Either that, or I am no good at guessing."

It was only after the captain had turned on his heel and left her that Cynthia realized that there had been no joy in the revelation of the most important secret of her life.

CHAPTER TWELVE

The Kissing Bough

The day of Lady Halifax's Christmas Ball dawned cold and clear, and the captain was glad when his father-in-law suggested, over the breakfast table to the male members of the party, that he would be happy to take them on a walking tour of the estate.

"That is an excellent idea, James," his wife said with evident relief. "I was wondering how to get you gentlemen out of the way so that Sophy and I can oversee the decoration of the hall for tonight."

"I say we take our guns with us," the marquess suggested jovially. "We might find a hare or two out in the South Meadow. And there are always pigeons down by the mill, of course."

"Now that would be wonderful, dear," the marchioness remarked encouragingly, apparently oblivious of the fact that the gentlemen had brought back over two dozen pigeons from their hunting expedition the previous afternoon.

The captain looked around the table and saw with some amusement that the four younger Monroyals were gazing at their uncle with undisguised eagerness.

"Does that mean you will let me use your gun again, Uncle James?" George demanded, his mind momentarily diverted from the heap of food on his plate. "I know I can bag a hare this time."

"You promised I might shoot today, Uncle James," Gerald interrupted, his mouth full of York ham. "And I am a better shot than George anyway."

"What a bouncer!" George exclaimed, glaring at his brother with disdain. "You have yet to hit a stationary target, much less a racing hare."

"I have, too," Gerald said loudly.

"Do not talk with your mouth full, Gerald," his mother said mildly. "And you know how I hate arguments at the breakfast table, boys."

"Gerald started it," George muttered darkly.

"That is quite enough," their half-brother drawled in a bored voice, passing his cup to his hostess to be refilled.

The captain listened with half an ear to this exchange which appeared to be a regular ritual when the four boys stayed at Halifax Park. His mind was upstairs with his wife, and he wondered whether she would put in an appearance at the breakfast table this morning before he left. She had not come down yesterday morning, and since he had spent the entire day out hunting with his host and a group of local enthusiasts, he had not seen her until tea-time. And even then she had not looked at him when she handed him his cup. It was little consolation that Cynthia had not glanced at the marquess either as he came up for his tea. They had stood there for a few moments but Cynthia had ignored them both in favor of Mrs. Frazier, an elderly relative who had captured her attention with a convoluted tale of a mysterious disease that was decimating her poultry.

Lord Monroyal had grimaced and moved away. "We are both in the doghouse, it seems," he murmured with that cynical little laugh that grated on Brian's nerves.

"With good reason, I should imagine," the captain had snapped back without thinking, regretting his words the instant he saw the marquess's lips curl into a sneer.

"Speak for yourself, old man," he drawled and sauntered away to join a group of gentlemen heatedly discussing the merits of a certain local pugilist who had recently been roundly defeated by one of Gentleman Jackson's protégés.

And now it appeared that he would have to begin a second day without seeing her warm smile, Brian thought. Unaccountably, the notion depressed him. Perhaps he should have gone to her last night, he mused. One night away from her should have been enough to express his displeasure, should it not? And it was becoming increasingly clear to him that prolonging his abstinence for a second night had been a mistake. Indeed, if he had had any sense at all, he would have listened to his heart instead of his bruised pride, and heeded that little appealing gesture his wife had made two evenings ago when he had confronted her with her perfidy.

"Ready, Sheffield?" His host's bluff voice recalled the captain to his present surroundings, and he rose to follow Lord Halifax out of the breakfast room, preceded by the four young Monroyals, who raced one another to be first into greatcoats and galoshes, fur-lined gloves and woolly scarves, for the tramp across the estate proposed by their uncle.

"Forgive me for saying so, old chap," he heard a silken voice drawl close to his elbow as the guests crowded into the front hall, struggling with their winter gear, "but you do not appear exactly overjoyed at the prospect of this invigorating exercise."

"Quite the contrary," Brian replied coldly. "I enjoy the rigors of country life."

"But not the rigors of marriage, I gather?" the marquess added softly, his smile not reaching his eyes.

The captain swung around, his fists clenched menacingly. "I shall thank you to keep your snide innuendoes to yourself, my lord," he said in a tight voice.

They stood, poised nose to nose, glaring at each other for what seemed like an age before Lord Halifax's voice broke the tension between them,

"Robbie, I am looking to you to keep a weather eye on George and young William, while the captain and I take on Gerald and Peter. It would never do to get one of the little rascals shot at."

It was not until they had traversed the Long Meadow adjoining the Park, crossed the rickety wooden bridge over a swift-flowing stream into the Home Wood, and emerged on the other side into a sloping stretch of grazing land known as the South Meadow, that the captain realized that his host had witnessed the flair of animosity between him and the marquess.

Lord Halifax was silent as the two men climbed over an ancient stile and started across the meadow. Ahead of them the four younger Monroyals were shouting and running around wildly, purportedly to scare up a hare or two. The marquess, their brother, his gun cradled in his arm strode after them.

"You must not mind Monroyal, Captain," Lord Halifax remarked quite unexpectedly. "He is too used to having his own way, of course, but he is neither vindictive nor unkind. In spite of his rather scandalous reputation, Cynthia has always doted on him. I still cannot understand why she would not marry him, but to tell you the truth, son, I am glad she did not."

"Thank you, sir," Brian said, not knowing what else to say.

"A little of Robert's company goes rather a long way," his lordship remarked shortly. "But tell me what ails my daughter," he continued in the same tone. "I know Cynthia well enough to tell she is mopish about something. It concerns Monroyal, I presume?"

When the captain made no response to this blunt interrogation, Lord Halifax laughed ruefully. "None of my business, of course, lad. But just remember that Cynthia turned her cousin down. And between you and me, one of the reasons she gave was that Robert was too old and jaded. Robbie did not like that a bit, I can tell you."

Lord Halifax chuckled, and Brian felt the first glimmer of humor he had experienced in two days. The lighter mood carried him through the rest of the day, but when it came time to dress for dinner, the captain took more pains than usual with the tying of his cravat. As he discarded the second ruined cloth, his batman snorted in disgust.

"Ain't never seen ye play the dandy afore, Capt'n," he grumbled. "Might save us all some time if ye was to call in that prune-faced bag of bones as rigs 'is lordship out in such prime twig."

Ignoring this impertinent reference to Monroyal's starched-up gentleman's gentleman—as Evans invariably called himself—the captain achieved a creditable variation of the Mathematical and descended to the formal drawing room where the guests were already assembling for dinner.

He had not expected his wife to be down early, but neither did he expect to see her enter the room on her cousin's arm, looking astonishingly lovely in a dark green gown cut daringly low across her bosom and glittering with silver sequins on a diaphanous overgown of silver net. Brian hardly noticed that Lady Halifax's arm was also linked through her nephew's and that she rivaled her daughter's beauty. He had eyes only for Cynthia and—for the first time since learning the news—he felt a surge of joy that this radiant female was carrying his child.

Suddenly he needed to tell her so, but before he had taken more than two steps towards her, Morgan's sonorous voice announced dinner.

Lady Cynthia had not wished to give her cousin the satisfaction of escorting her down to the drawing room that evening. She had half expected, half hoped that the captain would offer to accompany her, and she had taken particular pains to look her best. She knew her new ball gown of heavy green silk was both fashionable and becoming, and Annette had outdone herself in the stylish arrangement of dark auburn curls crowning her small head. In short, Cynthia felt beautiful and desirable, and wanted only the confirmation of it in her husband's blue eyes to make her happiness complete.

But the captain did not come.

Suppressing her disappointment, Cynthia had sallied forth in search of her mother, only to find the marchioness on the landing

with Lord Monroyal. The marquess had grinned broadly and offered his other arm, which Cynthia could hardly ignore without
seeming rude beyond reason. But she did not return her cousin's
smile, unable to forgive him the indiscretion that had cost her two
miserable days estranged from her husband.

"My dear Cynthia," the marquess murmured, glancing down at
her with open admiration, "you will outshine every other female
at the ball tonight, my love. Except for your lady mother, naturally," he added, casting a mischievous wink at his aunt. "Our
captain is indeed a fortunate man," he continued, with a sly
glance from hooded eyes.

Lady Halifax rapped him smartly with her fan. "You are a sad
rattle, Robbie," she said, evidently gratified by the flattery.

Cynthia ignored her cousin's easy banter, which normally
would have amused her and elicited some scathing rejoinder. She
was not in the mood for banter tonight, particularly not from her
handsome cousin. Her thoughts were on the captain and the
prospect of dancing with him later that evening.

"Methinks I am in my fair cousin's black book," Lord Monroyal complained in a mocking tone. "Tell me that it is not so,
love," he murmured. "And promise me the first waltz, Cousin. I
insist upon it."

"Wrong on all counts, Cousin," Cynthia responded coolly.
"And my first waltz is already promised," she lied, determined to
discourage her rakish cousin from flirting with her.

By that time they had entered the drawing room, but before
Cynthia could pick out the captain's tall figure above the milling
guests, her mother's butler had announced dinner and she found
herself placed between an aging uncle who was hard of hearing
and Sir John Biddleton, who relieved her of the need to do more
than nod at his endless flow of anecdotes concerning his latest
hunting exploits.

Captain Sheffield had been seated next to Lady Chester, a vivacious young matron recently married to the staid Sir William
Chester, whose small manor house lay on the other side of Eastleigh. Cynthia noted with some disgust that the young matron,
whose daring décolletage struck her as unnecessarily provocative,
was exerting her not inconsiderable charms to keep her dinner
partner amused.

Cynthia's gaze swept the dazzling expanse of Lady Halifax's
table and marveled, as she had done every year for as long as she
could remember, at the warmth and conviviality her mother
seemed to infuse into the annual holiday gathering of disparate

guests. Had her beautiful mother ever been anything but loved and cherished by the man she had wed more than thirty years ago? Cynthia wondered, her eyes resting affectionately on the object of her thoughts. She turned her gaze to her father at the other end of the long table. He was still undeniably a handsome man, she thought, wondering if her mother's heart had leapt with joy when she had been informed that she was to receive an offer from the young Viscount Holt, as Lord Halifax had been then. Had she fallen instantly in love with that stranger picked out for her by a careful father? Or had she grown to love him after he had initiated her into the rites of the marriage bed? After she had felt his child move within her? Or had her love grown and deepened over the years as they gave shape to their life together?

Of their own accord, Cynthia's eyes moved down the table until they rested on Captain Sheffield. Brian had been entirely her own choice, she thought with sudden satisfaction. And he had accepted her odd proposal even after she had been quite sure he would reject it. And he had kissed her, she remembered. Kissed her with astonishing and quite delightful thoroughness until her bones had turned to jelly. At the memory of that first kiss Cynthia's eyes strayed to her husband's mouth, softened in a slight smile at some witticism of Lady Chester's, and desire curled up inside her.

Sir John's voice droned on in her ear, but Cynthia's attention was focused on the captain's face. His strong profile delighted her, as did his rugged jawline, the small ears partially hidden beneath the riot of chestnut curls, the broad brow, and sensuously mobile mouth. And his eyes, she thought, their piercing blue, like no other blue she had ever seen, mesmerized her when they stared into hers. Cynthia stared back for perhaps a full minute before she realized that she was not imagining it; the captain was actually looking directly at her, and his mouth had broadened into a rather amused smile, even as his gaze dropped suggestively to her own lips. Her heart leapt at the unmistakable message in those eyes, and she returned his smile before the impropriety of their exchange caused her to blush and drag her attention back to Sir John, who was still waxing loudly on the merits of his favorite hunter for carrying him over some of the most difficult terrain in Melton Mobrey the previous November.

When Cynthia again dared to look down the table, the captain was talking to Lady Constance on his left, and Lady Chester's lovely countenance was marred by a definite pout. Still tingling with the warmth of her husband's gaze, Cynthia became aware of

Lord Monroyal's dark eyes fixed upon her. His sardonic expression made it abundantly clear to her that Robbie had witnessed the little scene between husband and wife. The thought of yet another intrusion from her disreputable cousin angered Cynthia, and she resolved to speak very seriously to him before the evening was out.

Instead of removing to the drawing room after dinner, the whole party repaired to the Great Hall, which had been decorated with festive greenery for the event of the Season. Cynthia could hear the musicians imported from London for the occasion tuning up their instruments in the minstrel gallery at the south end of the Hall. Families from the neighborhood not invited to the dinner were beginning to arrive, and Lord and Lady Halifax took up their positions at the head of the stairs to welcome their guests.

Two hours later, Cynthia had yet to dance with her husband, having done the honors, as protocol demanded, with several titled relatives and friends of her father's. She had seen the captain dancing with Lady Halifax and later with her Cousin Constance, but he had as yet made no attempt to approach her.

"The captain is an excellent dancer, Cousin," Lady Constance informed her as the two cousins stood in the shelter of a cluster of potted palms during a lull in the music. "I envy you, dear."

Cynthia repressed the urge to point out that she had as yet only enjoyed one dance with the captain and that before their marriage, but she held her tongue and surveyed the room again, hoping to catch her husband's eye. All she managed to attract was the marquess's attention and before she could escape, she heard her cousin's drawling voice at her elbow.

"You look as though you need rescuing from that army of old fogeys who have singled you out for their special attention this evening, my dear Cynthia," he murmured cynically. "And since our valiant captain is shirking his duty, allow me to play Sir Galahad to your Guinevere, love."

"Oh, do go away, Robbie," Cynthia said impatiently, her eyes still scanning the room for her husband. "You have caused quite enough trouble for me already."

In the awkward pause that followed, Cynthia heard her cousin's amused chuckle. Would nothing depress the unfeeling rogue? she thought with unaccustomed rancor.

"Whatever has my brother done to throw you into such a pucker, Cousin?" Constance demanded, her brown eyes wide with surprise.

"He has been his usual odious, overbearing self, of course,"

Cynthia replied shortly, annoyed at herself for allowing her temper to dictate her impetuous words. "He will insist upon teasing the captain, and—"

"Your husband has no sense of humor, love," the marquess interrupted in his bored voice. "A dashed dull dog, if you ask me—"

"I am *not* asking you," Cynthia shot back angrily. "And I will thank you not to—"

"Cynthia, dearest," Constance whispered in strong agitation. "You are making a spectacle of yourself. People will think you are arguing with Robbie."

"Well, I *am* arguing with him," Cynthia replied sharply. "And I will slap his smug face for him if he says another word against Brian."

The marquess gazed down at her speculatively. "Very well," he said with such meekness that Cynthia glanced at him suspiciously. "I promise to behave, love. Let us kiss and make up—"

"Robbie!" his half-sister exclaimed in shocked tones that drew several curious glances in their direction.

"Do not fly into a pet, my dear Constance," Lord Monroyal drawled, evidently enjoying the commotion he was creating. "I meant it figuratively, of course. I shall settle for a dance instead— if I must. If our dear Cynthia will dance with me, I promise not to—"

"I have already told you that the next dance is spoken for," Cynthia retorted sharply, her eyes roving around the room anxiously.

The marquess laughed. "If you are counting on Captain Sheffield to swoop down and save you from my nefarious clutches, Cousin, I suggest you put the notion out of your lovely head. The captain is at this very moment preparing to lead out the ravishing Lady Chester. Cannot say I blame him, of course, the wench's charms are all too obvious."

Ignoring Constance's shocked gasp, Cynthia followed her cousin's gaze and saw that he was correct. Her husband appeared to be engrossed by Lady Chester's vivacious chatter—or by her exposed bosom, she admitted viciously—and from the fatuous smile on his face did not seem in any hurry to seek out his wife.

Cynthia's joy faltered, but she forced herself to maintain her smile. On sudden impulse, she turned to Lady Constance and said brightly, "In that case, I think we should visit the refreshment room, Cousin. My mother's champagne punch is beyond anything delicious."

Lord Monroyal grinned and offered an arm to both ladies, and shepherded them towards the double doors of the ballroom. It took them several minutes to wind their way through the chattering crowd of guests, and it was not until they reached the hall outside that a sudden uneasiness assailed her.

The kissing bough, she thought. How foolish of her to forget that it hung, as it did every year, in the very threshold of the room where her mother always set up the long refreshment tables. And Robbie would know precisely where it was, since he had, together with her father, devised the notion of placing it where no one could avoid it. Her father had already claimed his kiss from Lady Halifax, another yearly tradition, earlier that afternoon, and now it hung there, the object of much giggling and teasing from the younger members of the family, and of furtive anticipation from those who had a specific victim in mind. But surely Robert would not be so shameless as to imagine he could . . . Cynthia glanced up at her cousin and saw, from the amused glint in his dark eyes, that he had read her mind and, worse yet, did indeed plan to steal a kiss from her.

Cynthia stopped in her tracks. "I do not feel like punch after all," she said when both her cousins looked at her quizzically. She glanced quickly up and down the hall, but the only guests in sight were two elderly gentlemen seated on a small settee at the end of the hall deep in conversation. The strains of a waltz issued from the ballroom, and Cynthia wondered whether Brian was dancing with Lady Chester. Perhaps he was even now looking for her, she told herself with false optimism. "I fancy I shall return to—"

"You would not deny your cousin a glass of lemonade, now would you, love?" Lord Monroyal murmured mendaciously, clamping Cynthia's arm in the crook of his and stepping towards the open door. "Very poor spirited of you, my dear."

Cynthia felt Robert's arm slip around her waist and shot a pleading glance at Lady Constance, who appeared to have just caught a drift of her cousin's intentions.

"Stop it this instant, Robert," she cried in a shrill voice. "I shall smack you myself unless you stop acting like a vulgar Jackstraw."

"He *is* a vulgar Jackstraw," Cynthia hissed furiously, trying to twist out of her cousin's grasp.

"I hate to say it, my dear Cynthia, but I fear you are correct," a cold voice said from immediately behind the marquess's broad shoulders.

Cynthia felt her cousin's arm drop abruptly away from her waist and closed her eyes. She could wish that the captain had not surprised her in this compromising situation, and had no desire to see the fury in his eyes. Half expecting a brawl to break out, she held her breath, praying that Robert would not say anything provoking.

"No harm intended, old man," the marquess murmured with none of his usual condescension. "Merely a Christmas pleasantry, nothing more."

To Cynthia's surprise, it was her normally reserved cousin who came to her defense. "Christmas pleasantry, indeed!" Constance jeered. "You are a shameless wretch, Robert. You must be in your cups to imagine that any decent female would wish to be mauled about in such a beastly fashion."

This uncharacteristic outburst caused Cynthia to open her eyes, and she saw that Robert was staring at his half-sister with a comical expression of amazement on his pale face.

Cynthia had never before seen the unflappable Lord Monroyal bereft of speech, and she stared at Lady Constance in awed admiration. Recovering himself with a visible effort, the marquess flashed his cynical smile.

"Just so, my dear," he murmured, offering his flushed sister his arm. "You will, I trust, allow me to procure you a glass of lemonade?"

And with a minimal nod in their direction, the unchastened rake sauntered into the refreshment room with Lady Constance.

Cynthia felt an arm go around her, and she glanced up at the captain, expecting to hear his condemnation burst over her head. Instead she saw an unexpected glint of amusement in his blue eyes, and her heart skipped in her chest.

"How very inviting," he murmured, his gaze dropping to her lips. "I see there are still some berries left up there. 'Twould be a pity to waste them, Cynthia. Would you not agree?"

It took her a moment to be sure she had heard aright. Then Cynthia smiled up at the man who could make her heart sing.

"Yes," she breathed, watching the captain's eyes changed to a darker shade of blue. "Oh, yes, indeed."

CHAPTER THIRTEEN

Secrets and Rumours

By the third week in January, Lady Cynthia had begun, tentatively at first and then with increasing confidence, to allow herself to believe in happiness again. Ever since their return to Milford Hall, the captain had delighted her with his renewed ardor and the tenderness of his nightly caresses, and surprised her with the unabashed pleasure he took in his approaching fatherhood. Only that morning he had urged her to lie abed for another hour or two, but Cynthia was not yet prepared to forego the novel experience of breakfasting with a husband who was not above discussing the daily events of the estate with her.

Lonsdale would never have dreamed of doing so, she recalled; in truth he had invariably brushed aside her attempts to interest him in the growing success of her horses, claiming that his experiments in sheep breeding would eventually bring in triple the income from the stables. Time had proved him wrong, of course, but that was small consolation to Lady Cynthia, who had always felt that the viscount had lavished more attention on his ailing flocks than on his wife and on populating his nursery. Perhaps if he had . . .

But no, she thought. Had Viscount Lonsdale made her a mother as she had hoped he would, she would never have conceived her immodest notion of seeking a younger husband, would she? And she would not now be married to Brian, who was in a fair way to fulfilling her every dream.

Of their own accord, Cynthia's eyes strayed to the other end of the table where evidence of the captain's presence still rested. He always had a hearty appetite in the mornings, she mused, and was not silent at the breakfast table as James had been. His enthusiasm over the progress of the horses being readied for the spring sale matched her own, and although the captain had strictly forbidden her to participate in the training sessions as she was wont to do, he appeared to welcome her presence in the arena when he was putting the three-year-olds through their paces.

She glanced at the morning post that had brought yet another missive from Lady Halifax, brimming as usual with disjointed though well-intended instructions, recommendations, and an occasional dire warning regarding the precautions to be followed by females in her daughter's delicate condition. Cynthia smiled as she recalled her mother's genuine delight at learning during their Christmas stay at Halifax Park that she would, at long last, become a grandmother. She had shared her mother's latest letter with her husband, as she always did, and had been touched by the amused tolerance mingled with serious concern with which he received her ladyship's advice.

With a sigh of pure contentment, Cynthia signaled the footman to refill her tea-cup and picked up the copy of *The Gazette*, which the captain had discarded on the table moments before. She scanned the social page but recognized none of the names in the marriage announcements. London was particularly thin of company at that time of year, so the reports of social events included none of the glittering gatherings normally to be found in these pages during the Season. Soon tiring of reading about people she had no interest in, Cynthia was about to cast the newspaper aside and go upstairs to don her warm cloak and fur bonnet the captain insisted she wear when joining him in the stables, when there was a discreet cough from the rotund butler.

She glanced up. "Yes, Turpin?"

"Begging your pardon, milady, but a groom has just arrived in a bit of a lather. He comes from Shropshire, he claims, and is demanding to see Captain Sheffield."

"The captain has gone down to the stables, Turpin," Cynthia said, wondering what could have occurred at Mulgrave Park to warrant sending a messenger all the way down to Surrey. "Have the message taken to him immediately, if you please."

Ten minutes later, while Cynthia was settling her new astrakhan bonnet over her auburn curls in her bedchamber, the door to the captain's room swung open and he strode in, looking so dashingly disheveled that her heart gave a lurch.

"My mother sends me a rather urgent message, love," he said abruptly, coming to a halt behind her and meeting her eyes in the mirror.

Cynthia paused for a moment, startled at the rush of emotion that shook her at the proximity of this man who had brought so much joy to her life. "I trust her ladyship is not taken ill," she said, inserting the hat pin she had been holding rather more forcefully than necessary.

"Oh, it is not her own health that prompts her to write. My mother never suffered so much as a megrim as far as I can remember. It is my half-brother, the earl." He turned and strode over to the window and stood looking out. "It seems he contracted a cold during the hunting season last November, which he refused to treat. I can well believe it. John never did have any patience with sickness. Mollycoddling, he calls it."

"How serious is it?" Cynthia wanted to know.

The captain turned back to face her, his expression dour. "Too serious to ignore, I fear. My mother begs me to come up for a week or two. It appears John's cold has gone to his lungs. The doctor claims it is influenza, which has set the whole house in an uproar. Margaret is not fully recovered from her last lying-in, so the brunt of the sickroom care has fallen to my mother. Besides which, two of the girls are down with chicken-pox, with the rest fully expected to follow." He smiled grimly and shrugged his shoulders. "Much as I dislike my brother, I cannot see how I can ignore my mother's plea."

"Of course, you cannot!" Cynthia exclaimed impulsively. "We must leave immediately. I shall tell Annette to start packing—"

The captain stepped forward and caught her arm. "Not so fast, love," he murmured. "I have no wish to drag you up to Shropshire in this weather and in your condition." He held up a hand when Cynthia opened her mouth to protest. "I shall send for you if I cannot cope with that houseful of females by myself, my dear."

"You promise?" Cynthia gazed up at him anxiously. The sudden warmth that flared in his blue eyes caused her to blush. The thought of being without him for even a week was unexpectedly painful, she realized, and two weeks seemed like an eternity.

He smiled then, and Cynthia's heart leapt. "I promise, but only if *you* promise not to go into the arena with those three-year-olds. I have told Waters he may bring in his two nephews to lend a hand while I am gone. Both lads are excellent with horses, so you must not worry your lovely head about them. Do you promise, love?"

If he spoke to her in those caressing tones, she would promise anything, Cynthia thought, smiling up at him.

"Will you drive the grays?"

He shook his head. "It will be quicker to ride. Hardy and I travel best that way."

"Then please take Tom-Boy," she said impulsively. "He is in prime twig and full of oats."

Cynthia was intensely gratified when her husband bent his head and kissed her on the lips. Assailed by the sudden impulse to fling her arms around his neck and pull his hard length against her, she hesitated, and before she could pluck up the courage, the captain had strode out of the room, shouting for his batman.

Less than an hour later, he was gone, and Cynthia settled herself down to write a long letter to Lady Halifax. And then she would write one to her husband, she thought, missing him already in the strangely silent house. She would write one every day, she vowed, surprised at her own eagerness to maintain this emotional contact with the father of her child.

And it was certainly time to write again to the Dowager Countess of Mulgrave. And to send her another bank draft. Cynthia had sent the first one several weeks before Christmas, under the pretext that she did not know the captain's nieces well enough to select appropriate gifts. The letter she had received in reply from the dowager had been as blunt as that lady herself, Cynthia recalled. Her gift would be used to put a decent holiday meal on the children's table, the dowager had explained, and to buy them some extra warm clothes which they seemed to outgrow far too quickly. Between the lines Cynthia had read a silent message that had touched her heart. The captain's family needed financial help, but to avoid bruising the Sheffield pride, Cynthia had entered into a conspiracy with the dowager, which neither of them acknowledged by so much as a whisper.

The second draft had ostensibly been sent to purchase pretty clothes for the twin baby girls, born in early January. The third was intended for the eldest girl, Matilda, for her seventh birthday, and now the fourth, larger than any of the previous ones, would be offered under the pretext of buying gifts for two of the younger girls, both born in February, but Cynthia suspected it would be put to more prosaic and pressing use.

Cynthia paused in midsentence, a faint smile curling her lips. She was delighted to have found this way of repaying some of the happiness the captain had brought her. And since she did not want his gratitude, it was better that he did not know.

Now, if only she could give him a son, she thought, perhaps she might touch that heart of his that he kept so well protected. Perhaps after he became a father, he might bring himself to speak of love.

With a sigh, Cynthia bent again over the half-filled sheet, her thoughts filled with romantical daydreams she had imagined long outgrown.

*   *   *

When the captain rode up the oak-lined driveway of Mulgrave Park two days later, his feelings were ambiguous. His heart lifted at the sweeter memories of his birthplace when his father was alive, but his mind, still seared by the darker side of his half-brother's character, cringed at the thought of facing John's contempt again. It was the thought of Cynthia that sustained him. She had, in her quiet, unobtrusive way, given him everything his own brother had taken away. He had a family again for the first time in over five years, and he owed it all to his wife. She had made him whole again. He smiled self-consciously to himself at this maudlin notion and brushed it aside impatiently, urging his tired horse up the snow-covered drive.

The place looked strangely deserted, and although the mid-January twilight was already falling, the stately brick house showed only a handful of lighted windows. Nobody opened the wide oak doors to welcome him, so he and Hardy rode around to the stables. It was there that Brian saw the first signs of decay. The big stable-yard was deserted and only the faint glimmer of a single lantern shone through the small windows of the head groom's lodging above the main stalls.

He let out a halloo as he swung down from Tom-Boy's back and heard the big chestnut snort wearily.

"I know just how you feel, old boy," he said, motioning Hardy to seek out a groom to unsaddle the horses. He led Tom-Boy into the nearest wing of the immense stables, stopping abruptly when he discovered it untenanted except for a motley-looking gray who stuck a misshapen nose out of the nearest stall and nickered invitingly. Someone had scrawled *Ned* above the gray's stall with a blunt knife.

"Well, Ned," the captain remarked in a tired voice, "there does not seem to be any shortage of stalls around here, so I will commandeer this one if you have no objection."

The gray nickered his consent, and the captain had unsaddled his horse and led him into an empty stall before Hardy returned, followed by an old man whose uncombed hair suggested that he had just been raised from his bed.

"Welcome home, Captain," he said in a somber voice. "'Ere, sir, let me do that," he added, moving to where the captain was rubbing his horse down with handfuls of straw.

"Cooper!" Brian exclaimed, relinquishing his task and extending his hand to the old groom. "What is going on hereabouts? Where is everybody?"

"There ain't nobody, Captain, sir," the old man muttered, turning to pick up fresh straw. "Times just ain't what they used to be around 'ere."

"Where are the horses?" The captain's voice sounded harsh to his own ears.

"Ain't no 'orses, sir," the groom replied shortly, without interrupting his task. "Except for old Ned 'ere, and 'e 'ardly counts as a 'orse, I'll 'ave to admit."

The captain felt his heart grow cold. "What do you mean there are no horses?" he snapped. "Where are they?"

"Gone, sir," the old man replied laconically. "All sold off to pay 'is lordship's debts, and that's a fact. I never thought to live to see the day when Sheffield 'orses would be auctioned off like so much dog meat."

"How did this come about, Cooper?"

The old man shrugged philosophically. "Don't rightly know, Captain. But 'twas a sad day around 'ere, let me tell you."

After a long silence, the captain asked, "I assume there is a room for my man?"

"Aye. Rooms aplenty, sir. There be ten of 'em standing empty next to me own. Take yer pick, me lad," he said to Hardy, who had unsaddled his own horse and was rubbing it down vigorously.

"Come up to the house as soon as you get settled in, Hardy," the captain said. "It could be that I shall be racking up here myself when his lordship discovers my presence," he added cynically.

What the devil was going on here? he wondered, striding up the uneven gravel path to the kitchen door. And the horses? The idea of Mulgrave Park without horses—horses he had raised himself—was preposterous. There had to be some other explanation.

The kitchen appeared deserted when the captain pushed open the creaking door and stepped in out of the cold. An indifferent fire burned in the old iron stove that had once roared with the energy needed to feed a houseful of hungry children. No plump, perspiring Cook stood over bubbling pots and sizzling skillets now, and no tantalizing smells of freshly baked bread, roasting capons, or sweet damson tarts welcomed the captain home. It appeared as though no evening meal had been prepared that day. His stomach growled in protest.

Brian stood quite still for a full minute, absorbing the unmistakable air of neglect. Something was definitely wrong here, he thought, alarm spiraling up inside him. The floor had not been swept recently, he noticed, and there were no pot-boys scrubbing their dirty skillets in the scullery and filling the air with their chatter. Scattered crumbs covered the heavy kitchen table, and a half loaf of bread sat beside a chunk of Stilton, the only signs of victuals in the room.

As the captain gazed around him, the pantry door opened and a stoop-shouldered servant shuffled in, carrying a tray of dirty dishes.

"Frost!" the captain exclaimed. "Perhaps you can explain to me the meaning of this." He swept a hand around the deserted kitchen.

"Master Brian!" the old man stammered, putting his tray down hastily and straightening his shoulders. "We were not expecting you, sir. No, and that we weren't—"

"Where are the servants?"

The butler stared at him and then lowered his eyes to the grease-spotted floor. "Gone, sir. Let go these six months past, most of them."

"Mrs. Collins, too?"

"Aye, sir. Poor Mabel was one of the first to go. His lordship claimed as how he had no need for another useless female eating his bread, sir. Fair broke her heart, it did. After nigh on thirty years at the Park—"

"My brother is gambling again, I take it?" Brian demanded.

"Aye, Master Brian. Leastwise he was before he took sick. And much worse than usual over the past twelvemonth. Fair put us all in the poorhouse, his lordship did, and that's a fact."

"Why was I not informed?" Brian said with mounting exasperation.

"Forbid it, he did," the butler said shortly. "Took off on one of his rampages, his lordship did, the moment I even suggested as how you should be told."

"And how is the earl?"

The butler's eyes slid away again. "Took to his bed over the New Year and ain't been up since, sir. The sawbones has it that his lordship should seek to appease his Maker. Daren't say it to his face, of course," Frost added hastily. "His lordship believes he is being mollycoddled, as he was used to do in the old days, Master Brian. As I am sure you remember. But this time it just ain't so, Captain. It just ain't so." His voice sank to a mere whisper as though he were suddenly very tired.

"My mother mentioned influenza. Has that been confirmed?"

"Aye, sir, it has. And his lordship is deceiving himself if he thinks he will get up from that bed, Master Brian. You only have to take one look at him to see that."

"Where is the dowager?"

"In her sitting room with Lady Mulgrave," the butler replied. And then, appearing to recall his duties, he straightened his shoulders again. "Unless you be changed beyond recognition, Captain, you must be starving. Let me bring up some cold meat for you; 'tis all there is."

"Anything will do," the captain replied. "And feed Hardy for me, will you, Frost. I can find my own way upstairs."

Taking the stairs two at a time, Brian burst into his mother's sitting room after the briefest of knocks.

"Brian!" the dowager exclaimed, a catch in her throat as she rose to embrace him. Lady Mulgrave also rose at his entrance and Brian, glancing at his sister-in-law over his mother's head, was startled at her pallor and lackluster eyes. Margaret had never been robust, and he guessed that the birthing of seven girls had taken its toll on her fragile health.

Although the captain had wished to get his first interview with his brother over as soon as possible, both ladies assured him, with an urgency he could not miss, that his lordship was presently sleeping and should not, under doctor's orders, be disturbed.

"John can get rather peevish when he is awake," his mother explained blandly.

"Still an overbearing, obnoxious bully, is he?" the captain replied, correctly interpreting her ladyship's discreet understatement. "Then let him sleep, by all means. I shall brave his temper in the morning."

Both ladies looked vastly relieved.

But when the captain was admitted to the earl's darkened bedchamber the following morning, by an unfamiliar, very nervous valet, he saw at once that the earl was not the man he had been back in July when the captain had returned from the Peninsula. His half-brother had always been a robust, corpulent man, blustering, irritable, and overbearing with all who dealt with him. The change was so radical that the captain stood for several moments at the foot of the huge bed, before convincing himself that this pale, flaccid creature was the same man.

The valet fluttered about ineffectually, straightening the bowls, glasses, and vials of medicine on the table by the bed, smoothing the eiderdown, twitching at the thick damask curtains shutting out the weak morning sunlight, all the while glancing apprehensively at the still figure in the bed.

"Is that you, Tucker or Turner or Trimble, or whatever the

bloody hell your name is?" the earl growled suddenly, in a voice the captain would never have recognized as his brother's.

"Tumball, milord," the valet replied, visibly quaking. "May I get you anything, milord?"

"Get my shaving things, I want to get up."

The valet went a shade paler and wrung his hands. "My lord, the physician has strictly—"

"The devil fly away with the bloody sawbones!" the earl exclaimed weakly, struggling to sit up. "And fix this infernal pillow. I cannot sit up properly."

Tumball flew to do his master's ungracious bidding, but his efforts only brought further reproof down on his head.

"Incompetent nincompoop!" the earl snarled weakly. "Now get out my new blue coat. I will breakfast downstairs this morning."

"You have already breakfasted, milord," the valet pointed out unwisely, causing the earl to fling a book at his head.

This fruitless exhibition of temper seemed to leave the earl without strength for further argument, and he closed his eyes, submitting with ill grace as the valet plumped up the pillows and drew the covers back into place around his master's chin.

"Oh, stop your fussing, Tucker, Turner, whatever it is. I will not be coddled, do you hear me?"

"Yes, milord," the valet murmured, and the captain marveled at the patience of the man.

From the foot of the great bed, the captain observed the feeble rantings of the sick man. Pity warred with dislike in his heart as he was forced to accept the possibility of his brother's death. John had always seemed invincible, indestructible, and it came as a shock to Brian to see in the ravaged face and closed sunken eyes the foreshadow of approaching death. The implications of such an event hit him with the suddenness of a thunderbolt and left him breathless. If John died . . .

"And what in blue blazes are *you* doing here?"

The captain snapped out of his meditation to find himself looking into the pale brown eyes he remembered so well, which still flared with their familiar contempt. So, he thought wryly, the earl had lost none of his mean viciousness after all. He forced himself to grin.

"Word has it that you are on your way out, old man," he said brutally, taking grim satisfaction in the grimace that twisted the earl's gaunt face.

"Hell and damnation! Cannot wait to step into my shoes, is that it?" the sick man snarled in a shadow of his former voice. "Well, I

ain't ready to stick my spoon in the wall yet awhile, m'lad. So
you can take yourself off to your fancy widow and leave me be."
He slumped back against the pillow, breathing with difficulty, but
the hatred in his eyes did not diminish. "Get out," he cried out
feebly, making a dismissive gesture with his shrunken hand. "Get
out, I say. Did I not tell you never to set . . . to set foot . . ." He
subsided again, and the valet fluttered around with damp cloths,
and smelling salts, and little exclamations of distress.

"I must ask you to leave, sir," he pleaded, anxious eyes flicking
between the captain and his patient.

Brian nodded. "Let me know when he revives, Tumball, I must
speak with him."

"Get out, get out, get . . ." The man in the bed expelled a long
sigh, and for a dreadful moment the captain thought he might
have given up the ghost then and there. Then he drew a quivering
breath and turned his head away.

More shaken by this experience than he would admit, the captain sought out the earl's steward, who confirmed what he had already surmised about his brother's affairs. The estates were
mortgage to the hilt, the Town house sold off, the stables dis-
banded at auction, his lordship's carriages sold at Tattersall's
three months ago, and the scant income from the estate siphoned
off to cover long-standing gambling debts. Mulgrave Park was
not—the steward said with no attempt to hide his bitterness—
what it once was and perhaps would never be again.

No wonder his half-brother had refused his aid last July, Brian
thought, beginning to understand something of what John must
have felt at the prospect of yet another drain on his vanishing re-
sources. The earl was not a generous man at the best of times, and
with the threat of ruin hanging over him, he had been more than
usually abusive, Brian recalled.

And now the tables were turned, the captain thought wryly. He
had a thousand pounds in his pocket, a ridiculous and quite unnecessarily vast sum to be taking on a short visit into Shropshire
he had protested, when Cynthia had given it to him. But she had
insisted and, to humor her, Brian had tucked the money into his
portmanteau. Now he was glad that he had. What he had thought
of as his wife's frivolity had turned out to be a necessity after all,
but as the captain went through the estate books with the steward,
he clearly saw that a thousand pounds would not begin to rescue
Mulgrave Park from bankruptcy.

Nevertheless, judiciously spread around, the money could bring
some immediate relief to the household, and so it was that the

family sat down to a cooked meal that evening, and the halls of the Park once again came alive with the muted comings and goings of a staff of servants.

After another aborted attempt to discuss the disastrous state of affairs with his brother, the captain was tempted to wash his hands of the earl and his rantings and return to the peace and quiet of Milford Hall and to Cynthia, whom he missed more than he had anticipated.

"I cannot see that I am any use to you here, Mama," he told the dowager that evening after dinner. "John refuses to discuss anything more important than the coat he will wear to breakfast tomorrow. If he is on his deathbed, as the physician seems to think, his lordship is not inclined to acknowledge the fact and may last for months. I cannot leave Cynthia so long alone in her condition."

The dowager sighed. "I sincerely trust that our dear Cynthia gives you a son, Brian," she remarked, handing the captain a cup of tea. "There are no sons in this house to inherit the title, as you can see for yourself, and I doubt that John will live to sire another child."

Accustomed as he was to his mother's bluntness, Brian glanced uneasily at Lady Mulgrave. She sat silently staring at the fire, a half-empty cup on her lap.

"You are distressing Margaret, Mama," he murmured.

"Oh, fiddlesticks!" the dowager exclaimed. "Margaret agrees with me that it is pointless to turn a blind eye on the facts. Do you not, child?"

"Yes, indeed," the countess agreed listlessly, setting her cup aside and rising to her feet. "And now if you will excuse me, Lady Agatha, I will go up to look in on John before I retire."

"Brian, you cannot leave us," his mother exclaimed the minute they were alone. "Poor Margaret is terrified that John will abandon her again as soon as he gets well and remove to London to that doxy of his. She is heartbroken, poor girl."

The captain laughed mirthlessly. "There is little likelihood of that happening, Mama, so do not tease yourself on that head. For one thing, there is no money for mistresses, and for another, even if John survives the disease, he will be an invalid for a very long time."

"But say you will not leave us so soon, dear. Until your sister Caroline returns from Scotland in April, you are the only comfort we can count on, you know. Margaret said as much to me just this morning."

Brian regarded his mother fondly. Although he had seen little enough of her during the past five years, and even less of his sister, who spent much of her time in Scotland with the dowager countess's family, she had written frequently, and he had a special place in his heart for her.

"There are several arrangements I must make before I can think of leaving," he remarked. "Not the least of which is the need to ask Cynthia for a loan to—"

"No!" the dowager cried with considerable agitation. "Do not, I beg you, Brian, bother your wife with our affairs. There must be a way to salvage the estate without begging."

"I have no intention of begging, Mama," the captain said in surprise. "My wife is a very generous woman—"

"Oh, I know that," his mother interrupted. "That is to say, I am sure she is, but I would rather not ask her for anything more, that is all."

The captain was stunned. "More than what?" he asked softly.

The dowager flushed guiltily. "Well, she did pay your gambling debts, or so I hear, and I would not ask her to pay your brother's as well."

Brian felt his face harden. "And who spread this interesting information about my affairs, Mother?" he demanded in accents so chilly that the dowager glanced up at him nervously.

"Why, I . . . It was John, I believe."

"You *believe*? Are you not sure?"

"Yes, it was certainly your brother."

"Then I must certainly demand an explanation of my dear brother," he said slowly.

"Oh, do not pick a quarrel with John, my dear," his mother pleaded. "He can become so ugly when he is crossed, you know."

"I know that only too well, Mama, but there are some matters that must be settled between us."

Much as the captain wished to confront his brother, however, it was not until the following afternoon that the physician allowed visitors in the sickroom. That morning the earl had suffered a relapse and his face was pasty white with fatigue when Brian came to stand by his bedside while the trembling Tumball attempted to spoon warm broth into his reluctant master.

"Take that hog swill away, Turner," the earl protested weakly, but for once he had not the strength to avoid the valet's persistence. "I am wasting away with these bloody slops you keep giving me," he cursed, turning his head fruitlessly away from the hovering spoon. As he did so, his eyes came to rest on his visitor, and Brian saw a flicker of fear in the dull brown gaze.

"Come to watch me die, have you?" the earl wheezed laboriously. "Well, I ain't dead yet, me lad. And I ain't likely to . . ." His voice gave out and his head sank back into the pillow displaying the scrawny neck of a much older man.

"Frankly, I do not care whether you live or die," the captain snapped impatiently, "but there are certain things we must—"

"What things, damn you?" the earl interrupted weakly. "My affairs are no concern of yours. Go home to that widow of yours." His thin lips cracked into a leer.

"Leave my wife out of this," the captain said sharply. "The Park is bankrupt, as you must know, and your steward tells me there is no money to put decent food on the table. Now that does concern me, John."

"If you are so damned concerned you can tell your widow to give me a loan until I get back on my feet." The effort of this speech seemed to drain his energy, for the earl sank back and closed his eyes.

The captain stared at the figure in the bed, who no longer resembled the man he has known as his brother, in silence for several minutes. Then he said, as gently as he could, "You are not going to get back on your feet, John. And the sooner we admit it, the sooner we can do something to salvage what we can of the estate."

"Get me a loan," the earl muttered without opening his eyes.

"No. I will not ask my wife to finance your mistress or your gambling debts, John."

"The devil fly away with you, then."

"Not so fast, Brother," the captain said, fighting to keep his temper under control. "There is much that needs to be done around the estate to improve the rents. That I might help you with—"

"I do not need your help, you insolent puppy," the earl interrupted in a stronger voice. "The widow's money has gone to yer head, has it?" He leered again. "I figure you must be earning it." The suggestive laugh that would have accompanied this statement turned into a hacking cough, which brought Tumball scurrying to the bedside with a bottle of green syrup and a spoon. The earl swatted feebly at the valet's hand, spilling green liquid on the white sheets.

"Get away with you," he exclaimed in the voice of a sick child.

Ignoring his brother's offensive remarks about Lady Cynthia, the captain forced himself to stay calm. "I have paid the servants what was owed them, and there is now a cook in the kitchen. I will not have my mother working in the house like a servant as she and Margaret have been doing for the past weeks. Two of your daughters are down with chicken-pox, but I suppose that should not concern me either."

"Damned brats," the earl mutter under his breath. "I should have turned that scrawny bitch out years ago and got me a wife with some fire in her." He paused and regarded the captain with hooded eyes. "Fancy her yourself, by any chance?" he leered. "Whey-faced, whining ninny. But I must get a son on her as soon as I get back on my feet."

Disgusted at the tack his brother's conversation was taking, the captain interrupted brusquely. "You can forget that, John. There's a strong chance you will never get back on your feet."

"And you would like that, I suppose?" the earl snarled weakly. "Itching to be lord of the manor, ain't you?" He drew a series of wheezing breaths before he could continue. "But if you think to see me turn up my toes so that you or that bastard cub your widow is breeding—"

"Watch your filthy mouth." The captain stepped forward, his fists clenched menacingly.

The earl regarded him for several moments in silence, his dull eyes showing a rare flash of cynical amusement. "Can it be," he said with obvious enjoyment, "that our pious and oh-so-gallant captain does not know he was gulled into marrying a slut?"

The captain felt himself go rigid. "I warn you, John, I shall not tolerate your insulting remarks about my wife and son—"

"Son?" the earl cut in. "So it is a son now, is it? Is that what she has told you? How convenient. You poor fool, Brian. Can you not see that the slut has taken you for a damned knock-in-the-cradle?" He closed his eyes and took several shallow breaths, while the captain stared at his brother as though he had come face-to-face with a basilisk.

Struggling to keep his fists from pounding the sick man into a bloody pulp, Brian said in a taut voice, "You were always an ugly, abusive liar, John. I find it oddly reassuring that you have not changed your spots." He paused to steady his racing pulse. "Naturally, I cannot tell if the child will be a son or a daughter. It does not much matter. I shall cherish it regardless of its sex."

The earl's gaunt face twisted into a leer. "You poor, deluded fool. You did not know, did you?" He lapsed into another spasm of coughing. "Did it not occur to you that fifteen thousand pounds was a premium price to pay for a penniless soldier?"

The captain's face must have betrayed his astonishment and chagrin, for his brother chuckled wheezingly. "How did I know? Why, the rumor went the rounds in all the clubs. Did you think it would not?"

"Lady Cynthia merely discharged my debts—"

The earl's expression cut him short. "Gambling debts, I understand. But what else was she buying, lad? Did she tell you? No, of course, she did no such thing."

"There was nothing to tell," Brian said coldly, fighting the growing apprehension that was making him feel faintly nauseated.

"Tell that to the Marquess of Monroyal."

There was complete silence in the darkened room for what seemed to Brian like an eternity. All his previous reservations, suspicions, and jealous assumptions about the notorious marquess came rushing back to plague him. His consternation must have been reflected in his face, for his brother grinned maliciously from ear to ear.

"No!" Brian exclaimed forcefully, willing himself to disregard his brother's ugly accusations as products of the vicious, envious mind he remembered so well from his childhood.

"Please yourself," the earl sniggered. "But rest assured that no bastard son of Monroyal's will ever be master here."

"That is an ungodly lie, and well you know it," Brian snarled in a voice that sounded oddly grating to his ears.

"Is it?" The leer was back on his brother's face, and the captain longed to plant him a facer.

"You know it is."

"Do I? Well, you had best ask the wench whose pup she is carrying. Although one would hardly expect her to tell the truth, now would you?"

The sound of his brother's choking, coughing attempts at laughter followed the captain as he slammed out of the room.

CHAPTER FOURTEEN

The Accusation

Cynthia signed her name with a flourish and sealed the letter with a blue wafer. There was so much more she had wanted to say to her husband, but had not dared. Private, intimate things, which she had never yet spoken aloud, even to herself. Not even in the warm intimacy of her bed had she dared to speak of what was in her heart to the man who had shown her that marital duty could be so much more than the ritual coupling she had known with Lonsdale. Perhaps tomorrow, in her next letter, she thought, setting the missive in the tray for Turpin to send down to the village. Perhaps tomorrow she would admit that she missed him most dreadfully and slept but fitfully in the cold bed every night.

Cynthia wished she might find the resolve to throw off the social decorum she had been taught to endure as a child, and accept as inevitable in a young matron. How else could a female hope to earn a gentleman's respect and devotion? her mother had often asked. How else could a wife deserve her husband's loyalty and win his regard? Her mother's reasoning had worked all too well with the viscount, she remembered. Lonsdale had never so much as touched her in anything resembling an intimate way in public, and even in the privacy of their bedchamber, he had always doused the candles. While Brian . . . Cynthia felt a delicious shiver run through her at the memory of how her second husband had changed the pattern of her nights.

There had been no doused candles for the captain, and Cynthia had seen more of him on their first night together than she had of Lonsdale in eight years of marriage. And she had been thrilled beyond her wildest dreams at her second husband's unabashed virility. The very thought of that virility caused a familiar warmth to start its slow spiral up inside her. She glanced around the room self-consciously. What could she be thinking of? she wondered. It was not yet tea-time, and here she was wishing that it were evening already and that Brian . . .

But this was idle dreaming at its most scandalous, Cynthia told herself firmly. The captain would not return from Shropshire for another sennight, and even when he did, Cynthia could not imagine herself giving vent to any of the unladylike emotions that had lately threatened her peace of mind. However much she might wish to be less decorous in her dealings with the captain, she knew that the mere confession that she missed him would tax her daring to the utmost. Any more intimate yearnings must remain unspoken, locked in her heart together with a host of other romantical notions more fitting for a schoolroom chit than a twice-married matron of impeccable reputation and advancing years.

Cynthia reached for another sheet, but before she could begin another letter to Lady Agatha, she heard the door open behind her. The thought flashed through her mind that perhaps today the post would bring a letter from the captain. Men were not as comfortable with letter-writing as females, her mother had consoled her when Cynthia complained that no word had come back from Brian since his departure for Mulgrave Park. It was very tiresome of them, to be sure, Lady Halifax had admitted, but what was a female to do? What indeed? Cynthia had agreed, not quite understanding her sudden desire to receive a letter from her husband, some tangible proof that he actually thought about her, written words—brief and prosaic as they would doubtless be—which might reveal something of his true feelings for her.

None had arrived, but perhaps today . . . She turned around and came to her feet with an irrepressible cry of joy.

"Brian!" She gazed in delight at the tall man standing silently in the doorway. "I did not expect you so soon." Impulsively, she started across the library towards him, her hands outstretched. But her joy dissipated abruptly when she noticed his scowl and the bleak expression in his eyes.

"Is something wrong?" she stammered, halting in midstride. "Has your brother . . . ?" She let the words trail off into silence.

The captain rubbed a hand across his eyes, like a man who would banish an unpleasant thought. "No," he said shortly. "At least not yet."

Cynthia was at a loss to know how to proceed. Repressing the immodest urge to touch him, to smooth the frown from his brow, she took refuge in social conventions. "You must be ready for your tea," she said with forced calm, as though her heart had not shriveled up inside her at the coolness in those marvelous blue eyes. "Will you join me in the small drawing room?"

"No," came the curt reply.

Cynthia drew back, her eyebrows raised in surprise.

"I am leaving for London within the hour," the captain said, turning abruptly on his heel.

Cynthia stood as if turned to stone, listening to the captain's footsteps striding along the hall, and then taking the stairs two at a time as though he could not escape her presence fast enough.

She glanced down at her hands, clasped tightly at her waist, and noticed they were trembling. The captain's harsh words still rang in her mind, but she could make no sense out of them. Go up to London? Whatever for? she wondered. Had he not just come through the Metropolis on his way down from Shropshire? *Leaving*, he had said. The word frightened her. It sounded so final. Fighting to contain her rising panic, Cynthia ascended the stairs, entered her bedchamber, and passed through to their private sitting room. The door of her husband's chamber was closed, but by this time, Cynthia wanted nothing so much as to convince herself that she had imagined that remote look in the captain's eyes, had misunderstood him to say he was leaving.

She opened the door and stepped inside. The sight of an open valise on the bed disabused Cynthia of any notion that she had not heard aright. As if to confirm this unwelcome news, the captain came out of his clothes-press with an armful of shirts and flung them into the valise in a haphazard fashion.

"Let me help you," Cynthia began.

"There is no need."

Ignoring this curt dismissal, she stepped up to the valise and attempted to impose order on the jumbled articles of clothing. Under the shirts she noticed a familiar red coat. "What is this?" she demanded, a snake of panic knotting her stomach.

"My uniform," the captain said shortly.

"Why are you taking your uniform?"

"I may be rejoining my regiment."

For a terrible moment, Cynthia felt that her heart had stopped entirely. She took a deep, shuddering breath. "Oh, I see," she murmured, not seeing anything at all. "Is that why you must go to London?"

"No." She thought for a terrible moment that he would say no more, but then he added, his voice harsh and grating. "I am going to seek an interview with Monroyal."

Cynthia felt stunned. None of this made any sense, she thought. "With Robert?" she stammered. "Why would you wish to see my cousin?"

He looked at her then, and Cynthia would have preferred that he had not. She quailed at the remoteness she saw in his eyes.

"I intend to wring the truth out of him," he said with such cold-ness that Cynthia's spirits sank to the soles of her slippers.

"The t-truth?" she stammered nervously. "What truth is this?"

"The truth about some ugly rumors that have come to my ears."

"Rumors?" she repeated, feeling positively stupid. "What rumors are you talking about?"

"Rumors about you, my dear." There was no trace of softness in the endearment, which jarred Cynthia's nerves with cynical echoes.

"About *me*?" She was so surprised she forgot to be scared. "Whatever are you talking about? What rumors are these?"

The captain glanced at her again, his eyes hooded. "I would rather not say," he said enigmatically.

"If these rumors concern me, I think I have a right to know what they are," Cynthia stated angrily. When he did not answer she added in a rush of words, quite forgetting her previous fright. "So, you do not trust me to tell you the truth? That is it, is it not? You cannot bring yourself to trust me, after . . ." She broke off, stunned to realize that she had been about to say *after all we have shared together*. Luckily she caught herself in time, she thought, mortified at being almost betrayed by her emotions into an un-seemly reference to their marital intimacies.

The captain slammed the valise shut and fastened the buckles. "You might say something like that," he said coldly, lifting the valise off the bed and setting it down on the floor.

"I insist that you tell me what the rumors are," she said, a note of hysteria in her voice. "Do they concern my cousin?" she added, with sudden premonition.

The captain gave a crack of laughter, harsh and cynical to her ears. "You must know that they do."

Cynthia made a moue of exasperation. "You are being quite ridiculous," she said crossly. "What has Robert to do with us?"

"That is what I intend to find out," the captain said grimly, picking up the valise and moving towards the door. "And if I find that I have been played for a fool, my lady, you may count on never seeing me again."

Cynthia stood rooted to the carpet for an interminable moment, listening to her husband's footsteps in the hall. Suddenly the im-plications of what he was suggesting dawned on her and she rushed out of the chamber towards the landing. The captain was halfway down to the first floor when she called to him. He turned and looked up at her, his eyes hard.

"What about your son, Brian?"

He looked at her for a long moment before answering, and Cynthia thought she had never seen such bitter sadness in any man's eyes.

"Is he my son, Cynthia?"

He spoke so softly that she had to strain to hear him. By the time she had registered the enormity of her husband's question, he had reached the first-floor landing and continued down to the front hall, where Hardy awaited him. In a daze, Cynthia watched Turpin help the captain into his greatcoat and open the front door.

She saw the cold wind ruffle the captain's chestnut hair before he clapped on his tall beaver and disappeared from sight.

As Cynthia heard the horses pull away from the house, she felt as if that cold January wind had blighted her soul.

For a week after the captain's precipitous departure, Cynthia walked about the house like a ghost. Some days she was able to convince herself that she had dreamed the whole incident. Surely she had imagined that Brian had returned before he was expected from Mulgrave Park? And if that were so, she must have also imagined that dreadful scene in his bedchamber, and the unthinkable accusation in his eyes, she told herself often enough to make it seem almost true. But then one morning early she opened the door to his chamber and looked inside.

The air was stale and the feeling of emptiness cut through to her heart. Slowly she walked over to the clothes-press and opened it. For a fleeting moment the faint smell of Holland water assailed her nostrils, and Cynthia choked back a sob. The clothes-press was empty except for a lone shirt, evidently dropped and forgotten in the rush of packing. Cynthia bent and picked it up, slowly folding the soft lawn and smoothing out the wrinkles. It was one of those she had ordered for Brian in the first weeks of their marriage. It was to be a surprise, she recalled, a smile hovering on her lips. She had sent one of his old shirts up to her mother, begging her to have Lord Halifax's tailor make up a dozen in the very finest cloth available.

Suddenly the sight of the abandoned shirt was too much for her. Distraught, she crushed it against her, destroying the neat folds she had been at such pains to achieve, and the tears that she had held back for the past sennight welled up and spilled over. Great noisy sobs shook her, and she threw herself on the captain's bed, burying her face in his pillow. The smell of him was stronger here, and when Cynthia closed her eyes, she could imagine that he was there with her, his dear head on the pillow beside her, his arm thrown across her hip to pull her closer. The vision seemed so real that Cynthia caught herself listening for his contented murmur against her neck, the whisper of his lips against her cheek.

She shuddered and sat up. This was maudlin beyond anything a sensible matron of her years should indulge in, she thought. Even in her most romantical dreams as a naive young girl Cynthia had never imagined that love could reduce a grown female to a whimpering ninny. Of course, some of Mrs. Radcliffe's heroines occasionally allowed themselves to be carried away by their tender emotions and behaved in a silly fashion, but Cynthia had never given any credence to such die-away damsels. In fact, she had always considered them poor spirited beyond bearing and twitted her mother when her ladyship—an avid reader of sentimental novels—would occasionally burst into tears at the trials these fictional females underwent in pursuit of love.

And there was no longer any doubt in Cynthia's mind that she loved her husband. She had never believed that balderdash about a heroine's heart breaking, of course, but her own was definitely hurting at the moment as if it wanted to break. She placed a hand on her bosom and felt the regular rhythm of that afflicted organ. No, it would not break, she thought, not if she had anything to say in the matter. But it still hurt dreadfully.

Resolutely Cynthia rose and examined her face in the captain's mirror. She looked a complete fright. She had not cried so bitterly since she was ten years old and her dog Sparky had been kicked by a horse and died. The memory was still painful, although she had not thought of Sparky in years. Now Brian was gone, too, was he not? But had she lost him as irrevocably as she had lost Sparky?

She dried her eyes and tucked a stray curl into her chignon. Perhaps she was making a big to-do about nothing, she thought, closing the captain's door softly behind her. Perhaps if she were patient and went about her tasks as a good wife was supposed to do, he would discover he had been mistaken and come back to her. Perhaps he needed to convince himself that Robert never had and never would have *that* kind of feeling for her. And she most certainly had never had anything but sisterly feelings for Robbie. Perhaps if Robbie assured the captain of his innocence—at least his innocence with respect to her, she amended quickly—then Brian would . . .

She paused as a sudden thought struck her. Of course, she thought, what a silly goose she had been not to see it before. She must write to Robbie immediately to warn him that a distraught husband was about to descend upon him. He would doubtless know what to do with distraught husbands; he must have had encounters with dozens of them. But this time he would be innocent, a novel situation she hoped he would appreciate.

Cynthia smiled to herself as she hurried down to the library and settled herself at the gate-legged escritoire. She would tell Robbie the whole, and he would rescue her from this dreadful muddle she had got herself into. As he had so many times in the past, she thought, remembering Sparky and her cousin's comforting presence during that most painful period of her life. No, she corrected herself, the loss of Sparky was no longer her most painful experience. Robbie had procured another dog for her. A floppy-eared, wriggly, silky-haired mongrel, who had licked her face with a warm tongue and made her cry all over again, partly from joy in the cuddly little creature, and partly at the memory of poor Sparky still fresh in her mind.

But there would be no replacing Brian. It had seemed almost indecently easy to replace James, but the captain was another matter entirely. He had taken over not just her life but her heart as well, and Cynthia grew increasingly aware, as the days dragged by, that life at Milford Hall without him would be flat and empty indeed.

She took what comfort she could in their child. Cynthia continued to think of it as *their* child, deliberately repressing the memory of those ugly words her husband had spoken. And when she had written to her cousin, laying the whole before him and begging his assistance, and to Lady Halifax, a tearful account of her hopes and fears, and lastly to the dowager countess, confiding, as calmly as she was able, the unhappy state of affairs that had motivated Brian's removal to the Metropolis, Cynthia felt confident that matters would soon be mended.

To her surprise, it was her mother-in-law who responded first, in a missive filled with scathing pronouncements about the idiocy of gentlemen who could not see the whole for staring at insignificant particles, and whose judgment was so distorted by pride that they could not always be counted upon to be reasonable. She admitted that she had already written a long letter to her son to that effect and begged Cynthia to inform her the moment Brian showed any signs of coming to his senses. She also offered to travel into Surrey to support her dearest Cynthia in her hour of need, an offer Cynthia seriously considered accepting.

Lady Halifax's response arrived two days later and Cynthia derived no small satisfaction from her mother's lengthy condemnation of the mindless eccentricities of gentlemen in general and of the infamous captain in particular. She announced that Lord Halifax had already removed to London to attend the opening of Parliament, and that she would follow immediately and make it her special business to seek out her errant son-in-law and give him a piece of her mind.

Cheered as she was by this show of support, Cynthia's real hopes lay with her cousin, but the marquess made no response at all to her plea. She was not surprised at his silence, disappointed yes, but not surprised. She knew Robbie was an indifferent correspondent, but she held on to the hope that he would recognize the urgency of her predicament and bestir himself to remedy her affairs.

A second letter from her mother-in-law confirmed what Cynthia had already suspected, that the captain had heard the rumors from his brother, the earl. According to the dowager, the sick man had boasted of the fact to his wife, and poor Margaret was beside herself with mortification and promised Cynthia to add her pleas to the dowager's for a swift resolution to this misunderstanding.

Do not fret yourself into ribbons over this insensitive rogue, her mother advised philosophically in a rambling letter from London. According to the marchioness, Lord Halifax had spoken to the captain at the Guards' Club and received nothing but a snub for his pains. It was being bruited about the clubs that the captain was behaving recklessly, drinking in excess and gambling with other young officers at the hells frequented by the least desirable elements of society. It was also rumored—although Lady Halifax could not confirm it since Robert had not yet returned to Town—that the captain had threatened to engage in fisticuffs with the marquess. She strongly advised her daughter to come up to London and see for herself the kind of man she was wasting her tears on.

Troubled by the news that her cousin had not yet received her frantic letter, which she had addressed to his London residence, Cynthia toyed with the idea of accepting her mother's suggestion and traveling to the Metropolis herself. The news of Robert's absence was particularly unsettling to her flagging spirits, and she would have written again had she known which of his numerous estates he had graced with his presence. So she wasted several days weighing the alternatives, and it was not until she received a terse note from her cousin Willy Hampton that Cynthia took any action.

Willy's letter, received in the same post as one from her London man of business, confirmed her mother's fears that the captain's reckless behavior would lead him into trouble. Captain Sheffield, her agent wrote without wrapping the matter up in clean linen, had incurred debts in the sum of three thousand pounds and had applied to him for payment. Did her ladyship wish him to cover these debts, Mr. Broadstone wanted to know, and up to what amount was he authorized to do so?

Cynthia had been sitting in the library—where she seemed to spend most of her time lately—writing to the dowager, when she received these disturbing missives, and her first inclination was to tear them both into shreds and consign them to the fire. Upon further reflection, however, she began to feel vastly misused by a man who had already cost her fifteen thousand pounds. Should she throw more good money away? she wondered, her mother's latest account of the captain's frivolous exploits still fresh in her mind. And what a nerve the man had, to be sure, to imagine that she would frank his excesses in Town while she languished alone in the country. And furthermore, she asked herself for the third time since receiving her agent's letter, was any gentleman worth nearly twenty thousand pounds?

The upshot of this solitary monologue was that Cynthia gradually threw off her inertia and worked herself into a towering rage. Why should she sit here in Surrey feeling sorry for herself, she wondered, while her husband cavorted about London, amusing himself at her expense in her own Town house? Incensed beyond endurance, she slammed the offensive letters down with such force that an empty tea-cup sitting on the leather top of the escritoire jumped into the air and shattered on the floor.

The door opened so swiftly that Cynthia knew that Turpin had been lurking in the hall.

"Is anything the matter, milady?" the butler inquired solicitously, his anxious gaze robbing Cynthia of her initial impulse to snap at him.

It suddenly dawned on her that the whole household must long ago have become aware of her unhappy state. Her simmering resentment at the injustice she had suffered at the captain's hands soared. So the villain did not trust her? she fumed. And thought so little of her that he could accuse her of the grossest deception a female could commit. Well, he had sadly missed his mark if he thought she would take these insults tamely. She was not some simpering miss quailing every time a gentleman so much as raised his voice. No, she thought, feeling a surge of relief as her

course became suddenly clear. She would cease this shilly-shally-
ing around and confront the captain with his iniquity. Make him
admit that he had made a terrible mistake. Force him to beg, yes,
to beg for her forgiveness. And if he would not beg . . . Cynthia
paused, not quite able to imagine what she would do if the captain
refused to beg. Impatiently, she brushed this aside.

"Nothing that signifies, Turpin," she replied calmly, gesturing
at the broken porcelain. "But please alert Annette that we leave
for London in the morning. Weather permitting, naturally," she
added, glancing out of the library window at the pale February
sunlight.

"The weather is supposed to hold for another three days at
least, milady," the butler responded, bending to gather up the broken cup.

"I sincerely hope so," Cynthia said, vowing silently that neither
sleet nor snow would keep her from confronting the man who had
caused her so much grief.

"I am sorry, sir," the starched-up butler said, staring at Captain
Sheffield down the inordinate length of his nose. "His lordship is
not in residence."

Brian uttered an oath under his breath. He had received the
same answer on the previous three calls he had made on the Marquess of Monroyal over the past ten days and his patience was
wearing thin.

"When do you expect his lordship to return to London?"

The butler's face remained impassive, but his eyes turned a
shade cooler. "His lordship does not inform me of his plans, sir."

Brian seriously doubted this, but there was nothing for it but to
leave his card again and trust that when the marquess did decide
to leave his pastoral amusement and return to the Metropolis, he
would realize the urgency of the matter.

"What? Still not back is he?" Captain Chatham drawled when
Brian joined him for lunch at the Guards' Club later than day.
"Can't say I blame the fellow, after all. Must be a deuced sight
more comfortable in the country than here in London with this
miserable weather. Particularly if his lordship has one of his little
bits of muslin with him tucked away in one of those cozy estates
he has so many of. Come to think of it, I ain't seen Prissy
Scanton-Jones in Town yet. Perhaps the ravishing widow is keeping his lordship warm in the wilds of Derbyshire or somewhere.
What's there to entice him back to Town, can you tell me?"

"I need to talk to him, that is why," Brian answered sharply.

"And I heard that Mrs. Scanton-Jones has a sister in Bath, so perhaps she has not taken that randy scoundrel's bait after all."

"No woman would be such a fool, Brian," Chatham offered cynically. "At least none that I know. Besides, I hear she succumbed before Christmas and so it is more than likely—"

"Oh, do let us talk of something more edifying than his depraved lordship's latest conquest," the captain snapped abruptly. His friend's continual harping on the marquess's success with the fairer sex only served to remind him of Cynthia. Not that he could think of much else, Brian had discovered since his angry departure from Surrey. No amount of drinking inordinate quantities of French brandy, or gambling recklessly with fellow officers at the clubs— although he had vowed to stay strictly away from Watier's—could banish her from his thoughts for very long. Not even that evening two nights ago when he had allowed himself to be persuaded to visit a fashionable house on St. James's where a lovely, graceful creature, impeccably gowned but shamelessly uninhibited, had bewitched him into the very lascivious conduct he so despised in the notorious marquess.

He had dreamed of the beautiful courtesan that night, but his pleasure had turned to ashes when he noticed Cynthia standing at the foot of the bed, watching him with eyes full of pain. He had awakened in a cold sweat, alone in the master bedchamber of his wife's Town house on Berkeley Square with the distinct impression that someone had just left the room. He had scrambled out of bed and rushed to open the connecting door to Cynthia's chamber, only to find it cold and empty. The lingering scent of lilac had brought his wife so vividly to mind that Brian had instinctively stepped up to her bed to convince himself that she was not there.

He had gone back to his own bed, shivering with cold and plagued by a nostalgia for his wife so overwhelming that he had spent the rest of the night wondering if perhaps he had not been overzealous in leaving her as he had. Should he not at least have stayed to hear her response to his parting question? he asked himself for the umpteenth time. But she had made no immediate response, he recalled, merely staring at him as if he had sprouted horns and a tail. The surprise, followed by shock and anguish that had flashed through those blue-green eyes had appeared so incriminating at the time, that he had turned away in disgust and fled the house without a backward glance. Now he was not so sure.

Later that evening he accompanied Chatham to a small soirée

at Lord and Lady Hereford's and, since he did not wish to dance, he soon drifted into the card room. He had imagined the stakes to be reasonably low at such a gathering, but as fate would have it, both he and Chatham found themselves at Lord Mansfield's table. He had met Phineas Ravenville, the Earl of Mansfield, at White's before his marriage to Cynthia and knew him to be one of the Seven Corinthians, a loose group of wealthy men who prided themselves on their clothes, cattle, and women. The earl was married now of course, and rumor had it that his new bride, a country vicar's daughter, had curbed his rakish inclinations. She had evidently not curbed his extravagant play, the captain thought wryly, seeing his losses mount at an alarming pace.

"You have cleaned me out, Raven," young Viscount Hart, the earl's brother-in-law, exclaimed disgustedly.

"Yes, it appears Raven has the devil's own luck tonight," drawled the elegant, blond Lord Gresham, leaning back in his chair and stretching his long legs, a bored expression on his handsome face. "How much do I owe you, Mansfield?"

Lord Mansfield glanced casually at the stack of vowels scattered on the table beside him. "About ten thousand, I would say, Robert," he said. "Tonight your mind must have been elsewhere." Several of the gentlemen smiled, but Lord Gresham's sudden frown did not encourage further comments. Brian had heard that, for perhaps the first time in his life, the dazzling marquess had been thwarted in his pursuit of a lady.

"Willy, you are out ahead, as usual," the earl said to Willy Hampton, who sat at his right hand. "I think I owe you around five thousand?"

Brian's heart sank as the earl passed over a stack of bills to the affable gentleman who was another of Cynthia's cousin. Hampton was eyeing him rather anxiously and the captain guessed that the jovial Willy had taken note that he had lost over three thousand pounds to the earl, most of it in scribbled vouchers.

His suspicions were confirmed when Hampton singled him out as the last guests made their way down the steps of Hereford House in the early hours of the morning.

"I have obtained your vowels from Mansfield, old chap," Hampton murmured. "Better to keep our debts in the family so to speak." He grinned affably as he spoke, but the captain took instant umbrage at this unwarranted meddling.

"And I suppose you intend to present them to Cynthia for payment," he snapped angrily. "I will thank you to mind your own bloody business, Hampton. Or do you think I am not good for the money?"

Hampton's cherubic face froze in a comical expression of dismay. "No harm intended, old man," he said hastily. "Thought it would cause less talk, that's all." He smiled, but his eyes were wary. "No need to settle right away, of course. Take all the time you need, Captain."

It did not help to know that Hampton intended it for the best. What galled Brian was the smugness of these wealthy men who had never denied themselves any luxury that money could buy. Not that he hankered after luxuries, of course, that was not his style at all. But he had been a self-indulgent fool to play with such men, he told himself. The knowledge that he had played the Jack again did nothing to sweeten his temper, and the thought of applying to Cynthia's agent for the extra funds to cover a debt he should never have incurred reminded him, in a roundabout way, of Lord Monroyal and the original gambling debt that had brought him into Cynthia's orbit.

And the memory of that ubiquitous nobleman rekindled all the ugly suspicions that lurked in the darkest corners of the captain's mind. He remembered how deliberately the marquess had baited him and drawn him into his net. There was no denying Brian had been flattered by the attentions of such a man, who had professed to a friendship with John. With the brash confidence of the very young and foolish, Brian had dared to consider himself a match for the notorious rake. Of course, he had been mildly castaway, but that was no excuse for allowing himself to be fleeced of fifteen thousand pounds that he did not own. The villain must have run straight to Lady Cynthia with the information that a Johnny Raw had practically thrown himself into their net.

And then there was the odd incident of Monroyal's unheralded appearance at Milford Hall during the first weeks of their marriage, and Cynthia's indiscreet letter to the marquess revealing her delicate condition, to say nothing of the role Lord Monroyal played in urging Brian to renew his offer, when Cynthia had, quite inexplicably, refused him. The haste with which the arrangements of the marriage itself had been conducted had not seemed unusual at the time, given the fact that this was not the lady's first nuptials. And if truth be told, the captain had been relieved to avoid the endless rounds of events normally associated with the marriage of a female of Lady Cynthia's rank and fortune. But now that same haste had taken on rather sinister implications.

Yes, the captain mused bitterly, he had thought himself fortunate indeed to have obtained a bride of such elegance and distinction. Cynthia was not a great Beauty, but her sweet nature and intelligence had been more appealing to the captain than any spoiled female whose face was her chief attraction. And there was no denying that his wife possessed a quiet loveliness and charm that he had grown to appreciate. No, he thought, it was much more than that. He had come to enjoy her company and to need the soft compliance of her body beside him at night. Cynthia had been everything he had wished for in a wife, or better said, she had been until John had told him she had been observed kissing Lord Monroyal in Hyde Park early one morning last October. Mere days before they had been wed. Perhaps even the very day he had offered for her.

The thought had galled him, but it would not have mattered had Cynthia's regard for the marquess been that of a cousin. But according to his brother, it was much more than that. And John had been at Oxford with Monroyal. They had been cronies, John had said, and it was only natural for old friends to discuss their dealings with females. And the marquess had, according to John, discussed his cousin Lady Cynthia at some length . . . Brian had not wanted to listen to this blasphemy, but John had only laughed at his scruples. What the devil did it matter if the wench was one of Monroyal's *amourettes*? the earl had demanded, his weak voice cracking with amusement. Who cared if the brat she was carrying was Monroyal's? The wench had more than enough of the ready to cover a multitude of such flaws.

And who was to know? John had sneered, his dull brown eyes glinting with malice.

The captain had not wanted to know. He still did not want to admit the possibility that his Cynthia had played him false. But his brother's ugly accusations refused to be silenced, and he had been assailed by the need to discover the truth, be what it may. He could pretend he did not know, could he not? an insidious little voice suggested from an unsuspected corner of his mind. He could call his half-brother a liar, and take his Cynthia in his arms again, and kiss her softly curving mouth until she moaned with pleasure. Or he might have done so had he not left her with that unthinkable question hanging in the air between them. Brian had realized, even before his carriage had reached the London toll-gate, that he had been unduly harsh with his wife. He should have turned back then, he thought, turned back to undo the harm he had done, both to Cynthia and to himself.

But pride had forbidden him to listen to that hidden corner of his heart, and he had come to London determined to wring the truth out of the marquess, if he had to beat the scoundrel's handsome phiz to a pulp to do so. But the marquess had not been in London, and Brian had grown more and more frustrated at the delay. As the second week dragged by, he began to realize that every day spent away from Cynthia seemed to lessen the chances of his return to Milford Hall and to the life he loved. To the wife he loved. The notion that he loved his wife was a novel one, which he admitted only in his most maudlin moments.

In such moments of brandy-induced self-pity, the captain seriously contemplated returning to Milford and throwing himself on Cynthia's mercy. He even practiced what he would say to convince her of his sincerity and to obliterate the pain he had seen in her blue-green eyes that day on the stairs. But in his more rational moments, he saw that this was impossible. He must finish what he had started, he told himself sternly, and if she proved innocent . . . Good Gad! he thought bitterly, whatever would he do if Cynthia were innocent? The thought appalled him, but he repressed it. There was no turning back, especially now that he had incurred quite unnecessary obligations that would place him, once again, heavily in his wife's debt.

The truth of the matter, the captain finally admitted to himself, was that he felt trapped between what he had set himself to do, and what that nagging, inner voice wanted him to do. So it was with mixed emotions that he paid yet another call on the marquess towards the end of his second week in London.

His lordship's starched-up butler's face relaxed infinitesimally when his gaze lighted on the captain.

"Yes, sir, his lordship is indeed in London," came the unexpected response to the captain's inquiry. "At the moment his lordship is not at home, however."

The prospect of finally getting his desired interview with Cynthia's cousin triggered all Brian's grievances against that gentleman, and he quickly scribbled a message on his card, urging an immediate encounter. Although his initial fury had abated considerably, he was so relieved that his quest was nearing its conclusion that he happily agreed to Chatham's suggestion that he gather a few intimate friends for dinner and cards at Berkeley Square the following evening.

"We shall celebrate Monroyal's return from his pastoral retreat," the jovial Chatham remarked as they sat in his family box at Drury Lane that evening, ogling a cluster of brightly gowned

Cyprians in a box across the way. "Leave the invitations to me, old chap. Company is a little thin this early in the year, but I know several fellows who are always game for a lark. And, of course, we shall have a few Cyprians to liven up the evening. What do you say, Brian?"

The captain grinned. "Anything you want, Dick."

"What do you say we invite old Monroyal to join us?" Chatham said unexpectedly. "I hear he is quite a hand at debauchery. He might teach us a thing or two."

"Over my dead body," Brian growled, his smile fading. "I trust you do not intend to stage one of your orgies, Dick," he added. "I should warn you that I am in no mood for debauchery. Much as I hate to confess it, painted London hussies are not my style, you know."

Dick Chatham grinned wickedly. "Never fear, old man. I shall invite an old Tabby for you, who will not transcend the bounds of decorum by so much as a hair's breadth."

"I was not aware you knew any respectable Tabbies," the captain quipped mildly, and was not surprised the following evening to find his dining room invaded by four gaily costumed actresses, none of whom remotely resembled a lady of decorum.

The dinner was the merriest the captain had enjoyed since his arrival, and he was feeling comfortably mellow when the ladies rose to leave them. The four gentlemen did not waste much time over their port, and when they entered the drawing room, the captain had the suspicion that the projected card-party would quickly become something far less sedate. The tone of the evening was set by the ladies, two of whom sat at the pianoforte playing lively drinking songs and jigs. The other two hung over the instrument, improvising new and excessively lewd verses to songs that had been anything but respectable when first penned.

"Which is the Tabby you selected for me?" Brian murmured under his breath to Chatham, as their two friends—the Honorable Theodore Thornton, generally known among his cronies as Toothsome Teddy, and the Honorable James Simmons, infamous for his failed attempt to abscond with an heiress noted for her buck teeth and eighty thousand pounds—joined the ladies around the pianoforte.

As the drinks flowed and the ditties became bawdier, it was not long before the tone of the gathering sank to the level of open debauchery. The actress who eventually attached herself to the captain, a curvesome wench with a merry laugh, a mop of fashionable blond curls, and an exquisite bosom peeking invitingly from her equally fashionable low neckline, revealed, to the delight of the other gentlemen, a vocabulary that made the captain's batman sound like a cleric. She confessed to the name of Babs, which Brian found very convenient for his wine-soaked brain to remember, since it vaguely resembled Tabby.

Although part of his senses was very conscious of the actress's warm arm around his neck, and her lithe body pressed suggestively against his right thigh, the captain's thoughts occasionally wandered from Babs's ribald chatter to the interview he had scheduled with the marquess on the next afternoon. This was not a difficult feat, since he soon found he was not expected to do more than nod and grin at her salacious repartee, or squeeze her comely posterior at regular intervals.

All four gentlemen had been divested of their coats and cravats in the course of the revelries, and Toothsome Teddy, living up to his reputation as a young blade ever ready to serve the fairer sex, was in imminent danger of losing his pantaloons as well to the teasing hands of an actress named Sally. Dick was engaged in rather more advanced stages of undress on the settee with his partner, and eventually slipped out of the drawing room, with a lewd wink at his host, presumably to seek more comfortable quarters upstairs. Young Simmons sprawled in a leather wing chair, with an actress on his lap, recounting for the fifth time that evening, the more salacious aspects of his aborted elopement with the heiress.

The captain listened with half an ear, discounting the more lascivious anecdotes as pure fabrication on the part of his friend, who was obviously deep in his cups. To tell the truth, he was not much in the mood for casual fornication, a confession he would have to make sooner or later to the eager Babs, who obviously was. Brian glanced down at the actress, who had undone his shirt and was now engaged in nibbling the hairs on his chest, amid what sounded like highly artificial squeals of delight. Cynthia had never nibbled his chest, he thought, shocked that he could entertain memories of his wife at a time like this. He drew a deep breath, but Babs's suddenly oppressive scent of roses only made his longing for Cynthia's delicate lilac fragrance all the more acute.

"Yer mind is wandering, luv," the actress chided in a voice husky with passion. "Ain't ye pleased with yer Babs, dearie?" She had slipped into the country brogue of her origins and stumbled slightly over her words. With a sigh, Brian reached up to untangle her arms from their stranglehold on his neck. The prospect of tumbling a female in her cups, however willing she might be, was unappealing. And in spite of being not entirely sober himself, he did not relish the mindless coupling Babs evidently had in mind.

"Of course I am, my sweet," he said quietly. "But it appears I am not in the mood to do you justice tonight."

Babs laughed throatily. "Never say that, luv. Babs can change any man's mood in a trice. Just take a gander at what yer'd be missing." She reached up quickly and pulled the scanty bodice of her gown down over a pair of really spectacular breasts.

Hoots of appreciation and encouragement echoed throughout the drawing room, and the captain was momentarily distracted from his intention to call it a night as he stared at the perfect pink globes offered for his inspection.

"Ravishing, my dear," he murmured, quite unable to tear his eyes away.

"Told ye so, didn't I, luv?" Babs said smugly, evidently taking his admiration for capitulation. " 'ere, 'ave a sample, dearie," she added, taking his left hand and placing it squarely on one of the firm mounds. "Now that's something like, ain't it?"

She gazed up at him triumphantly, and the captain wondered fuzzily how he could disengage himself without offending the lady. Or if he really wished to draw back from what had been so frankly offered.

Caught in this dilemma, Brian did not notice the door open until he heard the sudden silence in the room. When he did tear his gaze from the actress's breast, he found himself looking directly into the shocked blue-green eyes of his wife.

After the dead silence had extended for an unbearable length, during which the captain could not move so much as a muscle, Babs broke the tension with a tipsy giggle.

Her face pale, Lady Cynthia flicked her eyes contemptuously around the room, and Brian was all too conscious of the depraved spectacle they must present. Quite irrationally, he hoped that Teddy had not lost the tussle for his breeches.

"What an edifying spectacle," Lady Cynthia said, in a voice as arctic as the winter wind.

Then the painful scene was over, and his wife was gone, the door slamming resoundingly behind her.

CHAPTER FIFTEEN

Desperate Decision

After a cold and uncomfortable journey, Lady Cynthia was feeling definitely uncharitable towards her errant husband when she finally arrived in London, more than two hours later than she had anticipated. As a result of the lateness of the hour, not only did she miss her tea, but she found her mother dressing for dinner when she arrived at Halifax House.

"My darling Cynthia," Lady Halifax exclaimed when Cynthia was shown into her ladyship's dressing room. "What a wonderful surprise!" She took a closer look at her daughter after clasping her tightly in a perfumed embrace. "You look positively frozen to death, dear. Shall I ring for a pot of hot tea, or can you survive until dinner?"

"I *am* frozen to death, Mama," Cynthia replied, sinking down on the soft pink settee and stripping off her cold gloves. She removed her fur bonnet and shook out her flattened curls. "Tea would be lovely. But I cannot stay for dinner. I want to catch Brian before he goes out for the evening."

"I am glad you have come, Cynthia," Lady Halifax confided after a footman had found space for a small tea-tray on the rosewood table among an assortment of ribbons and trinkets. "That young man you insisted upon marrying has been raising quite a dust. Willy tells me that he dropped over three thousand pounds last week—"

"I know, Mama," Cynthia cut in. "Willy wrote me all about it. I have already instructed Mr. Broadstone to cover the debt." She was tired from the journey, and not really in any mood to discuss her husband's peccadilloes with anyone. She leaned forward to pour the tea, hoping her mother would change the subject.

"I am amazed that you are willing to frank the captain's excesses, my dear," Lady Halifax remarked. "Especially considering that the rogue has practically abandoned you."

"He has not abandoned me, Mama," Cynthia stated flatly.

"Oh? I was under the impression that he had done precisely

that." Lady Halifax glanced at her daughter searchingly. Apparently not liking what she saw, she sat down beside Cynthia on the pink settee. "It is senseless to make excuses for the villain," she said softly. "Gentlemen are very adept at doing that for themselves. It is up to us wives to decide how much philandering we are willing to put up with, dearest. I know this sounds coldhearted, but marriage—a relatively steady and comfortable arrangement with a gentleman who pleases us—is often preferable—"

"The captain is *not* philandering," Cynthia burst out, her voice quavering with indignation. And indeed the notion had never occurred to her. Not that she had any very precise understanding of a gentleman's baser instincts, of course, but she had always imagined—although she did not recall where she got the idea—that if a husband had a willing wife in his bed at home, he was much less apt to browse in other pastures. It had sounded reasonable to her at the time. It still did, but here was her own mother suggesting that Brian, *her* Brian, was out there with other women, touching them, kissing them, lying down with them, giving them the intense pleasure she had foolishly imagined was hers alone.

"No!" she exclaimed, as if she could banish the ugly thought by denying it. "He would not do that. Never!" She was appalled to hear the rising hysteria in her voice, and before she could stop it, a sob rose in her throat.

Lady Halifax laid a warm hand on her daughter's tightly clasped fingers. "Hush, sweetheart," she murmured. "Do not distress yourself, Cynthia." She paused, a faint smile on her beautiful face. "I see you have fallen in love with the rascal, dear. Well, I confess that the captain is a handsome rogue, and obviously nowhere near the rake our darling Robbie is, but he is very much a man, Cynthia, and it is a rare man indeed who cannot be tempted."

Cynthia stared at her mother in horror. "I will not believe a word of it," she choked. "Not Brian?" The last exclamation was part question, part denial, and when she saw the answer in her mother's eyes, she could no longer keep the tears from streaming down her face.

As a result, Cynthia not only stayed to dinner at Halifax House, but also had a long and comforting coze with her mother. Lord Halifax was more circumspect in his reaction to his daughter's marital difficulties than her ladyship, advising her to allow her husband time to come to his senses.

"Captain Sheffield has obviously been misinformed," he remarked as he accompanied the ladies into the drawing room after dinner. "He is a bit of a firebrand about matters that touch upon his honor, and I do not fault him for that. A man can never be too careful about his family reputation."

"But what about mine?" Cynthia wanted to know.

"That is precisely what I mean, Cynthia," Lord Halifax continued patiently in his best parliamentary intonation. "The captain feels compelled to defend your reputation, my dear, and I would not be surprised to hear he intends to call Robert out on the matter. I shall not permit it, of course—"

"Oh, fiddle," Cynthia exclaimed impatiently. "I fail to see how a duel will settle anything. I suppose you will claim that if Brian shoots Robert, I am proved innocent. And if Robert shoots the captain—which I truly hope he does"—she added the last in a repressed voice—"then I am declared guilty of every lewd rumor that is being bandied about. Is that it?"

Lord Halifax held up a restraining hand. "No, no, my dear," He said in the tone of voice he might use to someone of inferior understanding. "Naturally I do not expect a female to appreciate the finer points of honor," he began, beginning to sound uncomfortably pompous, Cynthia thought.

She decided it was time to get to the heart of the matter. "I may not appreciate the code of masculine honor," she said acidly. "But I do know that when a gentleman calls his wife a whore without the slightest shred of evidence—"

"Cynthia!" her father exclaimed, his face turning a deep purple. "I forbid you to use such vulgar language. I cannot believe the captain did any such thing."

"He questioned the parentage of my child," Cynthia said baldly. "And if that is not calling me a whore, I would like to know what is." Seeing the shock on Lord Halifax's face, she glanced accusingly at her mother. "Did you not tell Papa the whole?" she demanded, noting from her mother's alarmed expression what the answer would be.

"Not that part, dear," the marchioness confessed. "To tell you the truth I thought your nerves were overwrought. I cannot imagine the captain saying any such thing."

Cynthia stood up abruptly, her patience at an end. "Then I see I must proceed on my own," she said bitterly.

"If what you say is true, Cynthia," her father began.

"Why would I invent such an insulting story?"

Her father waved the question aside. "I had no idea it was that serious, my dear," he said more gently. "In that case, I suspect there might be ample cause for a legal separation . . ."

Cynthia did not hear the rest of her father's words. Her mind had frozen at the mention of separation. "No," she cried jerkily. "Surely the captain would not take matters that far?"

Lord Halifax stared at her in bemusement. "I doubt it, child. But what I meant was that *you* might have cause to seek a separation."

When Cynthia could find no words to express her consternation at the notion of being separated from the captain, her father added, "You may count on me to use my influence in the matter, Cynthia," he remarked calmly, as though he could not hear his daughter's world collapsing around her. "But think carefully before you take such an action, my dear. The separation of a man from his wife should not be taken lightly."

Half an hour later, when Lord Halifax deposited his daughter on the doorstep of Lonsdale Court, he reiterated his offer. "If you find you have been mistaken in the man, Cynthia, do not hesitate to call upon me to start the proceedings. I do not suggest divorce. That is an expensive and rather scandalous step to take. Rarely granted to a female, I might add . . ."

"Thank you, Papa," Cynthia cut in hastily, not wishing to hear anything more on the subject. "I shall call on Mama tomorrow, if things go well."

And if they did not, she would probably run to her mother anyway, Cynthia thought, waiting for her father's groom to knock on the door. It opened a crack to reveal the face of an astonished butler, who appeared to have turned to stone at the sight of his mistress.

"Good evening, Brooks," Cynthia said, waiting for him to allow her to enter the hall. "It is cold this evening," she added suggestively.

"Yes, indeed, milady," the butler mumbled, swinging the door open quickly and closing it behind her with a sharp click. "The captain did not let us know you were coming to London, milady."

"No, I am sure he did not," Cynthia said pleasantly, allowing the butler to remove her heavy fur cloak. "He did not know I was coming."

The butler stood, the fur cloak dangling from his fingers, staring at his mistress with something very like terror in his expression.

"Is the captain at home, Brooks?" Cynthia asked, wondering why the butler looked as though he had stumbled on a ghost.

"Yes, milady. That is to say, n-no," he stammered, glancing uneasily over his shoulder. "The captain has given instructions not to be disturbed, milady," Brooks added, when the unmistakable sounds of music and loud singing filtered down from the drawing room on the first floor.

Cynthia smiled. "I see," she said. "Have my trunks brought in, will you, Brooks. Annette is with me, and she will tell the footmen where to put everything."

The butler did not budge. "Do you intend to stay, milady?" he asked in a strangled voice.

Cynthia looked at him curiously. Perhaps the old man had been tippling down in the servants' quarters, she thought, a situation not entirely unheard of when the mistress of the house was away.

"Of course," she said briefly, turning to make her way up the staircase. "I hear there is a party going on upstairs. I think I shall join the company." She paused briefly to tuck a wayward curl into place but before she could proceed, Brooks had rushed to the foot of the stairs, waving his arms in apparent distress.

"Oh, I would not advise that, milady," he stammered, his eyes riveted on some point over her right shoulder. "I can send Mrs. Brooks up to your sitting room with a nice cup of hot tea, milady," he urged as if his very life depended upon it. "You will find a fire there, milady, and no doubt you are chilled to the bone." He looked at her then, desperate appeal in his eyes.

Something jangled in the back of Cynthia's mind, and a chill draught seemed to pass through her.

"No," she said brusquely, suddenly making up her mind. "I will join the captain in the drawing room."

Brushing the butler out of the way, she proceeded up to the first landing. Before she reached the double doors behind which the sounds of revelry were now clearly audible, Brooks appeared like a distraught phantom to block the way. She smiled at him.

"I beg you to reconsider, milady," he said desperately. "The captain and his friends are enjoying a masculine gathering, and I fear it has become rather, ahem, rowdy."

In the silence that followed this odd statement, Cynthia clearly heard the shrill crow of female laughter—such as Cynthia had never heard from a lady of quality—coming from the drawing room.

Her smile faded, and her voice turned icy.

"Step aside, if you please, Brooks," she said. "I fancy the party is not exclusively for gentlemen."

With a sigh of resignation, the butler turned and threw open the double doors. Cynthia stepped into the room, conscious of a sudden, paralyzed hush.

She gasped and held her breath, torn between shock and a blinding fury such as she had never before experienced. The scene before her could only be called an orgy. Cynthia had never witnessed an orgy before, but there was no mistaking the various stages of undress of the four gentlemen in the room, one of whom, she noted with a sick feeling of nausea, was Captain Sheffield.

Lady Cynthia stared at her husband as if he were some particularly repellent monster. His eyes were that dark, startling blue that she recognized as a sign either of anger or passion. She very much feared that at the moment they reflected the latter, and her heart froze.

It was then she noticed the female cuddling up to him in a most brazen manner. Cynthia drew a deep shuddering breath. The shameless hussy had pulled her bodice down to her waist—or had the captain done so? she wondered—and her husband's hand, the same one that had on so many occasions caressed her intimately, cradled one of the Cyprian's perfectly shaped breasts as though it were glued there.

Cynthia closed her eyes briefly. When she opened them, the sickening tableau had not altered a whit. Then the wanton of the bared bosom gave a tipsy giggle and the tension broke.

Cynthia cast a contemptuous glance around the room, not seeing anyone but her husband, still with the tart hanging on his neck.

"What an edifying spectacle," she said in a clear, arctic voice.

Unconscious of having made a move, she suddenly found herself walking unsteadily towards the stairs, and heard the drawing room door slam behind her with a satisfying crack that echoed throughout the house.

Lady Cynthia never knew how she got upstairs to her bedchamber. All she remembered was an overwhelming need to get away from that quite dreadful scene in the drawing room, to wipe away the heart-wrenching sight of the captain in another woman's arms. When she closed the door behind her, she felt drained of all emotion and indescribably tired. She stumbled over to the bed and was about to throw herself down on it when she noticed that it appeared rumpled, as though recently occupied. She bent down to straighten the damask eiderdown when a terrible thought occurred to her. Somebody had used her bed!

For perhaps a full minute, Cynthia stood there beside her bed, body rigid with slowly increasing indignation, eyes fixed on the telltale covers and on the pillows that in the dim light appeared faintly indented with a stranger's head. In a sudden rush of energy, she snatched the solitary candle on the dresser and swiftly applied it to all the candelabra she could find, never pausing until the room was lit as brightly as a ballroom. It was then that her terrible suspicions were confirmed: another woman had used her room.

Cynthia felt the bile rise in her throat as she stared around the familiar room, now abruptly cold and inhospitable. On the large dresser, her pots of cream, brushes, and powder box were in disarray, and the statuette of a shepherd lass that had belonged to her mother was lying on its side. Unwilling to believe this evidence of intrusion, Cynthia glanced away, only to be met by the incriminating sight of a pair of silk stockings tossed carelessly over the back of a chair. Gingerly she examined them. They were decidedly the kind of stockings she could imagine Cyprians wearing, black net with sequins festooned around the ankles. A large hole gaped in one stocking, as though it had been ripped rather than worn out, and Cynthia shied away from speculating on the cause of the tear. Had the intruder gone downstairs without stockings? she wondered. Another unpleasant suspicion caused her to jerk open one of the dresser drawers. Lace handkerchiefs, brightly colored scarves, ribbons, bows, gloves, and silk stockings were jumbled up as though an impatient stranger had rifled through them. Cynthia did not need to look further to know that a pair of her stockings would be missing.

The anger and humiliation that had been building in her since catching the captain *in flagrante delicto* consorting with a slut in her drawing room suddenly rose to fever pitch, and Cynthia started to tremble. She slammed the drawer closed but the bitterness of her husband's betrayal could not be dismissed so easily. She glanced around the room, searching for something upon which to vent her fury. It was then she noticed a red silk chemise peeping out from beneath the bed. Viciously she kicked at it, but the blatantly erotic garment seemed to defy her. Suddenly nauseated, she stumbled behind the screen in the corner searching for the chamber-pot, but what she saw there made her forget her nausea. The elegant Sèvres basin was full of dirty water, and a crumpled linen towel lay discarded on the floor beside the matching chamber-pot.

A fury such as Cynthia had never in her genteel, sheltered life experienced, shook her, and before she realized what she was about, she had grasped the basin of water, run to open the door—slopping the water on the Aubusson carpet in the process—and flung the offending object over the banister. For several seconds she waited, holding her breath, and then the sound of porcelain crashing on the tiled hall two floors below reached her, and she smiled grimly. Without waiting to find out what effect this unladylike and highly indecorous, uncharacteristic show of temper might have on the rest of the household, she ran back into her chamber and frantically ripped the bedclothes from the fourposter. Dragging the satin sheets behind her, she backed out onto the landing again and bundled the armload of bedding over the banister, leaning over this time to observe the fluttering descent of the peach-colored sheets—some of her best, she thought with renewed fury—as they came to rest in the hall below. They were followed immediately by the offending pillows.

That would teach the disgusting brute that she was not one of those complaisant wives who would turn a blind eye to his debauchery, she thought, standing in the doorway, glaring around her. The black stockings caught her eye, and she strode across to snatch them up, cringing instinctively at the touch of the silky fabric. Then she picked up the red chemise with two fingers and deposited both intimate garments over the banister. As she stooped to pick up the soiled towel, Cynthia's eye lighted on the squat chamber-pot. Why not? she thought furiously, the set was ruined anyway. With a flourish of desperation, she carted both items out onto the landing and deliberately threw them after the rest of the soiled articles, listening with a kind of bitter satisfaction as the chamber-pot shattered on the tiles below.

By this time signs of reaction from the household could be heard downstairs. She saw her butler's homely face staring blankly up at her, as though he had not yet fully comprehended the enormity of his mistress's actions. The sounds of running footsteps distracted Cynthia from her own horror as the implications of her unruly behavior began to penetrate her feverish brain.

"Are you unwell, milady?" a timid voice asked from behind her.

This innocuous question sounded so inappropriate that Cynthia had to control the insane urge to laugh.

"Yes, as a matter of fact I am, Mrs. Brooks," she replied in a tired voice, pressing a hand to her stomach which still felt queasy and wondering if she might not have harmed her baby with her wild exertions. With a faint smile, Cynthia turned to her housekeeper, who had—from the frazzled state of her gray curls and hastily tied tartan dressing gown—apparently been startled from her bed up in the servants' quarters. "But I shall need fresh linen in one of the guestrooms, if you please. I have no intention of sleeping in *here*," she added icily, indicating the dismantled room with a curt gesture. "And send Annette up to me, if you please."

This last request was not necessary for Annette appeared behind the housekeeper, her normally immutable expression replaced by one of apprehension. Although neither the abigail nor Mrs. Brooks mentioned the debacle that had so recently taken place in the drawing room, Cynthia saw that both were visibly shaken at the spectacle of their mistress acting like a bedlamite. As well they might be, Cynthia thought tiredly. She had never in her recollection been so lost to all sense of decorum as to behave like a Haymarket fishwife. A lady never, but *never* loses control of her emotions, she had heard her mother say a hundred times as a young girl. And never before had Cynthia had the least urge to give in to the tantrums, which she had always considered undignified and worthy only of the most unprincipled and manipulative females. Poor James had never driven her to such lengths, of course. How could he, when he had always been so magnificently aloof himself. But the captain had managed, in the short time she had known him, to upset her equilibrium so fundamentally that Cynthia no longer recognized herself. Why, she had actually longed to scratch that wanton tart's eyes out, she thought, suddenly aware of how close she had come to making a complete hoyden of herself. And slap that heavy-lidded expression of lust off her husband's face. The memory of it made her heart ache so acutely that she unconsciously pressed her hand to her breast.

"Are you feeling poorly, milady?" Annette demanded apprehensively. "Come along and let me get those heavy clothes off you," she added. "Brooks has already sent up all the luggage, so it will not take but a trice to get you changed and into bed."

"There is no need to unpack my trunks, Annette," Cynthia told her, once the housekeeper had gone off to oversee the preparation of a guest room. "I fancy I shall remove to Halifax House at first light."

"Very well, milady," Annette replied in a voice tinged with relief. "I shall lay out your night-things and have the bed-warmer brought up."

Once installed in a guest room, Cynthia only allowed Annette time enough to remove her traveling clothes and brush out her hair before dismissing the abigail, locking her door securely, and climbing gratefully into bed. Sleep did not come, however, for her nerves were still raw from the events of the evening. Much as she wished to put the captain out of her mind, her thoughts returned again and again to that devastating scene in the drawing room.

As she lay gazing at the flickering shadows of the candle on the ceiling, Cynthia heard the muffled noises of guests departing and wondered whether or not the captain would come searching for her to explain his abominable behavior. She half hoped he would, so that she could give him the set-down of his life; but when he did not come, and the house settled into silence, Cynthia could not decide whether she was sorry or relieved that she would not have to face him until the following day. She spent a considerable part of what remained of the night dreaming up suitable castigation for her debauched husband, and wondering if she should indeed accept Lord Halifax's suggestion for a separation.

The idea frightened her. Everything had seemed so simple last October when she had sought her cousin's aid in finding a young husband to give her the family she had been denied as Viscountess Lonsdale. Captain Sheffield had appeared to be the ideal candidate. He was young and vigorous, his breeding was impeccable, he had needed funds, and she had been more than willing to provide them. In exchange for his name, she had told him at the time. Only his name. But that had not been the whole truth, she thought. She had wanted a family, of course, but if she were entirely honest with herself, she would have to admit that she had wanted his lean, muscular body as well. Ever since that first kiss in her mother's Yellow Saloon, she had wanted to feel his hands on her, his hard body pressing her into the mattress, his lips caressing her as no other lips had ever done. Or ever would, she thought disconsolately, suddenly admitting what she had tried to deny for too long: that she wanted no other man in her life, no other father for her children. But now . . .

Her mother's prosaic words came back to her. How much philandering would she be willing to put up with? Cynthia wondered. Had Lady Halifax spoken from her own experience? For the first time, Cynthia considered the possibility that her adored father had been anything less than the perfect, attentive, and loving husband she had always taken him to be. Had Lord Halifax philandered, too, in the early years of his marriage? Had her beautiful mother loved him enough to turn a blind eye on those masculine aberrations? And to forgive him? Did Cynthia love her captain enough to do the same?

A spasm of pain shook her. Could she, knowing what she now

did about her own unsuspected jealousy of her husband, live with
the emotional distress his unfaithfulness would undoubtedly cause
her? And other than the separation her father had suggested, did
she have a choice?

These disturbing thoughts were not conducive to rest, and it
was almost dawn before Cynthia slipped into a fitful slumber.
When she awoke, bleary-eyed, unrested in body and troubled in
spirit, the pale February sunlight filtering into the room reminded
her that she was not in her own bed and that Brian was not with
her.

When she rang for her morning chocolate, Cynthia felt
strangely peevish and out of sorts. She had intended to rise early
to confront the captain, restored to her usual calm composure, but
she felt neither calm nor composed, and consequently in no frame
of mind to talk rationally to a philandering husband.

To make matters worse, when Annette came up with her
chocolate, Cynthia had an attack of nausea and could not touch it.

"Perhaps you should stay in bed this morning, milady," Annette suggested, looking askance as her mistress resolutely threw
back the covers and slid out of bed.

"There is nothing whatever the matter with me," Cynthia responded brusquely. She was certainly not about to admit that she
would much rather hide under the covers for the rest of the day
and avoid the confrontation she was beginning to dread. Her pillow had brought no counsel, and Cynthia felt woefully unprepared to make a decision that would affect the rest of her life. On
the one hand, she wanted her life with the captain to return to
what it had been during the first weeks of their marriage. In that
short period she had allowed herself to dream of happiness. But
that was patently impossible, she thought, slipping into the warm
green merino gown Annette held up for her. On the other hand,
she had no magic wand to make Brian's perverse accusations, and
his despicable behavior last night miraculously disappear.

No, Cynthia thought, staring moodily at herself in the beveled
mirror as Annette executed her swift, soothing strokes with the
silver-backed brush, willy-nilly she would have to make that uncomfortable decision. Oh, how she wished she had never come to
London, she thought. If she had stayed at Milford Hall, she would
not have known, she would not have seen that horrendous tableau
that would haunt her for the rest of her days, she was sure.

But she *had* seen, of course, and nothing could undo that. And
the worst part of this deplorable affair, she realized with a stab of

jealousy, was the indisputable fact that her husband's shapely little tart had been so young. Young and disgustingly beautiful, she mused. And with perfect breasts! Cynthia regarded her own face critically, vaguely surprised that it had not aged overnight. Could those be lines beside her eyes? She peered more closely. If not now, there inevitably would be, she thought morosely. She would soon be thirty. *Thirty!*

Deliberately, Cynthia put the thought aside.

"Would you send word to the captain that I wish to see him as soon as possible," she said quickly before she could find an excuse for putting off the interview. "Perhaps in the library in half an hour?"

Annette met her mistress's eyes in the mirror, her own expressionless. "Captain Sheffield did not sleep here last night, milady," she said in her driest voice. "He is not yet returned. And Mr. Brooks sent up to ask if you will want nuncheon served as usual, milady."

Cynthia did not hear the second part of this speech. Her breath seemed to have been suspended somewhere in the recesses of her lungs. Her mind struggled with the implications of Annette's information. Had he not so much as looked for her last night? Evidently not. And if that were true, had he gone off with his whore to take up where they had left off when she had interrupted them? The notion was too painful to contemplate, but what else was she to believe? What was she to do now? she wondered, her breath flowing again in jerky little gasps. Whatever was she to do?

Slowly and deliberately, Lady Cynthia rose to her feet. It was very clear that the captain wanted nothing more to do with her. She had been wrong all along. He *had* abandoned her. He had a young, beautiful substitute, had he not? What matter that she was a whore? This latest perversity was the last straw, she thought. And quite suddenly, with a painful wrench, Cynthia saw what must be done.

"Send down to Brooks to have my carriage brought round immediately," she said with terrible calmness. "And have the trunks loaded, if you please, Annette. We are going back to Milford."

But before she did, there were several matters that needed her attention, Cynthia thought. She must instruct Mrs. Brooks to put holland covers on the furniture and dismiss any unnecessary staff. Brooks must take the knocker off the door and close up the house. The captain's clothes must be packed and sent round to his old lodgings, if he still had them. If not, they would be sent to Captain Richard Chatham's apartments in Jermyn Street.

And then, only then, if Brian had not put in a suitably contrite appearance at Berkeley Square, Cynthia would call on her solicitor in the city. Mr. Broadstone would no doubt be surprised to see her, but he would be even more surprised, perhaps shocked, at the instructions she was determined to give him.

Calmly, deliberately keeping her emotions under tight rein, Cynthia sat down and dashed off a hasty note to that unsuspecting gentleman. After it had been sent off, Cynthia sat staring out of the library window, wondering where she would derive the strength to carry out the heartbreaking step she must take.

Her father would stand by her and give her support, of course, but the initial step must be taken on her own.

Then, and only then, could she return to Milford Hall and await the birth of her child.

And pray that it would be enough.

CHAPTER SIXTEEN

Counteraction

Captain Sheffield awoke well after noon the day following his wife's unexpected appearance in Town. Hardened by years of campaigning to rough bivouacs and unstable hours, he imagined for a fleeting moment that he was back in Spain. What a night it must have been, he thought wryly, passing a hand gingerly across his aching forehead. Judging by the infernal throbbing inside his head, he must have been more than three sheets in the wind when he came to bed last night. Hardy must have put him to bed, for Brian had no recollection of getting undressed and climbing into the four-poster.

He froze as memory began to return. Four-poster? He sat up abruptly and instantly regretted it. A blinding stab of pain made him groan. He was not in Spain at all, but here in London, a married man, in his own bed at home. Home? He looked about him uneasily. The room was smaller than he remembered, and definitely untidier. The only objects he recognized were his own clothes, folded neatly over a chair. Obviously he was not at home.

And then he remembered the dream and broke out in a cold sweat. He had been in the middle of a party at Berkeley Square with several friends. Some actresses were singing dirty ditties, and he had drunk more than he usually did. No, he told himself, as fragments of the previous night's orgy began to take shape. That part had been no dream, he remembered all too well that one of the girls—what was her name, Betsy or Babs?—had dropped her bodice and caused him to act rather foolishly. The nightmare had begun with the appearance of his wife. But Cynthia was not in London, so that part had to be a fabrication of his fevered mind. *It had to be.*

Unsteadily he crawled from the bed and rang for Hardy. The batman appeared so quickly with shaving water and a mug of tea that he must have been waiting for the captain's summons.

"Where the devil am I, Hardy?" the captain growled.

"Captain Chatham's establishment, sir," Hardy replied, imitating the dry tones and diction of the butler at Berkeley Square.

"And what the bloody hell am I doing here?"

Hardy cleared his throat. "We had a bit of a *contretemps* last night, Captain," he said, falling back into his own vernacular. "More like a full-scale rout, I would call it, sir. We decided it prudent to play least in sight, as they say, until things blow over." He handed his master the steaming mug of tea and stood back as the captain took a thirsty gulp. "So here we are racked up with Captain Chatham, sir."

The hot tea felt good in his queasy stomach and Brian took another long drink before focusing his mind on his batman's remarks. The suspicion that what he had written off as a nightmare might be uncomfortably close to the truth prompted his next question. "That *bit of a contretemps* had nothing to do with a female, I trust."

The batman grinned mirthlessly, his uneven teeth giving him a ghoulish appearance. "Oh, yes indeed, Capt'n," he said, rolling his eyes admiringly. "Damned near wrecked the 'ouse into the bargain she did, sir. Never saw no female toss a chamber-pot down the stairs with such gusto. Fit to burst the lady was and no mistake. Did me 'eart good to see it." His grin broadened. "Nothin' mealy-mouthed about 'er ladyship and that's a fact."

"Her ladyship?" the captain repeated uncertainly, conscious of a cold, clammy snake uncurling inside him. "Are you telling me that Lady Cynthia was at the house last night?"

Hardy nodded vigorously. "Aye, sir. And in fine fettle, if ye'll forgive the impertinence. Took an instant dislike to yer fancy piece, did 'er ladyship. Why, old Brooks says—"

"My *what*?" Brian shouted, cursing roundly at the excruciating pain that shot through his head.

"The little tart that was a'anging round yer neck when 'er ladyship walked in," Hardy explained patiently. "Threw a rare tantrum she did, or so Brooks tells me."

The captain stared at his valet in rising alarm. "Are you saying that my wife came into the *drawing room*?" he asked grimly, his brain flinching at the implications of such a ghastly event.

"Aye, sir," Hardy responded with evident relish. "And believe me, Capt'n, 'er ladyship ain't a female to turn a blind eye to such goings-on. Made of sterner stuff is 'er ladyship or me name ain't Nat Hardy. We ain't seen the last of this, let me tell ye, sir. Not by a long shot we ain't." The grinning valet gestured at a jumble of boxes, valises, and portmanteaux stacked haphazardly in a corner.

"Leastwise it did seem that way after I went over there this morning to get ye a clean shirt, sir. That pasty-faced looby Brooks sent me off with a flea in me ear. Seems as 'ow 'er ladyship has given ye yer marching orders, Capt'n, and that's a fact."

Throughout this rambling account, Brian had been staring at his luggage with foreboding. What the deuce was Cynthia doing in London? And what stroke of ill fate had brought her to Town only to stumble upon him in the company of Betsy or Babs or whatever her name was. He groaned. If she had but waited one more day, after his interview with Monroyal, this disastrous incident could have been put to rest. He might have been able to confess that he had been overhasty in believing John's ugly rumors about her son. *His son!* Brian cringed at his crass stupidity in ever doubting for a moment that the child Cynthia carried was his. He paused, uncertain in his own mind, as conflicting suspicions once more raised the specter of doubt. Of course, Monroyal was exactly the sort of cad to be amused at putting the horns to an unsuspecting husband, Brian thought grimly. And he had had the opportunity. And Cynthia? Always the lady—calm, composed, always in control of her emotions. Perhaps too much so, a perverse little voice echoed maliciously.

The captain stood up abruptly. Today he would see the marquess and settle the matter once and for all. "I will need a bath and a shave," he said curtly, glad to find that his life had not yet lost all purpose. "I shall call at Berkeley Square immediately, and then I have an appointment with the Marquess of Monroyal."

The batman made an unintelligible sound deep in his throat. "I would advise against that, sir," he said lugubriously. "Unless ye wish to 'ave yer ears pinned back, sir. Never git within spitting distance of a female in a fury, me old man used to say to us boys. There's no telling what a wench will do when she flies off the handle, Capt'n. So don't go saying I dinna warn ye, sir."

Ignoring this piece of homely advice, Brian decided to walk to Berkeley Square, but the closer he came, the more uneasy he felt about his reception. Most men he knew would bluster and bully their way out of a similar situation. But blustering and bullying would not do for Cynthia. He would simply tell her the truth, he decided as he rounded the corner into the Square. It had not been his intention to consort with Betsy or Babs, or whatever the tart's name was, much less fondle the Cyprian's bare bosom. Any other woman, the captain saw with sudden insight, meant nothing to him at all compared to Cynthia. He should have told her so long since.

He came to an abrupt halt, vaguely conscious that the simple truth might not be the best approach in his case. Perhaps he should leave out the part about the bare bosom. No need to rake up the coals. He continued to walk more slowly, wondering if perhaps Hardy had not been right after all. If he had not been so unaccountably eager to see his wife again, the captain thought, it might be wiser to allow Cynthia time to simmer down. But where Cynthia was concerned, Brian did not seem to be at all wise. His desire to touch her, kiss her sweet lips, and fold her into his arms again obliterated his common sense. He had been a bloody fool to allow his half-brother's malicious gossip to drive a wedge between them. He should have asked Cynthia herself, and when she denied it, as he knew she would have done, he should have believed her. The devil fly away with it, he believed her now, did he not? In his heart of hearts, Brian knew his wife incapable of such deceit. All he had to do was tell her so and beg her forgiveness. He would do so now, without delay. And then they could go home to Milford Hall together. . . .

The captain was standing before his wife's door when he realized that the knocker had been removed and the shutters were closed on all the windows. A warning bell went off in his head, and he rapped loudly on the carved oak panel. After a considerable elapse of time, the door opened and Brooks's round face appeared, his eyes openly hostile.

"Begging your pardon, sir," the butler said coldly. "Her ladyship is no longer in residence, and the house is closed."

The captain was not the man to tolerate such treatment. He pushed past the flustered butler into the hall.

"Then perhaps you can tell me where she is?" he said with deadly calm.

"I was not informed of her ladyship's plans, sir," the butler stammered. "But her ladyship did ask me to deliver this to you if you chanced to call."

Brian took the slim parcel proffered by the butler, but saw to his disappointment that the writing was not Cynthia's. Another warning bell went off, this time in his heart; he turned abruptly and stalked out into the street.

Shortly after two that afternoon, Captain Sheffield presented himself at the Monroyal residence on St. James's Square. Although his head had cleared somewhat, his emotions were chaotic, fluctuating between deep despondency and a simmering rage at his wife's unexpected ultimatum.

The marquess rose as the captain entered the elegant, book-lined study, but made no move to offer his hand. Neither did the host offer his visitor a drink. Brian chose to ignore the rudeness, indeed, he had half expected it. And he had far more important things on his mind than social niceties. During the past hour he had come face-to-face with a disturbing truth about himself. He needed the assistance, if not the friendship, of the man he had suspected of being his wife's lover.

Conscious of his host's unusually grim expression, Brian got straight to the point. "I have come to talk to you about Cynthia, my lord."

"So I understand," Lord Monroyal replied coldly, indicating a stack of letters on his desk. "My aunt, Lady Halifax, has been so good as to inform me—no less than four times to be precise—that you have abandoned your wife." He paused, his lips curling contemptuously. "I find it hard to credit that a man of your intelligence would do anything so addle-pated."

Bristling at the set-down, Brian forced himself to remain calm. "I did not exactly abandon Lady Cynthia, my lord," he said stiffly. "I had reason to believe . . ." He stopped abruptly, suddenly finding it impossible to accuse his host of seducing his wife. "Did her ladyship explain the circumstances?" he demanded.

"No," the marquess drawled, "but Cynthia did."

There was a sudden silence during which the two men glared at each other with growing belligerence. The captain was the first to speak.

"Cynthia wrote to you?" he inquired in a quiet, dangerous voice.

The marquess grinned wolfishly. "Of course, my dear Captain. Did you expect her not to?"

Brian had a furious urge to throw a punch at the handsome face that grinned tauntingly at him, but he restrained himself with an effort.

"I sincerely trust you have come to assure me that there is no truth whatsoever in my cousin's tale, Captain." As he spoke, the marquess strolled around his desk and came to stand before his visitor. There was no mistaking the menacing stance nor the challenging stare.

"Actually, I came to ask you the same question, my lord," Brian said deliberately. He saw his host's eyes turn to flinty slate, but he was unprepared when the marquess lunged forward and planted a punishing blow to his chin, knocking him down as though he were a raw novice.

"There is your answer, sir," the marquess growled, the muscles in his jaw twitching dangerously. "And if you will get back on your feet, I shall be happy to give you another for my cousin."

The captain remained where he was until he saw his opponent relax and step back. He had not come here to engage in fisticuffs, although at one point during this madness he had certainly contemplated doing so. "I take it that is a denial?" he said with grim humor, getting to his feet.

The marquess's fists clenched instinctively, but Brian raised a restraining hand. "I had to know if there was any truth to those rumors."

"What rumors?" Lord Monroyal's tone was sharp and dangerously quiet. "Are you admitting that you accused my cousin to her face of playing you false? With *me*?"

The captain prudently took a step back, wondering that he could so blithely jeopardize his life. "A man has a right to know . . ." he began.

"I should call you out for this, you insolent puppy," the marquess hissed, his expression glacial. "But for some inexplicable reason my cousin seemed to want you back alive."

"She does?" Brian could not keep the note of relief out of his voice and was mortified when the marquess laughed cynically.

"*Did*," he said dryly. "After the little fracas last night at Berkeley Square, I imagine she must wish to see you drawn and quartered."

The captain was suddenly on his guard again. "What do you know about last night?"

"By this evening the whole of London will know the sordid story," Lord Monroyal said disgustedly. "I ran into Teddy Thornton at White's this morning. He will dine out on the scandal for months to come, I imagine."

The captain blenched. What the devil had he done? he wondered. If this unsavory story got about, as he imagined it would if Teddy had his way, Cynthia would never speak to him again. He groaned softly and ran his fingers through his hair. He glanced at the marquess, only to find those flinty gray eyes fixed on him with open contempt.

"We have to do something to stop this from getting bruited about Town," he said harshly.

One of Lord Monroyal's eyebrows rose cynically. "*We*?" he sneered. "I beg to disappoint you, my dear captain, but this is none of my affair. As you should have known before you went off half-cocked."

Brian met his host's cynical stare, his mind working furiously. If it were the last thing he did, he must put a stop to this scandalous story. Cynthia should not have to suffer for his carelessness. Dick would not talk, of that he was sure. And Simmons was related to Chatham in some obscure way and might be made to see the harm such a story would cause. Thornton, unfortunately, was an avid tattler who delighted in his reputation about Town as the man who knew all the latest *on-dits*. He would need a more forceful incentive to keep his mouth shut.

"Yes, I see that now that it is too late," he said, sensing that the marquess would doubtless make him grovel, and knowing in his heart he would do it, if it came to that. For Cynthia, he would swallow his pride and beg.

"Chatham will not talk, and Simmons can be convinced, I am sure of it. The danger is Thornton. As you say, my lord, he thrives on scandal-broth." He paused, but the marquess merely looked bored. "Can you think of no way he might be persuaded . . . ?" He let his words trail off, uncomfortably aware that the only way to gain Monroyal's assistance was to invoke his wife again. "For Cynthia's sake, I would appreciate it," he added, the words sticking in his craw.

The marquess smiled humorlessly. "Ah, yes. For Cynthia's sake. There's the rub, Captain, is it not? My cousin is the one who stands to lose the most from this ridiculous start of yours." He paused, and Brian held his breath. "For Cynthia's sake, Captain, and for no one else's," he added meaningfully, "I have already taken care of Thornton. I warned him that if he so much as mentions last night's deplorable debacle, I would throttle him myself." He took a gilded snuff-box from his waistcoat, and flicked it open with a well-manicured thumbnail. "If I were you, Captain," he continued in a bored voice, helping himself to a pinch of snuff, "I would not count too heavily on getting back into my cousin's good graces. Females as straitlaced as Cynthia do not take kindly to being called whores—"

"I did no such thing—"

"Or to discovering their husbands consorting with Haymarket-ware," the marquess continued blandly, as though the captain had not interrupted. "So I advise you—though why I should bother is beyond me—to prepare yourself for a long spell of chill wind from that quarter."

"Oh, I was prepared for no less," the captain responded, relieved beyond measure to have brushed through this sticky encounter so lightly. "It is the other that I will not tolerate."

The marquess turned from the sideboard where he was pouring two glasses of brandy from the crystal decanter, and eyed his visitor quizzically. "Spare me, I beg of you, Captain. I have listened to enough of your foolishness for one day."

Ignoring the deliberate jibe, the captain savored the French brandy before replying. "It is your cousin's foolishness I am referring to, my lord," he said, feeling a wave of despair washing over him. "She is demanding a separation."

"A separation?"

Brian derived a bitter satisfaction at Lord Monroyal's evident amazement. He pulled the slim parcel from his pocket and offered it silently to his host.

After a careful perusal of the offending documents, the marquess raised his eyes, and smiled faintly. "Thirty thousand pounds? A respectable offer, I must admit, but I would advise you to demand fifty. Cynthia can well afford it."

For a horrifying moment, the captain thought he had not heard aright. But when his host's smile broadened into a cynical grin, he jumped up from the leather fauteuil, splashing his brandy on Lord Monroyal's Axminster rug. "This is not a laughing matter, my lord," he said coldly. "I am not prepared to sign a writ of separation."

"Fifty thousand is no small inducement," the marquess murmured. "Particularly given the state of your brother's health. As the next earl, my dear fellow, you will need that and more to set the Mulgrave estates to rights, I hear."

"The devil fly away with my brother and the cursed estates," Brian exploded. "I will not sign a damned separation, and that is final."

The marquess looked at him speculatively. "My cousin must be set on it, or she would not have had it drawn up."

"Why would a female wish to do such a thing?" Brian asked, feeling suddenly helpless to stop his life from disintegrating around him.

Lord Monroyal grunted unsympathetically. "Your behavior has hardly been exemplary, old man, would you say? Besides," he added dryly, "if I know anything about the fairer sex, Cynthia probably believes it is what you wish."

"What I wish?" Brian exclaimed in astonishment. "How can she possibly believe such farradiddle?"

"Very easily, I should say," drawled the marquess, and did not elaborate.

"Well, damn it, there is no truth to it," the captain stated with unusual forcefulness. "I want my wife back."

Even to his own ears, he sounded like a desperate man whose very lifeline had been threatened, and Brian was not surprised to see the familiar cynical grin on his host's lean face.

"Have you told her so?" the marquess inquired in a bored voice.

The captain regarded his host pityingly. "How can I?" he said miserably. "Cynthia will hardly receive me after last night, and furthermore, I have no idea where she is."

Lord Monroyal rose to his feet with a sigh, his handsome features set in their habitual expression of ennui. "I see that there is nothing for it but to accompany you to Halifax House," he drawled. "Undoubtedly my cousin has gone to her mother. She will see me, I imagine," he said with an arrogance that grated on Brian's nerves, "and I will put in a good word for you."

Much as the captain hated to admit that his lordship was probably right, he held his caustic retort in check, and followed the marquess out into the street. Twenty minutes later both gentlemen were admitted to Halifax House and received by Lady Halifax in her favorite Chinese drawing room.

"Do I detect a certain coolness, my dear Aunt?" the marquess said with what the captain considered an enviable degree of address in view of Lady Halifax's unsmiling silence.

"When I consider that, between the pair of you, you have brought untold grief down on my daughter's head," snapped her ladyship, "is it surprising that I have nothing to say to either of you?" She glared at the captain in particular, who found it impossible to answer her. "Had you come an hour earlier, Captain," she continued in an icy tone, "you would have found Lord Halifax at home, and believe me, his lordship has a good deal to say to you."

Giving silent thanks that he had not thought to call earlier, Brian sent an appealing glance at the marquess, and was surprised when Monroyal cut their fruitless visit short as soon as his aunt let it slip that Cynthia had already returned to Milford.

"I appreciate your efforts on my behalf," the captain said dispiritedly as the two men drove back to St. James's Square in the marquess's bright yellow curricle. "But it seems obvious to me that Cynthia has washed her hands of me."

"Which only goes to show—as I believe I have proved once before—that you know nothing of the female mind," Lord Monroyal replied caustically. "If half of what Thornton told me about my cousin's behavior last night is true, then there is every reason to believe that all is not yet lost."

The captain looked at his companion in surprise. "How do you come to that conclusion?"

The marquess grinned his wolfish grin. "My sweet cousin has rarely if ever raised her voice in anger or displayed any other outward signs of temper. That I can testify to from personal experience. If she behaved like a termagant last night, it can only mean that she was furiously jealous. By the way, did she actually throw the chamber-pot over the banister?" he added, sotto voce.

Brian nodded wryly. "And the basin, too. Raised the devil of a dust let me tell you." He regarded the marquess oddly. "Why do you ask?"

"In my experience, a jealous female is usually a female in love," he replied. "Has Cynthia ever given you reason to believe she loves you?" he added bluntly.

Much as the captain might have wished to answer in the affirmative, he could not honestly do so. Cynthia had always behaved with decorum and composure. It was difficult to believe that she was the same woman who had wrecked havoc in Berkeley Square last night.

"And what about you?" the marquess continued relentlessly.

"What about me?" Brian repeated apprehensively.

"How do you feel about my cousin?"

"How do you suppose I feel about her, damn it? She is my wife."

The marquess chuckled. "Believe me, Captain, I can sympathize with your reluctance to admit to such maudlin sentimentality. But you will have to do better than that if you wish to get your wife back. As for myself, I have never yet confessed tender feeling for any female, mainly because I have yet to be afflicted by those morbid emotions, but also because it is an exceedingly dangerous confession to make, even if true. A sort of bridge-burning that cuts off retreat too irrevocably for comfort. With any luck I shall never be brought to it. The females I frequent do not ask it, or if they do, they do not insist upon such farradiddle. But Cynthia is a different kind of female entirely."

"You are certainly correct there," Brian said with so much feeling that the marquess laughed outright. Unlike his companion, the captain suddenly recognized himself as a man only too willing to burn his bridges. For a female like his Cynthia. From whom he had no wish whatsoever to retreat.

"Yes, my cousin is a romantic at heart, even though she might not suspect it, and would be the first to deny it. And romantic females harbor secret dreams of true love and rot like that."

"How do you know so much about the secret dreams of females?"

"You forget that I have two very impressionable sisters fresh out of the schoolroom. To put it bluntly, if you have any warmer feelings for my cousin at all, Captain, I suggest you tell her as soon as we get down to Milford, and make an end to this Canterbury farce the two of you are playing out."

"We are going down to Milford?" the captain asked in surprise.

"Yes. Just as soon as you can pack a portmanteau and get on the road," the marquess said brusquely, pulling up his mettlesome chestnuts in front of Captain Chatham's lodgings. "I shall return in an hour. We do not want to spend the night on the road."

Barely giving the astonished captain time to jump down, Lord Monroyal turned his curricle and dashed off, with a practiced flick of his whip and a careless unconcern for two bulkier carriages proceeding at a sedate pace down Jermyn Street.

The captain stood looking after the marquess long after he had disappeared from sight, wishing he could be as optimistic about the outcome of their journey as his lordship appeared to be.

CHAPTER SEVENTEEN

Home Again

"If you are quite determined to pursue a separation, my dear Cynthia," the dowager countess remarked after the two ladies had repaired to the drawing room after dinner that evening, "I fear you will find life rather lonely and bleak without the father of your child, my love." Lady Agatha's tone indicated quite clearly her disapprobation of such a scandalous scheme, but Cynthia clung adamantly to the painful decision she had arrived at in London.

"Your son has practically disowned my child, my lady," she reminded her mother-in-law patiently. "I imagine that by now he must have signed the documents and deposited my draft in his bank. And there the matter must end," she added miserably, wishing that the dowager had not given utterance to her own despondent thoughts.

"Knowing Brian as I do, my dear, I can assure you that he will never accept a separation. He cares for you, Cynthia. I am sure of it," the dowager said with a confidence Cynthia wished she could share.

"Yes," she said with more bitterness than she intended. "He cares so much that he accuses me of playing him false, and then flies to the Metropolis to indulge in every sort of debauchery imaginable." She paused to swallow a lump that had formed in her throat. "I cannot believe he cares a fig for me or for his child."

The dowager patted her hand comfortingly, and Cynthia felt a sudden surge of affection for her mother-in-law, who had undertaken the arduous trip down from Shropshire in midwinter to lend her support. Cynthia had arrived home from London to find the Dowager Countess of Mulgrave installed at Milford Hall, and had to admit that the unexpected company of the older woman had proved most welcome. Instead of shutting herself in her chamber, as she had intended, to indulge in a bout of tears, Cynthia had been obliged to play the hostess, and in doing so, had been able to express some of her fears and relieve her heartache.

"Brian acted badly, of course," the dowager agreed. "I shall not deny that. But consider for a moment, my dear Cynthia. Would a gentleman who did not care a fig for you have flown into the boughs so unreasonably over your imagined preference for another man? I am willing to wager—if I had anything to wager, of course—that at this very moment my son is wishing he had acted less impetuously."

"And less lasciviously, perhaps?" Cynthia added sharply, feeling a blush suffusing her cheeks. The vision of her husband intimately embracing a female obviously lacking in morals of any kind had burned in her memory all the way down from London, and Cynthia had yet to reconcile herself with this unexpected side of the captain's nature.

The dowager smiled faintly. "Undoubtedly so, my dear. I imagine he must be feeling quite thoroughly ashamed of himself by now."

"He did not appear the least bit ashamed when I caught him embracing that . . . that . . ." She could not bring herself to say the awful word that sprang to her lips.

"Do not dwell upon it, love," the dowager remarked gently, taking Cynthia's cold hands in hers and rubbing them vigorously. "When it is all said and done, gentlemen are but weak creatures, my dear, much as we ladies would wish it otherwise. More often than not, it is we who must be strong, child. Only consider poor dear Margaret. In spite of every imaginable misfortune and excess on the earl's part, she is still in love with John, and no doubt will forgive him for leaving her penniless when he finally joins his Maker."

Cynthia drew her hands away and reached for the teapot, which Turpin had that moment placed before her. "I am not quite so forgiving, my lady," she said defiantly. "And if Brian has the nerve to show himself in Milford, I shall—"

"If you care for the rogue at all, you will forgive him, Cynthia," her mother-in-law broke in. "And you do love him, do you not?"

"No," Cynthia cried peevishly, her heart swelling with anguish at the thought of the captain returning home. "I *hate* him!" Her hand began to tremble so badly that she had to put the teapot down.

"I see," the dowager remarked gently. "I suspected as much. Here, dear, let me pour the tea." Deftly she poured two cups and handed one to Cynthia, who set it on the table beside her.

"But I *do* hate him," Cynthia repeated more emphatically. "How could I possibly care for a man who . . . a man who consorts with Cyprians in my own drawing room?"

"No, of course not, my dear," the other said soothingly. "But I hope you will not harp on that unfortunate incident when he arrives. Nothing is less conducive to a reconciliation than recriminations, my dear girl."

Cynthia stared at her mother-in-law as though her ladyship had spoken in Chinese. "Reconciliation?" she repeated. "What reconciliation can you mean, pray? I shall not receive the odious creature if he dares to come," she said forcefully. "Which I have no expectation of happening, of course." Cynthia hoped the dowager had not detected the wistful note in these last words that belied her sharp retort.

"Of course, dear," the dowager said calmly. "Now do drink up your tea before it becomes tepid, Cynthia. And then perhaps we might try a hand of picquet?" she added hopefully.

Before Cynthia could make up her mind whether she had the energy to pretend to enjoy a game of cards with her mother-in-law, she heard the unmistakable sound of the front door opening, immediately followed by masculine voices in the front hall below.

She glanced nervously at the ormolu clock on the mantel. "Who can be calling at such a late hour?" she murmured, rising abruptly to her feet and brushing at the creases in her deep blue merino gown. "I cannot receive anyone in this state, my lady," she appealed to the dowager. "I shall tell Turpin to deny us."

The older woman only smiled enigmatically, a gesture that sent shivers of panic racing through Cynthia's nerves. What if the dowager were right, and the captain had come home? The notion was ridiculous, of course. Brian had appeared too well entertained in London to brave the rigors of a winter journey into Surrey at this time of night. She was being uncharacteristically missish, she told herself, straightening her shoulders resolutely and moving to warm her hands at the fire.

"I fear I am very poor company this evening, my lady," she murmured through stiff lips. "The journey from London must have been more exhausting than . . ." Her voice tapered off as the drawing-room doors swung open abruptly to reveal not one but two travelers showing all the signs of having driven hard and fast through a snowstorm. Both gentlemen still wore their caped greatcoats, tall beavers, and gloves. The generous sprinkling of snowflakes on their hats and shoulders began to melt in the warmth of the room, causing the dowager countess to cluck her tongue disapprovingly.

"Good gracious!" she exclaimed. "This is no way to present yourselves in a drawing room, gentlemen. Turpin," she called imperiously to the butler, who had followed the visitors up the staircase, "pray help these gentlemen remove their traveling garments so they will not drip water all over the carpets."

After one horrified glance into her husband's startling blue eyes, Cynthia focused her gaze on the Marquess of Monroyal, her heart beating painfully. "Robbie," she murmured in a voice she did not recognize as her own, "whatever are you doing here at this time of night?"

Having handed his greatcoat and hat to the butler, the marquess strolled nonchalantly into the room, lifted Cynthia's limp hands, and kissed them warmly. "We did not fancy spending the night on the road, love," he said with unflappable calm, grinning down at her as if daring her to find fault with his logic. "We would have been here earlier, but it came on to snow after we stopped in Ripley for a hot toddy and a bite to eat. Ah, tea," he remarked, eyeing the tea-tray. "Just the thing to take the chill off, what do you say, my dear coz?"

Jolted out of her stupor, Cynthia remembered her duties as hostess and sent a footman down to fetch a fresh pot of tea.

Meanwhile the marquess had made his bows to the dowager, who regarded him—or so it appeared to Cynthia—with more than casual interest in her sharp eyes.

"I trust Lady Monroyal is well," the dowager said crisply before turning to her son, who still lingered near the door. "And you, sir," she added in a frosty voice, "I sincerely hope you have some rational explanation for your recent reprehensible behavior, young man. I, for one, shall be vastly interested to hear it."

An uncomfortable silence followed this blunt attack, and Cynthia risked a glance at the captain. She wished she had not done so, when she saw his pale face and taut lips drawn into a forbidding line. He looked so patently miserable and unhappy that, despite her determination to remain unmoved by her own tenderer emotions, Cynthia's resentment wavered. She noticed with a pang that her husband appeared haggard, although his shoulders were ramrod stiff, as though he were on parade. His glossy chestnut hair appeared disheveled, the reddish tints glinting in the candlelight. He looked so stricken and aloof that she felt the almost irresistible urge to go to him; her fingers ached to touch those tousled curls, to trace that rugged jaw until he relaxed into the smile she loved so well. And those lips . . . Cynthia shuddered at the memory of what the captain's lips could do to her.

But surely she was being absurdly fanciful to dwell on such delights, when her own eyes had seen him . . . Her mind shied away from what her eyes had seen her husband do. How could she live with that heart-wrenching memory? she wondered. Surely there was no truth in what the dowager had said about love and forgiveness? How could she possibly forgive *that*? Yet as she watched the captain flinch at his mother's blunt accusation, Cynthia knew, with sudden prescience, that if she wished to make her dreams of having a family come true, she would have to find a way. Because no other man would do, she reminded herself. No other man would do.

Cynthia glanced at her cousin and found the marquess regarding her with a knowing look in his dark eyes. Suddenly he winked, and Cynthia knew that he had read her thoughts. He turned back to the dowager with his most charming smile.

"I am sure that Sheffield can explain himself to your satisfaction, my lady," he said nonchalantly, bestowing another smile on the dowager that many a London Beauty would have died for. "And while he is doing so, I must beg the indulgence of a few words with my cousin." He took Cynthia firmly by the elbow and steered her to the door. "If you will excuse us for a moment?"

Taken by surprise at this odd development, Cynthia found herself out in the hall before she could react. She tried to protest, but Robbie paid no heed to her indignant murmurs until they were standing before the blazing fire in the library.

"Sit down, my pet," he said peremptorily, taking up a stand with his back to the hearth. "I have something of importance to say to you."

Cynthia glared at him. "You are too autocratic by half, Robert," she said hotly. "What do you suppose Brian will think of us sneaking off like this? As if I did not have enough disasters on my hands already."

The marquess only smiled. "In the first place, we did not sneak off, my dear Cynthia. In the second, I promised Sheffield I would put in a good word for him."

"Put in a good word for him?" she echoed, astounded at the extent of her cousin's effrontery. "I am sure that if the captain has anything to say to me, he can do so without your odious intervention," she snapped. "And I fail to see why you are here at all, Cousin, since you are partly to blame for . . . for e-everything." She gestured futilely with both arms, her voice threatening to break.

Dark eyebrows raised mockingly, the marquess sauntered over to pour himself a glass of brandy from the sideboard. "Much as you may wish me in Jericho, love," he murmured, "you have me to thank for bringing your precious captain home again." He lifted his glass in a silent toast.

"You?" Cynthia said scathingly, her heart cringing at the notion that Brian had been coerced into returning to her. "Are you saying that you dragged him down to Milford?"

The marquess expelled an exaggerated sigh. "You surely do not imagine I would do anything so exhausting, my dear, now do you? I had not credited you with such absurd flights of fancy, coz. Whatever do you take me for?" He brushed fastidiously at an imaginary speck of lint on the sleeve of his immaculately tailored coat.

"Then why *are* you here, Robert?" Cynthia demanded, impatient with her cousin's air of amused condescension.

"Believe it or not, my dear Cynthia—and I have a hard time believing it myself—I am playing Cupid." He gave a self-conscious chuckle.

"Cupid?" Cynthia repeated in astonishment. "*You?* Now that is a bag of moonshine," she declared without hesitation.

The marquess shrugged, as though suddenly bored with the conversation. "Well, it is true, nevertheless, coz. It was either that or allow the silly twit to rejoin the Army."

Cynthia could only gaze at her cousin, not trusting herself to speak.

"You may well stare, coz," the marquess drawled, helping himself to a pinch of snuff from his gilded box. "And I must say you did not help matters with that bird-witted notion of a separation, Cynthia. I felt that was truly beneath you, love. Like hitting a man when he is down sort of thing. Not sporting at all, let me tell you."

Quelling the irregular thumping of her heart, Cynthia took a deep breath. "You do not know the whole, Robbie," she whispered dejectedly. She dreaded having to repeat the painful tale of Brian's iniquity.

"Oh, but I do, love," the marquess said with unexpected gentleness, and when Cynthia raised startled eyes to his face, she detected none of her cousin's usual cynicism. "Rather tasteless of him, I will say that, but entirely to be expected under the circumstances." He grinned with renewed amusement.

"Expected of you, perhaps," Cynthia snapped crossly. "But I did not expect to see Brian in the clutches of some shameless hussy."

The marquess shrugged his elegant shoulders and took another drink. "Your esteemed captain is human, like the rest of us poor mortals, my dear," he said softly. "My advice is to accept him for what he is, love. If you expect him to be some silly hero from one of your romantical novels, he will always disappoint you. Believe me, my sweet coz, no man can live up to such ridiculous standards of perfection. You condemn us to failure in asking it of us."

Cynthia regarded her cousin with a rush of affection. This was a side to Robbie she had never suspected. She smiled shakily. "I never expected to hear you, of all men, admit to being imperfect," she said softly, repressing the urge to tease him on this extraordinary show of candor. "Thank you, Robbie. I appreciate your words of wisdom," she added, and meant it.

"I have no desire to spend the rest of my life being blamed for wrecking your marital bliss, my dear," he quipped, with a return to his usual flippancy. "So I gave the lad a good talking to and brought him back to you. The rest is up to you, Cynthia. And I wish you happy, my dear."

Cynthia was so choked up at her cousin's disclosure that she could not find the words she needed to express her deep affection for this childhood hero who, in spite of his cynicism and professed indifference to emotion, had proved himself a truer friend than she deserved. She smiled mistily and stepped forward with outstretched arms.

Gently but firmly, the marquess set her aside, his hands resting lightly on her shoulders. "This is precisely the kind of thing that will get us into trouble again, love," he said huskily. "The captain may be chastened, but I doubt he will take kindly to my kissing you, coz."

As if on cue, the door behind them opened and Captain Sheffield walked in.

"Finished talking to my wife, Monroyal?" he asked in a neutral voice.

The marquess winked shamelessly at Cynthia. "I have been given my congé, my dear," he drawled. He removed his hands from Cynthia's shoulders and sauntered out of the room.

After the door closed softly behind the marquess, an uneasy silence prevailed until, daunted by the enigmatic gaze in her husband's blue eyes, Cynthia turned to stare into the fire. For the life of her she could not think of a single thing to say to this man who had, in a few short weeks, turned her life upside down. Her brief conversation with her cousin had left her unsure of herself. *Accept him for what he is*, Robbie had said, which was in essence what her mother-in-law had counseled. *If you care for him, you will forgive.* Those were the dowager's very words, Cynthia remembered. And if one thing stood out clearly in her mind among the riot of emotions that had buffeted her over the past weeks, it was the deeply rooted conviction that she did indeed love her husband. There could be no other explanation for the rush of joy she felt when he looked at her. His silent presence in the room with her was sufficient to turn her mind into a tumultuous ebb and flow of erotic sensations she would blush to put into words.

The question was not whether she loved the captain, but whether she loved him *enough* to forgive the hurt he had caused her. And he had hurt her, Cynthia had to admit, deeply and unjustly. Then another unsettling thought jumped into her mind. Had the captain come back to be forgiven or—oh, horrible thought—did he merely wish to discuss their separation? The idea was so distressing that before she could stop herself, Cynthia had turned to face him.

"W-why are you here?" she murmured, noting that her voice sounded unnaturally strained.

Her question seemed to release the captain from his trancelike state, and a faint smile flitted briefly across his drawn face. He pulled a roll of papers from his pocket, and Cynthia—recognizing the legal documents Mr. Broadstone had drawn up for her so recently—felt her spirits drop into the soles of her blue kid slippers. So, her husband wished to discuss the separation before or even instead of what she most longed to hear.

The captain moved over to stand beside her, probably unaware, Cynthia thought bitterly, of the disturbing effect his nearness had on her tattered nerves. He held out one of the documents, which Cynthia recognized as a draft on her bank. Her signature stood out boldly on the cream vellum, and she wondered fleetingly what dark fate had driven her to tempt a man to desert her, particularly the only man in the world she wished to keep.

"How could you think I would accept this, Cynthia?" he said in a low voice, which sent quivers of delight trembling along her nerves.

Cynthia gazed at the proffered draft, her mind a maelstrom of unruly sensations. What exactly did he mean? she wondered. Why would he not accept thirty thousand pounds? She shook her head briefly to clear her thoughts.

"Is it not enough?" she whispered, forcing herself to look into his eyes again. At this distance she might easily drown in their dazzling blue depths, she thought giddily, her breath catching in her throat. They turned suddenly dark, and fearing she had aroused his anger, Cynthia blurted out, "Would you accept fifty, perhaps?"

The crack of cynical laughter that greeted this offer made her flinch. "You mock me, madam," he said brusquely. "Fifty thousand pounds indeed!" he repeated with a faint sneer in his voice. "I had no idea your freedom was quite that valuable to you, my lady. You must be desperate indeed to be rid of me if you are willing to throw that sum away." He regarded her with eyes that seemed—to Cynthia's befuddled mind—to be awash in despair. "And if I refuse?" he growled under his breath.

"Now it is *you* who mock *me*, sir," Cynthia flared back, sensing that her fragile composure would not withstand much more of this battering. "You have made it abundantly clear to me—and to all of London from what I understand—that you want nothing more to do with me or mine." Unconsciously her hands drifted to cradle the clearly defined swelling of her body, as if to protect the unborn child from the rejection of its father.

She saw the captain's eyes follow her movement, then heard him groan. He turned away to lean his elbows on the mantel, his head caught between his hands.

When he made no move to speak, Cynthia took what remained of her courage and forged on, determined to set the record straight. "I offered you the separation because I cannot find happiness with a man who does not trust me, a man who can disown his own child on the basis of a flimsy rumor from a mean-spirited troublemaker. The thought of my son growing up under that kind of stigma horrifies me, Brian." The sound of his name on her lips was bittersweet, and Cynthia wondered what Robbie had meant when he confessed to playing Cupid. Whatever it was, it did not seem to be working. On the contrary, everything she said seemed to drive the wedge more deeply between them.

When he made no reply, Cynthia glanced surreptitiously towards the door, wishing she might slip out and escape up to her room. But things between her and the captain remained curiously unresolved, and Cynthia knew she could not endure another such painful interview. If she were to forgive her husband, she must do so *now*. And she must make a push to tell him so. Cynthia's gaze returned to the tall man standing beside her, and of their own accord her eyes lingered hungrily on his beloved frame, her mind's eye probing beneath the tailored brown coat and champagne-colored breeches to the man beneath. The man who had brought her both happiness and despair. The man she did not want to give up, Cynthia realized with shocking clarity.

"Lady Agatha tells me that your brother is not expected to last beyond the end of February," she began tentatively. "When that happens, you will need funds to restore the estate. And there is Lady Margaret and seven nieces to support—"

The captain raised his head and looked at her, his eyes flat and expressionless. "The devil may fly away with the estate *and* my brother for all I care," he said with repressed fury. "Mama tells me the Sheffields have already benefited considerably from your largesse, my lady," he added evenly. "Was that another one of your secrets, Cynthia?"

"Not at all," she protested quickly. "I merely sent some trifling sums for the little girls. From what little Lady Agatha let slip in her letters, I gathered that things have not been easy at Mulgrave Park. I did not think you would mind . . ." Her voice trailed off uncertainly.

"And this?" He waved the legal documents in the air. "Did you imagine I would not mind this either?" When Cynthia made no reply, the captain continued in a bitter voice. "Or perhaps you did not care, is that it? Perhaps you were so disgusted with me, so repulsed by what you saw in London . . ."

He ran his fingers nervously through his hair, reminding Cynthia that it could be no easy feat for a man like her husband to admit the unpalatable truth about himself. Touched, she longed to reach out to him, to reassure him that all was not irrevocably lost. But she held her peace, praying for some sign that the captain truly regretted his mistrust of her. The other, much as it had pained her at the time, she could forgive, Cynthia realized with surprise. But trust was far more important to her, for upon it depended the success or failure of their future. Without it, there could be no true marriage, she thought, holding her breath as she watched her husband wrestle with his thoughts.

"I regret what happened in London far more than I can say, Cynthia," he said finally. "I cannot blame you for despising me. I deserve your contempt. But this?" He gestured hopelessly at the documents in his hand. "I cannot live with this, my dear." He paused, gazing at her keenly. "Unless, of course, it is what you truly wish, Cynthia."

Cynthia let her breath out slowly. This was not exactly what she wanted to hear, but it was a beginning. "No, it is not what I wish," she said firmly. "But when you denied your child and threatened to rejoin the Army, what could I think but that you wanted an excuse to be free again." Cynthia turned away, no longer able to prevent the tears from forming in her eyes.

There was a lengthy pause, and when he spoke, Cynthia clearly heard the tentative echo in his voice. "If you do not want the separation, my love, dare I hope that you can ever forgive me?"

My love. He had called her his love. Suddenly finding it impossible to utter a single word, Cynthia wrapped her arms about herself and bowed her head, fighting to control her tears. She would not cry, she thought. Gentlemen disliked watering-pots excessively, her Mama had always warned her, and with James it had been easy to avoid such missish starts. The viscount had never caused her even a shadow of the emotional upheaval she had suffered over Captain Sheffield. But then she had never been in love with James, she remembered wryly.

The captain must have mistaken her silence for denial, Cynthia realized, for quite suddenly she felt him move behind her, close enough that his warm breath touched her hair. The temptation to turn around into his warm arms was so strong that Cynthia felt the momentary dizziness of desire flow through her body.

"The title means nothing to me if I am to lose you, Cynthia," he murmured close to her ear. "And my brother could well defy us all and live for another twenty years. My home is here with you and my son. If you will have me, that is?"

"Your son?" she felt impelled to ask. "Which son is this? I understood you to say that—"

"This one, love," the captain murmured, slipping his arms about her and molding her stomach with infinite tenderness in his big hands. "I have said and done any number of foolish things where you are concerned, Cynthia. But perhaps the most heinous was doubting you, my love."

Cynthia felt the stiffness, the anxiety, the heartbreak of the past weeks drain out of her at her husband's words. Her body relaxed against his chest as his embrace tightened, and she let her head fall back as his lips traced a warm path down her cheek. All thought of tears miraculously vanished, and the blood danced in her veins.

"What if she is a daughter?" she whispered perversely.

The captain chuckled in her ear, and the sound was so infinitely comforting that Cynthia knew that she had done the right thing to forgive and forget. Lady Agatha had been right. She loved this man more than enough to accept him for what he was. And unless she were dreaming, it appeared entirely possible that he cared a little for her, too.

"Then we shall try again," the captain murmured seductively in her ear. "And again, my love. Until we get it right. There are more than enough Sheffield females in the world already. It is up to us to even the score, my pet. Do you not agree?" he added, nibbling deliciously on her ear.

"Whatever you say, my love," Cynthia moaned softly, tilting her face to find his lips. "Oh, Brian," she whispered against his mouth as he teased her with a flurry of light kisses. "I have missed you, you rogue."

He turned her about and pulled her roughly against him, burying his face in her neck. "I know, dearest. I love you, too."

Paralyzed at this unexpected confession, Cynthia drew back and stared up into her husband's eyes. The startling blue that had always been able to make her knees weak had darkened with passion, but the tenderness in their depths was unmistakable.

"You do?" Her voice was a mere whisper.

A slow grin spread over the captain's face and his eyes danced with amusement. "Yes, sweetheart. I discovered in London that I thought about you all the time."

Cynthia stared in disbelief. "*All* the time, sir?"

His grin broadened. "Every waking moment, Cynthia. At first I thought I was coming down with something. It was your esteemed cousin who made me see that I was sick indeed. Lovesick, my dear." He bent his head to capture her lips in a long, heated kiss that threatened to banish all other thoughts from Cynthia's head.

After some time, however, she pushed back and gazed up at him. "How did you know? About me, I mean?" she murmured, curious to find out how he had discovered her secret.

"It was the chamber-pot, love," he said, his lips curling into another grin.

Cynthia blushed. "The chamber-pot?" she repeated, at a loss to see how such an article could have anything to do with her secret feelings for her husband.

"Yes, love. The infamous chamber-pot. Monroyal assured me that you would never have thrown it over the banister had you not loved me to distraction. You were distracted, I gather, dearest?"

"I was furious," she retorted.

"Jealous," he clarified with such a devilish grin of male satisfaction that Cynthia's heart leapt with joy. "According to Monroyal, you were jealous, love. He made me see that I was jealous, too." He angled his head down to kiss her, but Cynthia placed a finger against his lips.

"And what else?" she insisted, quite sure that he had not completed his tale.

The captain raised an amused eyebrow. "What a tyrant you are, sweet. Your cousin told me that if I did not get myself down here and tell you I loved you, I would lose you."

Cynthia frowned. "So you came back because Robert told you to?" she wanted to know.

"I came because I wanted to, Cynthia. Because I love you," the captain corrected her. "But before I take you upstairs to give you a demonstration of just how much I missed you, love, there is something we must do." The captain turned to pick up the legal documents he had brought with him from London.

A glimmer of understanding flashed through Cynthia's mind as she stared down at the separation papers in the captain's hand. "What must we do?" she asked, half conscious of what his answer would be.

"Let me burn these, Cynthia. I cannot bear to have them in the house."

Cynthia smiled radiantly. "You realize that you may never have another chance to escape from me, Brian?" she teased, unable to keep her mind off the prospect of going upstairs with a decidedly amorous husband anxious to prove his feelings for her.

The captain's response was swift and irrevocable, dispelling any lingering doubts about his sincerity. With a dismissive flick of his wrist, he tossed the documents into the fire and turned to place both hands on Cynthia's shoulders, drawing her against him.

"I am very glad to be home again," he murmured against her eager mouth. "Home again with you, my love."

Cynthia released a long, satisfied sigh as she gave herself up to her husband's passion, his words echoing pleasantly in her ears.